An Armada Three-in

*Three Great
Enid Blyton*

ARMADA

The Rockingdown Mystery
The Rilloby Fair Mystery
The Ring O'Bells Mystery

Enid Blyton

ARMADA

This Armada *Enid Blyton Three-in-One* was
first published in the U.K. in Armada in 1988
by William Collins Sons & Co. Ltd

Armada is an imprint of
the Children's Division, part of
the Collins Publishing Group,
8 Grafton Street, London W1X 3LA

Published pursuant to agreement with
George Newnes

Printed and bound in Great Britain by
William Collins Sons & Co. Ltd, Glasgow

The Rockingdown Mystery

The Rockingdown Mystery was
first published in the U.K. in a single volume
in 1949 by William Collins Sons & Co. Ltd,
and in Armada in 1967

CHAPTER ONE

THE BEGINNING OF THE HOLIDAYS

" HALLO, Roger! "

" Hallo, Diana! Had a good term? "

The boy and girl grinned at one another, half-shy as they always were when they met again at the end of the school term. They were brother and sister, and rather alike to look at—sturdy, dark-haired with determined chins and wide smiles.

" My train came in twenty minutes before yours, " said Roger. " Bit of luck, breaking up on the same day

—we usually don't. I waited about for you. Now we've got to wait for Miss Pepper."

Diana groaned. She dragged her night-case, her tennis racket and a large brown parcel along with her. Roger had a racket and a case too.

" These aren't going to be very nice hols," said Diana, " with Mummy and Daddy away, and us poked down in the country somewhere with Miss Pepper. Whatever made Mummy ask her to look after us? Why couldn't we have gone to Auntie Pam?"

" Because her kids have got measles," said Roger. " Miss Pepper isn't so bad, really—I mean she does understand how hungry we always are, and she does know we like things like sausages and salad and cold meat and potatoes in their jackets and ice-cream and ginger-beer . . ."

" Oh, don't go on—you make me feel hungry already," said Diana. " What are the plans for to-day, Roger? I only know you were going to meet me and then we were to see Miss Pepper somewhere."

" I had a letter from Dad yesterday," said Roger, as they pushed their way through the crowds on the platform. " He and Mummy sail to-day for America. They *had* fixed up for us to go to Aunt Pam, but the measles knocked that on the head, so Mummy wired to her old governess, Miss Pepper, and got her to fix up to spend the hols with us—and we're to go to a little cottage somewhere that Dad managed to get hold of in Rockingdown—goodness knows where that is! "

" Where we're to moulder all the hols, I suppose," said Diana sulkily. " I think it's too bad."

" Well, there's a riding school not far off and we can ride," said Roger, " and I believe there's a river near. We might get a boat. And it's jolly good country all round Rockingdown for birds and flowers."

" All very nice for you because you're so mad on

nature," said Diana. " I shall feel buried alive—no tennis, no parties—and I suppose that horrid little Snubby is coming too."

" Of course," said Roger, digging somebody hard with his tennis racket. " Oh, sorry! Did I hurt you? Do let's get out of this awful crowd, Di. We seem to be going round and round in it."

" We've got into one that's rushing for a train," said Diana. " Let them go by, for goodness' sake. Look, here's a seat—let's sit down for a bit. When do we meet Miss Pepper?"

" Not for twenty-four minutes," said Roger, looking at the station clock. " Shall we go and see if we can get an ice-cream somewhere nearby?"

Diana immediately got up from the seat. " Oh, yes— what a brainwave! Look, there's the exit. There'll be a tea-shop or something nearby. We'll get ices there."

Over the ices the chatter went on. " You said Snubby was coming, didn't you?" said Diana as she ate her strawberry ice. " Little pest! "

" Well, he hasn't got any parents," said Roger. " That's pretty awful, you know, Di. He gets kicked about from one aunt to another, poor kid—and he likes coming to us better than anywhere else. He's not so bad, if only he wouldn't play the fool so much."

" Just our luck to have an idiotic cousin with an idiotic dog," said Diana.

" Oh, I like Loony," said Roger at once. " He *is* quite potty, of course—but he's a lovely spaniel, he really is! Loony's a wonderful name for him—he's an absolute lunatic, but honestly he's wizard, the things he does. I bet he plays Miss Pepper up! "

" Yes. He'll go off with all her shoes and hide them under a bush, and fight her Sunday hat, and get himself cleverly locked up in the larder," said Diana. " What about another ice?"

9

"If Snubby was more our age, it wouldn't be so bad," said Roger. "After all, I'm fourteen and you're thirteen —and he's only eleven—quite a baby."

"Well, he doesn't behave like one," said Diana, beginning on her second ice. "He behaves like a horrible little imp or goblin or something—always up to mischief of some sort—and thinking he can tag along with us. Oh, dear—what with Miss Pepper and Snubby these hols look as if they'll be awful."

"Gosh, look at the time," said Roger. "We shall miss Miss Pepper if we don't look out. I must get the bill and we'll go."

The girl brought him the bill, and he got up with Diana to go to the desk and pay. As they were going out of the door Roger glanced at Diana's hands. "Idiot! You've left your racket and bag at the table. I knew you would. You always do! It's a marvel to me you ever manage to bring anything home safely!"

"Blow!" said Diana, and went back to get her things, knocking over a chair in her impatience. Roger waited for her patiently, a grin on his good-looking face. Harum-scarum, untidy, impatient Di! He laughed at her, kept her in order, and was very fond of her indeed. He was fond of his cousin Snubby too, with his impudence, sense of fun, and his habit of doing the most surprising and annoying things.

Both Diana and Snubby would have to be kept in order these holidays, Roger was certain. Diana was cross and disappointed at being sent off with Miss Pepper to some place she had never heard of—she would be annoying and perhaps sulky. Snubby would be more irritating still, because he wouldn't have Roger's father to jump on him and yell at him. He would only have Miss Pepper, and Snubby hadn't much opinion of women.

Loony the dog was, of course, another problem, but a very nice problem indeed. He was a dog who only obeyed one person and that was Snubby. He had never outgrown his habit of chewing things, hiding them and burying them. He went mad quite regularly, racing up and down the stairs, in and out of every room, barking his head off with excitement, and thoroughly upsetting every grown-up within miles.

But he was so beautiful! Roger thought of the little black spaniel with his silky, shining coat, his long drooping ears that always went into his dinner-dish, and his melting, mournful eyes. How lucky Snubby was to have a dog like that! Roger had often smacked Loony hard for being wicked, but he had never ceased to love him. He was glad that Loony was to share the holidays with them, even though it meant having his cousin Snubby too.

" We've got to meet Miss Pepper under the station clock," said Roger. " We've got a minute to spare. Look —isn't that her?"

It was. The children took a good look at their mother's old governess as they hurried up to her. She was tall, thin, trim, with straight grey hair brushed back under a small black hat. Her eyes behind their glasses were sharp and twinkling. She had a very nice smile as she saw the children hurrying up to her.

" Roger! Diana! Here you are at last—and punctual to the minute too. It's a year since I saw you, but you haven't changed a scrap."

She kissed Diana and shook hands with Roger. " Now," she said, " we've a little time before we have to leave for our train at another station—what about a couple of ices —or have you grown out of your liking for them?"

Roger and Diana brightened up at once. Neither of them said that they had just had two ices each. Diana nudged Roger and grinned. Miss Pepper certainly was good at remembering to provide ice-cream and ginger-beer and the rest. She never failed in that.

" Now—I wonder where we can get ice-creams without going too far," said Miss Pepper, looking round the station.

11

" Er—let me see—isn't there a little tea-shop just outside the station?" said Roger.

" Yes—where they have lovely ices," said Diana. " Do you remember the way, Roger?"

Roger did, of course, and promptly led the way back to the little tea-shop they had left only a few minutes before. Miss Pepper's eyes twinkled. She wondered how many ices the two had already had whilst waiting for her.

Roger led his sister and Miss Pepper to a different table this time. He didn't want the girl to make some remark that would give them away. They ordered ices.

" When is Snubby coming?" asked Diana.

" By train to-morrow," said Miss Pepper. " With Loony, I fear. I don't like dogs, as you know, and I like Loony even less than most dogs. It means I shall have to lock up all my slippers and hats and gloves. I never knew such a dog for smelling out things! Never! Last time I stayed with your mother, Roger, I began to think that Loony could undo suitcases, because things I had put in disappeared regularly—and I always found Loony with them sooner or later."

" I expect Snubby had something to do with that," said Roger. " He was awful those hols you were there, Miss Pepper. As loony as his dog."

" Well, I hope Mr. Young will be able to keep Snubby in order," said Miss Pepper.

There was a sudden startled silence. Roger and Diana looked at Miss Pepper in alarm.

" Mr. *Young*," said Roger. " What's he coming for?"

" To coach you all," said Miss Pepper, in surprise. " Didn't you know? I expect you'll get a letter soon, if you haven't heard. Your father rang up your schools, you know, to find out what kind of a report you both had, because he knew he wouldn't get it before he left for America—and you've got to have coaching in Latin and maths, Roger, and you in French and English, Diana."

" *Well!* " said both children together. " How absolutely foul! "

" Oh, no," said Miss Pepper. " Mr. Young is very nice —and a very good coach. You've had him before."

" He's as dry as dust," said Diana angrily. " Oh, I do think it's hateful—holidays without Mummy and Daddy, at a place we don't know anything about—with Mr. Young and lessons—and . . ."

" Shut up, Di," said Roger, afraid that his angry sister would say something about Miss Pepper too. " You know we missed the whole of the Easter term because of scarlet fever—we're behind in a good many things. I meant to do some work anyhow these hols."

" Yes—but Mr. *Young*—with his beard and his sniffs and his ' My dear young lady! ' " cried Diana. " I hate him. I'll jolly well write and tell Daddy what I think of him for——"

" That's enough, Diana," said Miss Pepper in a sharp voice.

" Is Snubby having coaching too?" asked Roger, kicking the furious Diana under the table to make her stop working herself into a rage.

" Yes. Unfortunately he had a very bad report from the headmaster," said Miss Pepper.

" That's nothing new," growled Diana. " And I ask you—*can* Mr. Young do anything at all with Snubby? Snubby will lead him a frightful dance."

" Shall we have another ice?" said Miss Pepper, looking at her watch. " We've just time. Or do you feel too upset to have another?"

They certainly didn't feel too upset to have another ice and a ginger-beer on top of it. Roger began to talk cheerfully about the happenings of the last term, and Diana gloomed over her ice for a minute or two and then cheered up too. After all, it was holidays—and it would be fun to explore a new place—and there would be riding and perhaps boating. Things might be worse!

" Time to go," said Miss Pepper. " We're having dinner on the train. I hope you'll enjoy that. We shall be at Rockingdown by tea-time. Well, come along—and cheer up, Diana dear—I expect you'll enjoy the holidays just as you usually do! "

CHAPTER TWO

ROCKINGDOWN COTTAGE

ROCKINGDOWN VILLAGE was a tiny little place with a butcher's shop, a baker's and a general store, and plenty of farms and cottages around. The church tower showed above the trees, and the church bell could be heard quite clearly in the cottage where the children were to stay for the holidays.

This proved to be a very exciting little place. " It's more than a cottage," said Diana approvingly. " It's a jolly nice old house, with lots of rooms."

" It used to belong to a big mansion about half a mile off—this cottage is actually in the grounds of the mansion," said Miss Pepper. " It was what is called the Dower House."

" What's that?" asked Diana.

" It was a house set aside for the mistress of the big mansion when her husband died and her son and his wife came to take over the mansion," said Miss Pepper. " She was then called the dowager mother, and came to live here, in this house, with her own servants."

" It's very old, isn't it?" said Diana, looking at the oak panelling of the dining-room in which they were having tea. " And I like the wide staircase—and the tiny little back staircase that winds up from the kitchen. We could have wizard games of hide-and-seek here."

14

"I like my bedroom," said Roger. "It's got a ceiling that slants almost to the floor, and I've had to break away strands of ivy across one of the windows, Miss Pepper —it was so overgrown!"

"And I like the way the floors go up and down," said Diana. "And the funny little steps down to this dining-room and up to the kitchen."

They were just what Miss Pepper didn't like. She was rather short-sighted, and in this old house she seemed to stumble everywhere. Still, no doubt she would get used to it!

"This tea is wizard," said Roger approvingly. "Did you make the scones, Miss Pepper?"

"Dear me, no—I'm afraid I'm no cook," said Miss Pepper. "Mrs. Round made them. She's a village woman who comes in each day to do the cleaning and cooking."

"Is she like her name?" said Diana at once. Miss Pepper considered.

15

"Well, yes," she said. "She *is* rather plumpish—and her face certainly is very round. Yes—Mrs. Round seems a very good name for her."

The children explored the house after they had had tea—and a very good tea it was, with home-made jam, home-produced honey, scones, and a big fruit cake.

"This is the kind of fruit cake I like," said Diana, taking a third slice. "You don't have to look and see if you've got any fruit in your slice—there's plenty all over the cake."

"You're a pig, Di," said Roger.

"People are always pigs at your age," said Miss Pepper. "Some are worse pigs than others, of course."

"Am I a worse pig?" demanded Diana.

"Sometimes," said Miss Pepper, her eyes twinkling behind their glasses. Roger roared at Diana's indignant face.

"Miss Pepper, Di can eat a whole tin of Nestlé's milk by herself," he began, and got a kick under the table.

"So could I, once," said Miss Pepper, surprisingly. The children stared at her. It was quite impossible to imagine the thin, prim Miss Pepper ever having been greedy enough to devour a whole tin of Nestlé's milk by herself.

"Go on, now, finish your tea," said Miss Pepper. "I want to do your unpacking."

They explored, whilst Miss Pepper unpacked their school trunks, exclaiming over the dirty clothes, and looking with horror at the rents and tears in most of Diana's things. Anyone would think that the girl spent all her time climbing thorny trees, judging by the state of her clothes. Miss Pepper thought of having to unpack Snubby's trunk the next day, and shuddered. Really, children nowadays were quite impossible!

"Is the old mansion empty?" asked Roger that evening. "We saw it from a distance. There was no smoke coming from the chimneys. It looked a dead place."

"Yes. I believe it is," said Miss Pepper. "Roger,

16

where are all the socks you took back to school with you? It says you took back eight on this list, but I can only find one pair, very holey and dirty."

" I've got one pair on," said Roger helpfully. " That makes two."

" Miss Pepper, can we go and look over the mansion if it's empty?" asked Diana.

" No, I shouldn't think so," said Miss Pepper. " Diana, it says on your list that you took four blouses back to . . ."

Diana fled. It was dreadful the way grown-ups always put you through a cross-examination about clothes as soon as you got back from school. She and Roger rushed upstairs—and then tiptoed down the little back-stair and out into the garden.

Miss Pepper followed them upstairs in a moment or two, with another list of questions—but they had mysteriously disappeared. She looked round Diana's room and groaned. How could any girl make a perfectly neat room into such a terrible mess one hour after she had taken possession of it?

Roger was pleased that night when the two of them went up to bed. " It's going to be a wizard place for birds, this," he told Diana. " And there are badgers here too —in these very grounds. That old fellow we met told me. One of these nights I'm going to get up and watch for them."

" Well, don't badger me to come with you!" said Diana, and shrieked as Roger aimed a punch at her for her pun.

" You sound like Snubby," he said. " He's always making silly puns and jokes. For goodness' sake leave it to him!"

Their bedrooms were side by side under the slanting roof. Snubby's bedroom was across the landing, a tiny one looking to the back of the house, across the grounds. Miss Pepper slept on the first floor. Tucked away in another corner of the first floor were two other rooms.

17

"We'll have to meet Snubby to-morrow," said Roger, calling from his bedroom as he undressed. "And Loony."

"Yes. We'll walk over to the station," said Diana, flinging all her clothes on the floor one by one, although she knew perfectly well she would have to get out of bed and pick them up as soon as Miss Pepper arrived to say good night. "It's only about two miles. I could do with a good long walk. We can bus back if Snubby's got a lot of things."

The next day was brilliantly fine. Snubby's train was due in at half-past twelve.

"We'll go and meet him," said Roger to Miss Pepper. "You needn't come unless you want to, Miss Pepper. I expect there are lots of things you want to do."

They set off at twelve o'clock to walk to the station. They decided that the shortest way would be to go through the grounds of the old mansion. They were horrified to see how overgrown everything was. Even the paths were almost lost in the nettles and brambles that spread all round. Only one broad drive seemed to be at all well-kept, and that was now beginning to show signs of being covered with weeds.

"Funny," said Diana. "You'd think that whoever owned this place would want to keep it up decently, so that he could sell it at a good price, even if he didn't have any intention of living in it himself. Golly, how are we going to get through these brambles! I'll scratch my legs to pieces."

Here and there as they walked through the large grounds, they caught sight of the old mansion through gaps in the trees. It certainly looked a desolate place. Diana didn't like it.

"Well, I don't much feel as if I want to explore that," she said. "It would be full of spiders and creepy things and horrid noises and draughts from nowhere. A nasty spooky place."

They were out of the grounds at last and came to the

village. They stopped for an ice-cream at the little general store.

"Ah—you're the new people in Rockingdown Cottage," said the old woman who served them. "That's a nice old place. I remember old Lady Rockingdown going there when her son brought his wife home from Italy. Those were grand days—parties and balls and hunts and such goings-on! Now it's all dead and done with."

The children ate their ices and listened with interest. "Where did the family go, then?" asked Roger.

"Lady Rockingdown's son was killed in a war and his wife died of a broken heart," said the old woman, remembering. "The place went to a cousin, but he never lived there. He just let it. Then it was taken over in the last war, and some kind of secret work was done there —we never knew what. Now that's finished, of course— and the place has been empty ever since. Nobody wants it—it's so big and cumbersome. Ah—but it was a fine place once—and many's the time I've been up to it to help with a party!"

"We must go," said Roger to Diana. "Else we shall be late for the train. Come on!"

He paid for the ices and they ran off to the station. They got there just as the train was coming in. They stood on the platform waiting for Snubby and Loony to appear from a carriage. Usually they both fell out together!

An old market-woman got down. A farmer and his wife appeared. But nobody else at all. The train gave itself a little shake, preparing to start off again. Roger ran all down it, looking into the carriages for Snubby. Had he fallen asleep?

There was no one in the carriages except another farmer and a young woman with a baby.

The train steamed off importantly, and its one porter went off to his dinner. There was no other train for two hours.

It took the children a little time to find this out, because there didn't seem to be anyone else at the station once the porter had gone. No one in the tiny booking office No one in the stationmaster's room or in the waiting-room

"Blow Snubby! He's missed the train," said Diana Just like him! He might have phoned to say so—then we needn't have fagged all the way to meet him!"

They at last found a time-table that told them what trains there were. It took Roger a good ten minutes to discover that there were no more trains till the afternoon

He looked at the station clock which now said a quarter past one. "We've wasted nearly an hour here," he said in disgust. "Messing about looking for Snubby and hunting for somebody to ask about trains and trying to find out what the time-table says. Come on—let's go home. We'll catch the bus and perhaps we shan't be awfully late Miss Pepper said she'd make lunch at one o'clock—we should be back by about half-past."

But there was no bus for an hour so they had to walk The sun was hot and they were hungry and thirsty. Blow Snubby!

They arrived back at the cottage at two o'clock—and there, sitting at the table, looking very full indeed, was their cousin Snubby!

"Hallo!" he said. "You *are* late! Whatever hap pened?"

CHAPTER THREE

SNUBBY—AND LOONY

DIANA AND ROGER had no wish to fling themselves joyfully on Snubby; but Loony flung himself on them so violently that he almost knocked Diana over. He appeared from under the table, barking madly, and threw himself at them.

"Hey—wait a bit!" said Roger, very pleased to see Loony. The spaniel licked him lavishly, whining joyfully. Miss Pepper looked crossly at them.

"Diana! Roger! You are very late."

"*Well!*" said Diana indignantly. "Snubby wasn't on the train—and we waited and waited, and tried to find out when the next train was. It wasn't *our* fault!"

"We've had lunch already," said Snubby. "I was so hungry I couldn't wait."

"Sit down, Roger and Diana," said Miss Pepper. "Snubby, call Loony to you, for goodness' sake!"

Roger and Diana sat down. Loony tore back to Snubby and began to fawn on him as if he too had been away for some time.

"Still the same old lunatic," said Diana, holding out her plate for some cold meat-pie. "Snubby, what *happened* to you?"

"I suppose you were late for the train, and missed Snubby, and didn't see him or Loony on the road," said Miss Pepper. "I ought to have gone to meet him myself."

"They're not very observant," said Snubby, accepting another helping of tinned peaches and cream. "I mean —I could walk right past them with Loony, under their noses and they wouldn't see me."

21

Diana looked at him scornfully. "Don't be an idiot. You can't make out you passed us and we didn't see you."

"Well, but what else could have happened?" said Miss Pepper. "Snubby, I will not have Loony fed at meal-times. If you give him any more titbits I shall say he's to remain out of the room when we have a meal."

"He'd only scratch the door down," said Snubby. "As I said, my two cousins are not very observant, Miss Pepper. Fancy not even seeing Loony."

Loony jumped up in excitement whenever his name was mentioned. Miss Pepper made a resolve that she would never mention his name at all—only refer to him as "the dog." Oh dear—things were going to be twice as difficult with this mischievous boy and his excitable little dog.

"Snubby, you didn't come by that train," said Roger quietly. "What did you do? Go on—tell us, or we'll never go to meet you again."

"I got out at the station four miles before Rocking-down," said Snubby. "The train had to wait three-quarters of an hour there for a connection—so out I got, hopped on to a bus and here I was at a quarter to one! Easy!"

"Oh, Snubby!" said Miss Pepper. "Why couldn't you have said so before? It was so nice of your cousins to meet you—and all you did was to make them late for their lunch, and arrive cross and hot and hungry."

Diana glared at Snubby. "He's just the same horrid little boy," she said to Roger, speaking as if Snubby wasn't there. "Same old ginger hair, same old green eyes, same old freckles, same old snub-nose, and same old cheek. I'm sure I don't know why we put up with him."

"Well, I put up with you," said Snubby, wrinkling his turned-up nose and grinning, so that his face appeared to be made of rubber, and his eyes almost disappeared under his sandy eyebrows. "Sorry to upset you, cousins. Honestly, I didn't know you were going to meet me. I'm aot used to kind attentions of that sort from you. Are we, Loony?"

Loony leapt up madly and pawed violently at Snubby's knees, knocking his head against the table. He whined and yapped.

"Loony wants to go out," said Snubby, who used Loony as an excuse whenever he wanted to go wandering off by himself. "Can we go, Miss Pepper?"

"Yes," said Miss Pepper, thankful to be rid of them both. "Leave him outside in the garden when you come in again, and then go upstairs to help me to unpack your trunk. It came this morning."

Diana and Roger finished their meal in peace. Roger grinned to himself. What an idiot Snubby was—but it would certainly liven things up a bit to have him there —and Loony too. Diana mooned over her peaches and cream. She wasn't pleased. She would rather have had Roger to herself. She knew that Snubby admired Roger and wanted to be with him, and this always made her want to push Snubby away.

Except that Snubby found an outsize stag-beetle in the garden, which he insisted on displaying on the tea-table, and that he had arrived with another boy's trunk instead of his own, things passed off peacefully the first day.

He and Loony explored everywhere thoroughly by themselves. Snubby hated being "shown round." He liked to size things up for himself and go his own way. He was a most intelligent and sharp-witted boy, very clever at hiding his brains under a constant stream of tricks, jokes and general idiocies. He was adored by all the boys in his form, and was their natural leader—but the despair of all the masters who seemed to vie with one another in making biting remarks about his work and character in his reports.

His jokes and tricks were endless. All his pocket money was spent on ice-creams, chocolate—or his newest trick. It was Snubby who tried out all the trick pencils on the

23

various masters—the pencil whose point wobbled because it was made of rubber—the one whose point disappeared inside the pencil as soon as the unsuspecting master tried to write—the pencil that could be nailed to the floor and couldn't be picked up.

It was Snubby who experimented with stink-pills which, when thrown on the fire, at once gave out a smell like bad fish, and Snubby who climbed to the top of the school tower without falling. Everything was always Snubby—even when it really wasn't! But Snubby didn't mind. He accepted his punishments, rightful ones or wrongful, with pluck and resignation, and always owned up when tackled.

"A bad boy with a lot of good in him," said the head-master. "It's a pity he has no parents. If he had he would behave better because he wouldn't like to let them down. He'll turn out all right—but in the meantime he's a pest."

Snubby was pleased with Rockingdown Cottage and the garden and grounds of the old mansion. He could make plenty of good hidey-holes in the grounds for Loony and himself. They could play pirates, wrecked sailors, and Red Indians to their hearts' content under the thick bushes, and up in the tall trees—because Loony didn't at all mind being dragged up trees by the scruff of his neck. In fact, he didn't mind where he went as long as he was with his beloved master. He had even been known to crouch in a smelly dustbin with Snubby for an hour whilst Snubby waited to play a trick on the unsuspecting butcher's boy.

Snubby made up his mind to explore the old mansion. It would be locked and bolted and barred, but he'd get in somewhere all right. If Di and Roger would come, that would be fun—if not, he'd go by himself. He hoped Roger would come, though. He would like to be in Roger's good books—Roger was fine. Diana was a nuisance—but then, in Snubby's opinion all girls were a nuisance. Always in the way.

24

It was a terrible shock to Snubby to hear that he was to have coaching those holidays. Diana broke the news to him that night.

"You know you're to have lessons these hols, don't you, Snubby?" she said. "Mr. Young's coming to coach you."

Snubby stared at her in horror. "I don't believe you," he said at last. "Nobody could do that to me—make me learn things in the *summer hols*! I've never heard of such a thing."

"Well, you'll have to believe it," said Diana. "Daddy's arranged it. Roger is to have coaching in Latin and maths, I'm to be coached in French and English."

"What am I to be coached in?" said Snubby gloomily.

"Oh, I should think you want coaching in everything," said Diana. "I don't suppose you know your tables properly yet, do you, Snubby? And can you spell yet?"

"All right. I'll pay you out for that," said Snubby. "What about a worm or two under your pillow?"

"If you start doing that kind of babyish thing again I'll sit on you and bounce up and down till you cry for mercy," said Diana. "I'm much bigger than you are, baby-boy!"

This was quite true. Snubby was not big for his age and hadn't really begun to grow yet. Diana was a sturdy girl, and quite able to do what she threatened.

Loony appeared and rolled himself over and over on the floor. Snubby tickled him with his foot. The spaniel leapt up and fetched something in from the hall. Diana gave a shriek.

"Oh—he's got my hairbrush. Snubby, get it from him. Quick!"

"Why? You never use it, do you?" said Snubby, neatly getting back at his cousin for her jibes of a minute or two ago. "What good is it to you? You might as well let Loony play with it."

The brush was rescued and Loony got a few spanks

with it from Diana. He retired under the table, and looked
at her mournfully with big brown eyes.

"Now you've hurt his feelings," said Snubby.

"I'd like to hurt a lot more of him than that," said
Diana. "Now I shall have to wash this chewed-up brush.
Blow Loony!"

"Blow everything!" said Snubby dismally. "Fancy—
coaching with Mr. Young. I can't think of anything
worse!"

CHAPTER FOUR

CHANGED PLANS

But after all Mr. Young didn't come to coach the three
children. Two days later, when Roger, Diana and Snubby
had put out their school books neatly on the study table,
and had gloomily sharpened their pencils and found their
pens, the telephone bell rang shrilly.

"I'll answer it, Miss Pepper, I'll answer it!" yelled
Snubby, who adored answering the phone and pretending
that he was one of the grown-ups in the house. He rushed
to answer.

The others listened, bored. Probably it was the butcher
saying he couldn't send the meat, and one of them would
have to fetch it.

"Yes. This is Rockingdown Cottage," they heard Snubby
say. "Oh—who? Oh, Mrs. Young. Oh, yes, certainly.
Yes. I can give any message you like. Certainly. Dear,
dear, how very very sad. I'm so sorry to hear that. Well,
well, to think how suddenly these things happen! And is
he getting on all right? That's wonderful, isn't it? You
have my deepest sympathy, Mrs. Young—such a terrible

26

time for you. Yes, yes, I'll give your message. Certainly. *Good*-bye."

By this time both Diana and Roger were out in the hall, amazed at Snubby's telephoning.

"What is it? What are you saying? Who on earth are you pretending to *be*, Snubby?" demanded Diana.

"Nobody. I'm just being polite and helpful," said Snubby, beaming. "I *say*—Mr. Young's gone and got appendicitis and he's NOT COMING! What do you think of that?"

The others stared at him. "Gosh—we couldn't think what you were doing, talking in that idiotic way over the phone!" said Diana.

"It wasn't idiotic. It was only like grown-ups talk," said Snubby. "I can tell you I felt very sorry for poor Mr. Young—you know, having to go to hospital and everything."

"You didn't," said Roger. "You know you're always saying appendicitis is nothing, and telling us how you had it and enjoyed it. But I say—does this mean no coaching then? Of course, it's upsetting for Mrs. Young—but it does solve a problem for us. We can enjoy ourselves now."

Loony was barking round their ankles, sensing their excitement. Miss Pepper came down the stairs.

"What's all the excitement about? Who was that on the telephone? I hope it wasn't the butcher again."

"No. It was Mrs. Young," said Snubby. "Mr. Young is in hospital with appendicitis, Miss Pepper. He's not coming here to coach us."

"Dear, dear! I *am* sorry for poor Mrs. Young," said Miss Pepper in exactly the same voice that Snubby had used over the telephone. "Well—that does put us into a difficulty."

"*Does* it?" said Diana, astonished. "It seems to us that we've got out of one."

27

"Oh, dear me, no!" said Miss Pepper at once. "I shall get someone else to coach you. I can't imagine who, though. I shall have to go through my list of tutors. Snubby, stop Loony eating that rug. He's had more than half of it since he arrived and I should like a *little* bit left."

"He thinks it's a rabbit—it's a fur rug, you see," said Snubby.

"I don't care what he thinks it is," said Miss Pepper. "You heard what I said. Take Loony out of the hall at once. I'm getting tired of him already. I'm thinking of buying a whip—a nice strong whip."

Snubby stared at her in horror. What, whip Loony! Surely nobody could think of doing that! Smacking, yes —but whipping with a whip!

"He's run off with Mrs. Round's hearthbrush and left it somewhere. He's been in the larder twice. He's pulled every mat into a heap on the landing. And if I catch him under my bed again I shall BUY THAT WHIP," said poor Miss Pepper.

Loony suddenly sneezed and looked very surprised at himself. He was always surprised when he sneezed. He sneezed again.

"Now what's the matter with him?" said Miss Pepper. "Sneezing all over the place."

"He's had too much pepper," said Snubby at once. "That's what it is—too much pepper—it's got up his nose. There's a lot of it about these days."

Miss Pepper looked at him coldly. "Don't be rude, Snubby," she said, and went into the dining-room. Roger roared and Snubby grinned.

"Let's all sneeze when Miss Pepper gets peppery," he said. "She'll stop rowing us then. Loony, clear out. You really *will* get into trouble if you go off with any more of Mrs. Round's brushes. Besides, you're not to, anyway. She's nice."

Mrs. Round appeared at this minute. She was certainly

like her name, and her face shone like the harvest moon, it was so red and round.

"That dog of yours," she began, "if he hasn't got my hearthbrush somewhere now! And if I chase him off with my broom what does he do but think I'm playing a game with him. Loony by name and Loony by nature that dog is."

"What's for pudding to-day, Mrs. Round?" asked Snubby, changing the subject in his clever way. "Are you going to make us one of your smashing treacle puddings again? Honestly, I wish you'd come and be cook at our school. The boys would cheer you every day."

Mrs. Round beamed and patted the bun of hair at the back of her head. "Oh, go on with you now!" she said in her pleasant country drawl. "You keep that dog of yours out of my kitchen, and I might make you pancakes with raspberry jam."

"Loony! Don't you dare to go into Mrs. Round's kitchen to-day," said Snubby sternly, and Loony wagged his little black stump of a tail. He crawled humbly on his tummy to Snubby and lay quite flat in front of him.

"All humbug," said Diana. "He's as good at pretending as you are, Snubby!"

Miss Pepper came out into the hall. "Are you *still* here?" she said to Loony, who promptly went out of the front door at top speed. She turned to the children. "I'm going to telephone one or two coaches I know to see if one is free to come. Go and clear away your books now. There certainly won't be any lessons to-day."

They cleared away their books thankfully. Miss Pepper telephoned for some time and then came into the study. "It's no use," she said. "Everyone is either already fixed up, or is away. I'll have to put an advertisement in the newspapers."

"Oh, don't bother to do that, Miss Pepper," said Roger. "All this trouble for you! It's dreadful! I'm sure Daddy wouldn't want you to bother like this."

29

"Then you think wrong, Roger," said Miss Pepper, and began to draft out an advertisement. It went off by the next post, much to the children's annoyance.

"Goodness knows who we'll get now," said Diana gloomily. "At least we *knew* Mr. Young—and we *know* how to get him talking so that we didn't have to do much work ourselves. Blow!"

For the next three days the children were quite free to do what they liked. They found the riding school, and Miss Pepper arranged for one whole-day ride, and two hour-rides. That was fun. Loony was the only one who disapproved of it. He hated Snubby and the others to go off on horses, because sooner or later he couldn't keep up with them and dropped back. The stable dog, a big airedale, kept up with the whole ride easily and was very scornful of the little spaniel.

They found the river and hired a boat. They could all swim like fishes, so Miss Pepper didn't worry about them on the river. They explored the countryside, and enjoyed looking for uncommon flowers, unsual birds and queer beetles. At least the two boys did—Diana didn't do much seeking for birds and flowers—she "mooned along", as the boys called it, enjoying the smells, the sounds and the sights of the countryside—the smell of the meadow-sweet, the blue of the chicory, the queer little trill of the yellow-hammer, and the blue flash of the kingfisher as he flew past them, crying "tee-tee-tee!"

On the third day Snubby roused the scorn of the others. Diana was sitting beside the bank of the river, watching for the kingfisher again. Roger was lying on his back with his hat tilted over his eyes, listening to the high twitter of the swallows as they darted over the water, skimming the surface for flies.

Snubby was nowhere to be seen. He had crawled off to see if he could watch a few young rabbits who had unexpectedly come out to play in the daylight. Suddenly he came back.

30

"I say! Do you know what I've just seen?"

"A cabbage butterfly," suggested Diana.

"A dandelion," said Roger, not moving.

"A *monkey*!" said Snubby. "Yes, go on, laugh. But I tell you it *was* a monkey!"

"Don't try and stuff us up with one of your tall stories," said Roger. "We're not in the lower third with you."

"Look here—I tell you I *did* see a monkey," repeated Snubby. "It isn't a tall story. It was at the top of a tree and it swung itself down half-way, saw me—and disappeared. Loony didn't see it—but he smelt it. I could see his nose twitching like anything."

Diana and Roger stopped listening. Snubby had too many marvels to tell—wonderful things always seemed to be happening to him—this must be one of them! Diana shushed him.

"Sh! I think I can hear the kingfisher. He may come and sit on this branch."

"You are a disbelieving lot," said Snubby bitterly. "Here I come and tell you, absolutely solemnly and truthfully, that I've just seen a wizard monkey, and all you talk about is kingfishers."

Nobody said anything. Snubby sniffed scornfully. "All right—I'm going off by myself. And I shan't come back and tell you if I see a *chimpanzee* this time!"

He went off with Loony. Roger gave a gentle little snore—he was asleep. Diana sat with her chin on her knees, and was at last rewarded for her long wait. The kingfisher flashed down, sat on the branch just in front of her, and waited for a fish to swim along in the water beneath.

Snubby went gloomily through the wood behind. Loony trotted along at his heels, pondering over the inexplicable ways of rabbits that lived down holes too small for dogs to get into.

Then he stopped and growled deep down in his throat. "What's up?" said Snubby. "Oh—somebody coming?

I can hear them now. Wish I had ears like yours, Loony, though how you hear at all with those big ears flapping over your ear-holes, I really don't know!"

Somebody came through the wood, whistling softly, Loony growled again. Then Snubby saw the newcomer. He was a boy of about fourteen or fifteen, burnt very brown. His hair was corn-coloured and he had eyes so blue that they were quite startling to look at. They were set curiously wide apart and were fringed with thick dark lashes. He had a very wide mouth that grinned in a friendly fashion at Snubby.

"Hallo!" said the boy. "Have you seen a monkey?"

CHAPTER FIVE

BARNEY AND MIRANDA

THAT WAS the first time any of the three children saw the strange boy they were to know so well. Snubby stared at him, at his brilliant, wide-set blue eyes and friendly grin. He liked this boy immensely, but he didn't know why.

"Lost your tongue?" said the boy. "Well, I've lost my monkey. Have you seen one anywhere?"

The boy did not talk quite like anyone Snubby had ever heard. He had a slight American twang, and yet he sounded foreign?Spanish—Italian—what could it be? Nor did he look English, for all his blue eyes and fair hair.

Snubby found his tongue. "Yes!" he said. "I *have* seen a monkey. I saw one about five minutes ago. I'll take you to where I saw him."

"Her," said the boy. "It's a she-monkey. She's called Miranda."

" Is she really yours?" said Snubby. " I've always wanted a monkey. I've only got a dog."

" Lovely dog, though," said the boy, and he gave Loony a pat. Loony at once rolled over on his back and put all his legs into the air, doing a kind of bicycling movement upside down.

" Clever dog," said the boy. " Why don't you get him a little bicycle?" he said, turning to Snubby. " See how well he pedals upside down. Get him a bike with four pedals and you could make a fortune out of him. The only bicycling dog in the world!"

" Do you really mean it?" said Snubby eagerly. He was ready to believe anything wonderful about Loony. The boy laughed.

" No. 'Course not. Come on, where's this tree? I must find Miranda—she's been gone an hour!"

Miranda was in the tree next to the one that Snubby

had first seen her in. The boy gave his soft little whistle and the monkey leapt down like a squirrel, landing in his arms. He fondled her and scolded her.

"You know," said Snubby, trying to keep the excited Loony away from the monkey. "You know, I told my two cousins about the monkey and they absolutely refused to believe me. I suppose you wouldn't play a little trick on them for me?"

"If you like," said the boy, turning his blue eyes on Snubby with an amused look in them. "What do you want me to do?"

"Well—do you think you could make Miranda walk all round my cousins, or something like that, and then come back to you?" said Snubby eagerly. "Then I could go up and they'd tell me they'd seen a monkey too and I'd disbelieve them like they disbelieved *me*!"

"Not much of a trick," said the boy. "I'll tell Miranda to drop on them from a tree and then leap off again. Give them a bit of a fright."

"*Could* you make her do that?" said Snubby.

"You bet!" said the boy. "Where are these cousins of yours? Come on—we'll liven them up a bit. We won't show ourselves, though."

They crept towards the river. Snubby made Loony crouch down quietly. He pointed out Diana to the boy, and then Roger. The boy nodded. He said a few quiet words to the monkey who answered him in a funny little chattering voice and then sped up into the trees. The two boys watched. Loony looked most surprised to see the monkey disappear into the tree above him. Cats did that, but this creature didn't look or smell like a cat.

Miranda made her way to the tree immediately above Roger, who was still lying asleep with his hat over his face. The monkey leapt down and then jumped full on top of Roger. Diana turned in astonishment, her eyes almost falling out of her head when she saw Miranda leaping down on Roger and then leaping up into the tree again and disappearing.

Roger woke with a start and sat up hurriedly.

" What fell on me?" he said to Diana.

" A monkey," said Diana. " A little brown one."

" Oh, don't *you* start about monkeys," said Roger crossly. " Anyone would think this place was full of monkeys the way you and Snubby go on about them."

" But, Roger—honestly, it *was* a monkey," said Diana.

" You and Snubby can go on telling me all day long that you keep seeing monkeys, but I shan't believe there's a monkey about even if I see one! " said Roger.

And at that very moment he saw Miranda! He saw her sitting on the strange boy's shoulder, as he came along with Snubby, both of them grinning widely.

Roger had to believe in the monkey then. He was very astonished. " Is that your monkey?" he said to the boy. " Is it a pet?"

" Sure," said the boy. " You a pet, Miranda?"

Miranda chattered and put a little brown paw down the boy's neck. " Don't tickle," he said. " Shake hands with these people, and show your manners."

Loony sat by open-mouthed whilst Miranda gravely held out a little paw and allowed Roger, Diana and Snubby to shake it. The boy sat down beside them. Loony at once made a rush for Miranda. He was jealous.

Quick as lightning the monkey leapt off the boy's shoulder and on to Loony's back. She held on tightly and he couldn't get her off till he rolled on the ground. The children roared.

" Poor old Loony—nobody's ever tried to ride him before," said Diana. " What did you say her name was —Miranda? What a queer name for a monkey."

" Why?" said the boy. " I thought it was a mighty pretty name when I first read it, and it just suits Miranda —*she's* pretty too."

35

None of the three children thought Miranda was pretty, though they all thought she was sweet and amusing. Still, they were used to people thinking their pets pretty and marvellous even though they mostly weren't.

" She's cute, isn't she?" said the boy, as Miranda began to turn head over heels very fast indeed. " She can do no end of tricks. Turn cartwheels, Miranda."

Miranda turned dozens of cartwheels, going over and over on hands and feet without stopping. Loony regarded her solemnly. No—this couldn't be a cat. No cat he had ever seen behaved like this.

" What's your name?" asked Roger, liking this strange boy just as much as Snubby did.

" Barney—short for Barnabas," said the boy.

" Where do you live?" asked Snubby.

The boy hesitated. " Nowhere at present," he said. " I'm just tramping around."

This was puzzling. " What do you mean? Are you on a hiking trip, or something?" asked Diana.

" You might call it that," said the boy.

" Well, where's your *real home*?" persisted Snubby. " You must have a *home*! "

" Don't pester Barney," said Roger, seeing the boy hesitate again. " You're always so inquisitive, Snubby."

" It's all right," said Barney, and he rubbed Miranda's fur gently. " Actually I'm looking for my father."

This sounded queer. " Doesn't your mother know where he is?" demanded Snubby.

" My mother's dead," said Barney. " She died last year. I don't want to talk about that, see? I don't know much about her or about myself either, but I'm trying to find out. My mother was in the show business—you know, travelling around in a circus, and attending fairs and things like that. She was wonderful with animals. I thought my father was dead—but just before she died my mother told me she didn't think he was. He was an actor—acted in Shakespeare plays, she said—and she ran away from him after she'd been married three months. He doesn't know anything about me."

"Don't tell us all this," said Roger awkwardly. "It's your own private business."

"I want to talk to somebody," said Barney, looking at them with his startling blue eyes. "But there's been no one to talk to. Well, when my mother died I felt sort of lonely, and I couldn't settle to anything. So I thought I'd go off on my own—with Miranda, of course —and see if I could hear of my father. I'd like to know there was *some*body belonging to me, even if he turned out to be a disappointment."

"I haven't any father *or* mother," said Snubby. "But I'm lucky. I've heaps of other relations and they're jolly decent to me. I'd hate to have no one—only just Loony."

Diana couldn't imagine what things would be like without her mother. She was sorry for Barney. "What do you do for a living, then?" she asked him.

"Oh, just scrounge around," said the boy. "I can always go to a circus or a fair, you know, and earn some money there. There's not much I can't do. I've often been in the circus ring with Miranda here. I've just left the fair over at Northcotling. I'm at a loose end now, wandering about with Miranda. What I want to do is to get hold of some of Shakespeare's plays and read them. I suppose you can't lend me any?"

Snubby couldn't imagine why anyone should want to borrow Shakespeare's plays. Diana tumbled to it at once.

"You want to know the plays that your father acts in—or used to act in!" she said. "You want to know the things he liked and the parts he could play!"

"That's right," said Barney, pleased. "I've only read one of them—about a storm and a shipwreck, it was. It's where I got Miranda's name from."

"Oh, yes—*The Tempest*," said Roger. "That's quite

a good one to start off with. Do you *really* want to read the plays? They'll be jolly difficult for you. If you really do, I'll lend you some."

"Thanks," said the boy. "Where do you live?"

"Over at Rockingdown Cottage," said Roger. "Do you know it?" Barney nodded.

"Where are you living just at present?" said Diana curiously. It seemed odd to think of somebody without a bed at night.

"Oh—this weather I can sleep anywhere," said Barney. "Under a haystack—in a barn—even up a tree with Miranda so long as I tie myself on."

Diana glanced at her watch and gave an exclamation. "Do you know what the time is, boys? It's quarter of an hour past tea-time already. Miss Pepper will be all hot and bothered!"

They scrambled up. "If you come and whistle outside Rockingdown Cottage any time, we'll hear you and come out," said Roger. "I'll look out those plays for you."

"I'll see you to-morrow," said Barney, and stood watching them go, his blue eyes looking very far apart as he smiled and waved. Miranda waved a tiny paw too.

"I like him most awfully," said Snubby. "Do you, Roger? And hasn't he got queer eyes? Like somebody belonging to the Little Folk, not to us. That sounds silly —but you know what I mean."

They did know. There was something strange about Barney, something lonely and lost—and yet he was gay and had a most uproarious laugh, and the most natural manners in the world. "I hope we see a lot of him," said Roger.

He needn't have worried about that—they were going to see far more of Barney than any of them guessed!

CHAPTER SIX

MR. KING—AND AN EXCITING IDEA

The next thing that happened was that Miss Pepper found a tutor for the three of them. They were helping Mrs. Round to clear away breakfast when he arrived. He knocked and rang, and Mrs. Round scurried to open the door.

"Gentleman to see Miss Pepper," she announced to the children. "Name of King."

Diana hurried to fetch Miss Pepper, who took Mr. King into the study and remained there with him for some time. Then she opened the door and called the three children.

"Mr. King, these are the three I told you about—they are cousins—this is Roger, this is Diana, this is Peter."

Roger and Diana looked surprised to hear Snubby called Peter. They had quite forgotten that that was really his name. Mr. King grinned at them all. He was a stocky, well-built man about thirty-five or forty, with hair going a little grey, and a mouth that looked distinctly firm.

"They don't look too bad," he told Miss Pepper. She smiled.

"Appearances don't always tell the truth," she said. "Children, this is Mr. King. Subject to final arrangements, he is going to come and give you the coaching your parents want you to have."

This wasn't so good. The children's smiles faded away. They looked more carefully at Mr. King. He looked back. Did they like him—or didn't they? Snubby decided that he didn't. Diana wasn't sure. Roger felt that he might like him when he knew him better. Their hearts all sank when the thought of lessons morning after morning, just when they had got used to nice free days.

"Mr. King will start with you on Monday next," said Miss Pepper.

"Can Loony be in the room too?" said Snubby.

Mr. King looked a little startled. "Er—who is Loony?" he asked, wondering if it was another child, not quite so bright as these appeared.

"My spaniel," said Snubby, and at that moment Loony made one of his usual hurricane-like appearances. He came in at the door like a rocket, and hurled himself at everyone as if he hadn't seen them for a year. He even rolled over Mr. King's feet, too, before he realised that they were the feet of a stranger, and then he leapt to his own feet and growled.

"Oh—so this is Loony," said Mr. King. "Well— I don't see why he shouldn't be in the room, if he doesn't disturb us."

Snubby immediately decided that he liked Mr. King very much after all. Miss Pepper spoke hurriedly.

"I shouldn't make any rash promises if I were you," she said, trying to give Mr. King a warning look. He saw it.

"Ah—yes—I won't *promise*," he said, and then as Loony tore at his shoe and got his shoelaces undone, he firmly added a few more words. "In fact, we'll put Loony on trial first."

"I wish Miranda could come too," said Snubby. "She's a monkey, Mr. King—really a pet!"

Mr. King thought it was time to go before he was asked to put a monkey on trial too.

He went, and Miss Pepper spoke to the three children.

"He has the most excellent testimonials, and I think he should be a very fine coach. You'll begin on Monday —and if I hear of you misbehaving, Snubby, I shall put

40

Loony into a kennel at night instead of letting him sleep in the house."

This was a very alarming threat, and one that Miss Pepper was quite capable of carrying out. Snubby slept with Loony on his bed all night long, and the spaniel would be broken-hearted if he had to sleep anywhere else. Snubby didn't dare to argue with Miss Pepper about this. He sneezed violently, and then sneezed twice more, fishing for his handkerchief with a most concerned expression. " Whoooosh-oo! Oh dear—I'm so sorry—Whhoo-oooooooo . . ."

" Have you got a cold, Snubby?" said Miss Pepper. " I *told* you to take your coat yesterday evening."

" No—no cold, Miss Pepper," said Snubby, finding an extremely dirty handkerchief and sneezing into that. " Just —whooosh—oo—sorry just a little pepper up my nose. Whoooooooo . . ."

Miss Pepper made an impatient noise and went out. Diana and Roger roared with laughter. Loony joined in the excitement and tore round the table six times without stopping.

" Racehorse trick being performed," said Snubby, putting away his hanky. " All right, Loony—you've passed the winning-post about three times. Woa! "

" What shall we do to-day?" asked Diana, as she stacked up the breakfast dishes to take out to Mrs. Round.

" Let's go and peep in at the old mansion," said Roger. " Ask Mrs. Round if there's any way of getting in. I'd just love to poke round it, and imagine what it was like in the old days."

Mrs. Round didn't know very much. " You keep away from it," she said. " Folks do say that once a young fellow managed to get in there, and he couldn't never get out again. That might happen to you too. There's doors there that shut of themselves, yes, and lock themselves too. And there's rooms there still full of furniture, left by the last owner—my, they'll be full of moths and spiders!

A queer, creepy, place I wouldn't go into, not if you paid me a thousand pounds!"

This sounded pleasantly eerie. The three children at once made up their minds to do a bit of snooping that very day. They would meet Barney and take him too.

So, when they heard Barney's soft whistle they went out to see him. He had Miranda on his shoulder. She leapt into a tree and peered into a window nearby. Mrs. Round was in the room, sweeping. The monkey made a soft chattering noise.

Mrs. Round looked up, and was extremely astonished to see Miranda apparently about to jump in at the open window. She shut it at once, almost catching the monkey's nose.

Mrs. Round stood at the window, shaking her fist at the surprised monkey. She called to Miss Pepper. "You come here, Miss, and see what those children have collected now!"

Miss Pepper hurried in, wondering what caterpillar or beetle or mouse Mrs. Round had found. She was always finding something in Roger's bedroom. She was startled to see the monkey. Miranda disappeared down the tree.

"All I say is—if they starts bringing in monkeys I'm going," said Mrs. Round. "Loony dogs I can put up with, beetles and such I can deal with—but monkeys, no. It'll be elephants next, trampling up the stairs and down."

Miss Pepper hurried downstairs to solve the monkey mystery. She saw Barney with the others; Miranda was on his shoulder. He nodded his head politely to her when the children introduced him. "Miss Pepper, this is Barnabas, and this is Miranda, his monkey. Isn't she sweet?"

Miss Pepper wasn't going to go so far as to say that. In her experience, monkeys were full of fleas and apt to bite people. She eyed Miranda mistrustfully.

"I'd rather you didn't bring that animal indoors," said

Miss Pepper firmly. "Sweet or not, I'd rather she stayed outside."

"Yes, certainly, Mam," said Barney. "It isn't everyone that likes monkeys."

Miranda looked at Miss Pepper just as mournfully and pathetically as Loony sometimes looked at her. Oh dear —these animals! Why did they look at you like that? Miss Pepper ran to the kitchen, got a cucumber end and sliced it up. She ran out with the little slices on a plate.

"Monkeys like cucumber," she said. "Here's some for her. But please take her down the garden. Oh, do be careful Loony doesn't chew her tail!"

Miranda's tail hung down and Loony was eyeing it hopefully. It did look nice and chewy. He made a snap at it and Miranda gave a leap off Barney's shoulder and sat on his head, chattering.

"Loony! If you dare to chew Miranda's tail I'll let her chew yours," said Snubby. Loony promptly sat down on his as if he understood every word. Barney gave one of his uproarious laughs, and set everyone else laughing too. Even Mrs. Round opened the bedroom window and looked out to see what the joke was.

"Come on," said Roger to Barney. "Let's go down the garden. Oh, wait a bit. I say, Miss Pepper—Barney's keen on reading Shakespeare's plays. He's read *The Tempest* and he wants me to lend him another. What would be a good one for him to read next?"

Miss Pepper was most surprised. What with his monkey, and his queer blue eyes, and now his liking for plays, this boy was puzzling. He looked quite a nice boy, and Miss Pepper wondered where he came from. She would have to ask Roger about him when he had gone.

"Well—he could try *Midsummer Night's Dream*," she said.

"Oh, yes—that's a lovely play," said Diana. "We did it once at school. I was Titania."

43

They went down the garden to a tumbledown summer-house and sat there, with Loony on the floor trying to get another chew at Miranda's tail, and Miranda first on Snubby's shoulder and then Barney's—always swinging her tail just a *little* out of Loony's reach. She was very naughty. She took Diana's hanky out of her pocket and produced a horrible sticky mass of toffee from Snubby's shorts, which she proceeded to lick with great enjoyment before she threw the rest down to Loony.

" You're not to eat it, Loony," ordered Snubby. " You know what happened last time you ate toffee."

" What happened?" asked Barney with interest.

" He got his top and bottom teeth stuck together," said Snubby. " And he was in such a fright that he rushed straight out-of-doors and down the street and didn't come back for hours, till the toffee had melted and gone. For a whole day after that he was scared. It's the only day I've ever known him be really good from morning to-night."

" Miranda only licks it," said Barney.

" She's sensible," said Diana. " Loony isn't."

" Let's tell Barney what we want to do this morning," said Roger. " Barney, we want to go and walk round that big old mansion whose chimneys you can just see from here. It's empty now—nobody lives there—and there are all kinds of queer stories about it. We thought it would be fun to snoop round it."

They all got up, Loony too, his tail wagging. Were they going for a walk? He didn't like this sitting about. It was boring. They made their way through the overgrown paths, working their way steadily towards the old house.

" You almost have to hack your way through," said Roger. " We'll come to the drive soon—that's fairly clear. Look—now you can see the house—enormous, isn't it?"

It certainly was. Great chimneys stood up from the roof, scores of windows peered out dimly, half-covered with ivy and creeper, and there was an air of desolation and decay about the place.

"Come on," said Roger. "We'll explore—and I say —wouldn't it be fun if we managed to get inside!"

CHAPTER SEVEN

A LITTLE EXPLORING

THE FOUR CHILDREN and Loony came right up to the old house. A sparrow darted out of the thick ivy nearby and made them jump.

"It's so jolly quiet," said Roger. "Even the wind seems to have deserted the old mansion!"

"I don't like it at all," said Diana. "It's a horrid place."

They came to the great flight of steps that led up to the front door. The stone steps were cracked in places and weeds sprouted through the cracks. One step wobbled when Roger stood on it. The foundations had rotted away.

"It would need an absolute fortune spent on it to make it liveable in," said Diana. "Still—I can quite well imagine how gay and lovely it all was when it was properly kept up and a jolly family lived in it."

They came to the great front door. It was a double one, and had a lot of ironwork about it, which had rusted. There was no knocker, but a great iron bell-pull hung down beside the door.

Of course Snubby had to pull it. He found it very heavy and stiff to pull down and he almost hung on it to pull it. And suddenly a tremendous jangling broke out somewhere in the old house. It startled the children and Snubby let go the bell-pull. Loony barked madly and scraped at the front door.

45

" Gosh—that made me jump," said Diana. " Who would have thought the bell rang after all these years! I guess it gave a fright to any rats and mice in the house. You are an idiot, Snubby. For goodness sake don't go ringing all the bells you see. You might break one."

" I don't see that that would matter," said Snubby. " I'm the only person ever likely to ring the bells here! "

There was no letter-box so the children could not peep through that. But there was a crack in the door and by putting their eye to it the children could see into the vast, dim hall.

It was not a pleasant sight. It was covered in grey dust, and the walls were festooned with cobwebs. It looked lost and forgotten and dead. A great staircase loomed up dimly in the distance, at the back of the hall.

Roger shook the door hard, but he couldn't open it or budge it an inch, of course. Not that he really hoped to! Barney laughed at him.

" It would need a giant to force that door open! " he said. " Come on—let's look into the windows. There are plenty of them! "

They went down the flight of stone steps and made their way round the east side of the house. They came to some large french windows. The glass was dirty and streaked, but they were able to see in. It must once have been a ballroom, with a beautiful floor. Built-in mirrors still had their places on the walls. Most of them were now cracked. The children saw their ghostly faces reflected in the mirror opposite the window through which they were peeping. It made them jump.

" I really thought it was somebody looking at us," said Diana, scared, " but it's only our reflections in that cracked mirror. What a lovely room this must have been! What are those broken things in that corner?"

Roger squinted at them. " Broken chairs, I think," he said. " You know we heard this place was used in the last war for something or other. I expect this was one of the rooms used. Those look like office chairs or something."

They went on round the house, peeping into window after window, peering into dim, dusty rooms that had a look of utter forlornness. It made the children feel quite depressed. Even Miranda and Loony were quiet and subdued.

They came right round the house back to the front door again. Not one window had been found unfastened, nor even cracked or broken. One or two had had shutters fastened across them and these windows might have been broken. The children couldn't see.

They looked at the upstairs windows. They seemed tight-shut too—and again some had shutters fastened across them.

" Look! " said Diana, pointing. " There are two rooms there with bars across. They must have been the children's nurseries. When Roger and I were small we had bars like that across our windows too. We used to hate them."

Snubby was squinting up at the windows, blinking in his efforts to focus them clearly, for they were rather high up. " You know—it almost looks to me as if there are *curtains* at those windows," he said. " Can any of you see?"

Barney had the best eyesight of them all. His bright blue eyes fastened on the nursery windows. " Yes! " he said in surprise. " There *are* curtains there—almost falling to bits, I think! "

They all stared up at the barred nursery windows, Loony too. Miranda suddenly left Barney's shoulder, leapt up the ivy, bounded on to a window-sill, flung herself upwards again to a little balcony, and then there she was, sitting on the window-sill of the old nursery window, peering in!

" Golly—I wish *I* could do that! " said Snubby in admiration.

" I'm surprised you can't! " said Roger.

47

They were all watching Miranda. She sat on the window-sill, and then she suddenly got between the bars and disappeared! Everyone gaped.

"Where's she gone?" said Diana, amazed.

"Into the room behind!" said Barney.

"But—isn't there any window-glass there?" said Roger.

"Apparently not," said Diana. "Or she wouldn't have been able to go in! How queer!"

"Wait a bit," said Barney, squinting up at the window. "I think I can see where it's broken—just at one side, look. There's a hole there as if a stone's been thrown through it or something. That's where Miranda went through."

She appeared again and looked down at the interested children below. She chattered and waved her tiny paw.

"She's found something interesting up there," said Barney at once. "There—she's gone into the room again. Whatever can she have found?"

Miranda appeared once more—and this time she was holding something. She held it out and they all tried to see what it was.

"Throw it down, Miranda!" shouted Barney. And down through the air came the thing Miranda was holding. It fell beside Diana's foot. Loony pounced on it at once and Diana had to wrench it from him. She held it out to the others.

"A doll! A funny old-fashioned rag doll! Would you believe it! Fancy Miranda finding it in the old nursery!"

"She loves dolls," said Barney, and he took it and examined it. He shook it and dust flew from it in a cloud. He looked at it thoughtfully. "I wonder if there's anything else there?" he said. And as if Miranda could read his thoughts she appeared again at the window with something else in her paws. She held it out, chattering —then down it came, turning over and over in the air. Barney caught it. He gave an exclamation and showed it to the others.

"A soldier on horseback—carved most beautifully!" said Roger, taking it. "It's simply lovely. The colour's still showing. What lovely soldiers children must have had in the old days—I never had ones like this."

"Must be part of a hand-made set," said Diana. They all looked at the beautiful model and then gazed upwards again. And Miranda threw down yet another thing!

This time it was a book. It fell to pieces as Miranda threw it and the pages fluttered in the air. Diana picked some of them up. "What a funny old book!" she said. "It's rather like one Granny has, in her special bookshelf —she keeps a collection of children's books that are very precious because they are more than a hundred years old. I say—it's queer, isn't it, that there are still curtains to that room—and toys there? What do you make of it, Roger?"

"I don't know," said Roger. "Except that perhaps when the house was let, the nurseries were locked up—because of memories, or something—you know how grown-ups sometimes feel about those things. Think how Mummy keeps the first shoes you ever wore, Di—and the first tooth of mine that came out. She just won't part with them."

"Mothers seem to be like that," said Diana. "Perhaps the mother of the children who had these toys couldn't bear to let strangers use her nurseries—couldn't bear to part with the toys and things—and locked them up. Perhaps the rooms were forgotten. It's such a big house they might quite well have been."

Miranda appeared again. Barney called up to her. "No, Miranda. No more."

But one more thing came floating down, spreading itself out in the air. It was a small handkerchief. Diana caught it as it floated by her head. In the corner, beautifully embroidered, was a name in what once had been pale blue silk.

"Bob." Just that and nothing more. The children

looked at the name. Who was Bob? Was he grown-up now—or was he dead long ago? They didn't know. They pictured a tiny boy being told to use his hanky—the one with his name on. Diana could almost hear his nurse speaking to him.

"'Don't sniff, Bob, dear. Use your hanky—the one with your name on. I gave it to you this morning.'"

"Come down, Miranda!" called Barney. He turned to the others. "She'll throw down everything in the room if I don't stop her," he said. "And goodness knows how much more there is up there. I wouldn't be surprised if the nurseries are still furnished—with cots and things. Queer, isn't it?"

Miranda came leaping down. It was astonishing how she could come safely down the walls, by just clutching lightly at the ivy here and there.

Loony greeted her with a mad series of barks. He was jealous because she could do so many things that he couldn't. She settled on Barney's shoulder, and took hold of his right ear with her tiny paw. She made a funny whispering sound in his ear. He shook his head like a dog.

"Don't! You tickle!"

"What are we going to do with these things?" said Diana. "They don't belong to us."

"Well—we can't possibly put them back," said Snubby. "Unless we tell Miranda to—and surely she wouldn't have the sense to take them all back."

"Oh, yes, she would," said Barney. "She'll do anything I tell her. You don't know how clever she is. I should think she's just about the cleverest monkey in the world. If people knew how clever she was they'd offer me a thousand pounds for her—and I wouldn't take it."

They all gazed at Miranda with respect. A thousand pounds! "Why, that's more than *I'm* worth!" said Snubby.

"I should think so! About nine hundred and ninety-nine pounds, nineteen shillings and eleven pence three farthings more," said Roger at once. "Work that out, Snubby."

Snubby couldn't. He changed the subject and looked longingly up at the barred windows. "I wish *we* could get up there!" he said.

"Well," said Barney surprisingly. "That's easy—if you really want to."

CHAPTER EIGHT

BARNEY HAS AN IDEA

"WHAT do you mean?" said Roger, staring at Barney in surprise. "We can't possibly get up there—why, it's three storeys up—and jolly high storeys at that. No ladder we've got would reach there—even if we'd got one, which we haven't."

"And it would be too heavy to carry if we had," said Diana, remembering how heavy the longest ladder at home had been when she had tried to carry it with Roger.

"I'm not thinking of a ladder," said Barney. "I'm thinking of a rope."

They all stared at him. "A rope?" repeated Roger. "But how in the world are you going to get a rope up there? You'd want a ladder to take up the rope!"

Barney laughed one of his loud laughs. "No, no—I'd just send Miranda up with a rope. She'll do anything like that."

Still they didn't understand. Barney grinned at them.

"It's plain you've never lived in a circus or a fair," he said. "You get used to puzzles of this sort there. Now look—if we get a rope, we give one end to Miranda—and up she goes to the nursery windows with it. She sits on the window-sill and twists the rope over the bars—then she throws the rope down to us. It comes slithering down the walls—and down to us. We catch it—and we've got a double rope then, haven't we, with the middle held by those bars up there! And it's easy enough to test the bars by pulling on the rope."

" And then up we go to the window-sill! " cried Roger, seeing light. " Gosh—that's an idea. All the same, I don't think I could climb a rope all that way. I'm pretty good at gym, and one of the best on the ropes at school—but it's a terrific way up to those windows."

" I shall be able to manage it all right," said Barney. " I've been on the ropes at the circus many a time—on the tightrope too. You should see me walk along it back-wards! "

The others looked at Barney with a new respect. Could he really walk on a rope or a wire? Snubby made up his mind to get him to teach him during those holidays. He imagined himself setting up a rope across the gym and walking airily along it. That would make the others stare!

" Climbing up a rope's nothing," said Barney. " It's just a question whether those bars will still hold. Now the thing is—where is there a rope? I haven't got one—have you?"

Roger didn't know. His exploration of Rockingdown Cottage hadn't shown him any ropes or ladders.

" Even if there isn't a rope at home we can buy one," he said. " I say—this is exciting, isn't it? Do you think you really could get into that window, Barney?"

" Sure of it," said Barney. " Miranda can easily take up the rope. She knows how to put it over the bars—she's done that often enough in the circus. Then I'll go up and see what I can see. If there's a hole big enough for Miranda to get through, it will be big enough for me to put my hand in to slip the catch of the window—and in I'll go! "

" Let's go and buy the rope at once," said Diana eagerly.

With Loony rushing ahead like a mad thing, the four of
them made their way back through the grounds. They
went down the overgrown drive, as that was the shortest
way to the village. They had decided that it wouldn't be
much use looking for a rope at Rockingdown Cottage.
Miss Pepper would be sure to ask what they were looking
for and why they wanted a rope and a hundred other
things.

"Grown-ups are terribly inquisitive," said Snubby
plaintively. "Even if I'm doing absolutely nothing at all
people come and ask me what I'm up to."

"I don't blame them," said Diana. "You're always
up to some kind of mischief as far as I can see. By the
way, was it you who put my bedroom slippers on the top
of the cupboard last night? I couldn't find them for
ages."

53

" I expect I put them there out of Loony's way," said Snubby.

" Well, don't. Just shut my bedroom door if it happens to be open—then Loony can't go in," said Diana. " I'm not going to hunt all over the place for my slippers every single night! "

They decided to have an ice-cream at the little general store when they got there. They sat down at the one and only table and ordered vanilla ices. The old lady came bustling out with them.

" And how do you like Rockingdown Cottage?" she said. " Nice little place, isn't it? No queer stories about it, like there are about the big house."

" What queer stories are there?" said Roger, paying for the ice-creams.

" Oh, I wouldn't scare you with such tales," said the old woman, beaming. " That old place has fallen on evil days. Seems as if a curse was on it, somehow, the things that happened."

This sounded interesting. " What happened?" asked Roger.

" Oh—folks were killed—and two children died—and . . ."

" What two children?" asked Diana. " Was one called Bob?"

" Well, there now—fancy you knowing that! " said the old woman in surprise. " Yes—that was Master Robert. His sister, little Miss Arabella, fell out of the nursery window and was killed—then only Master Robert was left. So they barred the windows up. And then if he didn't go and get scarlet fever and pass away too."

" What happened then?" asked Diana, after a pause. Poor little Bob! She actually had his small hanky in her pocket. He hadn't lived to grow up—but his hanky was still there. And his soldier and book.

" The nurseries were shut up just as they were," said

54

the old woman, trying to remember. " The nurse was given orders to leave everything as it was—everything! She was so upset, poor creature—she loved those two children like her own."

" What happened to the father and mother?" asked Roger.

" Lord Rockingdown was killed," said the old woman. " Yes, and his lady died of a broken heart—no husband, no child left. Wasn't I telling you this the other day? I'll be boring you, repeating myself like this! The place went to a cousin after that, but he never came near it."

The children now had a picture of what had happened to the unlucky house and family. Diana felt sad. She pictured the big house gay and lively, with Lord and Lady Rockingdown giving parties, going off to hunt, choosing ponies for their two small children, Arabella and Bob—planning all sorts of things for them as they grew up.

But they didn't grow up. The time came when the gay, happy family was no more—the house was empty and unloved. Only the nurseries with their toys, and goodness knew what else, were left to guard the memories of the little family.

Diana's eyes had been wandering round the crowded little shop. It really was a most interesting place and Diana felt sure that there was practically nothing that couldn't be bought there. Pails, deck-chairs, lengths of garden hose, saucepans, kettles, rugs, crockery—everything seemed to be there, muddled up together. Things hung down from the ceiling, and were piled on shelves round the walls.

" Do you know exactly what you've got in your shop?" asked Diana curiously. " There are so many things— surely you don't know them all."

" Ah, indeed I do," said the old woman, beaming all over her wrinkled pink face. " There's not a thing I don't know, and I could put my hand on anything you like to mention! "

"Well—could you put your hand on a good, long, strong rope?" said Roger at once.

"A rope? Now, let's see," said the old dame, frowning. "Yes—second shelf to the right, near the end. That's where it should be."

"I'll look for you," said Barney, getting up. "Don't you go climbing about on those shelves!"

The second shelf was near the ceiling. Barney leapt up like a cat, found the rope, and leapt back again.

"What it is to be young!" said the old woman admiringly. "You ought to be in a circus, you ought!"

Everyone grinned, but nobody said anything. The old woman looked at the price on the rope. "Do you really want a rope?" she said. "Don't you go doing nothing dangerous, now. This rope's expensive—but then it's good and strong. Perhaps a cheaper one would do for you. What do you want it for?"

"Oh, this and that," said Diana quickly. "I think this strong one would be best. Pay for it, Roger."

Roger paid, thinking it was a good thing it was the beginning of the holidays and he had plenty of money! They said good day and went off with the rope. As they went down the street the church clock struck loudly.

"Half-past twelve already," said Diana. "We shan't have time to do any more exploring this morning. We'd better meet you this afternoon, Barney."

"Right," said Barney.

"What are you going to do about dinner?" asked Snubby, suddenly realising that Barney had no nice-smelling meal to go home to—in fact, not even a home.

"I'll buy myself some bread and cheese," said Barney. "And I'll get Miranda an orange. She loves oranges."

He went off with Miranda on his shoulder, after arranging to call for the children at half-past two. Diana made up her mind to ask Miss Pepper to give them a picnic tea —one they could share with Barney.

She was worried about Barney. Was it comfortable to

sleep under a haystack at night? Did he have enough money to buy himself the food he wanted? Suppose it rained? What did he do then? He didn't seem to have any clothes except those he had on. What a strange life he must lead with Miranda—just the two of them, wandering about together. She looked up.

"It's going to pour," she said to the others. "I hope Miss Pepper won't say we're to keep indoors this afternoon."

"It'll hold off until the evening," said Roger, looking at the clouds. "We'll be all right this afternoon, I think. There may be a storm to-night."

Miss Pepper was pleased to see them punctual for once. An appetising smell filled the house as they went in.

"Sausages—and onions," said Roger. "I hope there are chip potatoes."

There were—and fried tomatoes too. The children were hungry and soon cleared the big dish. Diana wished that Barney could have shared such a meal. She pictured him sitting on a grassy bank somewhere, munching bread and cheese, with Miranda beside him, eating an orange.

"Never mind—he'll be with us this afternoon—sharing our tea—and a jolly fine adventure!" she thought.

CHAPTER NINE

BARNEY was outside at half-past two, whistling. "There's that boy with the monkey again," said Miss Pepper. "I do hope he's a *nice* boy, Roger. I don't want you to make friends with anyone who will lead you into bad ways."

Roger grinned. "It's much more likely that *Snubby* will teach *him* bad ways," he said. "Barney's all right,

Miss Pepper. Shall I ask him in for a meal sometime, then you can judge for yourself?"

"Yes. That would be a good idea," said Miss Pepper. "Well, you'd better go, if he's waiting for you. I've got your picnic ready for you. It's on the kitchen window-sill. Ask Mrs. Round for it."

Snubby went racing out to the kitchen, Loony at his heels. "Roundy, Roundy, where are you? Have you got our tea for us?"

Mrs. Round looked up from her after-dinner cup of tea. "Now, don't you be cheeky," she said. "Calling me Roundy like that! I've told you of that before, Master Sauce-Box!"

"Roundy's a lovely name for you," said Snubby, and gave the plump Mrs. Round a sudden squeeze. "I can't help calling you Roundy. It's a pet name. You needn't mind."

Mrs. Round didn't. She thought Snubby was what she called a "caution," and she didn't seem to mind what he said or did. She was even putting up with Loony a bit better now, in spite of his habit of taking all her brushes out into the garden.

"That dog and you are a pair," she said, putting her hair straight after Snubby's sudden squeeze. "Get down, Loony. Where did you put my carpet brush, I'd like to know? Wait till I find it and I'll give you such a hiding with it."

Loony picked up a duster and ran off with it, shaking it as if it were a rat. Snubby yelled at him and Miss Pepper appeared in the doorway.

"Snubby! Stop that noise. What's the dog got now? Drop it, Loony. I'm so sorry, Mrs. Round—that dog is completely mad."

"That's all right, Miss," said Mrs. Round graciously. "I'm getting used to him now. He's not so bad, take him all round. Just puppy-like."

Miss Pepper was relieved to hear Mrs. Round taking

things so calmly. She gave Snubby the basket of tea-things and sent him off. He tore into the garden with Loony.

Loony greeted Barney riotously, and Miranda sat on her master's shoulder and watched. She suddenly slid down and caught hold of Loony's ear. She gave it a good tug and leapt back again to Barney's shoulder almost before the dog knew what had happened. He yelped.

The children laughed. They always enjoyed these bits of by-play between Loony and Miranda. " We've got the tea," said Diana. " And the rope. Come on! "

Feeling rather excited the children made their way once more through the grounds to the old mansion. Miranda made a little chattering noise when they came near. She remembered her adventure of the morning.

" Blow! It's beginning to rain! " said Roger. " Just as we've got a picnic tea too! "

" We can have it on that veranda place," said Snubby, pointing to where a veranda showed on the south side of the house, almost hidden by hanging creepers. " We could drag away some of those creepers to let a bit of light and air in."

They put the tea-basket on the veranda. It certainly was a dismal place. Diana felt sure it would be full of spiders and earwigs, and very damp. She hoped they wouldn't have to have tea there.

The boys were longing to get on with the exploring. They were already walking round to the part of the house where the nurseries were. They looked up at the barred windows. Miranda was off Barney's shoulder and away to the nursery window-sill immediately. Barney called her back.

" Here, Miranda! Come back. We've got a job for you to do! "

Snubby and Roger undid the rope. It certainly was a good strong one. " I believe it will be too heavy for Miranda to pull up behind her," said Roger weighing it in his hand. It certainly was very heavy.

" I thought of that," said Barney, and he took some string from his pocket. " We'll play the old trick of letting a string pull the rope! "

The others watched whilst he tied some string to the rope-end. Then he found a stone with a hole in it and tied the other end of the string to it.

" What's that for?" said Diana.

" You'll soon see," said Barney. " Now, Miranda— are you ready? Take the string up—twist it over the bars just as you do when you go up to one of the trapeze swings in the circus—and let the other end of the string drop! "

Miranda listened, her brown eyes gleaming intelligently. She chattered softly back. She really was a remarkable little monkey.

She took the stone in her tiny paw, and leapt off Barney's shoulder. She bounded to the little balcony, the string pulling up behind her. Up the ivy, on to another window-sill, and up the ivy again to the barred windows. The string unravelled swiftly behind her.

Miranda sat on the window-sill, peering in at the window again. Barney called to her, " Go on, Miranda. Do your stuff! "

The others watched breathlessly. Would Miranda really " do her stuff?"

She did! She slipped the stone over the top bar, and let it drop down the other side of the bars—the window side. The stone fell, dragging the string behind it. More string unravelled and ran up the wall, as the stone with its tail of string dropped down to the ground.

Barney caught the stone as it fell and pulled at the string. " Now, watch," he said to Diana. " You'll soon see the rope go up."

He pulled hard at the string, and it travelled over the bars of the window and down the wall to his hand—dragging behind it the rope that was tied to it. Up went the rope after the string, round the bars, and down to Barney's hand, as he pulled.

"It's very, very clever," said Diana, much impressed. "Barney, I should never have thought of that."

"Oh, there's nothing at all in that," said Barney, smiling. "Any circus kid could do that from the age of two. Hallo—Miranda's gone into the room again. I'd better go up before she starts showering us with all kinds of things!"

He twisted the rope as the two strands hung from the bars to the ground. He twisted it so thoroughly that the two strands looked like one. They would be very strong, and give him a good hold.

"Now let's hope the bars will hold all right," said Barney. He put all his weight suddenly on the rope and pulled hard. There was an ominous grating noise.

"Oh dear—the top bar's giving way," said Diana in alarm. "Look out—it may fall!"

Barney put his weight on the rope again. The top bar came out of the wall at one side, and hung down crookedly. The rope slid down to the next bar. There were five bars altogether.

"Well—that's one bar gone," said Barney. "Perhaps the next one will hold. "Again he put all his weight on the rope. The second bar gave a very little bit, and then held.

"I'll try going up now," said Barney. "Don't worry if this bar breaks. The rope will just slide down to the next one—and if that one breaks it'll go down to the fourth one."

"Yes—but, Barney, suppose they all break?" said Diana in a panic.

"By the time that happens I'll be on the window-sill," grinned Barney. "Don't worry. I'm like a cat, I always fall on my feet."

He suddenly swung on the rope, slid up his legs, holding the rope between his feet, and then hauled himself up strongly. "He's going up!" said Snubby, and Loony leapt at the rope in excitement, barking.

" The bar's breaking! " screamed Diana. " Look out, Barney—it's breaking! "

Sure enough, it suddenly gave way and dropped out from the wall, striking the stone sill as it fell, and just missing hitting Loony on the head. He jumped away in fright and went to hide under a bush. Barney felt the rope drop a little and got a jerk as it came to rest on the next bar. He hung still for a moment. What about this bar?

That held for a few seconds only, and then it too broke from its place. It didn't fall but hung down to one side and the rope slid down to the fourth bar.

" Barney, come down! All the bars will break and you'll hurt yourself! " shrieked Diana, really frightened. Barney took no notice. He went on hauling himself up the rope, intent on reaching the window-sill before the last bar broke. Once the fourth one broke, there was only one bar left.

The fourth one broke just as he reached the window-sill. With a light catlike motion he was over the last bar and on to the broad sill. He sat there, grinning down at the others, the rope swinging below him. Diana was pale with fright.

" Well, I'm here! " called Barney, getting his breath back after his long climb. He glanced into the window behind him to look for Miranda. He looked into the room there for what seemed a long, long time to the children below.

" Barney! What can you see?" called Snubby impatiently, longing to see everything himself.

" It's weird! " called down Barney at last. " The room in here is a proper nursery -rocking-horse and all -and there's a meal laid on the table. Gives me a funny feeling! "

Diana shivered a little. It certainly did sound strange. " Can we come up the rope too?" she called. " Can you tie it to something in the room?"

"You're none of you coming up the rope," said Barney. "You can't climb like me. You'd kill yourselves."

He put his arm in at the hole in the glass of the window —the hole Miranda used when she went in and out. He felt about for the window-catch. Would it be too old and rusty to move? He didn't want to have to break the window much more.

He found the catch. It certainly was stiff—but he moved it at last. Then the window stuck, of course! It took a lot of shoving and pushing to make it move a little way. Barney almost fell off the window-sill in his efforts to open it.

But at last it was open far enough for him to squeeze in. He disappeared, whilst the children below watched eagerly and impatiently.

Barney looked round the room. It had a carpet on the floor, almost eaten away by moths. The window curtains were also in holes, destroyed by moths. A nursery table, covered by what had once been a gay-patterned cloth, stood in the middle of the room. Coloured nursery chairs stood about. A big rocking-horse stood near the window. Barney touched it with his foot. It rocked, creaking to and fro. It sent a queer shiver down his back.

A big doll's house stood on a low shelf. A box of bricks was upset on the floor nearby. Books stood on a bookshelf, mostly picture books. Bob and Arabella apparently had not been very old. A nurse's rocking-chair stood by the fireplace, where the old, dead embers of a coal fire still showed.

"It must have been left and shut up very suddenly," thought Barney. "Nothing tidied up—nothing cleared away—just left exactly as it was when Bob was taken ill."

He saw another door leading out of the nursery and went to it. It was half-open. There was another room beyond. In this room were two small beds—evidently one for each child. A low dressing-table and two little chests

63

of drawers stood near the window. Yet another door opened out from this middle room.

Barney looked into that. This must have been the nurse's room. It was neat and tidy, covered with dust, and not so much eaten up by clothes moths. The bed stood in the corner with its once-white cover now grey with dust. It was all very strange indeed. Barney felt as if he had stepped back years and years.

A voice came up from below. " Barney! BARNEY! What are you doing? You might come and tell us what's up there! "

CHAPTER TEN

IN THE OLD FORGOTTEN HOUSE

BARNEY went back to the window through which he had climbed. He leaned out.

" It's all jolly queer," he said. " There are three rooms up here—still furnished. Wait—I'll come down and tell you all about it. Somehow I don't feel as if I want to shout."

" Barney! There's only one bar left! " shouted Diana in a panic. " Don't risk that. Tie the rope to something else in the room."

Barney tried the last bar with his hand. It broke at once. It was the rottenest one of all. Thank goodness he hadn't had to trust his weight to that one. Then he looked sharply at the rope. It was almost in two! It had pulled against something jagged on one of the bars and was cut practically to the last thread. Even as he took it up it fell in half. He made a grab at it—but down it went.

There was a dismayed silence. " Now what's going to happen?" asked Diana. " The rope's in two! "

"We can knot it, silly," said Roger. Barney leaned out of the window and pointed up to the sky.

"Look there—there's a rainstorm just about to pour down. You'll all get soaked if you mess about knotting the rope and sending Miranda up with it. I think I'd better see if I can get out of this room and into the main part of the building. Then I can open a door or something from inside and let you in."

"Right," said Roger. "We'll go and wait on that veranda, Barney. It's beginning to pour now."

Roger, Snubby, Diana and Loony ran round the house to the horrible veranda. As Diana had feared, there were spiders and earwigs, and many other insects she felt she had never seen anywhere else. The floor was slimy and

65

the place felt very damp. It was quite impossible to think of having tea there.

"I hope Barney will find some way of letting us in," said Snubby with a shiver. "It's jolly cold now."

He sneezed.

"Pepper up your nose," said Roger, trying to raise a laugh. But the veranda was too gloomy a place for a joke or a laugh.

What was Barney doing in the old house? Was he finding a way to let them in? He was certainly doing his best.

He went to the outer door of the first nursery. It was not locked. In fact, the key was in the keyhole inside the room. He opened the door and looked out on a long dark passage. Surely these rooms had been locked—not left open for anyone to come into?

He went down the passage, disturbing the dust on the floor. It rose in a light cloud. One or two long cobwebby strands hanging from the ceiling brushed against his face and made him jump. They felt like soft fingers. He didn't like it at all, and wished he had a torch with him. The passage was so very dark.

He came to a stout door at the end of the passage. He tried it, turning the big handle this way and that. No use. The door wouldn't open. It was well and truly locked on the other side. Of course—that was how they had sealed off the nurseries—by locking the door that led to all three rooms. Nobody could go near them.

How could he get into the main part of the house? He considered the matter carefully. He could not possibly kick this stout door down, and the lock was strong. It looked as if he couldn't leave this passage at all.

A thought struck him. What about the key he had seen in one of the nursery doors? Would that by any chance fit this door? It was worth trying.

He went back quickly, almost choking as he kicked up the dust. Miranda clung to his shoulder in silence. She didn't like this. It was strange and dark and queer. She held on tightly to Barney's shoulder.

He looked at the three doors in the other rooms. Each had a key in it. He looked at the keys. They seemed more or less the same to him, but perhaps they weren't. He took them back to the passage door.

The first key slid in easily, but wouldn't turn. However he tried, it wouldn't turn more than half-way. He was afraid of forcing it in case the key broke in the lock. He tried the second one. That would only turn half-way too. Without much hope he tried the third key.

And it turned! True, it was stiff, and grated protestingly as he turned it slowly and carefully—but it suddenly clicked back the old lock. He could open the door!

He turned the handle and pulled at the door. It came open and a cloud of dust arose again, making him cough. He was looking out at a broad landing. Doors opened on either side of it. Barney went to them, walking on tip-toe, he didn't quite know why.

He pushed open the doors, one by one, and looked into the rooms. They were completely empty. Not a chair, not a book, not a rug, remained in any of them. Only dust covered the bare floors, and cobwebs hung everywhere. Large spiders scuttled over the ceilings as he opened the doors, terrified to be disturbed in the midst of their long dark peace.

Most of the rooms were dark, or at least dim, because of the ivy that grew across the windows, allowing only a small amount of daylight in. The rooms smelt musty and old.

Barney went down the bare stairs. Dust rose from each stair, fine dust, like grey flour, that made him choke whenever it reached his nose. He didn't touch the banister rail as he went down, for fear of disturbing even more dust.

Down to the first floor. Here there were more doors that

opened on to miserable dark rooms, dusty and silent. From the first floor down to the ground floor the staircase descended from each side of the great landing, and then joined its two flights together to sweep down in one huge curve to the enormous hall.

Now Barney was in the hall, which he had seen through the crack in the front door. He tiptoed into a big room to the right. It was the ballroom. The mirrors gave back a dozen reflections of his dim, shadowy figure and made him feel uncomfortable. He left the ballroom and went into another room. This must have been used by people during the last war, as well as the ballroom, for here, again, there was broken furniture, old papers strewn about and the remains of a broken telephone receiver. It was dusty but the dust was not so thick as in the upper floors.

He went into another room, and saw that it was the room leading out on the veranda. He made out the figures of the three children and Loony, standing patiently outside, waiting for him. Perhaps he could open the veranda door. He went over to it and knocked on the glass with his knuckles. All three children jumped violently and then turned to see what the noise was.

"It's Barney!" cried Diana gladly. "Oh, Barney—you were able to get out of the rooms upstairs, then!"

Barney could just make out what she said. He struggled with the veranda door-bolts and managed at last to push each one back. He unlocked the door, and forced it open. The children outside rushed in, and Diana caught hold of his arm.

"Barney! You *are* clever! We were getting so cold out there, and the rain comes sweeping in on the veranda."

Loony tore round and round the room, kicking up dust as he went. "Shut up, Loony," said Roger sharply. "You'll choke us all—and yourself too."

Miranda still clung to Barney's shoulder. She was very

68

glad to see the other children. They all looked round at the silent, dusty room. Diana took a few steps forward and then screamed, making the others jump.

She had walked into a cobweb, which had swung softly against her face. " Someone touched me," she yelled.

" No. It's only a hanging cobweb," said Barney with a laugh. " There are plenty of those. Has anyone got a torch?"

Snubby had. He usually had everything. It was really amazing what his pockets could hold. He fished out a torch and switched it on. Immediately a horde of spiders went this way and that and Diana screamed again. She couldn't bear spiders. The children saw the big webs everywhere and the long strands of web hanging down from the ceiling.

" I don't like this much," said Roger. " It's an awful place to have our tea in. What's the place upstairs like, Barney? You haven't told us anything yet."

Barney told them quickly what he had found, and how he had got out of the rooms and downstairs. " I think we'd be better up in the nurseries really," he said. " They are frightfully dusty too, but at least there are chairs to sit on—and it seems lighter up there. Let's go up."

So they all went up, climbing first the two-branched stairway to the first floor and then the smaller one to the second floor. They came to the passage door and went through it.

" This must have been the nursery wing, all on its own," said Barney. " A very nice place it was too, with a wonderful view over the countryside. Look!"

He swung open the nursery door and the children peered in. They fell silent when they saw the rocking-horse standing motionless as if waiting for some child to ride it—the toy cupboard door open to show the toys still sitting there—the dolls' house on the shelf—and the plates and dishes on the table, set out ready for a meal.

" Weird," said Diana. " Weird to look at and weird to feel. I'm not sure I like it. Still, the house feels a bit happier here than it did downstairs."

" We'll have tea here," said Roger. " That's if nobody minds sitting down in dust inches thick! Come on! Where's the basket? I'll feel a lot better when I've got a few slices of cake inside me."

CHAPTER ELEVEN

A VERY GOOD IDEA

THE STORM came whilst they sat eating their tea. Thunder suddenly rolled over the sky and lightning forked across, dazzling the children for a moment and making them jump and blink.

" Well—I'm glad we're not out-of-doors picnicking! " said Roger, trying to be cheerful. But nobody felt terribly happy. Still, they felt a lot better when they had eaten every sandwich, every cake and biscuit, and drunk the gingerbeer too. Loony had his share. Actually he was a real nuisance in that dusty room, because his four feet scraped the dust up so much. Miranda stayed sedately on her master's shoulder, nibbling slices of cucumber sandwich.

The children explored the three rooms again after tea. It seemed queer to think that they had never been used since little Bob had been taken away with the fever so many, many years ago. " I suppose the mother couldn't bear to come into the empty rooms again," said Diana. " Poor thing! She couldn't even bear to have them touched. I wonder if anyone knows about them but us. They might quite easily have been forgotten by now. I mean, people might have thought that door in the passage outside, that was locked, was only a door to a box-room or something."

" I think you're probably right," said Barney. " My word, hark at the rain pelting down! "

It certainly was pouring hard. The thunder rolled still, but sounded farther away, and the lightning flashed but not so vividly. Diana glanced at Barney. Where would he sleep that night? Surely not under a haystack.

" Barney—you won't sleep out in the open to-night, surely?" she asked him at last, putting away the ginger-beer bottles in the empty basket. " Everywhere will be so wet."

" No, I shan't," said Barney. " As a matter of fact, I had thought of sleeping here."

The others looked at him in amazement.

" What, *here*! By yourself! In this awful old empty house, with its spiders and dust! " cried Diana horrified. " How could you *dare* to? All alone too! "

" I shall have Miranda," said Barney. " And I'm not easily scared, you know. I've slept in much worse places."

Diana couldn't think of any worse place to sleep. She shuddered. Miranda put her little arms round Barney's neck and chattered to him.

" She says it's all right, she'll be with me and chase any spider away," said Barney with a grin.

" I think it's a good idea," said Snubby. " After all, the beds are still good, even if the bedclothes fall to bits! The nurse's room didn't look too bad. Why don't you take that for your own room, Barney? You'd be quite comfortable there."

" I know! " cried Diana, getting up and looking in various cupboards. " I'll see if there's a brush and a dust-pan somewhere—and I could perhaps clear up some of the dust in the nurse's room."

It was Loony who found the brush, of course! He

darted into the bottom of a cupboard and brought out a carpet brush, whose bristles had gone soft. "Just the thing!" said Diana, wrenching the brush away from Loony. "Thanks, Loony. I'll have it. Snubby, keep him away from me—he's kicking dust up all over the place."

"Better put something round your hair, Di," said Roger, seeing how the dust flew up round Diana's head as she began brushing dust into the pan. "Here's my hanky. It's a big one. Tie it round your head."

So, whilst the boys amused themselves by looking through the old toy cupboard and picking out more of the beautifully carved old soldiers, and Miranda tried on various dolls' bonnets, Diana got very busy.

She took the bedclothes off the nurse's bed and carried them down the passage to the landing. She shook them well. They were full of dust, of course. The bedspread and one of the blankets fell to pieces and were no use—but one blanket seemed quite good. Diana carried it back to the bed and laid it on the mattress. There were no sheets. Perhaps those had been removed by the nurse. The pillow was full of moths. They flew out as she punched it. Grubs had eaten the pillow almost to nothing.

"Barney will have to do without a pillow," she thought. "We must bring him an old coat or something, to roll up under his head. Or perhaps an old cushion."

She swept the dust off the dressing-table, the washstand and the chest-of-drawers. It choked her and she began to cough. She had to wait for the dust to settle a little before she went on. She went to the window and struggled to open it. The room was so musty and dusty—a little fresh air would be good. She got the window open at last and a shower of raindrops came over her as she pushed back the thick sprays of ivy.

That gave her an idea. She picked some of the rain-wet sprays and sprinkled the dusty floor with the raindrops. "That will help to lay the dust a bit," she thought, rather pleased with herself. It certainly did. She was able to

72

sweep the floor carefully without raising too much dust now.

In the end she took up the moth-eaten carpet and stuffed it into a cupboard. It fell to pieces in places as she brushed it. It was easier to brush the bare boards beneath.

She called Barney when she had finished. " It's the best I can do," she said. " It's not nearly so dusty now—and you've got one fairly decent blanket to sleep on—or under. I don't know what you'll do for water though."

" There's probably an old well somewhere—or a pump in the kitchen," said Barney cheerfully. Things like that didn't worry him at all. " Anyway, I always swim in the river each morning."

" There's a bottle of ginger-beer left," said Roger. " We'll leave you that. Well—I hope you'll be all right, Barney—sleeping here all by yourself! "

" It's fine," said Barney. " Better than a wet barn or a dripping haystack any day! "

" Will you leave the veranda door unlocked and unbolted?" said Roger. " Then we can get in and out as we like. So long as the door is shut no one will guess anything. We could use these rooms up here as playrooms in wet weather."

" I'm glad Barney's got somewhere sheltered to sleep," said Diana. " And Miranda too, of course. Where is she?"

They went to look for her. She had watched Barney stretching himself on the bed and had considered him carefully and then bounded out of the room. Now she had disappeared!

It was Loony who smelt her out. He rushed over to the wall opposite the window in the day nursery and barked madly. There was a doll's bed there, with a doll in it.

Beside the doll lay Miranda, her big brown eyes looking wickedly up at Loony. She was in bed too! If Barney had a bed, she would have one as well!

73

"Oh, Miranda!" cried Diana. "You really look a darling there. Barney, isn't she sweet? Don't, Loony. You've pulled the covers off Miranda. That's unkind."

"I think we'd better go now," said Roger, "or Miss Pepper will be ringing up the village policeman."

"I'll come down with you," said Barney. "Then I'll leave the veranda door unlocked and unbolted as you suggested, Roger. Nobody will know it's open. It's obvious that no one ever comes here."

He saw them safely through the veranda door, Miranda sitting on his shoulder, wearing a doll's hat she had found. She fancied herself in it very much, and wore it back to front. Diana ran across the spidery veranda and down the steps to the wet grass.

The three of them got very wet going home through the thick undergrowth. Everything was dripping with silvery raindrops. The sun was trying to struggle out now. It might be quite a nice evening.

Miss Pepper was very concerned about them when they came in. "Oh, dear—how wet you are!" she said. "Go and put on something dry at once. I do hope you sheltered during that storm."

"Oh, yes," said Roger. But they didn't tell her where! No—that was their own very private secret. Nobody was going to know what they had been up to that afternoon.

When they went to bed that night the three called cautiously to one another, with Loony rushing as usual out of one bedroom and into another, sending all the mats sliding this way and that.

"Do you suppose Barney's in bed? Do you think he's all right?"

"*I* wouldn't like to sleep in that awful old deserted house at night!" That was Diana, of course.

"I wouldn't mind if Barney was with me."

"I bet he's in that bed and sound asleep! I bet he'll sleep sound till the morning!"

Barney *was* in bed and asleep. Miranda was in her little

dolls' bed. She usually slept with Barney, cuddled up to him, but the bed appealed to her funny little monkey-mind very much. She was there, under the blanket, hugging the old doll.

Barney slept soundly till half-past two in the morning—and then he awoke with a jump! Miranda had leapt on top of him, and was cuddling into his neck, trembling, chattering in a tiny voice in his ear.

Barney sat up.

"What's the matter, Miranda? What's frightened you? You're shivering all over. Were you lonely?"

Miranda clung to him and showed no signs of going back to her own little bed. Barney came to the conclusion that something had frightened her badly. But what? Was it a noise? It couldn't have been anybody coming into the nursery, because there was nobody to come!

He thought he heard a far-away sound then. He sat there on the bed, and listened, feeling his ears pricking like a dog's. Was that a sound? Or was it his imagination?

It must be his imagination! He lay down again, with Miranda still cuddled into his neck—and then he sat up straight in one quick movement.

He *had* heard a sound! Quite a loud one. Bang! He listened intently, and heard it again.

Bang! Then the wind blew in at the window and the ivy rustled against the glass. It made Barney jump. He realised what the rustling noise was at once—the wind in the ivy. Could the other noise have been caused by the wind too? Was it a door banging somewhere? Or was it perhaps the veranda door that had swung open in the wind and was banging?

Barney debated whether to go and see. He wasn't afraid, but he definitely didn't want to get up in the middle of a dark night, and go wandering down dark stairs and along dusty passages without a light.

75

" If I hear the noise again I'll go down," he decided. " If I don't, I won't. I bet it's that beastly veranda door banging. I can't have shut it tightly enough."

He heard no more noises at all, except that the wind blew an old ivy leaf into the room and made it shuffle along the floor in a very hair-raising manner. For a moment poor Barney thought somebody was in the room— but Miranda knew it was only a leaf, and didn't move. So Barney decided it was just something being blown along the floor.

He lay down again and shut his eyes. He listened for a few minutes longer, but all he heard was the monkey's little heart pattering fast against his neck.

Then he fell asleep and didn't wake till the sun pushed through the ivy leaves in the morning.

CHAPTER TWELVE

MR. KING ARRIVES

IMMEDIATELY after breakfast the next morning Diana wanted to go and see if Barney was all right.

"You've got to help make the beds and clear away the breakfast," said Roger. " We'll let Snubby go with Loony. I'm just about fed up with Snubby this morning. He put a worm in each of my shoes and put treacle or something on my sponge. If it's going to be one of his tiresome days we'd be better off without him. Let him go and plague Barney. Barney will know how to deal with him."

So Snubby was told to take some bread and butter and tomatoes and a bottle of milk to Barney. He set off in glee, Loony running at his heels. He had got half-way over the grounds when he discovered that Loony was carrying Miss Pepper's hair-brush. So back he went and stood beneath Miss Pepper's bedroom window. He threw the brush up and it went straight in at the window.

There was an agonised yell and Snubby took to his heels. " Well, how was I to know she was standing in the way?" he argued to himself. " Just like a woman."

He looked down at Loony, who was again at his heels. This time he was carrying Mrs. Round's old shoe-cleaning brush. Snubby stopped and addressed Loony fiercely.

" What do you think you're doing? Do you suppose I'm going to spend half the day taking back your silly brushes? You're a very bad dog. Take it back! Grrrrr! "

Loony stared up at Snubby out of melting brown eyes, his tail down.

" Take it back! Don't you understand plain English when it's spoken?" yelled Snubby. " TAKE—IT—BACK! "

Loony wagged his tail and darted off. Snubby was pleased. " Clever dog that," he said to a couple of sparrows nearby. " Understands every word I say."

He petted Loony when the dog came back. " Good dog. Took it all the way back to the kitchen and dropped it at Roundy's feet, I bet! Cleverest dog in the world."

Loony was very pleased. He had just dropped the brush down the nearest rabbit-hole. Well—if Snubby was so delighted with him, he'd drop plenty of other things down the rabbit-hole too.

The two went on together, Loony making a dart at anything that dared to move—a leaf, a swirl of dust, a bit of paper. Grrrrr! He darted at Snubby's shoe-laces, tripping him up. He behaved, in fact, just like the lunatic dog he was, and pleased Snubby very much indeed.

Snubby got to the old house at last and made his way round to the veranda. The door was fast shut. He pushed against it. It was so hard to open that he had to put down the basket that he was carrying, and push against the door with all his might. It obliged him by suddenly flying open and sending him headlong into the room. He sat down abruptly. Loony flung himself on him and licked him wildly.

"Hallo! It's you, is it?" said Barney's voice. "I heard an awful row and came to see what it was. You're early. But why sit on that dusty floor?"

"Get off, Loony," said Snubby, pushing the excited spaniel away. He looked up at Barney and grinned. "I found the door shut so hard I couldn't get in. So I had to barge against it with all my might—and it flew open unexpectedly. And I flew in!"

"I see," said Barney. He spotted the basket outside. "I say—anything to eat? How super! Bread and butter and tomatoes! Are they for me?"

"Of course," said Snubby, brushing himself down. Barney took the basket into the room and shut the door. He pulled at it when he had shut it. It certainly did shut very tightly indeed. He looked puzzled.

"What's up?" said Snubby, noticing Barney's looks. "Anything wrong with the door?"

Barney told Snubby about how frightened Miranda had been the night before, and how he had heard noises.

"I thought it must be the wind blowing open this door and banging it again," he said. "But I don't think it was now. The door fits so tightly."

They went up to the top rooms together. Snubby felt a little nervous. "I'd have hated that," he said to Barney. "Lying up there in the dark, hearing noises—and not able to put a light on. Brrrrrr!"

"You might lend me your torch for to-night," Barney said. "I could do a little snooping round then, if I hear any more noises."

Snubby handed out his torch at once. He sat and watched Barney eat. "It's a gorgeous day," he said. "What about going to the river and getting a boat?"

"Yes, I'd like that," said Barney. "When do you start this coaching of yours? Monday? We'd better make the most of our time then. I've been reading that play Roger lent me, this morning, up there in bed. It's grand."

"Well, better you than me," said Snubby, making a face. "I never could make out why Shakespeare wanted to write in such a funny way—you know, all the lines the same length. Seems a queer idea."

Barney laughed. "I wish I could come and listen to you all being coached," he said. "I bet I would enjoy it! I bet I'd learn a lot."

"Well!" Snubby looked at Barney as if he were quite mad. "You must be crazy. Fancy wanting to come and be coached! Well—I don't see why you shouldn't come and listen if you want to. But fancy *wanting* to! Do you hear that, Loony? Here's a chap madder than you are!"

They walked to the door, their footsteps showing clearly in the dust. All their footsteps were there, Loony's as well. Snubby pointed them out.

"There's Loony's marks—and mine—and these must be yours. Those are Di's, they're small. And there are Roger's—he's got the biggest feet of the lot."

They went out of the veranda door and Barney pulled it fast behind him. He pushed at it. It didn't open. He had to barge against it hard before it flew open. It couldn't have been this door banging last night. He must find out which door it was—if it was a door. It was a bit of a mystery!

Barney didn't sleep in the old house for a night or two after that. It was suddenly very hot weather again and the children hired a boat for a day or so. Barney had the idea of sleeping in the boat, with a rug over him, and the boat-cushions for a bed.

"Do you mind if I do!" he asked the others. "It will save you the bother of taking it back to the boatman and I should love to bob about all night long on the water."

"Right," said Roger, pleased. "You do that. It's

very stuffy up in those dusty old rooms this weather— much better sleep out if it's going to be hot and dry."

Monday came all too soon, and with it came Mr. King, armed with text-books and a suitcase. He was apparently going to stay at Rockingdown Cottage! The children hadn't realised this. They were shocked.

"Gracious! Have we got to have him for meals and everything?" said Snubby, dismally, seeing him go up-stairs to one of the rooms on the first floor, accompanied by Mrs. Round and Loony.

"Oh, don't be silly, Snubby," said Miss Pepper, impatiently. "He lives too far away to come over every day. And I may have to go away for a day or two, so I shall be glad to know there's someone responsible in the house to see to you."

A gloom settled on the children. Barney peeped in at the window and raised his eyebrows.

"Yes. He's come," said Diana. "*And* he's living here. Isn't that frightful? We shall have to behave more than ever."

"Well, I shan't," said Snubby.

"You never do," said Diana. "Barney, do you really want to come in and listen to us being coached? Honestly, you'll be bored stiff. Honestly!"

Barney nodded. He had a real thirst for book know-ledge, and thought the three children very lucky in their education, and their possession of so many books.

"All right. You come and knock at the door in about ten minutes' time," said Diana. "Then when you come in you can be surprised to see us all working so quietly and . . ."

"He can apologise and back out," said Roger, enjoying this little plan. "And I'll say, 'Oh Mr. King, would you mind if Barney sits here and waits for us?' And every-thing will be O.K."

"Right," said Barney, and disappeared with Miranda just as Miss Pepper came into the study with Mr. King.

"Ha! All ready and waiting, I see," said Mr. King. "Very good. We'll just see what standard you've all reached and then I can tell how to proceed with you."

In about a quarter of an hour's time Barney passed the window. He walked in at the open hall door and came to the study door. He knocked.

"Come in," yelled all the children at once, before Mr. King could say a word. In came Barney, looking unexpectedly tidy, his hair wet and brushed back, and his hands and face clean.

"Oh—er? I'm sorry," he said, as he saw the three children sitting with Mr. King at the table. "I don't want to interrupt. So sorry, sir."

He began to back out of the room, looking hot and bothered. Diana thought he was doing it all very well! Snubby choked back a giggle. Roger spoke earnestly to Mr. King.

"Oh, Mr. King—would you very much mind if our friend Barnabas sits down here and waits for us?" he said. "He won't be any trouble."

"Certainly," said Mr. King graciously. "By all means. Sit down by the window, Barnabas. Have you a book to read?"

Mr. King was pleasantly surprised to see that Barney had a book of Shakespeare's plays. He turned his back on the boy and went on with his coaching. Loony was lying quietly at Snubby's feet, rather exhausted by a mad race he had had up and down the stairs. Mr. King congratulated himself on a nice quiet class. Miss Pepper had warned him he might not find things too easy—but nothing could be easier than this.

Snubby wondered where Miranda was. Barney hadn't brought her in. He must have shut her up somewhere—probably in the shed. He yawned. Things were getting boring. Even Loony was subdued.

Then things happened quickly! The door was slightly ajar and Miranda came shuffling in quietly. She saw

81

Loony lying under the table asleep. Unseen by anyone, she went under Snubby's chair and came to the spaniel. Ha—her enemy was asleep! She took hold of both his long floppy ears and pulled them hard, making a loud squawk as she did so. Loony woke up in a hurry and yelped madly. He leapt out from under the table, and snapped at Miranda, who hung on to the tablecloth to get out of his way. The cloth slid to the side and books fell off with a crash. Then a battle royal developed under and round the table, and Mr. King leapt up in alarm, his chair falling on Miranda, who happened to be chasing round it. She gave a howl and leapt on to his shoulder, pulling his ear hard.

Snubby rushed after Loony, who had fallen into the fireplace, bringing the tongs and the shovel down on himself with a clatter. He almost leapt up the chimney in fright. Barney yelled at Miranda.

Snubby knocked a vase over as he tore after Loony, and Miss Pepper and Mrs. Round, talking about meals in the kitchen, looked at each other in amazement.

" What can they be doing?" said Miss Pepper and rushed to the study door, to be met by a crazy spaniel and an equally crazy monkey, both intent on devouring one another if they possibly could.

Miranda disappeared upstairs and hid. Loony crept back to Snubby, who had yelled at him without ceasing, partly to get him to come, and partly to make as much noise as he could.

" Well! " said Miss Pepper, annoyed. " I suppose this is what comes of letting Loony be in the room with you, Snubby."

" It was nothing to do with Loony," said Snubby indignantly. " He was asleep under the table. It was Miranda."

" Er—I think—I think you must take the dog out of the room," said Mr. King, trying to recover himself under the prim disapproving eye of Miss Pepper.

"But, I tell you, it wasn't Loony's fault," almost yelled Snubby. "That's not fair."

"I cannot have either a dog or a monkey in my class," said Mr. King with great dignity and sudden firmness. "They've both had a trial. It was not successful."

"But Mr. King—Loony was fast asleep," wailed Snubby. "Didn't you hear his little snores?"

"No, I didn't," said Mr. King. "Take the dog out, Peter."

Snubby took Loony by the collar to lead him out. He faced Mr. King, his face as red as a beetroot.

"All right," he said, in a choking voice. "If you don't like my dog, I don't like you. You'll be sorry you didn't give him a chance—when he was fast asleep too!"

He went outside with Loony, who was quite scared now. Miss Pepper took him from Snubby. "Now don't be so *silly*, Snubby," she said. "Acting like a seven-year-old. I'll take Loony to the kitchen with Mrs. Round."

"I'll pay Mr. King out," said Snubby, darkly. "See if I don't. He'll be sorry, Miss Pepper. He will, really!"

CHAPTER THIRTEEN

SNUBBY GETS A SURPRISE

MR. KING didn't like the next few days very much. Snubby produced his vast collection of tricks and became a perfect nightmare to the coach.

Poor Mr. King was given a rubber that wouldn't rub out but made strange yellow marks on the paper. He was provided with a ruler that was mysteriously wrong in its measurements and astonished him considerably. This ruler was one of Snubby's pet tricks and had been confiscated at school, times without number, by irritated masters. But somehow or other it always found its way back to Snubby.

Books fell suddenly to the floor in a cascade, though Snubby was quite a long way from them. Mr. King did not see the cunningly laid string that tipped up the bottom book when pulled, and sent the whole pile crashing down near him. The wall blackboard continually fell down in a most amazing way, and when Snubby was sent to clean it at any time a thick cloud of horrible-smelling dust appeared. It would have been a good thing if Mr. King had examined Snubby's duster occasionally, but he didn't seem to think of things like that.

" Considering he has been a master in a boys' school he's pretty innocent," said Roger, who was very amused at all Snubby's idiotic tricks. As for Barney, he couldn't contain himself when Snubby perpetrated yet another foolish joke, and his uproarious laugh sounded all over the house.

Barney seemed to be the only one who really enjoyed the morning lessons. He didn't actually join the class but sat in the window, apparently reading. Mr. King's back was to him, so he was unaware that the boy was absorbing everything that went on—listening to the explanations of mathematical problems, taking in the French lesson, enjoying the readings of English literature. There was nothing that Barney didn't enjoy. He had an extraordinary memory, and quite annoyed Roger by the way he could repeat the Latin phrases and declensions, when poor Roger himself was struggling to do the prep that Mr. King gave him.

Mr. King was not really a good teacher, Diana thought. He didn't seem interested enough. Nor could he keep Snubby in his place, but often seemed inclined to be amused at his silly tricks. Snubby sulked. He hated Loony being kept away from him, and he was determined not to have Miranda sneaking in at any time. The little monkey was shut up in the shed whilst lessons were going on, but she sometimes managed to escape. She would find some crack or crevice and squeeze miraculously out of it—then she would appear silently at the window.

She would look for Loony, and then cuddle down with Barney. But at once Snubby would point her out to Mr. King. "There's Miranda, Mr. King. Can I get Loony in here?"

And Miranda would then have to go. Barney didn't bear any resentment towards Snubby for this. He liked the red-haired, freckled little pest, and always watched for his next trick.

Mr. King was with the children in the mornings, and had all his meals with them—but he disappeared for the rest of the time.

"You're awfully fond of walks, aren't you?" Roger said, one afternoon, when Mr. King set off with his stick and a book. "Where do you go?"

"Oh, anywhere," said Mr. King vaguely. "Down to the river—through the village—and yesterday I visited that strange old mansion."

The children pricked up their ears at once. Blow! Would he discover their secret? Would he see the curtained windows they had seen, and notice the marks of their feet on the ground below?

"It's a very desolate place, I believe," said Diana, after a pause. "Not worth looking at!"

"I thought it was very interesting," said Mr. King. "It's very old—has quite a history. I wish I could go over it."

This was worse than ever. Had they better lock and bolt the veranda door in case Mr. King found that it could be opened? What a nuisance he was!

But if they did that they wouldn't be able to go in and out themselves if they wanted to—and as Barney was once more sleeping up in the nursery at the top of the old house it was useful to have that door left unlocked, so that they could use it if they wanted to.

Barney was quite used to sleeping in the old bed up in

the little bedroom now. Diana had provided him with a garden cushion for a pillow, and an old rug. He had taken some of the nursery crockery for himself.

Diana had managed to get rid of most of the dust and Barney enjoyed his little hiding-place. Nobody would ever guess he was there! On wet days the children went up to the three rooms and amused themselves there. They had once thought of playing hide-and-seek, using the front stairs and the back ones—but somehow it didn't work. Nobody liked hiding in the gloomy old place, and it was horrid tiptoeing along to find the hiders!

" I feel as if somebody is going to jump out and grab me all the time! " said Diana, with a shiver.

Barney had not heard any more noises. Miranda would not sleep in the doll's bed any more since she had been frightened the first night, but cuddled up with him. She only went into the doll's bed in the daytime when she got bored with the children's games. Then she would leap in, draw the bedclothes over her, and apparently sleep soundly with the old doll!

The only one who had really thoroughly explored the house and gone into every cupboard and corner was Loony, of course. His paw-marks were everywhere! He sniffed here and snuffled there, choking with the dust, and scraping madly at doors to make them open.

One night Snubby thought of going to sleep at the old house with Barney. The idea just came into his head. " But why?" said Diana. " What a horrible idea! In that dark old place—I wouldn't sleep there for anything."

" I'd like to," said Snubby obstinately. " Anything for a bit of a change. I call these hols too dull for words."

So that night, when he was supposed to be in bed and asleep, Snubby dressed again, and went out on the landing and listened. Downstairs the clock struck half-past eleven. Was Mr. King in bed? He usually went up at eleven, about the same time as Miss Pepper. Mrs. Round didn't sleep in the house. She came in from the village each day.

Diana and Roger knew that Snubby was going to go to Barney for the night of course—but they hadn't bothered to keep awake to see him go. Snubby had borrowed Roger's torch, because he had lent Barney his. He switched it on and off, whilst he stood on the landing, to see if it worked all right. Yes, it did. It was a good torch, better than Snubby's.

Loony was at the boy's heels, his tail-stump wagging. He liked this kind of thing. He pressed against Snubby's legs, and didn't make a sound. He could be quiet and good if he wanted to—and he wanted to now, in case Snubby left him behind.

Snubby decided that Mr. King was safely in bed. Anyway, in case he wasn't he'd go down the little back stairs. Then nobody would hear him. He crept to where they began and went down on tiptoe. He knew that the third and the seventh and the thirteenth stairs creaked, so he counted carefully, and missed those out. He had his hand on Loony's collar to stop him tearing downstairs as he usually did.

Now he was at the bottom. Good. He cautiously opened the back door and looked out. It was a fine starry night. There was no moon, but the stars were so bright that it was possible to see the trees outlined against the sky. Now for the walk across to Rockingdown Hall. The children had made quite a path of their own now by hacking away branches and bushes.

Silently Snubby shut the door behind him and then he and Loony began their walk across the grounds. He could soon see the black mass of the old mansion looming up against the starry sky. It looked much bigger than it did in the daytime.

Loony made several little excursions into the undergrowth, and scared a good many rabbits who were not expecting him at all. He would have liked to chase them, but he wanted to keep with Snubby. It was night-time, and his master must be protected—against what, Loony

87

didn't know. He just felt that he must keep close to him.

Snubby whistled softly. He wasn't scared but he felt it would be nice to whistle a little tune. He came out on to what had once been a great lawn—and then he stopped very suddenly indeed, and his hand closed over Loony's collar.

He could see a light moving near the house! He screwed up his eyes and tried to see what the light was. It must be the light of a torch! It moved here and there as if the owner were looking for something. Was it Barney? Snubby didn't like to whistle and find out, in case it wasn't.

And then Loony told him quite plainly that it wasn't Barney. He growled ominously, deep down in his throat. Snubby shook him a little to make him stop. He didn't want the person with the torch to know he was there with the spaniel. Loony would never growl at Barney. Snubby knew that. This was a stranger then. Whatever could he be doing? Or was he a tramp, seeking a way in to get a night's shelter?

Snubby crept nearer with Loony. The dog now knew he was to keep quiet, and Snubby relaxed his hold on his collar. He had switched off his own torch. He followed the light of the other torch. Whoever held it was going systematically round the house, examining doors and windows. Suppose he came to the veranda door and found it open? Would he go in?

The man went round a corner of the house and Snubby saw his outline clearly. He gazed in real amazement. Why—he knew who this night prowler was—surely it was Mr. King!

CHAPTER FOURTEEN

A MYSTERIOUS NIGHT

SNUBBY was full of astonishment. What in the world was Mr. King doing prowling round the old house in the middle of the night, when he was supposed to be in bed? He stood still in the shadow of a big bush and thought about it. He couldn't make head or tail of it at all.

He made up his mind to make his way to the veranda door, go in as quietly as he could and run upstairs to warn Barney. He would lock the door behind him, so that Mr. King couldn't get in. The man was now on the opposite side of the house to the veranda, the north side. If Snubby was quick he could get in without being seen or heard. He set off quietly for the house with Loony padding at his heels.

On to the veranda he crept, and had to put on his torch to see the handle of the door. He turned it and pushed. The door was easier to open now that the children had used it a good deal, and it swung inwards without much noise. Snubby went in with Loony and shut the door behind him. He shot the bolts and locked the door as well. Now Mr. King wouldn't be able to get in!

He tiptoed into the hall and across into another room, standing by the door to see if he could spot Mr. King's torch shining on the opposite side of the house. Yes, there it was!

Snubby shot upstairs to the first landing, then up again to the second. He went to the door that led into the passage to the nurseries. He turned the handle.

The door was locked! Snubby was puzzled. Why was the door locked? Barney left it unlocked usually, so that the children could go in and out as they pleased. He rattled the door gently. Then he heard Miranda chattering softly on the other side.

"Miranda!" he said, in a low voice. "Where's Barney? Fetch Barney."

The door was unlocked immediately and Barney stood there with Miranda on his shoulder. He pulled Snubby into the passage and locked the door. In silence he led the way to the room where he slept.

"Why did you lock the door?" whispered Snubby.

"Because there's somebody about," said Barney in a low voice. "Didn't you bump into him?"

"Yes, almost! I know who it is, too," said Snubby.

"Who?" said Barney.

"Mr. King!" said Snubby. "Yes—that's surprising isn't it? But it is. He's snooping all round the house trying to get in, I should think."

"Miranda woke me up a few minutes ago," said Barney. "I knew there was something up the way she was chattering, and pawing at me, patting me on the cheek and putting her paw down my neck. So I got up and looked out of the window—and I saw somebody down below, using a torch!"

"Why didn't you rush down and lock the veranda door?" asked Snubby.

"Because I thought this fellow would have been at the door just about the same time as I would," said Barney. "So I locked the passage door instead. Then you came along, and I got a bit of a fright. I thought you must be the man—or another man perhaps. It was only when Miranda began her friendly little chatter that I guessed it was one of you three. Are the others here? Why have you come to-night?"

Snubby explained in whispers. "I just had a sudden idea I'd like a bit of an adventure so I came along to spend the night with you—and I saw this man just as I came up to the house. I was awfully surprised when I saw who it was. The others aren't here. They're in bed."

"What do you suppose he's doing?" said Barney, puzzled. "What's he after?"

"Can't imagine," said Snubby. "By the way—have you heard any more noises in the night, Barney?"

"None," said Barney. "I think it must just have been the wind banging the door, that's all."

He went to the window and looked out cautiously. There was nothing to be seen. "He may be at the other side of the house," said Barney. "Well, now that the veranda door is safely locked we know he can't get in. Let's go down the passage, unlock the door there, and see if we can find out where Mr. King is now."

Off they went, very quietly. Miranda was on Barney's shoulder, chattering softly in a whispery voice. Loony trotted along with them, enjoying himself.

They unlocked the passage door and went down the stairs quietly to the rooms on the next floor. There was one with a bay window that jutted out—they would stand in the bay and see if they could spot Mr. King's torchlight.

They spotted it at once—moving slowly along below, as if he were examining every window catch. What *was* he doing? Why did he want to get in?

And then—just as they stood there quietly watching, they heard a noise.

Bang! Thud! Thud! Bang!

They almost jumped out of their skins. Evidently Mr. King heard the noise too, for he switched off his torch at once. Snubby clutched Barney in a fright. Loony growled loudly and Miranda sat quite still, listening.

"That's the noise I heard the first night," said Barney in a low voice. "Is it a door banging, do you think?"

"Well—it *might* be," said Snubby, listening.

Bang!

"There it is again," said Barney. "Where is the noise coming from?"

"Downstairs," said Snubby, his teeth beginning to chatter. He was ashamed of himself for being afraid, and

tried to shut his mouth firmly to stop his teeth from behaving in such an idiotic way. He badly wanted to go
upstairs again, and lock the passage door and go into the
nurseries and lock their doors too! He was shocked
to find that he wasn't nearly as brave as he had always
thought he was.

Barney was quite calm and didn't seem afraid at all. He
stood there listening. The noises came again. Yes—they
were definitely from downstairs.

There was no sign of Mr. King's torch. Either he was
in hiding or he had gone—or had he joined the persons
who were making the noise? Barney thought it was very
likely that that was the reason he had come along that
night—to join friends of his somewhere about here!

He stood there, puzzling it out, waiting for more noises.
There came a curious whining, half-screeching noise that
made all Snubby's hair slowly stand upright on his head,
much to his surprise—and then dead silence. Not a bang
or a thud came again.

"Well," said Barney at last, moving from the window,
"I think the show's over for to-night, whatever it was!
Mr. King's disappeared, and the noises off have stopped.
Let's go and explore downstairs and see if we can find out
what made them."

Snubby was horrified. What! Go down in the dark
and snoop about to see what made those terrifying noises?
Barney must be mad. He clutched at his arm.

"No, Barney! Let's go upstairs and lock ourselves in!"

"You go," said Barney. "Take Loony with you. I'll
go and explore myself."

But poor Snubby didn't dare to go upstairs by himself
—no, not even with Loony at his heels! He thought that
of the two evils, going with Barney was the lesser—he
couldn't possibly go anywhere by himself at the moment!

Feeling very panicky Snubby went down the stairs with
Barney. Loony pressed against his heels, and that was

comforting. Snubby wished he were a dog too. Dogs never seemed really afraid!

" I think the noises came from the kitchen part," said Barney, in a whisper. " Let's just stand here in the hall and listen once more."

They stood there—and then, to Snubby's horror something touched his hair! He almost yelled in fright. Then the something *pulled* his hair—and Snubby nearly died with relief. It was only Miranda putting out her paw from where she sat on Barney's shoulder, and being affectionate!

They went into the great kitchens. Barney switched on his torch, and the beam played over the room in front of them. Shadows seemed to flee into the corners as the beam of light moved round the room. Snubby trembled and Barney felt him.

" You frightened?" he said in surprise. " Don't worry, Snubby. Miranda and Loony would soon let us know if there was anyone near. There can't be anyone about now or Miranda would chatter and Loony would growl."

That was true. Snubby felt relieved at once. There was nothing to be seen in the great kitchens at all. The beam of light travelled over the floor and showed footmarks—but only those of the children and the dog, where they had once gone across the rooms. No other footsteps showed at all.

" Nobody has been here," whispered Barney and he went into the scullery. This was a big room with a pump for water as well as taps in a sink. Nobody had been there either. Not even the children's footsteps showed here in the dust on the floor. They had never been into the scullery.

It was very puzzling. How could people make loud noises downstairs and yet leave no footmarks or any sign of having been there?

" It's a bit spooky, isn't it?" said Snubby at last. Barney laughed.

" Don't you believe it! Those noises were made by people—there was nothing spooky about them. Surely you don't believe in spooks! What a baby you are! "

" Well—it's all jolly funny," said Snubby. " All those noises—and nothing to show for it. Not even a footmark! Can you tell me how anyone could make such a row down here, and yet not leave the dust disturbed? "

" No, I can't," said Barney. " But I'm going to find out! That's quite certain. There's something strange about all this—very strange—and I'm going to solve the mystery! "

" Do you think Mr. King's in it, whatever it is? " asked Snubby.

Barney considered. " I shouldn't be surprised," he said. " Ask him a few questions to-morrow, Snubby, and see what he says. Ask him if he slept well—ask him if he heard any noises in the night—ask him if he ever walks in his sleep! "

Snubby grinned in the dark. ' Right! I'll just see what he says! I say, is the show really over now, Barney? I'm frightfully sleepy."

" Yes—it seems to be over," said Barney. " Come on, Miranda—to bed! Are you really going to sleep here to-night, Snubby? "

" Well, nothing would make me go back to Rocking-down Cottage in the dark to-night," said Snubby. " Can you make room on your bed for me? "

" I suppose that means Loony too! " said Barney. " Yes, I expect the bed will take four of us. Come on! "

They went upstairs again, carefully locking the passage door and the nursery doors, and went into the little third room. Snubby felt sure it would take him ages to go to sleep—but his eyes shut tight as soon as his head was on the pillow. And there the four of them slept soundly till the morning—Miranda cuddled in Barney's neck and Loony on Snubby's feet—what a bedful!

CHAPTER FIFTEEN

SNUBBY IS A NUISANCE

SNUBBY was up and about very early, anxious to be back at the cottage before anyone else was up. Barney went with him and sat in the tumbledown summer-house. Snubby promised to see if he could manage to smuggle him out some breakfast.

But Mrs. Round caught sight of Miranda outside the summer-house as she hurried to the cottage to do her morning work and get breakfast. She peeped in and saw Barney.

"Ah—another one to breakfast, I suppose!" she said. Barney grinned. He and Mrs. Round understood one another. He often did little odd jobs for her—unstopping her sink when it got stopped up, putting up a new clothes-line for her and so on. She thought, he was a very handy, obliging boy, though she couldn't bear Miranda.

Barney had breakfast with everyone else. Miss Pepper didn't mind. One more didn't make much difference, and Barney seemed a nice boy, if a little strange. Mr. King was there too, looking a little tired. He came in very late for breakfast.

Snubby was ready and waiting for him. He had told Diana and Roger the happenings of the night before, and they had listened, thrilled and astonished.

"Lucky fellow—having all that fun with Barney in the middle of the night!" said Roger. Snubby didn't tell him how frightened he had been—now that it was daylight and the sun had chattered and his hair had stood on end. He was boastful and brave now—aha, he had had a marvellous night whilst the others had been fast asleep in bed!

They had been amazed to hear that Mr. King had been on the prowl in the night too. Roger whistled. "What on earth was he up to? He's a dark horse, isn't he? Why didn't he say anything about it?"

Mr. King made his apologies for coming late to breakfast and helped himself to cornflakes. Snubby began at once.

"Did you have a bad night, Mr. King?"

Mr. King looked surprised at this concern on Snubby's part. "No," he said. "I had a very good one, thank you."

"I didn't," said Snubby. "I was awake a lot. Didn't you hear noises in the night?"

Mr. King looked rather startled. He glanced at the innocent-looking Snubby.

"What noises?" he said, cautiously.

"Oh—just noises," said Snubby. "Perhaps you slept too well to hear anything, Mr. King."

"I certainly slept very well—in fact, as you know, I

over-slept," said Mr. King. "Miss Pepper, will you have the mustard?"

Snubby wasn't going to have the subject changed like that. He persisted with his questions.

"I thought I heard somebody about last night. It might have been somebody walking in their sleep. Do *you* ever walk in your sleep, Mr. King?"

"Never," said Mr. King, shortly. "These are very nice sausages. Miss Pepper."

"I wonder who it was getting up in the night," said Snubby, innocently. "Did you, Roger? Did you, Diana?"

"*We* didn't," said Roger and Diana, enjoying all this baiting of poor Mr. King.

"And you didn't either, did you, Mr. King?" said Snubby, turning to him. "Unless you were walking in your sleep, of course."

"I've already told you I don't walk in my sleep," said Mr. King, exasperated. "Now, will you kindly let me talk to Miss Pepper? If this is your latest idea of being funny, think of something else. It's puerile."

"What's puerile?" asked Snubby at once.

"I'll tell you in your Latin lesson," said Mr. King, in a voice that promised a very harassing lesson for Snubby that morning. "Though I should have thought you already knew what "puer" meant. It's a pity you're so backward."

Snubby winked at the others. He had found out what he wanted to know. Mr. King wasn't going to admit that he had been out last night—that was his own business evidently. He was going to keep it a secret—which probably meant he was going snooping again sometime. It would be fun to keep an eye on him in that case.

"Are you going for a walk to-day?" asked Snubby, addressing himself to Mr. King again. "Can I come with you?"

"I *am* going for a walk—but I certainly don't want you with me in your present tiresome mood," said Mr. King.

Snubby at once made up his mind to follow him on his walk. Loony, who was under the table, quietly began to chew Mr. King's shoelace. Miranda had been left in the shed in case she and Loony started one of their mad games with one another.

Snubby was even more tiresome in lessons than he had been at breakfast. He was told to make up three sentences and write them down in French. He produced the following sentences and read them out gleefully.

" Ils étaient de bruits dans la nuit—There were noises in the night."

" Je me promene dans mon sommeil—I walk in my sleep."

" Je ne parle toujours le vrai—I do not always speak the truth."

Mr. King listened to these peculiar sentences in silence. He looked consideringly at Snubby and seemed about to break out angrily. Then he apparently changed his mind.

" Full of the most elementary mistakes," he said coldly. " Please write three more. If those are also full of mistakes you can write yet another three."

Snubby decided not to bait Mr. King any more. He wrote three innocent French sentences which were perfectly correct in every way. This was not surprising as he had taken them from his French book. Mr. King did not seem to be up to little tricks of this sort. Snubby wished fervently that his French master at school could be taken in so easily. Unfortunately Monsieur Rieu was apt to smell out a trick before it was even played.

After dinner the children met together in the summer-house. They giggled when they talked about Snubby's cheekiness that morning. " All the same, Mr. King's pretty peculiar," said Roger. " Why all the secrecy about his prowling? He could easily have said that he couldn't sleep and went for a walk."

" I'm going to track him this afternoon," said Snubby. " Aren't we, Loony, old chap?"

Loony agreed eagerly, leaping up on Snubby's knee and licking his nose lavishly. He then tried to lie on his back, fell off with a bump, saw Miranda and raced after her till she bounded up a tree and sat there chattering at him.

"The names Miranda calls him!" said Barney, pretending to be shocked. "Wherever did she learn them!"

Mr. King set off on his walk at half-past two, taking with him a map and a stick. Snubby, who was on the watch, let him get a good way ahead and then went quietly after him. Loony, having been told to keep quiet, nosed along at his heels.

Mr. King struck across country towards the river. Snubby was a little disappointed. He had hoped that he would go snooping round the old mansion again. If so he might possibly get in, as the veranda door was not locked. Most unfortunately the key would not lock it from the outside.

Snubby followed Mr. King carefully, occasionally sinking down flat with Loony if the tutor stopped, or looked round. This caused great astonishment to an old lady who was near Snubby when he did one of his disappearing acts. He lay down flat, hissing to Loony to lie down too. The old lady went up in concern.

"Are you all right, little boy?" she said. "Do you feel ill?"

"Sssssst!" said Snubby, annoyed. He crawled sideways into the hedge like a crab and the old lady looked at him in alarm. The boy must be mad. Then an idea came to her.

"Are you playing Red Indians?" she asked.

Mr. King had now walked on. Snubby got up cautiously and stalked down the other side of the hedge. "I'm Chief Red-feather," he said to the relieved old lady. "Be careful of my men. Don't let them scalp you, whatever you do!"

He left the old lady looking out for his "men," and went on after Mr. King, frightening several cows by suddenly flattening himself out on the ground whenever Mr. King stopped again to consider his way. Snubby thoroughly enjoyed himself. He was getting his own back nicely on Mr. King.

They came to the river eventually. Mr. King glanced at his map again and then made his way up the river. There was a very wild part just there, and both Mr. King and his pupil found the going difficult. In fact Snubby, having fallen into a marshy piece two or three times, and having had to haul poor Loony out of the mud at least six times, almost gave up.

Steep hills now rose up on one side of the river. A stream came into it from the east, and to Snubby's surprise Mr. King now left the main river and began to follow the stream. Poor Snubby groaned. This was much worse than he had imagined. It must already be nearly tea-time—and there was all that way to go back!

To make matters worse, Mr. King suddenly sat down on a nice dry spot, pulled out a packet from his pocket, and opened it, displaying a very fine array of sandwiches and cake! Snubby could have cried! Why hadn't he had the sense to find out if Mr. King meant to get back to tea or not?

He had to lie under a rather prickly bush and watch Mr. King devour every sandwich and two pieces of Mrs. Round's fruit cake. Loony whined when the smell wafted towards him on the wind. He thought his little master was extremely foolish not to have brought something to eat too. Snubby saw Mr. King raise his head when he heard the whine, and he hissed at the surprised spaniel.

"Shut up, idiot! Not a word!"

Loony looked at his master for a moment, made up his mind that Snubby was temporarily mad, and curled himself up in disgust to go to sleep. Snubby was very glad when Mr. King folded up his sandwich papers and put them back into his pocket. Now perhaps he would go home!

But he didn't. He followed the stream instead, and Snubby had to give up the chase because the country was now too bare for him to follow without being seen. All that way for nothing!

Wait a minute, though. Mr. King was standing still now, looking with great interest at something. What was it? Snubby was full of curiosity. He saw Mr. King bend down to the stream and touch something. Then he bent very low, almost disappeared, and remained practically out of sight for a few minutes. He then reappeared again, and took out some fieldglasses. He swept the countryside with them. What could he be looking for? And what had he found in the stream? Snubby made up his mind to go and see, even if it made him hours late for supper!

CHAPTER SIXTEEN

SNUBBY IS NOT VERY CLEVER

MR. KING at last went off in another direction altogether, much to Snubby's surprise. He took a look at his map and set off to the south, across rough country—hilly country too. Snubby who hadn't the faintest idea where he was, and felt that he was miles from home, looked after Mr. King with exasperation.

"Now where's he going? What a wild goose chase this is!"

He waited till Mr. King was out of sight behind a small clump of trees and then went as quickly as he could to where he had seen him stop by the stream. There was a tiny creek there—a little backwater, with trees and bushes overhanging. Pulled right back in the creek, almost hidden under a bush was a boat. It had no name. A couple of oars lay in it, and a coil of rope. Nothing else. How mysterious!

Snubby gazed at the lonely little boat. Who owned it? There didn't appear to be a house within miles. What a strange thing to leave a boat here, on this stream, hidden like that. Why? Who used it? And where did the owner live? Snubby wished he had field-glasses like Mr. King. Then he could have swept the countryside with them and found out if any cottage or house was hidden in a corner of the hills.

By the time he had finished examining the boat, which told him absolutely nothing, Mr. King had completely disappeared. Snubby couldn't see a sign of him anywhere. He looked down at the patient spaniel.

"Could you track him, Loony, do you think?" he asked. "Then we could follow him without getting lost."

Loony looked up intelligently and wagged his tail. "All right—track him then," said Snubby, waving his hand vaguely in the direction in which Mr. King had gone.

Loony started off eagerly, for all the world as if he knew exactly what Snubby meant. Snubby was delighted.

"He's the cleverest dog that was ever born," he said to himself, as he followed after the pattering spaniel. But when Loony had led him to eight rabbit-holes in succession, he began to change his mind.

"You're daft," he said to Loony, gloomily. "Do you really think I said 'find rabbit-holes'? Do use a little common sense, Loony."

Loony barked and wagged his tail, and started off to find yet another hole. But Snubby had had enough. He was tired, muddy, hungry and thirsty. In addition he felt most annoyed with Mr. King. His tracking had taught him nothing except that Mr. King liked long and apparently aimless walks—and he had seen a hidden boat which didn't seem to belong to anyone at all. Mr. King had enjoyed a jolly good tea and had now completely disappeared into the blue. Snubby would get lost if he tried to follow his trail. He must go back to the stream, follow it to the river, then follow the river to the part he knew, and so get home.

It seemed a long long way to poor Snubby and even Loony's heart sank as they began to stumble back down the marshy banks of the little stream.

Snubby didn't arrive home till eight o'clock. He found everyone in a terrible state about him, even Mr. King. He glared at the tutor, feeling that it was all his fault he had had such a terrible afternoon and evening.

" How long have you been back?" he asked.

" Oh—since about half-past five," said Mr. King, to Snubby's intense astonishment. Half-past five! Why, Mr. King had got back from the stream in about half an hour then—or less. But how had he done it? Snubby couldn't make it out at all. He was almost in tears with tiredness and hunger.

Miss Pepper suddenly took pity on him and forgot her worry and anger over his being so late. She hustled him up to a hot bath, and got him into bed—then she brought up a dish of Mrs. Round's delicious tomato soup, a plate of corned beef and salad and another plate of fresh peaches and cream. Snubby was in the seventh heaven of delight. What a feast! Honestly, it was worth going through those awful hours of hunger and thirst to get all this!

He said very little to Miss Pepper about his long absence. " I went for a walk and lost my way," he said. " That's all."

" Where did you go?" asked Mr. King, curiously.

" I really don't know," said Snubby, politely. " Where did *you* go?"

" Oh round and about," said Mr. King. " But I was sensible— I took my tea with me. Pity you didn't come across me, I could have shared it with you."

Snubby grinned to himself. Little did Mr. King know that he had been hidden under a bush near enough to him to see what he ate! Not until Miss Pepper and Mr. King had gone downstairs did Snubby tell the others exactly what had happened. They were very interested indeed.

" Fancy a boat there, hidden under the trees, with no

visible owner anywhere," said Roger. "A mystery!"

"Yes. But what seems to be much *more* mysterious is how did Mr. King get back here so quickly?" said Snubby. "I mean—it took hours to *get* to that boat, you know—and yet it seems only to have taken Mr. King under half an hour to get back home!"

"Well—he must have taken a short cut back," said Roger. "Let's have a squint at a map and find out."

He went downstairs, found a big map of the district, and put his finger on Rockingdown Village. "Here we are—here's the village, see—and there's the way to the river. Now you went *up* the river, you say—like that."

"Yes. And we came to a stream—quite a big one where it entered the river," said Snubby, stabbing a piece of corned beef with his fork. "Is the stream shown?"

"Yes, here it is—Rocking Stream," said Roger. "You say you went up it a good way—right, here we go," and he ran his finger up the stream.

Diana gave an exclamation. "Well! It's quite easy to see how Mr. King got home so quickly! Look—he had walked almost round in a circle—and by taking a short cut across this hill, he came out quite near Rockingdown Cottage. See—it's hardly any distance."

Diana was right. Because of the way the river curved, Snubby had walked in a half circle, and then up the stream, which made a three-quarter circle—and the other quarter of the circle lay over the hill to Rockingdown Cottage. Easy!

Snubby let out a long sigh. "Gosh! I was certainly a prize idiot! There I was, only a little way from here, and I go and walk miles and miles the long way round. But I didn't know."

"You want to take a compass with you," said Roger. "Anyway, if you want us to see the boat, it won't take long to get there—we'll take this path here, and go over the hill, across this bit of marsh to the stream—and the boat will be somewhere there!"

It all looked very easy and simple, when the map lay before them. Snubby felt really exasperated when he saw what a long and unnecessary walk home he had had. What a lover of walks Mr. King must be to struggle along through marshy ground and overgrown paths, up the stream! Well, it was the last time he would ever do any tracking. Mr. King could go walking every day if he wanted to—but as far as Snubby was concerned he would go alone!

Snubby fell asleep immediately after he had finished his supper. What with his disturbed night, and his long and tiresome walk, he was tired out. There were going to be no excursions for him to-night!

Barney played a game with Roger and Diana till it was time for them to go to bed. The map they had all been looking at lay unheeded on a nearby table.

Barney, who was out of the game for one or two turns, glanced idly at the map. His eye followed the river—then followed the stream—and he looked at it, puzzled.

"Here's a funny thing!" he said to the others, suddenly. "Look!"

"What?" said Diana, throwing the dice out of the shaker. "A six—good! Just what I wanted."

"Look," went on Barney. "See this stream? The one where Snubby found the boat. Look where it goes."

They all looked. "Well, I don't see anything wonderful about it," said Roger. "It just runs close by Rockingdown Manor—then goes off northwards to those hills—where it apparently has its source."

"Yes—but don't you *see*," said Barney. "Have you ever seen any stream in the grounds at all? The old house is set right in the middle of very big grounds. Well, this map apparently shows the stream very close to the house indeed—but you know as well as I do that there is no stream to be found here in these grounds."

The others stopped their game and looked more closely. Yes—it certainly seemed as if the stream ran very close to

105

the house indeed. The map was on a large scale and the stream was shown, or seemed to be shown, actually in the grounds.

And yet what Barney said was quite true. None of them had seen any stream in the grounds at all, and yet they had explored them very thoroughly indeed.

Miranda dropped down on the map and they pushed her off. They were interested now. Where was the stream? They tried to figure it out.

"It's not near our cottage, that's certain. It's not any-where near the village itself, or we'd have had to cross over a bridge or something. It must be on the other side of the old house. We'll look and see."

"If it isn't it must simply have dried up or altered its course or something," said Roger.

"We can easily find out," said Barney.

"How?" asked Diana.

"Use your brains!" said Roger.

"Oh, of course, we can follow the stream all the way up from the river!" said Diana. "I never thought of that. How stupid of me!"

"Yes. We can easily follow it and see what its course is," said Barney. "Not that it matters really. I was just suddenly interested to notice how near it came to the old house, when I was looking at the map."

The subject was dropped and a new game begun. Miss Pepper put her head in at the study after a while. "Barney, it's time you went. It's raining hard. Is it far for you to go to your lodgings?"

Miss Pepper thought Barney had lodgings somewhere. He had told her he had a room to sleep in and she imagined it was one in the village. Nobody undeceived her. They couldn't possibly tell her where Barney really slept.

"No. Not far, Miss Pepper," said Barney, rising to go. He really had very good manners. "I'll be seeing you to-morrow," he said to Diana and Roger. "So long!"

He went off with Miranda as usual on his shoulder, Loony escorting him to the door, sending a few barks after him, which were really meant for Miranda. " Good riddance to bad rubbish! " was what his barks meant. Then back he trotted to the others, pleased with himself.

Barney went cautiously through the grounds, wondering if Mr. King—or anyone else—was about. But he saw no one. All the same, he locked the veranda door *and* the passage door too—he didn't mean to be disturbed in the middle of the night again!

CHAPTER SEVENTEEN

BARNEY DOES SOME EXPLORING

ALL the same, it was a very disturbing night for Barney. He was awakened suddenly by Miranda chattering to him in fright, pulling at his hair and ears. He took her in his arms and sat up in bed.

Bang! Thud!

There were the noises again. Blow! What *was* going on in this empty old house? Should he get up and see, or should he lie down and sleep again? Apparently nothing happened except noises. There was nobody actually *in* the house, otherwise there would be strange footprints to find. And there were no footprints except their own.

The noises came again, and then the queer whining, half-screeching sound. Miranda was absolutely terrified. She tried to get inside Barney's shirt, and made little whining noises of fear. He comforted her automatically, listening hard. What was making those noises? And where were they being made? They simply *must* be inside the house!

Barney sighed. He was tired after his disturbed night the night before, and he dearly wanted to go to sleep. But he felt intensely curious about all this. He was not in the least frightened, and he threw off the blanket and went across the room feeling for the door. He did not put on his torch for fear of the light being seen by anyone who might perhaps be outside.

Miranda tried to pull him back. She leapt down to the floor and pulled at his legs, chattering wildly. Barney laughed. " You'll be all right with me, Miranda. I'm not afraid! Don't be a little idiot. Now—be quiet, or you'll be heard."

He went down the passage and unlocked the door there quietly. He wondered how the person or persons who made those noises could possibly get into the house—and if they did where were the footmarks they made? He gave it up. It was a real puzzle.

" I'll solve it somehow though," thought Barney. " I don't know what's going on, but something is! And what's more I believe that Mr. King's in it too, whatever it is.

Maybe he can get into the house somewhere we haven't found—and it's he who makes those queer noises."

Thud! Thud! There it went again, deep down in the house. One thud was so loud that Barney was really startled.

He went right down to the kitchen, feeling his way cautiously, not daring to put on his torch. All was quiet there. Barney switched his torch on and off very swiftly, gazing at the floor as he did so. No fresh footprints were there, nobody had been in the kitchen.

He went into the scullery. No footprints there either. And yet it honestly seemed as if the noises came from this direction. As he stood there, waiting, a noise came again.

Thud! Thud! And then the whining sound, and a queer guttural noise that Barney hadn't heard before. He felt a moment's fear. That was a strange noise—what could it be? It didn't sound at all human. Could there be dungeons or something under the scullery floor? Was the house old enough for those? What about cellars? Where were they? There must be plenty in an old house of this kind.

Barney wondered why he hadn't thought of cellars before. They ought to be explored! Probably the explanation of the noises lay in the cellars.

He went through the scullery and came to some stone-paved outhouses—one was a washhouse, the other must have been a dairy at one time. It had shelves of marble all round to hold pans of cream.

His torch swung over the floor and the beam showed up dust again. Not a footprint anywhere! Not even Loony's. The doors to the outhouses had been shut, so Loony hadn't gone through them. Barney looked carefully over the floor. He found what he was seeking—a square place where a trapdoor lay, its handle sunk into a groove of the wood, so that no one would trip over it.

That's where the cellars would be—under there. Well, he wasn't going down there to-night. Whatever was going on could go on without him. Fearless as Barney was he had no wish to explore dark cellars at that moment— especially cellars that gave out such peculiar noises!

He would tell the children in the morning and they would all do a little more exploring. It would be exciting! Barney went back to bed, yawning. A few more noises came up to him as he lay in bed, but he took no notice of them. Miranda didn't either. She was cuddled up to him half asleep, her tiny front paws down his neck.

In the morning Barney told the children what he had heard, and how he had gone into the outhouses and seen the trapdoor.

"The washhouse and the dairy open out of one side of the scullery," he said. "We've never been into them. There's a trapdoor in the dairy—I bet it leads down to cellars. We'll explore there this afternoon. I'm sure there's something queer going on there, though I can't for the life of me imagine what it is!"

This was so thrilling that nobody could pay much attention to their coaching that morning. Fortunately Mr. King seemed a little bored with it too, and appeared to be working out calculations of his own on a sheet of paper.

Loony crept in unnoticed and lay at Snubby's feet. He began to gnaw the edge of the tablecloth that hung just by his nose. He made a chewy kind of noise and Mr. King looked up.

"Stop making that silly noise, Snubby," he said. Snubby hastily kicked Loony to stop him chewing, and there was peace again. Everyone was thankful when the morning came to an end. Mr. King noticed with a start that Loony had apparently suddenly materialised under the table, and was just about to make a stern remark about it, when Snubby fell on Loony and fondled him extravagantly.

"How did you know we'd just finished! How clever of you to come in just at the right moment! Mr. King, wasn't he clever to know it was the right minute to come in?"

Mr. King said nothing. He just looked sternly at Loony and even more sternly at Snubby. Before he could make up his mind exactly how to answer Snubby, the boy rushed from the room with Loony, yelling like a Red Indian. "Come on, Loony, walkie-walks!"

The other three children grinned at one another. They had known perfectly well that Loony was under the table all the morning, and had wondered when Mr. King would find it out.

"Can Barney stay to lunch, Miss Pepper, can he, can he?" shouted Snubby, who always yelled at the top of his voice for about ten minutes after finishing his coaching. "It's cold chicken and salad and Roundy says there is enough."

"All right, all right," said Miss Pepper, putting her hands over her ears. "Why must you shout so? And didn't I tell you to go upstairs after breakfast and change out of that disgustingly dirty shirt?"

"Oh—so you did," said Snubby. "Well, need I now? I shall probably get awfully dirty this afternoon."

"Why? What are you going to do?" asked Miss Pepper. "You came home filthy yesterday too. Is it *necessary* to do all the dirty things you seem to do?"

"Yes—it's absolutely necessary," Snubby assured her cheerfully. "Well, I won't change my shirt then. I don't want Roundy to have any more washing to do. I wish I was like Loony, and just wore my own coat of hair and nothing else."

"You wouldn't manage to keep yourself as clean as Loony does, even then," said Miss Pepper. "I really do think you are the most filthy dirty child I have ever . . ."

"Dear old Pep!" said the irrepressible Snubby and swung her round, trying to do a foxtrot with her.

She was half cross, half amused.

Mr. King came in suddenly, looking as black as thunder. "Snubby! Did you tie that bit of string between the gateposts in the garden? I've almost broken my ankle over it. Miss Pepper, I'm going to buy a cane this afternoon—a nice thin one that goes wheeeee in the air."

"Do," said Miss Pepper. "Lend it to me to use some time, will you?"

Snubby didn't like this. It wasn't good when Miss Pepper and Mr. King both sided against him. He looked pained. "I'm sorry, Mr. King. I was practising jumping. You must have fallen over my jumping-string."

"Snubby, that kind of thing is stupid and dangerous," said Miss Pepper. "I shall make you go without your pudding at dinner to-day. I've told you before about dangerous tricks. I will not have them played."

"Aha—no pudding for you then," said Mr. King, pleased. "Serves you right, you little pest."

Snubby lost his high spirits and looked sulky. He couldn't do anything if both Mr. King and Miss Pepper were in league against him. There were all sorts of nasty punishments they could think up. He scowled at their retreating backs.

"I'll have to set them against one another," he thought and sat down to worry out a plan. It didn't take him long. He went into the kitchen and got the kitchen pepper-pot when Mrs. Round's back was turned. He slipped it into his pocket. He tiptoed out again, Loony sniffing at his pocket. Then the spaniel suddenly sneezed.

"Pepper up your nose?" said Snubby, loudly, so that Miss Pepper could hear. "Poor little dog. Pepper's awful, isn't it?"

Dinner was soon ready. There were big bowls of steaming pea soup. Mrs. Round was good at making soup, and she knew the children liked it. It filled them up too, when there wasn't much meat to go round, like to-day.

Snubby had a few words with Roger, who grinned and nodded. They all sat down. Roger tasted his soup.

" Wants salt and pepper," he said. " Pass the pepper, Di. Mr. King, will you have some?"

Just as Mr. King took up the table pepper-pot to sprinkle a little on his soup, Snubby left his place and went to pick up his table napkin ring. As he passed behind the unsuspecting Mr. King he whipped the kitchen pepper-pot from his pocket and tossed pepper round Mr. King's head.

Miss Pepper didn't notice anything. Nor did poor Mr. King. He finished sprinkling pepper and salt on his soup, and was about to take up his spoon when he felt an enormous sneeze coming. He got out his handkerchief hastily.

" Whooooosh—oo! I beg your pardon, Miss Pepper. A—whoooooosh—oo! Oh dear me! Here's another one coming. Really — I — I — whooooosh—oo! "

Miss Pepper looked at him. What an extraordinary paroxysm of sneezing! Mr. King was now purple in the face, wondering whether to leave the room or not.

" A—whooooosh—oooosh—oo! " he began again. " I do apologise. It must be a little pepper up my nose! "

The children roared with laugher. Good old Mr. King! He had said the exact words that Miss Pepper hated.

Miss Pepper looked at Mr. King coldly. How dare he make fun of her like this—in front of the children too. She didn't believe in his sneezes at all, now that he had said the fatal words. " Perhaps you would like to leave the room till your er—indisposition is over?" she said, in an icy voice.

Mr. King got up and went. The children heard him still coping with his sneezes in the bedroom above, and Diana was almost helpless with laughter. Every time she ate a spoonful of soup she laughed and choked. Miss Pepper got really angry.

" Now stop it, Diana. It's an old joke now and a silly one, this pepper joke. It's not even funny."

Snubby made his face solemn. " I think it was rude of Mr. King to say that in front of you," he said, righteously.

" I mean—it's all very well for *us* to say silly things like that, Miss Pepper—but Mr. King shouldn't forget his manners, should he?"

" That's enough," said Miss Pepper. " Not a word more from you. And when Mr. King comes back we shall not refer to this again."

Mr. King came back shortly looking very sheepish, not understanding his fit of sneezing at all. He was upset to find Miss Pepper so cold to him. Was she cross because of his sneezing at table? Well, anybody might do that! Sneezes were like hiccups—you just couldn't stop them.

The meat course came in and then the pudding. Snubby was supposed to go without—but because Miss Pepper was still annoyed with Mr. King she quite forgot to leave Snubby out when she served the pudding—and he got his usual big helping.

And poor Mr. King, who remembered about it, didn't dare to remind Miss Pepper! Snubby grinned. He had got on top as usual.

CHAPTER EIGHTEEN

A VERY EXCITING AFTERNOON

THE exploration that afternoon proved very interesting indeed. They all arrived at Rockingdown Manor at just after half-past two, full of anticipation. What would they find in the cellar?

Snubby had forgotten his fears of a night or two ago. He was once again brave and fearless, entering the old house first of all, and even shouting loudly in it to make the echoes come.

Barney laughed at him. Snubby always amused him with his silly tricks and ridiculous ways. They all went to the big kitchens and out into the scullery. Then through the door that led into the outhouses. The washhouse first and then the dairy with its marble shelves.

"Here we are," said Barney. "And look, there's the trap-door. I bet that leads down into the cellars. And I bet they're pretty big ones too."

Roger took the iron handle and gave it a tug. Nothing happened at all.

"It'll be stiff," said Barney. "It can't have been used for years. Let me try."

He couldn't budge the trapdoor either. Loony went and scraped madly at it as if he could open it that way. They all sat back and panted after their exertions.

"Where's that rope we had?" said Barney, suddenly. "Let me see—what did I do with it? I believe it's up-stairs in the nurseries, Snubby. Go and get it."

Snubby shot off with Loony—but when he got to the passage door, he heard noises beyond. He stopped, frightened. Who was it? He tore down the stairs again and into the dairy. "There's somebody upstairs. I heard them."

"Don't be silly," said Barney. "You're a little coward, Snubby! There's nobody there."

"There *is* I tell you—I heard them," said Snubby. Barney got up.

"I'll go," he said, and up he went. He came down with the rope—and with Miranda too. He was grinning.

"It was Miranda up there," he said. "She'd got a box of skittles and was throwing them all over the place. That's what you heard. Baby!"

Snubby went very red. The others laughed at him whilst Barney slid the rope through the handle of the trap-door. He twisted the two strands into one.

"Here you are," he said to the other three. "Take hold, all of you, and we'll pull together. Miranda, you pull too!"

So, with Miranda pulling as well, and looking extremely proud, the children pulled together with all their might.

And, of course, the trapdoor opened so very suddenly that they all sat down in a heap, and Roger, who was last, got a terrific bump that shook all the breath out of him!

They got up and went to peer into the dark hole under the trapdoor.

"Steps," said Roger. "Stone steps. They go down to the cellars, no doubt about that. Got the torch, Barney?"

"I'll go first," said Barney, and down he went, flashing the torch carefully in front of him. The steps curved a little towards the bottom and ended in a stone floor. Barney felt it with his feet to see if it were slimy. No, it was quite dry.

A musty smell of old casks and barrels came to his nose. He flashed his torch round. It was, as he had suspected, a most enormous cellar. Boxes, casks, barrels, old cobwebbed bottles lay about everywhere. Wooden shelves showed where wine had once been stored.

Everyone was now down the steps. Miranda would not leave Barney's shoulder, and held on to his hair as he made his way into the depths of the cellar. The others followed, flashing their torches too. Loony, surprised at this new place so unexpectedly opened in the depths of the earth, ran about sniffing. Any rabbits down here? Not even a smell of one!

The children explored the old cellars from end to end. They opened the old boxes but found nothing in any of them. They knocked on the casks and barrels and decided they were absolutely empty. "Not even a full bottle of gingerbeer," said Snubby, mournfully. "Very dull."

Mice or rats scurried away into corners as the torches lighted them up. Loony had a lovely time chasing them, and got a bite on the ear. Miranda wouldn't chase rats. Loony got a rat in a corner behind a cask, and began to scrape there after it. The cask fell, and three more fell too, making a terrific noise in the old cellars. Everyone jumped.

"It's only Loony," said Roger, relieved. "I say, Barney—I wish we could hear those queer noises now. We should know what part of the cellar they came from."

"I think it's very queer," came Barney's voice from another corner. "There doesn't seem anything here to account for those noises at all—and honestly I can't see any signs of people being here— there's dust in quite a lot of places, but no footprints again—no cigarette ends—nothing!"

"Well—how can we solve the mystery?" demanded Snubby.

"I think I shall come down here one night when I hear the noises and watch," said Barney. "Or better still I could hide myself *before* the noises begin."

"Would you *dare*?" said Snubby, in horror. "Gracious, you must be brave."

117

" Yes. I certainly wouldn't dare to do that," said Diana, soberly. " Would you, Roger?"

Roger thought about it. " No, I don't think I would," he said. " And what's more I don't think you'd better, Barney."

" Well, I'm going to," said Barney. " I can't make all this out. I'm going to find out what's going on. "

They sat silent for a few minutes on one or two old boxes whilst Loony snuffled round them. Barney pricked up his ears. " Can you hear anything?" he asked the others.

They listened. " Well," said Diana doubtfully, " I *think* I can hear a little noise occasionally—but I don't quite know how to describe it—rather a *gurgly* sort of noise! "

This didn't please Snubby at all. He got up. He had no wish to hear any noises, least of all " gurgly " ones. Anyway he was tired of this awful dark, musty cellar. He wanted to be out in the daylight again.

" Come on—don't let's listen for gurgles or gobbles or guzzles," he said. " Let's go."

The others laughed and got up too. Barney listened for a moment or two more and gave it up. " Probably my imagination," he said.

They went up the stone steps, chattering, with Loony bounding in front. At the top he stopped and growled. The children ceased talking at once and Diana clutched Barney. Now what?

There was the sound of men's voices! " Did we lock that veranda door?" whispered Roger. " Gosh—we didn't! What idiots! Now someone has got in! "

" I'll go and see," whispered Barney. " Keep Loony back and don't let him growl or bark, or he'll give us away."

Snubby put a hand on Loony's collar and the dog stopped his low growling. Barney went quietly through the outhouse and into the scullery. He stopped and listened. Nobody was in the kitchen beyond. He went to

118

the kitchen door and peered through the crack of the door there into the hall.

What he saw surprised him very much! Mr. King was there with two other men. Both were strong, burly men, and had their backs to Barney. They were talking together.

"See all these footprints?" Mr. King was saying. "That tells you something, doesn't it! We'll have to find out whose they are. And who left the veranda door ajar too? Look at the footmarks going up the stairs. Crowds of them! Looks as if there are troops of people using this place for their own purposes! And yet there's never anyone to be found here when I come—and not a light to be seen anywhere. Where do they go?"

"Beats me," said one of the men. "Anyway this is the place all right. We'll get going now, no doubt about that."

Barney had heard enough. He slipped back to the others. "It's Mr. King—with two others," he whispered. "I don't believe they're up to any good here, really. There's some queer plan or something going on—and Mr. King's in it. I don't believe he's a tutor at all. He's a fraud!"

This was amazing news. Diana clutched at Barney. "Will they find us down here? What shall we do?"

"We'll get out, shut the trapdoor, and steal out of the kitchen door," said Barney. "We can take the kitchen key, so that we can get in again if we want to. You can bet anything you like that those fellows will search the house now to find out who's made those footprints everywhere—and when they go they will see that every door and window's fastened so that we can't get in again."

"But we'll have the kitchen door key, so we can if we want to!" said Snubby, trembling with excitement. "Is it safe to go now?"

Barney went to see. He came back in half a minute. "They've gone upstairs. I wonder if they know about those nurseries. Anyway the passage door is locked and

119

I've got the key. They may think it's only boxrooms or something."

"We'll steal out now then," said Diana, who was very anxious to go. They all got out of the opening in the floor, and then quietly shut the trapdoor. They made their way into the kitchen, Loony as quiet as the others.

Over to the kitchen door they went—and Barney unlocked it. He took the key from the lock and opened the door. It creaked a little but not much. They all went out into an overgrown yard, where an old dustbin still stood. A dog-kennel stood nearby, almost falling to bits. Loony went over to it and sniffed in it inquisitively. But there was no dog smell left.

Barney locked the door behind them. He put the key in his pocket. He looked up at the windows. Could anyone see them if they made a dash for it now? No. Trees overhung the backyard and screened it from overhead.

"Come on," he said. "We'll run for it now. Keep under bushes and trees and don't show yourselves at all."

They ran from the back door, across the yard and into the bushes. There had once been a kitchen garden on the other side of the yard, but it was so overgrown with weeds that it would have been impossible to know what it was now, if it had not been for the apple trees showing here and there, struggling against the ivy that was slowly choking everything.

The children soon found a part of the grounds they knew and quickly made their way home, astonished and puzzled. Was Mr. King really a fraud? Ought they to tell Miss Pepper? What was he doing here? And what had Rockingdown Manor and the queer noises to do with everything? It was all very puzzling indeed.

"I think we ought to tell Miss Pepper," said Roger, at last. "We'll sleep on it first—and then tell her in the morning."

CHAPTER NINETEEN

MR. KING IN CHARGE

BUT that night something happened which upset all their plans. A telephone call came for Miss Pepper and after she had answered it she came into the study, looking very upset.

"Children—I have to leave you for a few days. My sister is very ill—dangerously ill—and I must go to her. I must leave you in Mr. King's charge. You will be quite all right, and I shall put you on your honour to be as good as you can."

"Oh, Miss Pepper—I'm so sorry about your sister!" cried Diana. "Is there anything we can do? Are you leaving to-night—or to-morrow morning?"

"To-night, I think. Oh dear, I *can't* make up my mind what to do. Can I catch the last night-train, or not? There is my packing to do—and I must see Mrs. Round before I go."

"You can give me any messages for Mrs. Round," said Diana. "You know I'll help her all I can. And I can do your packing for you too, if you'll put out the things you want. The boys can ring up for a taxi. You will easily be able to catch the night-train."

"What a kind, good child you are!" said Miss Pepper, almost in tears. "Very well. I'll go to-night. Come up and help me to pack whilst I tell you what I want you to say to Mrs. Round."

Roger rang up for a taxi. Diana did the packing and listened to the instructions for Mrs. Round. "I'll telephone to her to-morrow to tell her how things are getting on," said Miss Pepper. "Did I pack my hair-brushes?

And a clean blouse? Now what have I done with those shoes?"

"They're in your hands, Miss Pepper," said Diana, taking them from her. "Now, do take things easily. You've plenty of time for your train—and I expect your sister will feel much better as soon as she sees you."

"I must talk to Mr. King too," said Miss Pepper. "Thank goodness I can leave him in charge of you. He seems very dependable and responsible."

Diana said nothing to that. Because of what she now suspected about Mr. King there didn't seem anything to say except things that would upset Miss Pepper and probably upset her plans too! So she went on packing and made no remark.

Mr. King came up to condole with Miss Pepper. He had been out for one of his walks. He was very sweet to her and she felt comforted.

"I feel quite safe to leave the children with you and Mrs. Round," she said. "I only hope they'll behave themselves—but I think they will, Mr. King. They always come out well in an emergency and are really very trustworthy."

She went off in the taxi, still looking very worried. Everyone waved cheerily to her.

"Well!" said Mr. King, shutting the door. "Poor Miss Pepper! I hope everything goes all right for her. Now children—we've got to make the best of one another! You'll have to put up with me in charge of you!"

He beamed round at them. They looked away. "Er— we shall do our best, Mr. King," said Roger, feeling that somebody certainly ought to say something. Mr. King looked faintly surprised at the children's lack of response, but put it down to their being upset at Miss Pepper's sudden going.

He looked at his watch. "My word—we *are* all late to-night!" he said. "I think we ought to go to bed. Off with you! Lights out in ten minutes, please."

The three of them had their lights out in ten minutes. They wondered about Barney. He wasn't going to sleep in the old house to-night. They had taken cushions and a rug to the old summer-house for him, hoping that it would not rain. The summer-house was not very weatherproof nowadays.

When they were sure that Mr. King was in bed they stole down the back stairs to find Barney in the summer-house, and tell him the news about Miss Pepper's leaving.

" We haven't been able to tell Miss Pepper what we suspect," finished Roger. " That must wait till she comes back. In the meantime—we must keep our eyes and ears open! "

" I wonder if I ought to go back and sleep in the old house to-night," said Barney. " Just in case there's something being planned there by Mr. King and the other men."

" No don't," said Roger. " Mr. King is indoors now— look, you can see his light through the curtains of his bedroom window. If he has any idea of wandering over to the mansion again to-night, he will have to pass near the summerhouse—and then you can follow him."

" Yes. There's something in that," said Barney, snuggling down in his rug. " I don't really feel like scrambling through the grounds again at the moment. I feel jolly sleepy."

" Well, we'll go back now," said the others. " Good night Barney. See you to-morrow."

It seemed queer without Miss Pepper the next day. Mrs. Round arrived and heard the news. " Dear, dear— she's so fond of her sister too," she said. " Well, we must hope for the best. Now you don't need to bother your heads about anything except just to do a bit of shopping for me now and again, and make your own beds and give a hand at times."

They all had their coaching as usual, though Mr. King seemed lost in thought. If they hadn't been on their honour to behave themselves they could have played any amount of tricks on the absent-minded tutor. But not even Snubby thought out any. Barney sat as usual in the window, listening. He looked earnestly at the back of Mr. King's head and thought about him. What was he doing at Rockingdown Manor? What was he interested in there? It must be something important or he wouldn't have gone to the trouble of taking the job here as coach—which meant that he could live near the Manor, and find it easier to carry out his plans.

Barney couldn't imagine what those plans were. He wondered if by any chance the three men had done anything in the house after the children had escaped in such a hurry—had they hidden something there, perhaps? Or found something they were looking for?

He slipped out of the room before the end of the lesson. He felt that he wanted to go and see if anything had been done at the old house—the men certainly hadn't got in for nothing.

He saw nothing at all on the ground floor except for the footmarks of the three men in every room. He took the trouble of going into the outhouses to see if the trapdoor had been discovered.

It was wide open! The wooden trapdoor was swung back, and the flight of stone steps was plainly to be seen.

Barney went to the open trapdoor. He listened. All was quiet below. There was no one down there now. But obviously the three men had been down to search for something.

He went up to the first floor and saw the prints of the men there, in every room. They had walked to every cupboard. Some of the doors were left open. What *could* they be looking for? A secret hiding-place?

Up the stairs to the second floor went the boy, feeling certain that the locked door at the end of the passage would have been opened.

It had been burst open! Somebody had either kicked it

or flung himself hard against it. The old lock had given way, and the door was swinging wide open.

" Now my hiding-place is discovered! " thought Barney. He went into the nurseries. The three beds had been stripped and the covers thrown to the ground. The chests had been looked through, the cupboards opened. Even the linoleum in the day nursery had been taken up.

The rooms were in a dreadful state now. It would need a good morning's work from Diana to get them straight again. Barney wondered if it was safe for him to sleep there any more. Well, as long as the good weather lasted he could sleep comfortably in the old summer-house at Rockingdown Cottage.

It was all very puzzling. Barney made up his mind about one thing straight away. He would certainly go down into the cellars and wait for those noises that night! He meant to get to the bottom of those. Had the three men anything to do with them?

He went back to the children after he had bought himself some bread and cheese at the village shop. He gave Miranda some plums to eat. She liked those. She pulled each plum in half, took out the stone, threw it away, joined the halves together, and then nibbled the plum in delight.

" You want a bib, Miranda," said Barney, with a laugh. " Those plums are so juicy that you're getting sticky all down your chest! "

After his meal Barney went to see the children. He told them what he had discovered in the old house—the open trapdoor, the footmarks everywhere, the burst-open door, and the rifled nurseries. They listened in amazement.

" How *dare* Mr. King do all that! " said Diana. " After I'd made everything so tidy for you too. It's too bad. I've a good mind to tick him off."

" No. Don't you say a word," said Barney, quickly. " Don't put him on his guard at all. As long as he thinks we don't suspect anything wrong about him he won't try to hide his doings. If he guesses what we know, he may go off—and whilst he is here we have at least got him under our eyes!"

"Yes, that's true," said Diana. "Well, I won't say a word. Barney, I hate the idea of your going to watch down in the cellars to-night. Wouldn't you like one of us with you?"

"Of course not!" said Barney with a laugh. "What do you think could happen to me down there? Nothing, of course!"

But for once in a way Barney was wrong.

CHAPTER TWENTY

DOWN IN THE CELLARS

NONE of the three children at Rockingdown Cottage felt very friendly towards Mr. King, and he was puzzled. Even Loony sat with his back to him whenever he could! The spaniel always knew when Snubby was doubtful about anyone, and if his master would not be friendly towards someone, then Loony behaved in the same way.

Mr. King looked at the children three or four times during their midday meal. How odd they were all of a sudden! Anyone would think he had offended them in some way, he thought. They wouldn't look at him, and hardly smiled at all. They hardly spoke to him either.

"Anything the matter?" he said at last. "You seem to be a very gloomy lot to-day. Are you worried about something?"

"Well—yes," said Diana. "We're worried about Miss Pepper's sister, of course."

"Dear me—I didn't think you even knew her," said Mr.

King, in astonishment. " Well, do cheer up. I'm sure you'll hear that things are all right."

Miss Pepper did ring up shortly after that, but the news was not very good. Her sister was still very ill and Miss Pepper didn't know when she would be back. " But I'm sure you'll be all right with Mr. King," she said. " And Mrs. Round is very good too."

Mr. King kept trying to cheer the children up. He offered to take them for a walk. He offered to fix up a riding lesson for them. He even suggested going down to the river to bathe as it was a hot day. In the ordinary way the last two suggestions would have been hailed with glee—but nobody felt that they wanted to take any favours from Mr King at the moment. He was a fraud. They weren't going to like him any more. He was " Up to something," and they wanted to know what!

Mr. King gave up his efforts at last, decided that the children were sulky and cross, and could jolly well look after themselves. Loony annoyed him most. He couldn't believe that a dog would sit with his back to him on purpose, but it really did look as if Loony meant to!

Barney stayed to tea. The children had it out in the garden, hoping to get away from Mr. King. But he most annoyingly came and had it with them. He seemed to feel that he must look after them every minute, now Miss Pepper was away. So the children couldn't talk freely at all, and Diana grew very sulky. She was the worst of them all at hiding her feelings.

" You really are a set of miseries! " said Mr. King. ". Take that sulky look off your face, Diana—it doesn't suit you at all! "

Diana immediately looked twice as sulky. Barney felt that Mr. King would really begin to suspect something if they all behaved like this, so he began to talk to the coach, relating all kinds of tales, and livening things up considerably. Miranda also did her best by behaving very badly with Loony—snatching away a biscuit Diana was giving him, and throwing plum-stones at him.

Everyone laughed at her ridiculous antics except Loony, who was very hurt. Mr. King felt quite relieved to find that they *could* laugh!

They escaped from the coach after tea, and went to the village to buy ice-creams. The old lady in the general store seemed to keep her shop open till all hours at night, and it was possible to get ice-creams from dawn to dark at her exciting little shop.

" Don't let's go back to supper till we've got to," said Diana. " I just can't bear Mr. King now that I know he's a fraud. Let's go over the grounds and see if we can find that stream."

" Oh yes—that's a good idea," said Roger. " I've been puzzling my head where it is. It's shown so very close to the old house on the map."

They explored the grounds very thoroughly indeed, north, south, east and west—but there was no sign of a stream at all!

" There's not even a dried-up bed, or ditch," said Roger, puzzled. " The map must be wrong."

" I suppose it must be," said Barney. " Anyway, as I said, we can always trace where it goes by following its course up from the river. Still—it's not important."

" I don't like to think of you down in those cellars to-night," began Diana again, as they made their way back to the cottage. " I really don't. You'll take your rug and cushion down there with you, won't you? You may as well be comfortable. That floor will be hard and cold."

" Yes. I'll take them," said Barney. " And look—I've bought myself a new torch—grand, isn't it! "

He showed his torch to them. It certainly was a nice one and gave out a very good light. " I shall be all right with this! " he said.

Mrs. Round had left enough supper for Barney, so he

stayed. He always enjoyed his meals with the children. Afterwards they played a game, whilst Mr. King read.

"I'd better be going," said Barney at last. Mr. King looked up.

"Where do you sleep at night?" he asked, and he spoke the words in such a pointed way that the children felt sure he suspected Barney of sleeping up in the nurseries of Rockingdown Manor.

"I slept in the summer house last night, sir," said Barney, politely. "And last week I slept in the boat with a rug and a cushion. I haven't a proper home, and lodgings are expensive."

"I see," said Mr. King. "Well—so long as you don't get into mischief! I suppose you're sleeping in the summer-house again to-night as it's a hot night—well, look out for a storm, if so!"

"Yes, sir, I will," said Barney. His eyes gleamed as he looked at Mr. King. What would the coach say if he knew he was sleeping in the cellars of the old house?

Barney went off with Miranda. The children went with him to the gate, Loony too. He was always glad to see the back of Miranda!

Diana watched Barney out of sight. She was worried. "I do hope he'll be all right," she said.

"'Course he will!" said Roger. "Nothing will happen to old Barney. Anyway, he's like a cat—he'll always fall on his feet. He'll look after himself all right."

Barney unlocked the kitchen door of the old house when he got there, and let himself in. He took a quick glance round the ground floor. Nothing had altered since the morning. He went upstairs to get his rug and a cushion. The nurseries were just the same as when he had seen them that morning—untidy and higgledy-piggledy, drawers and cupboards open everywhere.

Barney picked up his rug and the cushion. He went downstairs with Miranda, yawning. He thought he would

129

get a little sleep straight away, then if the noises began he would be wide awake and fresh.

Miranda was astonished to find that Barney was going to sleep down in the dark cellars. She was not at all pleased. She chattered angrily and pulled at the rug as if to say " No, no—come upstairs! This is all wrong! "

" Sorry, Miranda—but this is where we sleep to-night! " said Barney, firmly. " Now—where do you think would be a good corner?"

All the corners were equally dirty. In the end Barney thought it would be quite a good idea to lie on one of the wooden shelves that had once held bottles. Wood would not be so cold or hard as stone.

He climbed up on a shelf, put the cushion down for his head, and wrapped himself up in the thick rug. The cellars were cold, but it was a very warm night. Barney thought he would be all right in the rug, with Miranda cuddled to him like a hot-water bottle! She snuggled down protestingly.

Barney fell asleep at once, hard though his bed was. A spider ran over his face but didn't disturb him. When it ran over Miranda's hairy little face she put up a quick paw and caught it. Then she too went to sleep.

Barney slept peacefully on. Half-past ten came, eleven o'clock, half-past eleven, midnight. Then Barney was awakened by the hardness of his bed. One of his arms was aching through being bent underneath him on the hard board. He shifted his position, remembered where he was, and sat up to listen. Were there any noises at all?

The cellars were very, very quiet—and in the silence Barney again thought he caught the faint noise he had heard once before, with Diana. Was it a kind of gurgle? It had gone before he had made up his mind. Well—it was so faint and far-off that it was quite impossible to tell what it was, if it was anything.

He switched on his torch and shone it round. Nothing
130

to be seen except a pair of frightened rat's eyes gleaming. Then the rat scampered away to a corner and disappeared.

Barney lay down again and Miranda snuggled into his neck, putting her paws inside his shirt for warmth. Barney liked the feel of the tiny monkey-hands. He patted Miranda affectionately, and she nibbled the skin of his neck, also affectionately. She had some funny little ways!

Barney soon fell asleep again. One o'clock came—two o'clock—and then Barney was awakened suddenly.

Thud! Bang!

He shot up straight and Miranda fell off the shelf. The boy listened intently.

BANG!

The noises were very much louder down here. But they couldn't be in the cellars! They sounded too far away for that.

Barney listened hard. When he was sure that the noises were not in the cellars he switched on his torch. He flashed it all round—no, there was absolutely nothing to be seen. But the noises went on!

Bang! Thud! And then there came the whining noise, and after that a curious grating sound, guttural and harsh. Then Barney felt sure he could hear voices. But they were muffled voices—as if there was a wall or two between them and Barney.

"Well! This is certainly where we do a spot of exploring," said Barney to Miranda, and he threw aside his rug. He jumped down from the wooden shelf and stood listening. He must go in the direction of the noises.

They came from the right. He went in that direction and came up against a stone wall. The noises seemed to be on the other side. But how could they be? There was no way of getting through to the other side.

Barney ran his torch along the stone wall on his right. It was just the same as the rest of the cellar walls, except that it was glistening with damp.

Thud! That noise really did sound as if it were behind the wall. Well then, there must be some place behind there! Barney shone his torch again.

And then he found what he was looking for! He wouldn't have seen it but for Miranda—it was really she who found it for him.

CHAPTER TWENTY-ONE

QUEER HAPPENINGS

AN OLD BOX stood against the wall. Miranda saw something moving there—was it a spider—a moth? In a trice she was after it! She slid down behind the box, and Barney moved it out to see what she was after.

And there in the wall he saw an iron handle. It was low down, and very rusty. He had to kneel down to look at it closely.

Why was there an iron handle so low down in the wall? Surely it wasn't meant to be used for anything? Perhaps in the old far-off days this cellar was used as a dungeon and prisoners had been tied to the iron ring.

Barney looked at it. He set down his torch, put both hands to the ring and tugged. It was very fast in the wall and would not move. He pushed. No result. He tugged again whilst Miranda sat close by and watched with great interest.

It was quite by accident that he found the secret of the iron handle. He discovered that it turned round and round. So he turned it with a screwing motion—and something happened!

Barney never found out quite what did happen. The screwing round of the handle seemed to work some kind of lever—and suddenly the stone next to the one in which the iron ring was set began to move, very very slowly! It moved inwards, towards Barney, grating a little as it ran over hidden grooves. He stopped twisting the handle in surprise, and the stone stopped moving. It was half in, half out of the thick wall. Shaking with excitement Barney twisted the iron handle again and once more the stone next to it began to move.

It came right out from its place, leaving a small gap between itself and the wall. Barney looked at the gap. It would take him easily, or a small man. A big man would have difficulty in squeezing through. He flashed his torch to the gap, but it was impossible to see what lay behind it.

"Shall we get through?" said he to Miranda. She did not wait to answer, but slipped neatly through herself! She came back at once, chattering.

She was not frightened, so Barney decided there couldn't

be much behind the sliding stone. He would go and see. The noises might have their origin behind it somewhere.

So he squeezed in through the gap. On the other side of the wall was pitch darkness! Barney shone his torch round to see what was what.

He was in a very curious place indeed. It was very small, not much bigger than a boxroom, and the ceiling or roof was so low that Barney could not stand upright. The walls were running with damp, and there was a very damp smell there too.

Barney looked round this strange little place in surprise. What in the world was it? There was nothing there at all, as far as he could see.

And then he heard one of the " noises." My goodness, it was so loud that he almost jumped out of his skin! It sounded almost in the little room, but not quite.

It seemed to come from under the ground. Barney flashed his torch on the floor—and how he stared!

Not far from him was a dark hole, quite round and very narrow. It went down for some way because his torch could not pick out the bottom of it. He could see the remains of an old iron ladder going down this curious shaft —and it was up this hole that the noises came!

They sounded very loud indeed when he stood at the top of the hole. Miranda was terrified. She bounded back to the gap in the wall and shot through it, gibbering with fright. Barney called her back, but it was a long time before she would come. He had to go to the gap and coax her gently.

She came through again at last, and then something really dreadful happened! Barney must have touched some hidden lever, or pressed on some spring—because the stone that had moved out to make the gap, began slowly to move back again. At first Barney did not realise what was happening. He was fondling Miranda and trying to make her less frightened.

Then a small noise made him look up—and to his horror

he saw that the gap was almost closed! He tried to catch
hold of the moving stone and push it out again—but it was
heavy and he couldn't stop it going right back into its
place.

Barney got into a panic then. He was cold and damp
in that horrid little space with its streaming walls. He
hunted frantically for any iron ring or lever that would
set the stone moving again, so that he might squeeze
through the gap. He was a prisoner if he couldn't find it!
There must be some way of getting the stone to move from
this side—or wasn't there? Surely this could not be a
horrible little dungeon where unwanted prisoners were
hidden long ago?

Another noise boomed up through the strange hole.
Warm now with his exertions at trying to find some way
of moving the stone out again, Barney stopped to listen.

If men were causing that noise, then there must be a
way of escape down that hole! But where in the world
did it lead to? Barney didn't want to go down it at all. It
was so black and narrow and the iron ladder was not safe.

He made some more frantic efforts to find a way to move
the stone, but it was no use. It couldn't be done. He
walked the three steps to the hole and looked down it.
Again he thought he heard voices. Were they really
voices? If there were men down there they might help
him—except that whatever they were doing must be very
secret, and probably against the law. They would certainly not be pleased to see him!

Supposing Mr. King was down there too! That would
be a funny state of affairs! Well—not funny. Things were
far from funny at the moment—in fact they were horribly
serious.

There was nothing for it but to begin climbing down
that fearsome shaft. Barney knelt down on the stone floor
and gingerly put one leg down into the hole. His foot
felt about for the ladder. He found a bar and let his
weight go down on it.

It broke at once! Well—this was going to be very difficult indeed if the ladder wasn't going to hold him!

He felt for the next rung. His weight pressed down on it—and that broke too! Barney began to feel panic-stricken again. Miranda chattered in fright, clinging on his shoulder.

Then Barney felt for the sides of the rungs. Were there staples there, or nails—or even bits of broken rung?

He found a sharp piece of iron, the bit of rung that was driven into the wall of the shaft. He decided that it would be best to tread on the ends of the rungs, because then possibly they would not break. They would certainly break if he trod in the middle of them. So, very carefully indeed Barney felt about for another rung and trod gingerly at the very edge of it, where it was driven into the shaft wall. Each one held now, and Barney breathed more easily.

Soon his whole body was in the hole, his feet feeling for the edges of the rungs, his hands holding on to the ones above his head. Down he went and down. Where did the hole lead to? One of the noises came up as he descended and Miranda nearly fell off his shoulder in fright.

The hole was about twelve feet long. It came to an end at last. Barney felt his feet on solid ground. He let go and turned himself round. There was a kind of doorway in the shaft wall behind him, low and narrow. Barney stooped and went through it.

Now he could plainly hear the voices of men, shouting and calling to one another. Then he jumped. He heard that screeching, whining sound. He guessed what it was now. It was some machine—a winch perhaps being worked.

He squinted round, not yet daring to put on his torch again. He had switched it off as soon as he found his feet on solid ground. He stood there in the dark, listening, not wanting to take a step forward or backward in case he fell down yet another hole!

Then he became conscious of another sound—a sound that went on and on all the time—a quiet sound that occasionally became louder. The sound of water!

"Yes—that's it—it's *water*!" said Barney to himself in amazement. "Where is it? It sounds awfully near."

He switched his torch on and off quickly for a moment. He was in a narrow passage that slanted down from the shaft-hole. At the end of the passage was the gleam of water!

"Well!" said Barney, in amazement. "What is it? An underground pool?"

He walked cautiously down the narrow passage and came to the water, shading his torch with his hand so that its light would not easily be seen. Yes—there was the water, black and gleaming—and flowing along!

Flowing along! Then it must be a river of some kind— no, a stream, because it wasn't wide enough for a river.

And then, in a flash Barney knew what it was! It was Rocking Stream—the stream shown on the map as flowing near, very near, Rockingham Manor! Not only did it flow near—but it must flow practically *under* the old house! No wonder the wall near the shaft-hole was damp.

Forgetting to be cautious he flashed his torch on the stream. It flowed in a rocky bed, and there was an arched rocky roof to it, that was very low in places. Beside it, on the side that Barney stood, was a ledge, wide enough to walk on. There was no ledge at all on the other side.

What an extraordinary thing! A river flowing under the house—and men working by it in the tunnel, making weird noises underground that sounded up in the old house—muffled and distant, but still easy to hear!

Barney wondered if the men knew that their noises could be heard. Still, even if they knew, they wouldn't care, because they thought the old house was completely deserted—there would be no one there to hear!

From some way down to the left, the way the stream was flowing, a dim light showed. It was from there the sound of voices and other noises came. Barney made his way carefully along the rocky ledge beside the stream, crouching when the roof swept down low. He came out on the other side of the low roof, and saw that the stream curved to the left. Round the corner the light was brighter —that was evidently where the men were.

Barney began to feel more cheerful. If men knew a way in to this place, then there was a way out! And he would be able to find it and escape. But before he did that he was going to see what was happening down here!

He came to the place where the river curved to the left, and peeped cautiously round the corner. He was astounded at what he saw. The narrow tunnel, in which the stream ran, suddenly widened out into a great, low-roofed cave, and here men were at work with a winch, which was giving out the whining, screeching noise that Barney had so often heard. Another winch was at work nearby, and that had a harsh guttural sound, which was magnified very much in the tunnel.

Barney could make out three men. They were shouting above the noise of the winches. Whatever were they doing? If only he could find out!

CHAPTER TWENTY-TWO

ANY WAY OF ESCAPE?

BARNEY stood hidden by a rock that jutted out from the tunnel, and watched in astonishment all that was going on. The stream flowed quickly past him, gurgled along at one side of the big low cave, and disappeared again into another tunnel, leaving the cave behind.

Men were working at a couple of winches, which made loud harsh noises as the rope was wound up on each winch. One of the men gave a shout: " Lights up! "

A bright glaring lamp was switched on near the stream. Another man appeared from the far tunnel with what looked like a pitchfork in his hand. The winches went on winding. And then a large object appeared, coming out from the far tunnel, bobbing about on the swift-flowing stream, whose current was against it.

Barney stared, his mouth open in surprise. The men were winding in big crates from the far tunnel where the stream disappeared on its swift course. Barney could not make out quite what these crate-like objects were—great boxes of something? Cases of something heavy? It was impossible to see.

The four men rushed to the crate and it was dragged right in to the cave. Bang! Thud! It was shifted into place, and was obviously very heavy indeed, judging by the thuds it made when it was turned over and over to be put into place.

Barney craned round as far as he dared to see where the crate was being put. He thought he could see other cases piled together. This must be a hiding-place—or sorting-place? It was obviously some very secret spot, used for very secret things.

The winches wound again and another crate came bobbing up the tunnel—and yet another. Barney guessed they must all be tied together in some way. There must be a long line of them down the far tunnel! The man who held what looked like a pitchfork disappeared into the tunnel each time a new crate appeared, guiding it deftly as it bobbed along. Barney guessed there was a narrow little rocky ledge by the side of the river there, just as there had been in his part of the underground tunnel.

"That's the lot!" shouted the man with the pitchfork, as the laste crate was man-handled into place: "Now let's clear off! I'm dead!"

Barney crouched back against the rocky side of the tunnel, hoping the men would not come near him. They didn't. They walked off the other way, clambering along the rocky ledge of the distant tunnel and disappearing in the dark, their torches shining out for a time and then vanishing.

The whole place was now in pitch darkness. Miranda, on Barney's shoulder, chattered into his ear. She was cold and tired. She didn't understand this curious adventure at all.

Barney switched on his own torch again, glad he had such a powerful one. He made his way to the low-roofed cave. It was even bigger than he had imagined! It was, in fact, a vast, underground cavern, its walls gleaming with phosphorus here and there.

Piled against one wall were crates of all kinds and sizes. There were names on them that Barney did not understand—were they names of places or people? He didn't know.

He wandered round the big cavern. Right at the end he found what was evidently a kind of workshop or sorting place. Here were empty crates that had been unpacked. There was nothing to show what had been in them except for a stack of dull leaden-looking bars. Barney picked one up.

It certainly was very heavy. He thought it must be a bar of silver—silver that had been melted down and made into a bar.

"Perhaps stolen silver articles are melted down into these bars," thought the boy. "Perhaps this is a kind of central receiving place for stolen or smuggled goods—what a wonderful hiding-place! Nobody would ever guess where it was!"

He wandered all round the big cavern. He found something that pleased him very much—an old mattress with rugs and a pillow—and, even better, a ledge on which were stacked tins of meat and fruit!

The men evidently had meals down here sometimes in the middle of a big job—and maybe even slept here on occasion. Well—Barney would sleep here too, if he had to—*and* would have a meal as well! If he couldn't find a way of escape at once, he could make himself comfortable till he did find one. In the meantime he would find out all he could.

He looked at the winches. They were powerful ones. They needed to be to drag those crates against the fast-flowing water—and how far did they have to be dragged? Barney began to wonder about that too.

He decided not to explore any more for the present. He was tired and cold and he had had enough adventure for the time being. He would lie down on the mattress and sleep. Miranda would wake him if she heard anyone coming.

He lay down and was soon asleep, Miranda cuddled up to him once more. He did not know how long he slept for he had no watch, and, as it was always dark in the underground cavern, he could not tell, on waking, if it was daytime or not.

But he felt as if it must be, when he awoke. He was hungry so he went to the collection of tins. Ah!—tins of ham. He would open one of those—if there was an opener! He saw a pile of tin plates and dishes nearby, with a little heap of cheap knives, forks and spoons. With them were two tin-openers.

Barney was soon enjoying a meal of tinned ham, and peaches from another tin. He hid the empty tins behind a rock so that if the men came back they wouldn't suspect anything.

He felt a good deal better after that—in fact he felt fit for anything! Miranda, who had gobbled up four half-peaches in delight, was also ready for anything. She bounded round the cave, examining this and that—and then, quite suddenly, the place was flooded with a dazzling light.

Barney leapt to his feet, blinking, expecting to see the men returning. But nobody appeared. Then how did the light come on so suddenly?

He laughed—of course, it was that monkey Miranda. She had come across the light switch and turned it on, flooding the cave with light! She loved meddling about with any switches she found, and had often got herself into trouble over this. He called to her.

" Naughty Miranda! Don't meddle! Turn it off again."

Miranda made a chattering noise, full of glee. She switched the light on and off several times. Finally she switched it off and left the place in darkness again, except for Barney's torch.

" Come here, Miranda," called Barney. " It's time we got out of here. We're going down the river—if the men have a way of escape there, so have we! "

Miranda leapt to his shoulder and held on to his right ear. Barney went to where the stream disappeared into the far tunnel, and flashed his torch down it. Beside the water ran a very narrow ledge of rock, much narrower than the ledge he had scrambled down before. Also at times it was not above the level of the stream, but below, which meant wading through the cold water for some way.

The tunnel did not run straight, but curved about, and the stream curved with it. It was a weird journey, walking beside the black water, on a terribly narrow ledge of rock. At one place the tunnel roof was so low that Barney was forced to go on his hands and knees, and Miranda screamed in terror. She didn't like water.

After about ten minutes of this Barney was quite fed up. But he had to go on. On he went for another fifteen minutes—and then he saw a dim light in front of him. What was it? He hurried along as fast as he could, hoping it was daylight.

He came to a great iron gate! Beyond the gate was daylight, obscured by enormous strands of greenery that hung down over the bars! This was where the stream flowed out from underground into the open. Barney stopped and stared at the iron gate. It was very old, very stout, very overgrown. It could never have been meant to open. It had been built from the low roof of the tunnel right down to the bed of the stream, allowing the water to flow out between the bars.

Barney did not even try to shake the gate or move it in any way. It was quite plain that nobody had gone out that way—nobody could! It must have been built years and years ago, to stop people exploring up the underground stream, so curiously flowing out of the hill on which the old house stood.

The boy stood looking through the thick curtain of greenery that dimmed the daylight. Brambles, ferns, and creeping plants climbed across the iron gate. It was impossible to get out of this strange prison behind the bars!

"The men can't have escaped through this," thought Barney. "Well—where *did* they go, then? I must have missed their way of exit. I'll go back."

So back he went, stumbling along the rocky ledge again, looking carefully everywhere to see if he had missed the men's way of departure from the tunnel.

And then Miranda suddenly gave one of her little excited chatterings. She had seen something! It was about half-way up the tunnel. Barney flashed his torch all round. but at first could see nothing but the rocky sides of the river tunnel, and the ledge he was standing on.

Then Miranda suddenly left- his shoulder and swung herself over the water. She grasped something in mid-air and rocked to and fro! Barney flashed his torch on her. She was swinging on a rope!

"Gosh! A rope! Where does it come from?" said Barney in astonishment. His torch picked out the thick, sturdy rope. It ran up to the roof of the tunnel—and there, in the roof, was what looked like flat pieces of board. Barney stared, puzzled. A rope—hanging down from boarding in the roof of the tunnel!

He puzzled it out. There must be a hole in the roof of the tunnel there—either a natural one, or man-made. It was possible that there was a dip in the ground above

143

and that the surface was quite near the tunnel-roof. A hole had been found—or made—the river below discovered and explored—and the cavern found.

"The men must have used this as their way of escape," thought Barney. "Once the boards are taken up, and they climb through the hole, they are above ground. I wonder if this is the place where the crates are brought, and lowered down to the water. It must be."

He swarmed up the rope, hanging above the water. But he could not move the boards lying in place across the hole in the roof. Something heavy must be put on top of them, to hide them. He dropped down disappointed.

He worked out what the men did. "They bring the crates and boxes here at night—they remove the boards that hide the hole in the tunnel-roof. They drop the goods down into the water and fasten them to a wire rope that runs up the stream to those winches. Then it's just a question of dragging them up the water, guiding them as they go! What a very ingenious idea—nobody in the world would guess such a hiding-place!"

But working out the ingenious idea didn't help Barney to escape! There he was, a prisoner underground, and with no way out at all!

CHAPTER TWENTY-THREE

WHERE CAN BARNEY BE?

NEXT day the children wondered what in the world had happened to Barney. He didn't appear for breakfast, though he had said he would. He didn't even appear when the time came for lessons, and that was very disturbing. Barney never missed his morning's listening!

"Where is he?" wondered Roger. "I hope he's all right."

Diana was very worried indeed. When Barney didn't appear at dinner-time she was quite beside herself. " I *know* something's happened to him! " she said. " We must all go and look for him in the old house—we'll go down to the cellars and see if we can find out anything there."

Mr. King couldn't make the children out at all. They obviously had some worry, but they wouldn't tell him a thing, and when he came near they stopped talking at once.

" I must say I think your behaviour is peculiar," he remarked to Diana. " Why don't you tell me what's wrong? I might be able to do something. Where's Barney?"

" He'll probably turn up," said Roger at once. Certainly they were not going to tell Mr. King their worries. As for peculiar behaviour—well, what about his?

So they told him nothing, and he felt very cross. Miss Pepper telephoned to say that her sister was better. Perhaps it would not be very long before she could come back. Mr. King was relieved. Maybe the children would behave in a more normal way when Miss Pepper was back.

After dinner they set off for the old house. Loony was very pleased to be out. He didn't like it when the children stayed in the house and went into huddles over something, and talked earnestly and worriedly, never noticing him at all.

First of all the three went up to the nurseries with Loony. They had wondered at first how to get in, but had found that Barney had not locked the kitchen door, whether purposely or not, they didn't know. The untidy, dishevelled nurseries shocked Diana very much. How dare Mr. King mess them up like this?

" Don't bother about putting them straight now, Di," said Roger. " We'd better go over the whole of the house and down into the cellars straight away—just in case Barney's ill or hurt, and wants help. You never know. It's so strange that he has not turned up to-day."

They went all over the house. Nothing to be seen. Then

they went down to the kitchen, through the scullery and into the outhouses. The trapdoor in the dairy was wide open.

" Well—down we go," said Roger, switching on his torch, and down they went, carefully descending the steep, stone steps. Now they were in the dark cellars. They called Barney.

" Barney! Where are you? Are you here?"

Echoes answered them queerly. " Here! Here! Here! "

" He's not here," said Roger. " Loony, go and look for him."

Loony was soon sniffing into every corner. It was he who found the wooden shelf on which Barney had slept the night before. He stood by it and barked loudly. The others hurried up. They saw the rug and the cushion on the shelf at once.

" There! That's where he slept last night! " said Roger. " But where is he now? And where's Miranda?"

The children sat down on a box to think what to do next.

Whilst they were sitting there Loony ran sniffing round the cellars, trying to smell where Barney had been. He came to the corner where the iron ring was, low in the wall. He scraped at it, whining, smelling Barney's smell there.

Snubby ran over to him. " What is it, Loony? What have you found? I say, you others, what do you think this is?"

They all knelt down in the corner and examined the iron ring set in the wall. Just as Barney had done they pushed and pulled. But unfortunately nobody thought of turning it round and round, so they did not discover the secret of the moving stone. They gave it up after a time.

" It's nothing," said Roger. " It's not worth bothering about. I expect Loony's only excited because he can smell rats there or something."

So they left the iron ring and went up the steps into the dairy. It was nice to be in the daylight again.

"Well—Barney's not here," said Snubby, dolefully. "Let's go. This house gives me the creeps to-day. It really does."

"What shall we do about Barney?" said Diana to Roger. "Do you think we ought to report that he's disappeared?"

"Not *yet*," said Roger. "We'd feel awfully silly if we did that and then Barney walked in with Miranda, grinning all over his face as usual!"

"All right," said Diana. "We won't then. But if he doesn't turn up by to-morrow I really think we ought to tell somebody. I wish Miss Pepper was at home. We can't possibly tell Mr. King. And we don't know anyone else here."

They went soberly out of the kitchen door and pulled it to. They began to make their way through the grounds. "What shall we do for the rest of the afternoon?" said Roger.

"Well, we won't go riding or swimming," said Diana. "Just in case Barney comes in to tea. I want to be about when he does come, in case he's got any news for us."

"I know," said Snubby, suddenly. "We could take the short cut to that stream I saw the other day when I was tracking Mr. King—and we could follow it up and see where it does go to. We could find out where the map goes wrong."

"It's not a very exciting thing to do—but we may as well do it," said Roger. "Come on, Loony—leave that rabbit-hole alone. You'll never get down it. You're too fat!"

Off they went with Loony at their heels. They went to Rockingdown Cottage for the map, and discovered that Mr. King had gone out, Mrs. Round told them.

"He went off over that way, with his stick," she said, pointing down the hill. "He said he'd be back for tea."

" Blow! That's the way *we* want to go," said Roger, looking at the map. " See—we take this path—and then go down there, round that little wood—then on down the hill, till we come to the stream. This spot must be about where Snubby saw the hidden boat. We'll make for that and then follow the stream upwards and see where it goes."

They set off with Loony, who was very pleased at the prospect of a second walk. Perhaps he would find rabbit-holes big enough to get down this time! That was always Loony's biggest hope.

It didn't take them long to find the stream. " Where's the place where the boat was hidden, Snubby?" said Roger, standing beside the stream that flowed swiftly by.

" See that bunch of willows over there? That looks like the place," said Snubby. They went on again over the marshy fields, Loony cleverly leaping from tuft to tuft of wiry grass; the children, less clever, walked into sodden ground from which they had to pull their feet with a plop-plop-plop.

" I don't like this much," said Diana. She stopped and surveyed the big flat field. " It's rather a desolate sort of place—there are trees only where the stream runs. You can easily see its course by the willows and alders on its banks."

" Look—this is the place where the boat was hidden," said Snubby, when they came near to the clump of willows he had pointed out.

The boat was not there! The little backwater was empty.

" Now where's the boat gone?" wondered Snubby.

" Oh well—I suppose whoever owns it has gone for a row!" said Diana.

" But *who* owns it?" demanded Snubby. " Look all round you—there isn't a single house or cottage in sight! "

There wasn't. What Snubby said was perfectly true. It was really very odd to think of a boat in a little hidden
148

creek and nobody within miles to own it. Anyway the boat was gone now. It wasn't any good puzzling about it.

"Let's follow the stream upwards now," said Roger. "Come on, Loony. This way. Get him, Snubby, he'll fall into the water. He's seen a vole or something."

Snubby rescued Loony from a watery bed and propelled him in front of him. Loony promptly rolled over on his back.

"Right," said Snubby. "If you want to spend the afternoon like that, do! Good-bye!"

Loony soon followed, forgetting his vole. The four of them went along the banks of the stream. It flowed downhill and the current was quite swift. The little stream twisted and curved about as all streams do, making the children walk twice as far as they need have done.

They followed it for about fifteen minutes, and then a steeper hill towered in front of them. "If the stream flows down that it will come pretty fast," said Roger. But it didn't flow down the hill. It suddenly disappeared behind a curtain of greenery. In fact, it went underground.

"Gosh—it's gone to ground!" said Roger. "Well— *that* explains the map then, when it showed the stream so near the old house—it must flow almost underneath it, underground."

"Yes—of course," said Diana, quite excited. "That's what the explanation is—it's an underground stream as far as here—and then it pops out and flows across the marshy fields."

They clambered to where the stream came out from the hill. They could not see the iron gate that shut it off because of the thick curtains of brambles and fern and ivy. But Roger, thrusting his hand through the ivy, felt the iron bars.

"There's something here," he said, and began to tear away the ivy strands. "Yes—a gate or barrier of some sort. To stop people going up the stream, I suppose. Perhaps it's dangerous."

149

" Oh, what a pity! I'd have loved to go up the stream underground and see where it goes," said Snubby. " What a pity Barney isn't here—he would have loved this."

Not many hours before, Barney himself had stood only a yard or two away from where they were—but on the other side of the barrier! They didn't know that. They peered through the thick green curtain, but could see nothing but darkness there.

" Well—we've solved *that* mystery," said Roger, climbing down from where he had clung to see through the ivy sprays. " We'd better go back."

" Look—is that a little backwater there?" said Diana, pointing to the other side of the stream a little way down from the iron gate. " Let's see if it is."

" Well—we really ought to go home," said Roger, looking at his watch. " Still—we'll just see if there's anything interesting there. We might even find the mysterious boat."

They did! They followed the queer little backwater between a row of alder trees. It curved round very suddenly and entered a dip in the ground where it opened out into a pond. Ducks were on the pond and—the boat was there, tied to a tree! Snubby was sure it was the same boat because it again had no name!

In a hollow was a farm-house. Barns rose around it, mellow and with moss on the tiles. It was a lovely place.

" Well—what a surprise! " said Diana. " A farm-house up here, lost to the world! That's where the boat belongs. No mystery about it at all! "

They went towards the farm-house. A man came out from a barn and saw them. He looked extremely disagreeable.

" You clear off! " he shouted. " Do you hear? We don't allow hikers here. Be off at once, or I'll set the dogs on you."

Three or four dogs now set up a terrific barking and

150

Loony barked back. But he did not venture any nearer. He was afraid of so many dogs at once!

"All right!" called Roger indignantly. "We're going! Don't worry."

He and the others turned to go back. What a horrid fellow! They made their way back down the stream to the backwater—and there they had another surprise.

Mr. King was there, gazing earnestly at the iron gate, the barrier covered with green!

CHAPTER TWENTY FOUR

A VERY GREAT SURPRISE

MR. KING was just as surprised to see the three children and Loony as they were to see him. Loony was so astonished that he quite forgot the feud that seemed to lie between Mr. King and the children, and hurled himself at him to greet him.

"Well!" said Mr. King, in surprise. "Who would have thought of meeting *you* here!"

"Yes. Odd isn't it?" said Roger, politely. *Now* what was Mr. King up to? Had he followed them? What was he doing, snooping round in that part of the world again—staring at the iron gate covered with greenery as if he knew some secret about it! Perhaps he knew where Barney was!

"Well, we might as well walk home together," said Mr. King, looking at his watch "We shall be a little late for tea, but I don't expect Mrs. Round will mind."

The children didn't want to walk home with him but there was nothing for it but to agree. So off they all went, Loony rather subdued. He had suddenly remembered that Snubby was not friendly towards Mr. King, and he wished he hadn't given him such a welcome!

"Isn't Barney with you?" said Mr. King, sounding surprised. "Where's he got to to-day? Don't you know?"

"Oh, he's got all sorts of things to do," said Roger. "He's about somewhere, I expect. Haven't *you* seen him, Mr. King?"

"You haven't quarrelled, I hope?" said the coach. This was too silly a suggestion to be answered. Snubby made a noise that sounded rather like "Pooh." It would be difficult to quarrel with the good-tempered Barney.

Barney was not waiting for them at tea-time. Mrs Round said he hadn't called at all. They ate their tea with Mr. King, and began to be really worried again about Barney. What could have happened to him?

"We'll wait till to-morrow morning and then we'll go to the police," said Roger, desperately, when bed-time came and still Barney had not appeared. Diana was almost beside herself with worry. She was very fond of Barney. But Snubby looked the most miserable of them all.

That night Roger woke up with a jump. He had heard something. He sat up and thought for a minute. What had the sound been like? Could it have been made by Barney? What did it sound like—yes—it sounded like someone closing the front door very, very softly!

Roger was up in a trice. Without putting on slippers or dressing-gown he went quietly down the stairs. He ran out of the front door, leaving it open. He saw a figure moving down by the gate. There was a little moon that night, and Roger could make out who it was—Mr. King!

Yes—Mr. King on another of his mysterious night prowls. All right—Roger would follow him and see where he went—he might even lead him to Barney. Roger felt that Mr. King was villain enough to keep him prisoner somewhere, for some secret reason of his own!

It was not nice walking in bare feet, especially as Mr. King went through the grounds of the old house. He must be going there. Carefully—and painfully—Roger followed him, biting his lip as he trod on a thorn or stone with his bare feet.

Mr. King stopped. Two men materialised out of the bushes. They all began to talk in low voices. Roger strained his ears, but could only catch a few sentences.

"We got him all right—but he won't talk." Then there was some conversation Roger couldn't catch.

"Oh yes—it makes a very good cover! I'll say it does— nobody would ever guess that."

More low talk, and then a sentence from Mr. King again. "Well—if those kids I coach guessed what I'm really up to, they'd pass out!"

Roger froze into the bushes. Had they got hold of Barney then? What cover were they talking about—the old house? "All right, Mr. King, you think we don't know anything, but we know *you're* a bad lot all right!" thought Roger, grimly.

The men talked a little while longer, and then walked towards the old house. Roger had heard enough. He would go to the police to-morrow and tell them all he knew, and beg them to find Barney. He'd tell them to arrest Mr. King too, the fraud! He didn't want to follow the men any farther. His feet were sore and bleeding. He must go back. Anyway he knew enough to spike Mr. King's guns now, and stop his little game, whatever it was!

He went home to bed, but not to sleep. He puzzled things over in his mind, trying to make out what Mr. King was doing, why he had captured Barney, and hundreds of other things that gradually slipped into dreams, and gave him nightmares. He awoke in the morning, anxious and exhausted with his worried sleep.

He told the others what he had planned to do. "I'm off to the police," he said. "You sit down and begin lessons as usual with Mr. King, so that he doesn't suspect anything. Just say I've gone to do some urgent shopping for

153

Mrs. Round. I know she wants some potatoes. I'll tell her I'll go and get those!"

So Snubby and Diana sat down alone with Mr. King. No Barney, no Roger. Diana was pale and looked worried. Mr. King looked at her and at the restless Snubby. What *on earth* was the matter with these three kids ever since Miss Pepper had been away?

At about eleven o'clock footsteps came up to the front door—*two* pairs of footsteps! Diana began to tremble. Had Roger brought back a policeman? She couldn't see who it was from the study window.

The door opened and in came Roger, looking extremely important. Behind him came a burly policeman. Diana gave a gasp. Mr. King looked amazed.

" What's all this?" he said, in astonishment. " Roger— you haven't got into trouble, have you?"

" *I* haven't," said Roger.

" It's like this, sir," said the policeman, taking out a note-book and flicking over the pages. " This boy here came and made a report to me, sir, this morning. Seems as if a friend of his has been missing for two days—name of Barnabas, surname not known. And Master Roger here seems to think you know something about his disappearance."

" This is absurd," said Mr. King angrily. " Roger, what do you mean by it?"

" Well, we know all about your night prowlings, and your queer walks, and your explorations of the old house," said Roger boldly. " You went into Rockingdown Manor and looked everywhere—you messed up the nurseries and threw everything all over the place. You meet strange men at night—you're plotting something with them. We don't know what it is—but we're sure you've got something to do with Barney's disappearance—so I went to the police this morning and reported everything."

" That's right, sir," said the policeman, stolidly. " It's a queer story, sir, and I'd like some kind of explanation, *if* you please—most particularly about this here breaking into Rockingdown Manor. Serious business that, sir."

Mr. King was frowning. He glared at Roger, who looked him straight in the face. " Aha! " said Roger's look, " what have you to say to all this, fraud of a Mr. King! "

Mr. King stood up. He looked rather taller and more imposing all of a sudden. He spoke in a crisp, commanding voice.

" Constable, take a look at this, will you?"

He held out something in his hand. The constable took a look, and his face slowly went red. He shut up his notebook and backed away hurriedly.

" I beg your pardon, sir. I'd no idea, sir, none at all. I never got any notification from headquarters, sir."

" That's all right," said Mr. King, still in his new, crisp voice. " It was thought better to say nothing locally. You can go. I'll deal with this matter now."

The constable went. Even the back of his neck was red, Diana noticed. She was completely overcome with amazement. As for Roger and Snubby they couldn't make head or tail of anything. They stared at Mr. King, bewildered. He sat down again.

" Sit down," he said, and Roger sat. Mr. King took out a cigarette from his case, tapped it on the table, and got out his lighter. Nobody said a word. Mr. King looked round grimly at the three.

" So you were spying on me, were you? What for, I should like to know? And why not come to me straight away and tell me everything, instead of going to a village policeman? Exactly what do you know?"

Nobody answered at first. They felt completely in the dark.

" Mr. King—what did you show to the constable, please?" said Diana, at last.

" I showed him something that told him I was somebody considerably higher up in the police force than he
155

was," said Mr. King, after a pause. " I'm here on an important investigation. I'm sorry you thought I was the villain of the piece. I assure you I'm not."

There was another silence. Roger felt more foolish and more embarrassed than he had ever felt in his life before. What was Mr. King then—a detective—a secret agent—or what? Roger didn't even dare to ask him!

" I'm very sorry, sir," he said at last. " It—it was only because I was so worried about Barney disappearing that I went to the police—and—and—well—told them what I suspected about you. I'm very sorry."

" I should think so," said Mr. King. " But what *is* all this about Barney disappearing? I didn't know you were really worried about him. Look here—you've been snooping about just as much as I have, evidently—and maybe you know things I don't. We'd better pool our knowledge and help one another instead of working against each other—though I'm blessed if I knew anything about your secret activities at all! Little criminals, the lot of you!"

He smiled, and the children's hearts lightened. He had a nice smile. How could they have thought he was a fraud, a villain? He was somebody important, somebody intensely interesting, somebody unexpectedly commanding and altogether admirable.

" We've been idiots," said Snubby, finding his voice suddenly. " Absolute super-idiots."

" Smashing ones," agreed Mr. King, with a wider smile. " I've been a bit of a fraud though, I must confess. I'm not really a coach! I know enough to teach three ignoramuses like you, though it's not a job I like. I took it because I needed to be somewhere in this neighbourhood, as you have probably guessed by now."

" Yes, we did guess you were a—fraud in that way," Diana agreed, blushing. " Shall we tell you all we know, Mr. King? Then perhaps you can help us with Barney."

The three of them told everything. Mr. King listened

intently. " Well—there's not much I don't know in all you tell me," he said. " Still, it all helps. Now, I'll tell *you* something—and you'll please keep your mouths shut about it."

The three of them listened, thrilled.

" There's smuggling going on in this neighbourhood," said Mr. King. " It's been suspected for a long time. There's a mysterious aeroplane that lands somewhere at night and takes off almost immediately. There's a motor-launch, also mysterious, that appears at times in this neighbourhood, on the river. We think there's a kind of receiving headquarters here—where the stuff is hidden till it's safe to dispose of it—or where it is sorted out into small bits for sale and disposed of immediately, somewhere, somehow. But where this hiding-place is, and who are the chief men concerned we don't know. We've got one of the smaller men, but he won't talk. We had an idea that the old house, Rockingdown Manor, was the centre—but we've gone through it with a tooth-comb and there's nothing to show that it is. Nothing at all."

" What about those noises?" said Roger, in excitement. " The ones Barney was going to find out about?"

" Ah—those are very, very interesting," said Mr. King. " And I think young Barney's disappearance is due to his curiosity about those noises! He's paying for his inquisitiveness, I fear."

" Oh dear," said Diana, going pale. " What—what do you think has happened to him? Where is he?"

" I've no idea," said Mr. King. " But we'll find him as soon as we can. There are such a lot of loose ends about all this—that Rocking Stream, which runs underground, might lead us to the heart of the mystery—but no, it's blocked up with a completely impassable barrier— so we have to rule *that* out! "

" It's a good thing Miss Pepper is away," said Snubby, suddenly. " She'd have a blue fit about all this."

"Yes—she'd certainly go up in smoke," agreed Mr. King. "Now—will you leave me alone for a bit. I must think, and I must remake my plans. I'll see you at dinner-time, and tell you what I'm going to do. So long till then —and cheer up, do, for goodness' sake!"

CHAPTER TWENTY-FIVE

EVERYTHING IS VERY DIFFICULT

AT dinner-time Mr. King told the children his plans.

"I'm pretty certain Barney's disappearance is the result of his poking his nose into this smuggling affair," he said. "We'll have to find him, or things will be serious for him. These men are rogues—real bad fellows who stick at nothing."

Diana was frightened. She stared at Mr. King with wide, scared eyes. "What are you going to do then?" she asked.

"First of all go through Rockingdown Manor again, top to bottom—especially the bottom, where the cellars are." said Mr. King. "I feel you're right when you say those strange noises have something to do with all this—and Barney must have stumbled on the cause, and now he's disappeared because of it. Though I must say it beats me how the noises are made, and where they come from. If they don't come from the cellars, where *can* they come from?"

Mr. King went on explaining his plans. "I must also find out who that boat belongs to, and have a look at the farm-house you told me about—and I must examine that gate or barrier thoroughly. It certainly looks as if nobody has moved it for centuries—but we must see. And if *we* can't get up past the barrier, well, I'm pretty certain nobody else has been able to push by it!"

" We'll come and help," said Roger eagerly. He looked hard at Mr. King. It was puzzling to think how he and the others had been so certain he was a villain! He seemed such a very admirable person now—really a very thrilling person indeed. Roger felt quite proud to know him! And yet he had been so scornful of him a short time ago. It just showed how careful you had to be in judging people.

They all spent a very busy and exciting day, but without much result. Rockingdown Manor was searched once more from top to bottom. Two men appeared from the grounds on the way over, and joined them. They were the two men Roger had heard Mr. King talking to the night before. They turned out to be men under him, detailed to help him.

" Meet Jimmy and Fred," said Mr. King, introducing them to the children. " The terrors of the police force— hunters of rogues and scoundrels and my very good friends! "

The children grinned. Jimmy and Fred were strong and well-built, but otherwise quite ordinary-looking except for their quick observant eyes. They were both dressed in plain clothes.

" And Jimmy, Fred—meet Roger, Diana, Snubby— and Loony," said Mr. King. " Terrors too, all of them, especially this young limb, Snubby. Watch out for him, or he'll play one of his frightful tricks on you; he's a real pest. Actually, Loony is the best of the lot—and quite the most intelligent."

This was the kind of foolery the children understood and liked. They laughed. They began to feel that things really must turn out all right if Jimmy, Fred—and Mr. King— were all on the job. Barney would soon be back!

Down in the cellars at Rockingdown Manor Mr. King looked at the rug and cushion on the wooden shelf. He also looked at the iron ring in the corner, but, like the children dismissed it as nothing. It did not occur to him to screw the great ring round and round.

"Nothing here," he said at last. "I think either Barney left the cellars and went up into the grounds and was captured—or else the men came down here for some reason and found him. In any case he can't be anywhere near us, or he would yell and we would hear him."

Jimmy was sent to make enquiries about the boat, and Fred was sent to examine the iron gate barring the way to the underground stream. The children wanted to go too but Mr. King said no—he didn't want a whole crowd of people about, in case the men got wind that something was up. Where they were he didn't know—but obviously they must be hidden somewhere about the countryside.

Jimmy came back and reported. "I've been to the farmhouse, sir. Said I wanted to buy some eggs. There was a boy there, in the boat, messing about on the backwater. He said the boat was his—he' : had it from his uncle for a present on his last birthday. Seemed quite honest, sir—I don't think there's an, reason to disbelieve him."

"Well—there goes the mystery of the boat, then," said Mr. King. "It belongs to a small boy who plays about in it! Ah—here's Fred. Perhaps he has something more interesting to report."

Fred hadn't. He had been to the iron gate and had done a lot of dragging-away of greenery, pulling off enormous strands of ivy.

"No one has entered that wa, sir," he reported. "It's impossible. Short of blasting out the gate by dynamite we'd never make an entry there. The solid earth has settled all round the gate, and it's absolutely immovable. I don't think that stream has got much to do with this case."

Mr. King rubbed his chin and frowned. "It's a real mystery, this," he said. "We know a mysterious aeroplane lands somewhere in that field—probably in the dry, flat area in the middle of it. We know a strange motor-launch haunts the spot where that stream joins the river. We suspect smuggling on a large scale here—and yet we can't find out where the stuff goes, or how it comes out again from wherever its hiding-place is. And on top of all this a boy disappears into thin air—with a monkey—and we haven't the faintest notion where he's gone! "

" Do the men at the farm-house know anything of this affair, do you think?" asked Roger.

" So far as we know, they don't," said Mr. King. " The farm is run by an old farmer who has been there for years —man called Daws. His father had the farm before him, and they've a very good name. We've checked up on him all right—and we've had a quiet inspection made of the whole farm—sent a man there who was apparently a Food Inspector, you know—and old Daws took him unsuspectingly round the farm, showing him every nook and cranny, most indignant that anyone should think he didn't keep on the right side of the law in every way! "

" Well—we really are at a dead end," said Roger. " There doesn't seem anything else we can do at all."

" I do wonder where Barney is," said Diana. " I keep thinking of him. What's he doing? I'm sure he must be very miserable and frightened."

" Barney's never really frightened," said Snubby. " He's one of these naturally brave people—he doesn't turn a hair when everybody else is shivering with fright."

All the same, Barney was not feeling very brave at the moment. He was not having a good time at all! He had spent the day before exploring everywhere, trying to find a way of escape, but without success.

As we know, he explored as far as the iron gate and gave that up. He discovered the rope hanging down from the hole in the rocky roof of the tunnel—and gave that up too as a way of escape. The only thing left to do was to explore *up* the tunnel, and see where the stream came from. Maybe it flowed into the tunnel at a place where he could get out. On the other hand, of course, it might actually have its source underground, and not go into the open air at all until it poured out through the close bars of the iron gate. That really seemed rather more likely.

"Still, Miranda, we won't give up hope!" said Barney to the little monkey on his shoulder. "Come on—up the stream we'll go—but before we do that, what about finishing that ham and opening another tin of fruit?"

After a meal of ham and tinned pears the two of them set off up the stream, instead of down. Barney came to the little passage that led to the shaft down which he had come the night before. He passed that, and went on up the stream, keeping to the little rocky ledge. Once the ledge stopped altogether, and Barney had to leap to where it began again, hoping he wouldn't fall into the water and be soaked through!

He went on for about fifteen minutes, flashing his torch round his feet to make sure of his next step. In places the ledge was slimy and slippery and he had to tread carefully. In other places the roof suddenly dipped down and he knocked his head against it before he realised it.

And then he came to a full stop. He couldn't go any farther. The roof had slanted down to the water, and there was no tunnel left—only a gurgling channel of water, hurrying through, pressing along, washing against the rock that completely hemmed it in. It was almost as if it were in a great pipe.

"Unless I get down into the water and make my way through it, completely submerged, head and all, I can't go any farther," thought poor Barney, in despair. "And I daren't do that! I don't know how long the channel is before it becomes a tunnel again, with a ledge to walk on, and a roof above my head. I'd have to hold my breath under water for goodness knows how long, and probably I'd drown. As for Miranda she wouldn't come at all. In any case she'd be swept away at once."

There was nothing for it but to go back the way he had come. He was very disappointed. When he came to the

little slanting passage leading from the tunnel to the shaft
he turned up it. He would climb up the shaft and get into
that tiny room above—he would have one more shot at
moving that queer stone!

So up the passage he went with Miranda, and climbed
the shaft to the top. He clambered out into the little room
—but no matter how he tried he could not make anything
work that stone out of its place! He didn't know the
secret, he didn't even know if the stone *could* be moved
from this side. Probably it couldn't. Poor Barney—he
really didn't know what to do next!

CHAPTER TWENTY-SIX

MIRANDA GIVES THE GAME AWAY

NOBODY came into the underground tunnel that day.
Barney was there all alone with Miranda. He didn't like
it at all, and wished hundreds of times that he had a
watch. He had no idea whether it was twelve o'clock in
the morning or six o'clock in the evening! Actually it was
then about half-past five in the afternoon. Outside was
broad daylight and bright sunshine. Down in the cave it
was pitch dark unless Barney had his torch on.

He didn't like to keep it on too long in case the battery
went. He knew how to turn on the big lights that flooded
the cavern, but he was afraid of doing that in case the
men came back unexpectedly and saw them. Then they
would know that an intruder was there and hunt for him.
Barney certainly didn't want to be discovered!

" What *I* want is to find a way of escape and go and tell
the others all I've found out," thought Barney. " Then I
suppose we'd have to go to the police—and what a surprise
they would get! "

He had another meal, and Miranda ate some pineapple
chunks from a tin and was extremely greedy over them.

So was Barney. They both liked them very much. Then the boy went to stretch himself out on the mattress.

"This is very, very boring, Miranda," he told the monkey. "Gracious, are you *still* eating pineapple. You'll turn into a chunk if you don't look out! Miranda, what are we to do? Can't *you* think of something?"

Miranda chattered away, sucking at the bit of pineapple. She had got used to her strange surroundings now—and as long as she had Barney, and tinned peaches, pears and pineapple she was quite prepared to stay in the tunnel for a long, long time.

"No books to read—nothing to do," groaned Barney, punching the pillow to fit his head. "It's frightful. There's only one thing to be said for this stay down here, Miranda—and that is I'm not spending any money! I've got precious little left, you know. We'll have to get a job soon, Miranda."

Miranda didn't mind that. She liked "jobs" especially when it meant being dressed up in fine clothes and having people clap and cheer her in the ring, or at a fair. That was grand!

Barney fell asleep about eight o'clock: He slept for four or five hours and then was awakened by Miranda pulling at his ear, and chattering.

He sat up, wondering where he was. He felt about for his torch and put it on. Of course—he was in that cavern, a prisoner who couldn't get out! He gazed round, wishing that he knew whether it was night or morning. It really was odd not to know.

"What's up, Miranda?" he said. "Stop grabbing my ear, silly!"

But Miranda had heard something that Barney had not. She was warning him. He suddenly realised it, when he heard a heavy sound coming up the tunnel. He sprang to his feet.

The men were at work again. Then it must be the middle of the night—his second night there. They must be

lowering stuff into the tunnel—soon some of them would
be coming along to work the winches.

Barney knew he must hide. He decided to get behind
the crates and spy on the men from there. He could hear
their talk too. Taking Miranda on his shoulder he made
his way to the side of the cavern where the big crates were
stored, both full and empty ones. He found a place inside
an empty crate. He could peer through the cracks.

Soon lights appeared down the tunnel and came nearer
—the torches of the men walking up the tunnel. Then
Barney heard their voices. There were five men this time.
One or two were evidently foreigners, and spoke with a
strange accent. Barney could barely understand what they
said.

He gathered that more crates had arrived that night—
dropped by an aeroplane somewhere not far off. Some-

165

how they had been transported to the tunnel—and were now about to be pulled up the stream by means of the wire rope wound up by the powerful winches.

And then Barney realised something he had not guessed before. The crates were not dragged up in the water just as they were—but were apparently put on narrow, solid and very strong little rafts of wood. It was these rafts that the man with the pitchfork guided. The crates were heavy, the current was swift, and the rafts and crates bobbed about as they came up against the stream.

Barney watched breathlessly, peering through the crack in the empty crate. The men were soon hard at work, working the winches, which whined and screeched, shouting to one another, pulling in the boxes and crates and cases as they appeared on their bobbing rafts. There were six of them.

Soon they were piled up with the others. Then one of the men, one of the chiefs, or perhaps a foreman, gave an order. Two men manhandled a crate from the store, and opened it.

It was full of bales of what looked like silk. Barney tried hard to see, but it was difficult. Then another crate was opened and Barney saw revolvers being thrown out in a heap. A third crate was opened, and the dull, leaden-looking bars Barney had seen before, were flung out on the floor of the cave.

From another corner a man brought small boxes, and what looked like small canvas bags. The goods were rapidly packed in these. Barney guessed why. They would now be quietly disposed of in small quantities here and there. They were thrown on one of the bobbing rafts and the man with the pitchfork guided the raft down the stream, soon disappearing from sight.

Another raft was loaded and another. Then the men stopped work and had a meal. Barney hoped they wouldn't discover that some of their tins were gone! They didn't. They opened a tin of chicken, a tin of meat and three tins of fruit. They found some bottles and opened those too, drinking from them without bothering about glasses or cups.

They lighted cigarettes and talked. It was difficult to hear what they said, and Barney could only catch a word now and again. They talked about horses and cars and food and the cinema, as far as he could tell.

Miranda watching from Barney's shoulder, saw one of the men toss an empty peach tin away. To Barney's horror she leapt from his shoulder, squeezed out of the crate and bounded over to the tin. She picked it up, chattering with pleasure because there was still some juice in it.

The man turned and saw her. His mouth fell open in amazement. He rubbed his eyes and looked again. Miranda was now licking out the tin.

" Hey, Jo," called the man. " Look here! "

Jo turned—and he too gaped in astonishment at the sight of Miranda. He got up at once.

" Look, you fellows—a monkey! Now where in the name of goodness did it come from?"

All the men gathered round Miranda. She looked up at them impudently. One of the men stroked her gently. In a trice Miranda was on his shoulder, pulling his hair.

The men began to laugh. They gathered round the little monkey, teasing her, petting her, and even opened another tin for her.

" How did she get here?" said Jo, in the greatest wonder. " We've never seen her before. Where did she come from? Surely she hasn't been here all the time."

" 'Course she hasn't. Don't be a fool, Jo," said a big man with a scar right down his face. " What I want to know is—did she come with anyone?"

Now it was Jo's turn to laugh. " That's a funny joke, that is! How would anyone get in here? There's only one way in and that's ours—and no one but us knows it."

" Well, how did the monkey get here then?" demanded the man with a scar.

" Oh—monkeys squeeze in anywhere," said Jo. " Artful little things, they are. Look at this one, eating a bit of peach just like you might—holding it in its hand and all! "

Barney watched Miranda angry and afraid. Little idiot! She might give the whole game away now—betray the fact that he was there, in hiding.

She sat there, eating the peach, gradually getting very full indeed. In fact, she was now so full that she felt she could not eat the fine half peach that one of the men gave her as soon as she had finished the piece in her hand.

She suddenly thought of Barney. She would give him the peach. He liked peaches too! So she leapt away from the crowd of admiring men and went straight to the crate in which poor Barney was hiding! She disappeared inside, chattering.

" Is that her hiding-place?" said Jo, and went to peep in at her, flashing his torch. Then he gave a tremendous shout.

" HEY, LOOK HERE! "

The men came running up. They saw Barney crouching in the empty crate—with Miranda trying to push the peach into his mouth!

The men pulled him out roughly. " What are you doing here? How did you get here, into this tunnel? Go on, you tell us everything or we'll make you very sorry for yourself! "

Barney looked round at the angry, glowering men. Now he was done for—silly little Miranda, her greed had made her give him away to the men. Jo shook him hard and Barney almost fell over.

" You tell us how you got in," said Jo, between his teeth. " Go on—quick! "

" All right," said Barney. " I'll show you. Let me go— I've not done any harm. I was only exploring a bit. Come on—I'll show you where I got in."

CHAPTER TWENTY-SEVEN

MIRANDA DOES HER BEST

BARNEY led the men up the tunnel, and then up the little passage to the shaft-hole. "I came down there," he said.

"Well—we know all about that old shaft," said the man with the scar. "It leads up to a little stone room and that's all."

"Yes—but there's a movable stone in the wall there, that gives on to the old cellars of Rockingdown Manor," said Barney. "I moved the stone by accident when I was in the cellars, and got through the gap. But the stone closed up again and I couldn't get back. So I came down the shaft and into the tunnel. I hid there. That's all."

"Anyone know anything about this movable stone?"

169

said the man with a scar, sharply, looking round at the men. They shook their heads.

" I'll go up with you," said the man, and he climbed up the shaft. Jo pushed Barney up behind him and then followed. " Go on up—you show him this wonderful stone! "

Barney showed the man the stone that had moved. He looked it over carefully and then swung his torch all over the wall. He called to Jo to come up.

" Jo—see that stone? It's worked by a lever somewhere. Look for a little groove in the wall and a staple or something jutting out, almost unnoticeable. Destroy the mechanism. I'm not having anyone else find this queer way in! "

" So that's the explanation of this mysterious room," said Jo, elbowing Barney aside. " It must have been secretly built when the old house was first put up, two or three centuries ago—with a secret way in. What a nice quiet way of disposing of your enemies! "

" Very," said the man with a scar, in a dry voice that Barney didn't like at all. " Now get down the shaft, boy—and we'll decide how to dispose of *you*. Good heavens, is that monkey still on your shoulder?"

Back in the cavern the man questioned Barney carefully. When he heard that the boy was more or less a tramp, going from fair to fair and circus to circus, and had slept in the old house because he needed shelter, his face cleared a little.

" I see. Then you heard these noises, I suppose, and came down to explore—and found the secret of the moving stone. Well—you seem a likely enough lad—the kind we can train in our way of business—bit of smuggling now and again. Like to join us?"

" No," said Barney.

That was quite the wrong thing to say. The man was taken aback. He scowled at Barney and then gave him a sharp box on the ears.

" Right! If that's the way you feel about it, you can

170

keep out. But you won't like it. You'll be kept here till we can get you out, and then you'll be taken abroad in an aeroplane, and got rid of somewhere in a foreign land. We'll sell you to somebody who'll be glad of your help!"

"Anyway he can work for us now," said Jo. "There's always plenty to do. The only difference will be that he works for nothing because he's a fool, instead of working for good pay."

Barney felt his heart go cold. How long would these men keep him here, working underground for them? He felt sure they would not allow him to go up into the daylight with them. He would always be left behind here, in the dark, with the sound of the stream for company.

"How long are you going to keep me here?" he asked, as boldly as he could.

"Maybe four weeks—maybe four months—it might even be four years," said the man with the scar, enjoying frightening the boy. "Depends how long our job goes on. You'll soon get quite fond of this place, won't you!"

Barney didn't think he would at all. He said nothing more. He was afraid of these rough-looking, scowling men, afraid they would beat him or ill-use him. He wasn't going to learn their illegal business—but he could quite well see that he would have to turn to and do a lot of the dirty work for them, or else have a very bad time indeed. They would make as much use of him as they could.

Certainly the men made him keep hard at work that night! He had to help to guide the rafts up the stream, he had to help to take the crates and boxes to the side where they were stored, and he was given the job of undoing those that were to be sorted and repacked at once. He said nothing but did what he was told, though as slowly as he could.

His brain was working hard. How was he to escape? There must be some way. If only he could get a message through to the others! They must be very worried about him by now. They would have gone down to the cellars to look for him—and have found his rug and cushion—but nothing else to show where he had gone! They couldn't tell Miss Pepper—and they certainly wouldn't tell Mr. King.

Barney had been surprised that Mr. King had not appeared underground with the men that night. Perhaps he directed operations from above ground. Well, if he came, Barney meant to tell him what he thought of him, even if it meant a beating! What a fraud, what a hypocrite, what a humbug! Barney spent quite a lot of time thinking bad things of Mr. King. Little did he know what different ideas the other children had of him now!

The men worked for several hours, and then went. They left Barney underground, of course. "We'll be back to-morrow night," said Jo. "And you'll have to work hard again, so sleep for the day!"

"I don't know if it's day or night down here," said Barney, sullenly. "It's always pitch-dark."

He spent a very miserable day indeed down in the darkness, switching on the big lamps at times to give him a change, though the men had forbidden him to do this. But he was not going to spend every hour in darkness. His torch was getting a little dim. He must save it.

He slept all the afternoon, though he did not know it was that time of day. He awoke about five o'clock and had a meal with Miranda. He had quite forgiven the little monkey for giving him away. He was very glad she was with him, to amuse him with her ridiculous ways and to keep him company.

He felt very wide awake when he awoke, and wondered if it was night or morning. Perhaps it was morning as he felt so lively. He would have been surprised to know that it was getting on for the evening!

He began to think of some way out of his difficulties. There simply *must* be some way. He looked at Miranda.

172

She had found a pencil belonging to one of the men and was scribbling on a piece of paper taken from an empty packing case. She showed her scribbles to Barney, evidently thinking she had been very clever.

Barney pretended to read it. "'Please rescue us—we are in an underground tunnel.' Very clever, Miranda! Very clever indeed—and beautiful writing."

He was just handing back the paper to her when a thought suddenly struck him. Miranda was used to taking notes or articles to people. Could she—could she possibly take a message from him to the others? She was a very tiny monkey—if she knew she was to go on a message, wouldn't she be able to find *somewhere* to get out from this tunnel, somewhere to squeeze through? She was so very small.

Barney had taught Miranda the trick of taking notes in the way that all good trainers teach their animals—by coaxing and reward. Many a time he had petted her and fondled her, and said someone's name over and over again, so that she would know where to take the note to—and when she had found that person and delivered the note, she had always been rewarded well by the one who received it.

Would she be able to find Snubby and take a note to him? Would she be able to squeeze out *somewhere*? It was worth trying even if nothing came of it.

Barney had a note-book in his pocket. He took it out and borrowed the pencil Miranda was using.

He began to write. He told briefly what had happened to him and where he was. "How you can rescue me I don't know," he wrote. "I don't even know how you're to find the place in the roof where the men enter, dropping down on a rope. All I can say is it must be some place where there is a dip in the ground—some spot where the tunnel is very near the surface. Do what you can."

When he had finished the note he folded it two or three times, took some thin string from his pocket, and tied it up carefully. Then he felt about for Miranda's collar which was buried in her thick neck-fur, and he tied the note firmly to it.

"Snubby," he said to the little monkey, fondling her. "Take it to Snubby. You know Snubby, don't you? Snubby, my friend who likes you so much. Take it to Snubby, to Snubby. Go find Snubby, Miranda. Snubby!"

Miranda listened, patting Barney's hands with her little brown paws. She knew quite well what he meant. She was to take the letter that Barney had put round her neck to his friend Snubby—the nice boy with the dog.

She leapt off Barney's shoulder and bounded over the rocky floor to the tunnel. Barney watched her. Where was she going? Did she know a way out? He couldn't believe that she did because she had not been away from him for even a minute!

Miranda went up the tunnel, not down. Barney was surprised. There is no way out there, Miranda! But in about twenty minutes she was back again, the note still round her neck. She had been up the shaft and into the little room at the top, remembering that that was the way they had come in—but of course there was no way out for her there, so after scrambling round for a while she had come back.

Barney petted her again. "Go on, find Snubby," he commanded. "You can find a way out if you try. Find Snubby, Miranda. It's very, very important!"

Miranda went off once more—and this time she didn't come back. Barney wondered about her. Had she found a way out? If so, where was it? He was quite sure that if there was some hole or cranny through which she could squeeze she would certainly find it.

Miranda had remembered the other place she had been to with Barney—the iron gate. She had sensed the daylight on the other side, and now she remembered it. Snubby would be somewhere out in that daylight. She must find him.

She arrived at the barrier. More daylight came through now, because Fred had torn away so much of the overhanging greenery, and had pulled at the ivy that clung so thickly to the bars. Miranda climbed lightly up the gate.

The bars were set very close indeed, too close even for Miranda to squeeze through. She tried her hardest. She almost got stuck in one place, and in her fright tore herself free so roughly that she made her leg bleed.

She sat down to lick it, chattering comfortingly to herself. Then, feeling tired with her efforts she curled up in a corner and fell asleep. She slept for two or three hours and then awoke. She stretched herself and then felt the note round her neck. Ah—she must take it to Snubby. Barney had said so.

She looked consideringly at the barrier. She felt a little afraid of it since it had hurt her leg. She chattered rudely at the gate, and then leapt on to it once more. She made a really good examination of it, from top to bottom, seeking for a way of escape.

And, at the bottom, she found a place where a bar had broken away at the surface of the water. Miranda got soaked as she squeezed through it. It was a tight fit, but she managed it! Now she was on the other side of the gate, in the dusk of evening. Snubby! She must go and find Snubby. But which way was she to go?

CHAPTER TWENTY-EIGHT

A THRILLING NIGHT

THE three children went to bed feeling down in the dumps that night. Even Mr. King had confessed that he didn't know which way to turn. Barney really did seem to have vanished into thin air, and there appeared to be no more steps they could take either to find him or to clear up the mystery.

"I don't want to go to bed," said Diana. "I know I shan't go to sleep."

"Oh, yes, you will," said Mr. King firmly. "Off you go. It's ten o'clock already. Good gracious me, what would Miss Pepper say if she knew how late I have kept you up!"

They all went off, grumbling. Loony raced ahead of them. He never seemed to mind going to bed. He tore into Mr. King's room, found his bedroom slippers, which were fleece-lined, and lightheartedly tossed them down the stairs. He then growled at all the rugs, dragged them into a heap where Mr. King would be sure to fall over them, and left them there. Then he shot up the stairs as if a tiger were after him, landing on Snubby's bed in one last mad leap.

"Loony dog," said Snubby, who was taking off his socks. "Loony! Mad! Daft! Potty! Crazy!"

"Woof," said Loony happily, and flung himself on Snubby to lick every bit of him that he could.

Diana did fall asleep quickly, though she had felt certain she wouldn't. So did Roger. Snubby lay awake a little time and then slid off into a peculiar dream about Barney and Miranda.

He was awakened some time later by Loony. Snubby

sat up in bed and felt for his torch. Blow, where was it? The moon shone into the room through the trees, and gave a dim light, so he tried to see by that.

Loony was at the window, growling fiercely. He was on the window-seat just inside the window, and kept making darts at something outside, snapping and snarling.

"What's up, Loony?" said Snubby in surprise. He wondered if a burglar was trying to break into his bedroom. No—of course not—no burglar would face a growling dog like that!

Then something leapt right in through the window, sprang on to the top of a picture, and then up to the top of the window-curtain with a flying leap.

"Miranda! Oh, Miranda! It's *you*!" cried Snubby, recognising the tiny creature as she leapt across a ray of moonlight. "Where's Barney?"

Loony was now barking the place down, very angry to think that Miranda should dare to leap in at his master's window at night, when he, Loony, was on guard! Snubby threw a book at him. "Shut up, idiot! You'll wake the whole household. Shut *up*, I say!"

Loony subsided at last, and sprang on to the bed jealously. Miranda was now on the bar of the bed at the back. Snubby got out of bed and switched on the light, just as Diana and Roger, awakened by the noise, switched on theirs. Roger appeared sleepily at the door.

"Whatever's the matter with Loony? Has he gone mad or something?"

"No—look, Miranda's back!" cried Snubby, and at her name the little creature sprang to his shoulder, cuddling into his neck. Snubby put up his hand to pet her, and at once felt the note tied to her collar.

"I say—what's this? A note! I bet it's from Barney!" he cried. He took off the note and undid the string round it. He opened it out. Roger came to read it with him, and Diana too, eager to join in the excitement.

"*Well*!" said Snubby, when they had all finished read-

177

ing it. " Fancy all this happening to Barney. Gosh—what a pity nobody can get that stone down in the cellars to move now. Fancy to think Barney's down underground where the river is. Would you believe it! "

" We'll have to rescue him somehow," said Diana at once. " I say—won't Mr. King be thrilled to hear of this! "

" Better go and tell him," said Roger, and all three went racing down the stairs, bursting into Mr. King's room after a very quick knock. He was asleep.

But he woke up completely as soon as he read Barney's note. " My word! This is news! So that's where the goods go to—where Barney is now. In some cavern underground, reached by way of the stream in the tunnel. But how can we find where that hole in the roof is, the one the men use to drop the goods down? I see it all now . . . the only missing link is the bit where the hole in the roof is. We've got to find that, and all is clear! "

" Can we do something about it to-night? " asked Snubby, excited.

" I can—but you're not going to," said Mr. King firmly, to the bitter disappointment of all three children. He got out of bed and went down to the telephone. Fred and Jimmy and two other men were told to come along to Rockingdown Cottage. " Things are moving! " said Mr. King.

He shooed the children away and dressed. He was ready by the time the other men came. The children said good-bye so meekly that Mr. King ought to have guessed they had something up their sleeves—but he didn't.

Under their dressing-gowns the children were fully dressed! They meant to follow Mr. King and the four men, and to see " the fun " as Snubby put it.

Before he went off with his men, Mr. King took a long look at a map he had. He put his finger on a certain spot. " We know that the hole in the roof of the river-tunnel is in some place where the ground dips considerably," he said. " That means a hollow somewhere—and there's only one place where there is a hollow on Rockingdown Hill, and that's where the farm-house is built that you went to the other day, Jimmy."

" Right," said Jimmy. " That's it! The job is worked from there. Old Daws doesn't know anything about it, of course—he's too old—it's all done under his nose and he doesn't suspect a thing! I reckon it's that son-in-law of his who's in with the gang. He's a nasty piece of work."

" Well—we're going there now," said Mr. King. " We'll be quite a surprise-party! We might even catch them red-handed. But if they're not there we've got to find that hole in the tunnel-roof and do a little dropping-in ourselves. Well, children—we'll see you in the morning! "

They said good-bye to the three children and strode off in the night. " We needn't hurry," said Roger to Snubby, seeing him begin energetically to strip off his dressing-gown. " We know where they're going. We mustn't follow too close behind in case they spot us and send us back. We'll go in about five minutes' time."

So they waited, very impatiently, for about five minutes, and then, with Loony at their heels, they set off. Miranda had gone again, though nobody saw her. They looked for her and came to the conclusion that she must have gone back to Barney.

They knew the way to the farm well now, and picked the best route they could. Once they got to the little back-water that led to the pond in the farm-yard they knew they were getting very near. They crept alongside the water and came to the pond.

" Look--do look—that must be Mr. King and his men —seeking everywhere with torches," said Snubby in a whisper. " They haven't waked anybody at the farm yet. Funny the dogs aren't barking."

" Let's hide somewhere safe," said Roger. " Look— here's an old barn. We'll go in there and hide in some straw."

They went into the old barn. A great heap of manure
179

was in one corner. A pile of straw was in another. The children slipped into the straw and pulled it over them. They could wait there till things boiled up a bit—then they would creep out and see what was happening. The moonlight slanted into the barn and filled the place with light and with black shadows. It was all very exciting indeed.

Loony was as quiet as a mouse. Snubby's hand was on his collar. "I simply can't think why the farm dogs don't bark," began Snubby in a whisper. "What's happened to them?"

"Don't know—either somebody's keeping them quiet, for some reason, or they're not here," said Roger, also puzzled.

His first idea was right. The farm dogs were being kept quiet by someone who had spotted Mr. King and his men—someone who wanted others to escape before the dogs barked, when he would have to come out into the open, and answer Mr. King's awkward questions!

Suddenly the barn-door was pushed slowly and softly open. Roger saw it and clutched Snubby and Diana, whispering into their ears. "Look—someone's coming in. Keep Loony quiet."

A man came in, silently, and slunk over to the manure heap. Another followed and another—a whole line of them. Who were they? Where had they come from? The children had no idea. Loony stiffened and the fur on his neck rose up, but he made no sound.

Roger regretted bitterly that he had come into the barn with the others to hide. There might be a fight in here, when Mr. King and his men came seeking with their torches—and Diana might get hurt.

He peered out of the straw. The men had pitchforks and were moving the manure heap rapidly. Then one knelt down and loosened something in the floor. He took out what looked like boards. Then he swung himself down and disappeared. All the men followed him save one. He

180

stood there alone, panting as he pitchforked the manure back into place.

The children watched silently, their hearts beating fast. The hole in the roof of the tunnel! Why, it was here, in the floor of the barn—just a little way away from them. The men had gone down into the tunnel—the river must flow directly under this old barn. It probably fed the pond and the backwater in some way, as well as going on and on down to the iron gate.

The man who was left threw down his pitchfork on the manure and crept to the door. He went out and disappeared. A minute or two later the dogs of the farm began to yelp madly, and a voice called out sharply.

"Who's there! Come out and show yourselves. What are you doing on my farm at night?"

Then Mr. King's voice answered sternly, and there was quite a meeting in the middle of the farm-yard. The old farmer did not appear. He was sound asleep. It was the son-in-law who did all the talking.

"What nonsense! I know nothing about smuggled goods—nothing about entrances to underground rivers. You must be mad. Haven't the police anything better to do than look for things that aren't there and never have been? I tell you, you can go all over the place from top to bottom and you'll find nothing suspicious at all!"

Roger suddenly flung aside the straw in which he was hiding and ran to the door. Mr. King might be wild with him for coming here, when he had forbidden him—but he had to say what he knew. He shouted at the top of his voice.

"Mr King! Mr. King! We know where the hole is. It's in here, in the barn. And a lot of men have just escaped down it, waiting for you to go—then they'll come out again."

There was an astonished silence. "Well—you little pest! You've come after all—and the others too, I suppose," said Mr. King. He strode over to the barn with his men.

Roger pointed to the heap of manure. "It's under there. You'd never have guessed. Fork it aside and you'll see! Gosh—isn't this EXCITING!"

CHAPTER TWENTY-NINE

THE END OF IT ALL

BARNEY was in the cavern when Miranda came back without the note. He petted her, very pleased. He gave her a big piece of pineapple from a tin as a reward. Now the others knew where he was—they would think of a way to rescue him.

And then things began to happen very quickly indeed. The men arrived in a hurry, queerly silent. They didn't work the winches. They brought no rafts with cases on them. They clustered together in the cavern, their faces anxious. They seemed to have forgotten all about Barney.

He didn't like the look of them. Supposing they had been driven underground because Roger had got on to the police, and they had got wind of it? They might guess that Barney had had something to do with it, and might turn on him. He decided it would be a very, very good thing to hide.

But where? Not in the empty crates—they would think of that at once. He would climb up the rocky wall of the cavern at the back and find a ledge to lie on. Barney silently crept away right to the back of the vast cavern and made his way up the wall, carefully feeling for jutting-out bits to hold on to with his hands and feet, climbing up bit by bit.

He found a very narrow ledge, so narrow that he almost

rolled off if he took a deep breath. But it was hidden from down below. He lay there with Miranda, listening.

And now came other voices, shouting and calling commands. Barney could hear Mr. King's loudest of all, and was astonished. *Mr King*! Had he come down to be with the other men too then? Barney had no idea that the coach had nothing to do with the men. He was most amazed to hear all that Mr. King shouted.

"You may as well give in! We're armed, and we know all about you. Either you surrender now, or we seal up the hole in the roof and leave you to starve."

"We won't surrender," Barney heard Jo say to the others. "We've got plenty of food here. We shan't starve."

"And how long will that last us?" said the man with

the scar. " A week at the most. Don't be a fool, Jo. We're caught here like rats in a trap. Why did we ever come down? If we had thought for one moment we'd have known that we had done for ourselves as soon as we came down here! "

They talked again, heatedly, urgently, some for surrender, some for staying down. Mr. King shouted again.

" I'll give you five minutes. Stay down if you like, whilst we get hold of your chief up here—yes we know all about him—and he'll talk all right to save his own skin. He's talked before, you know. We'll come and collect you when you want to be collected. A little starvation diet won't do you any harm."

" I'm giving up," said the man with the scar. " It won't do us any good to try and shoot it out, or to refuse to surrender. You all know we're caught. We've had a good run for our money. Well, I'm off to surrender. Anyone coming with me?"

" What about that boy?" said Jo suddenly. " Can't we do a bit of bargaining over him? Can't we say we'll keep him down here with us and starve him to death?"

" I'd forgotten about him! " said the man with a scar. " Where is he? Find him."

But they couldn't find him. They didn't see him lying precariously on a high ledge at the back, trying not to breathe.

" Well," came Mr. King's stentorian voice, " your time is up. We're getting out—and the hole will be sealed up. A man will be on guard in the barn. Knock three times on the boards over the hole if you want to surrender."

Then the men got panic-stricken. They surged towards the tunnel, forgetting Barney.

" We give in! " shouted Jo. " You're on top, and we know it all right. We're coming."

" One at a time, round the corner of the tunnel," came the directions. " Hands up as you come, or we fire."

So, one at a time, round the corner of the tunnel went

184

the men, holding their hands as high as they could, stumbling over the rocky ledge. And one by one they were hauled up the hole, and had handcuffs neatly clicked on their wrists as soon as they were in the barn. Jimmy and Fred greeted one or two of them by name.

" Well, if it isn't Jo! You just can't stay out of trouble, can you, Jo? And here's Frisky again, large as life and twice as natural—to think you're in this racket too! And who would have thought of meeting *you* here, Scarface?"

The last man was out. Mr. King spoke sharply to him. " Where's the boy who had the monkey? If you've harmed him things will go hard with you."

" I don't know where he is," said the man sullenly. " He's not there. We looked for him."

Roger could keep quiet no longer. He went to the hole and peered down it. " Barney! BARNEY! Miranda! Come along, we're here. Everything's safe."

Barney was already coming along the tunnel. He had watched the last man go, and reckoned it was safe for him to appear again. He heard Roger's yell and yelled back.

" I'm coming! I'm coming! "

He was hauled up. The three children and Loony fell on him and almost suffocated him. They were overjoyed to see him.

" We got your note! Miranda brought it! "

" The hole in the roof was under a manure heap—in this old barn! "

" Are you all right? Are you hungry?"

The handcuffed men eyed the children in amazement. Where had they sprung from in the middle of the night? How very extraordinary. The chief, who had sent the men down into the hole, and covered up the boards with manure, looked sullen and downcast. He was the old farmer's son-in-law, and under cover of getting in men to help on the farm, and to do repair work, he had brought in these villains, persuading them to help him in his illegal doings.

"And now," said Mr. King, looking quite sternly at the four children, "it's really time you behaved like children and got yourselves to bed. Barney, I'm glad to see you safe—but you've had a very narrow escape, I think. As for you others, how you dared to follow me after I'd said you were not to come amazes me—and if you hadn't unexpectedly been of the very greatest help, I should have a lot more to say about disobedience. As things are I shall probably not say anything."

He grinned suddenly, and the children grinned too. Good old Mr. King! "I suppose we can't stay any longer then?" said Roger.

"Not one moment," said Mr. King. "And *this* time I expect complete obedience to my orders. Get back home and get into bed. I'll see you in the morning. I've got to stay here and see this little lot safely put away for the night!"

Barney, Roger, Diana, Snubby, with Miranda and Loony, took a last look at the sullen men, and then stumbled back home, Snubby yawning loudly, and setting everyone else off too. Then he sneezed.

"Oh dear—don't say you've caught cold," said Diana in alarm. Snubby's colds were awful, and he sniffled dreadfully.

"No—just pepper up my nose," yawned Snubby. "Oh my—what will Miss Pepper say—and Roundy—when they hear what we've been up to!"

They all got into bed eventually. Barney was given one of the spare-room beds and cuddled down into it with Miranda, marvelling at its softness.

In the morning they could hardly believe all the happenings of the night before. Barney was thrilled to wake up and find himself in the cottage instead of in the dark cavern. There was such a tremendous chattering upstairs that Mrs. Round came up to see what was the matter as soon as she arrived.

She listened, open-mouthed. She couldn't say anything

at all except, "Well, I never—you young limbs! Well, I never!"

When Mr. King arrived in time for breakfast she regarded him with the greatest awe. She cooked him a very, very special breakfast of ham and eggs. She never once took her eyes off him, even backing out of the room so that she could look at him till the last moment.

"What in the world have you told Mrs. Round?" said Mr. King, half-irritated. He looked tired but pleased. He tucked into his breakfast eagerly.

The children finished their own breakfast, which was not quite so special as Mr. King's, and waited patiently for him to push away his plate and light his cigarette. Ah—there he was at last, puffing away.

"Well—it's all tied up nicely," he said. "Very, very nicely. Tanner, the son-in-law of the old farmer, and incidentally a very bad lot, has spilt the beans—in other words has told us everything. It has saved us quite a bit of trouble. I'm afraid, however, he'll get into a spot of trouble himself when he's out of prison, because the others won't easily forget how he betrayed them!"

"Serve him right," said Snubby, who hated disloyalty.

"It was a very pretty little plot," said Mr. King, puffing at his cigarette. "All kinds of goods were flown here from different countries—the aeroplane touched down in that field you know of—threw out the goods and made off again. The cases were manhandled to the stream, and put on the little rafts Barney has probably told you about. They were pulled up-stream by two men rowing the little unnamed boat that presumably belonged to the farmer's boy."

"In the dark, I suppose?" said Roger.

"Oh, yes—always at night," said Mr. King. "They were then manhandled again to the barn and dropped down the hole into the water—the rafts were dropped first, of course, and it wasn't very difficult to arrange the cases safely on the rafts, tie them to the wire rope, and then

187

wind them up to the cavern by means of the winches. Once there, the cases were perfectly safe and could be unpacked, and the goods sorted and repacked in small packets and bags, ready for sale secretly."

"They must have made a lot of money," said Roger.

"They did," said Mr. King. "They made just a few mistakes, though. They hired an electric launch which came slinking up the river to collect all these small packages and parcels, and they didn't pay the owner what they owed him—so he talked a bit—and his talk came round to us. That's what really made us suspect there was something going on, on a rather big scale."

"What other mistakes did they make?" asked Roger.

"Well—they didn't realise that thuds and bangs underground are often magnified when a building stands overhead," said Mr. King. "Though even if they did realise it they would probably think that as the house was empty, nobody would hear them. But the *biggest* mistake of all . . ." He paused and lighted another cigarette. The children waited impatiently. "The *biggest* mistake of all was that they didn't realise there were four tiresome children, to say nothing of a monkey and a dog, who were going to suspect their poor old tutor, and snoop round him and his doings, and fall headlong into the mystery themselves! Aha—that was a very big mistake indeed!"

They all laughed, and Loony tugged madly at Mr. King's shoelaces. "No good, Loony," said Mr. King. "They're special ones, made of leather, quite unchewable."

"What *will* Miss Pepper say?" said Diana. "She's coming back to-day!"

Once she had recovered from her amazement, Miss Pepper said rather a lot. She rounded on Mr. King for deceiving her regarding his ability to coach. "All those wonderful testimonials!" she said. "I'm shocked, Mr. King."

188

" Don't be," said Mr. King. " These kids have learnt a lot since I've been here. As for the testimonials, they were all true—I did do some coaching before I took up my present job. Cheer up, Miss Pepper—at least you weren't here when all this blew up."

" I *should* have been," said Miss Pepper. " It is scandalous that all this should happen when I was away."

" Yes. We ought to have waited till you came back," said Mr. King, and that made everyone laugh.

" Well, I'm glad it's all cleared up happily," said Miss Pepper. " What a tale! What will their parents say."

" You don't need to bother about that," said Mr. King. " I'm going to see them when they come back, and tell them everything myself. I can assure you that they will not blame you for anything, Miss Pepper."

" I can't stay on at the cottage after all this," said Miss Pepper. " Not that I meant to, anyhow—because I'm taking my sister away to the sea, and I mean to take the children too. It will be *so* much nicer for them—bathing, sailing, fishing—much more to do than there is here."

This was fine news. The children were thrilled. " What about Barney? Can he come too?" Snubby asked.

" Well, there isn't really room, but I dare say we can squeeze him in," said Miss Pepper. " He certainly seems one of us now."

But Barney shook his head. " No, thank you," he said. " I've got a job. I'm joining a fair to-morrow—it's on its way through Rockingdown Village to-day. I met someone I knew who told me about it when I went to the village for Mrs. Round this morning. It's time Miranda and I earned our living again! "

This was disappointing, very, very disappointing. They would miss Barney terribly. Would they ever see him again? Would he find his father some day? Now they would never know!

But when the children heard that the fair was actually

189

coming to the seaside place where Miss Pepper was taking them, in ten days' time, they cheered up. They would see Barney then!

" And I also must say good-bye," said Mr. King. " I have my living to earn as well—but not as a coach, I am thankful to say. I must get back to headquarters, and forget this pleasant little interlude with children, and monkeys and dogs! "

" Only one monkey and one dog," said Snubby.

" And quite enough," said Mr. King, pushing Miranda off his shoulder and Loony off his feet. He stood up.

" I'm saying good-bye now. You were my bitter enemies at first—but I hope we're friends now! "

" Oh, *yes*," said everyone, and then he was hugged by Diana, and banged on the back by the boys, whilst Loony barked madly.

Barney went down the front path with him, having said good-bye too. The children watched them go, feeling rather sad that such a wonderful adventure had come to an end.

" All the same, I feel that we'll have more adventures with Barney and Miranda some day," said Snubby, picking Loony up and squashing him till he squealed. " I feel it in my bones."

And I shouldn't be surprised if he's right!

The Rilloby Fair Mystery

The Rilloby Fair Mystery was
first published in the U.K. in a single volume
in 1950 by William Collins Sons & Co. Ltd,
and in Armada in 1967

CHAPTER 1

FIRST DAY OF THE HOLIDAYS

"'Morning, Mother! 'Morning, Dad!" said Roger, and ruffled his father's hair as he passed him, and dropped a kiss on his mother's curls.

"Don't *do* that, Roger," said his father impatiently, smoothing his hair down. "Why are you late for breakfast? And where's Diana?"

"Can't imagine," said Roger cheerfully, helping himself to an enormous plateful of porridge. "Asleep, I suppose."

"Never mind," said his mother. "It's only the second day of the holidays. Roger, you can't *possibly* eat all that porridge—with sausages to follow."

"Oh, jolly good," said Roger, sitting down in front of his great plateful. "Any fried onions with them?"

"Not at breakfast-time, Roger. You know we don't have onions then."

"I can't imagine why not," said Roger. He began to eat his porridge, craning his neck to read the back of his father's newspaper.

As the newspaper was folded in two, the reading matter was upside down for Roger, and his father glanced at him irritably.

"Roger! What are you screwing your head round like that for? Have you got a stiff neck?"

"No—only just reading that exciting bit in the paper about the dog that . . ."

"Well, don't. You know it's bad manners to read a paper when someone else is reading it," said his father. "Don't they teach you manners at school?"

"No. They think we learn them at home," said Roger cheekily.

Mr. Lynton glared over the top of his newspaper. "Well, then, perhaps I'd better teach you a few these holidays," he began. And just at that moment Diana burst into the room, beaming.

"Hallo, Mother! 'Morning, Dad! I say, isn't this a heavenly day—all daffodils and primroses and sunshine! Gosh, I do love the Easter hols."

"Get your porridge, dear," said her mother. "Roger, you haven't taken *all* the cream surely?"

"No, there's a spot left," said Roger. "Anyway, it won't hurt Diana to have plain milk. She's too fat."

"I'm *not*! Am I, Mother?" said Diana indignantly. Her father gave an exasperated click.

"Sit down, Diana. Eat your porridge. If you *must* be late, be late quietly. Breakfast is at eight o'clock—and it's now half-past!"

Mr. Lynton gathered up his newspaper, put it beside his wife's place, and went out of the room.

"What's the matter with Dad this morning?" asked Diana, pulling up one of her stockings. "Blow this stocking. It keeps coming down. Why is Dad so mouldy, Mother?"

"Don't talk like that, Diana," said Mrs. Lynton. "There's nothing wrong with your father except that he does like you two to be punctual for meals—and also he's heard that his Uncle Robert is coming to stay. You know the dear old fellow bores your father terribly."

"Oh my goodness—is Great-uncle Robert *really* coming?" said Roger. "Whatever for? And where are you going to put him? Snubby's coming to-morrow, isn't he—and he'll have the only guest-room."

"Well, he can't now—he'll have to sleep in your room," said his mother. "I'll have a bed put up there. I'm sorry, Roger—but it's the only thing to do. Uncle Robert must have the guest-room."

"Oh gosh—Snubby sleeping with me—and playing his fool tricks all the time," groaned Roger. "I shan't mind having Loony in the room—but Snubby's awful."

"I'd very much rather you didn't have Loony sleeping in the bedroom with you," said Mrs. Lynton. "He's a very nice spaniel, I know, although he's completely mad—but I do *not* like dogs in bedrooms."

"Mother! You say that every single time Snubby and Loony come to stay," said Diana. "And you know quite well that if you turned Loony out into the kennel Snubby would go too, and sleep with him there at night."

"Yes, I know," said Mrs. Lynton with a sigh. "I don't know which is worse—Snubby or Loony."

Snubby was a cousin of the two children, and owned a black cocker spaniel called Loony, short for Lunatic. Snubby's parents were dead, so he spent his holidays staying with various relations. Mrs. Lynton was sorry for him and fond of him, and he came more often to her house than to anyone else's.

"He's coming to-morrow, isn't he?" asked Diana. "I'll order a big bone for Loony to-day when I go by the butcher's. Dear old Loony. I wonder if he's still mad on brushes. Mother, last summer hols he took every single brush he could find. He put some of them down a rabbit-hole. We found quite a collection there one day."

Mrs. Lynton hurriedly made up her mind that she would warn the household to keep all brushes out of Loony's reach. Oh dear—what with Snubby and Loony and Uncle Robert, it looked as if things would be much too hectic for the next few weeks.

"I wonder what Snubby will say to Great-uncle Robert," said Diana with a giggle, helping herself to sausages. "Oh, Mother—I just can't see them together, somehow. Uncle Robert's so haw-hawish and pompous—and Snubby's so mad and idiotic."

"You'll just have to keep Snubby and Loony out of your uncle's way, that's all," said her mother, getting up from the table. "Well, I'm sorry I can't wait for you two any more. I see you've finished up the toast and have begun on the loaf of bread. When you've finished that perhaps you'd like to call it a meal! I cannot imagine how you can put all that away."

"Easy," said Roger, and grinned at his mother as she went out of the room. She smiled back. It was nice to have the children at home again, but it did take a little time to get used to their enormous appetites, careless ways and constant sparring.

Silence fell when Mrs. Lynton had gone out of the room. The two munched away hard, gazing out of the window. Daffodils danced at the edges of the lawn, and wallflowers shook the scent from their velvet petals. Sunshine flooded the garden and the two children felt happy and excited. The weeks stretched before them—no lessons, no rules—only day after day of sunshine and holidays, enormous meals, ice-creams—and Loony, the dog, to take for walks.

"Heavenly," said Diana, coming out of her daydream. Roger knew what she had been thinking, and he agreed.

"Yes. Super," he said. "I wonder how Loony will get on with Sardine."

Sardine was their big black cat, so-called because of her great fondness for the tinned fish called sardine. The grocer was always astonished at the amount of tinned sardines Mrs. Lynton bought—fancy a family eating as many sardines as that! But it was Sardine the cat who ate it all, and waxed fat and sleek on it.

"I should think Loony will give Sardine a frightful time," said Roger, scraping out the marmalade dish.

"I shouldn't be surprised if Sardine doesn't hold her own quite well," said Diana. "Let me have a scrape of that marmalade, Roger. Don't be a pig."

"I wish Great-uncle Robert wasn't coming," said Roger, handing over the marmalade pot. "I wonder why he's coming. He doesn't usually come in our hols. It's the last thing you'd think he'd want to do, considering he thinks all children are perfect pests."

"Diana! Haven't you two finished *yet*?" called Mrs. Lynton from upstairs. "Come along. I want you to help me with Snubby's bed. I'm putting the play-room divan into Roger's room. Roger, come and give me a hand with it."

"Never a moment's peace!" said Roger with a grin at Diana. "Come on. Let's give a hand."

They tore upstairs, falling over Sardine as they went. The big black cat fled up in front of them, tail in air, green eyes gleaming wickedly.

"Sardine! Do you *still* lie on the stairs, you wicked cat?" shouted Roger. "You be careful to-morrow, or Loony will get you if you don't look out!"

"Loony'll get you if you don't look out. Loony'll get you if you don't look out!" chanted Diana, and skipped into Roger's room to help her mother. Sardine was sitting on the window-sill there, her long tail waving from side to side.

"What have you two been doing to make Sardine so cross?" asked her mother.

"Well, I like *that*! She was lying doggo on the stairs waiting to trip us up!" said Diana indignantly.

"Lying catto, you mean!" said Roger with a chortle.

"Oh, Roger—you sound like Snubby when you say things like that!" said his mother. "Diana, make Roger's bed whilst he and I bring in the divan."

They were all busy that day, preparing for Great-uncle Robert and Snubby—what an odd pair! Great-uncle Robert was so old and polite and pompous, correct in every way—and Snubby was so very much the opposite, cheeky, idiotic and unexpected in all he did. Mrs. Lynton had quite a few qualms when she thought of them in the house together.

As for Loony, he would probably drive the old man mad. All the same Loony was a darling, and Mrs. Lynton, like everyone else, had fallen under his spell. Dear, silky-coated, melting-eyed Loony. There was probably only one person in the household who would regard Loony with bitter dislike—and that was Sardine.

At last the two rooms were done. The guest-room looked nice and bright and clean. Flowers arranged by Diana stood on the dressing-table, bright yellow daffodils matched by the yellow towels hanging by the basin.

Roger's room looked different, now that it had the extra divan in. It wasn't very big anyhow, and looked very crowded now, with the divan and an extra chair. Mrs. Lynton also added an old rug in one corner for Loony to sleep on.

"Oh, Mother! What's the good of that?" said Roger. "You know where Loony always sleeps—on Snubby's feet."

His mother sighed. It looked as if these holidays were going to be just a little bit *too* exciting. She was quite right —they were!

CHAPTER 2

SNUBBY ENJOYS HIMSELF

SNUBBY was pleased to be going to his cousins' home for the holidays. He liked Mrs. Lynton, their mother, and he quite liked Mr. Lynton, though he was secretly afraid of his sudden tempers. It would be good to see Diana and Roger again.

His luggage had gone in advance. He only had a small bag with him—and Loony, of course. He was now waiting for the train, a snub-nosed, red-haired, freckled boy of twelve. He whistled tunelessly as he waited, and Loony pricked up his ears as he always did when his beloved master made a noise of any sort.

The train came in with such a roar and rumble that Loony was startled. He jerked away in alarm, and rushed into the waiting-room, where he cowered under a seat.

Snubby followed, indignantly. "What do you think you're doing, idiot, rushing away like that! Anyone would think you'd never seen a train before. Come here! "

The train gave a piercing whistle, and Loony cowered back still farther. Snubby had a job to get him to move.

"Look here—the train will be gone before we've caught it if you don't look out! " shouted Snubby, exasperated. "Come OUT, I tell you. What's come over you?"

He dragged poor Loony out at last, lumped him into his arms and staggered to the train. The porter was already slamming the doors.

"Hey you—get in quickly!" yelled the man. "Train's just going!"

Poor Snubby had no chance to choose his carriage carefully as he usually did. He liked a completely empty one, so that he could occupy each corner in turn, and look out of any window he liked. There was no time to look into even one carriage now. He wrenched open a door, threw Loony in, and fell in himself, landing on hands and knees. The porter slammed the door, and the train moved off.

Loony retired under the seat. Snubby glared at him. "Idiotic dog! You nearly made us miss the train!"

He got up and dusted himself down. He looked round the carriage. Only one other person was there, thank goodness.

The one other person stared at Snubby in annoyed surprise. He was an old man with a head of silvery-white hair, a real mane. His eyes were a faded blue and he had a small pointed beard, also very white.

"My boy," he said, "it is most inadvisable to leave so little time for catching a train."

"I've been waiting for twenty minutes," said Snubby indignantly. "Here, Loony, come on out. You'll get filthy under there."

Loony appeared, his tail well between his legs. The old man looked at him with dislike.

"Dogs!" he said. "I think they should travel in the guard's van. They always smell. And they scratch themselves in such an objectionable manner."

"Of course dogs smell," said Snubby, sitting down opposite the old man. "It's a nice smell, a doggy smell. So is a horsy smell. And I like a cow's smell too. And as for ..."

"I don't think I want to discuss smells," said the old man. "I do *not* like the smell of dogs, and I do *not* like the way they scratch themselves."

"Loony never scratches," said Snubby, at once. "A dog only scratches when he's got heaps of fleas. I keep Loony jolly clean. Brush him every single day, and ..."

Loony put himself into a peculiar position and began to

202

scratch himself very hard indeed, making a thumping noise against the floor of the carriage.

Snubby pushed him crossly with the toe of his shoe. "Shut up, idiot. Didn't you hear what I just said?"

Loony looked up politely, and then began to scratch himself again. The old man looked disgusted. "Do you mind taking him to the other end of the carriage?" he said. "Bearing in mind your remark about dogs only scratching themselves when they have a large number of fleas, I don't feel too happy about having him in quite such close proximity."

"What's that mean?" asked Snubby obstinately, not moving. "I tell you, he hasn't got fleas, he's never . . ."

"I don't think I want to discuss fleas," said the old man stiffly. "Well, if you won't move your dog, I must move myself. But I must say that children nowadays are not remarkable for their good manners."

Snubby hastily removed Loony to the other end of the carriage, feeling rather ashamed of himself. The spaniel tried to climb up the seat, but the old man looked so very disapproving that Snubby changed his mind about letting him.

Loony fortunately went to sleep. Snubby undid his case and took out a paper-covered book. He settled down to read. The old man looked to see what Snubby was reading. The book had a most lurid cover and an extraordinary title. It was called *SPIES! SPIES! SPIES!*

Snubby curled himself up, lost to the world. The old man was astonished to see such a peculiar title.

"What is your book about?" he asked at last.

Snubby thought that was a silly question, considering that the book's title was plainly to be seen.

"It's about spies," he said. "Stealing old maps and plans and things like that."

The old man gazed at Snubby and then made a curious remark. "Spies! I never thought of that! It might have been spies."

Snubby looked up, astonished. "Funny old fellow!" he thought. "What's he talking about now?"

"It's strange you should be reading a book about old documents being stolen," said the old man. "Because I've just left a place where there's been a theft of that kind. Terrible, terrible!"

Snubby stared at him. "What exactly was stolen?" he asked.

"The letter of Lord Macaulay, of maps of the county of Lincolnshire, and the correspondence between Lady Eleanor Ritchie and her sister," said the old man, shaking his head solemnly. "And the old recipes of the Dowager Lady Lucy, and . . ."

This was all Greek to Snubby. He began to think the old man was pulling his leg. All right, he could do some of that too!

"And I suppose the pedigree tables of all the dogs went too, and the letters written by Lord Popoffski," he said, solemnly and sympathetically.

Now it was the old man's turn to stare. "Ah—I see you don't believe me," he said with dignity. "Well, let me tell you this, young man. The thief got into a locked room without unlocking it. He got into a room with every window fastened and didn't unfasten one. He left no fingerprints, he made no noise."

Snubby didn't believe a word. He looked disbelievingly at the old man.

"Well," said the old fellow, "that's a queer story, isn't it? Too queer for me. I've left the house where it all happened, and I'm not going back there. I don't like thieves who go through locked doors. Do you?"

Snubby put down his book. If there was to be a bit of story-telling, well he would do some too.

"Funny you should tell me this, sir," he said earnestly. "I'm running away too. I've unearthed a Plot, sir, a very sinister Plot."

"Good gracious!" said the old man, alarmed. "What kind of a plot?"

"Sort of atom-bomb plot, sir," went on Snubby, enjoying himself. "They tried to get me, sir—and they very nearly did."

"Who tried to get you?" asked the old man, amazed.

"Sh!" said Snubby mysteriously, looking all round the compartment as if he thought "They" were listening. "It's the Green Hands, sir—surely you've heard of that gang?"

"No. No, I can't say I have," said the old man. "Who are they?"

"An international gang, sir," said Snubby, enjoying himself more and more, and marvelling at his powers of invention. "They've got the secret of the atom bomb, sir—and I stumbled on it by accident. They captured me and wanted me to work for them."

"What—a boy like you?" said the old man.

"They can use boys," said Snubby. "For experiments and so on, you know. Well, I didn't want to be blown to bits, did I?"

"Good heavens!" said the old fellow. "This is incredible. You should go to the police."

"I'm running away," said Snubby, sinking his voice to a whisper. "But They're after me, sir—the Green Hands. I know they are. They'll track me down. They'll get me in the end."

"But this is unbelievable!" said the old man, mopping his forehead with a big white silk handkerchief. "First I stay in a house where thieves go through locked doors and fastened windows—and now I travel with a boy hunted by—by what, did you say—the Green Hands. Do they—do they have green hands?"

"They wear green gloves," invented Snubby wildly. "Beware if you ever see anyone wearing green gloves, won't you? Man *or* woman."

"Yes. Yes, I certainly will," said the old man. "My poor boy—have you no parents to look after you?"

"No," said Snubby, telling the truth for the first time in five minutes. "I haven't. I'm fleeing to the country to stay with my cousins. I hope the Green Hands don't track me there. I don't want the whole lot of us blown up."

"Good heavens! Incredible! The things that happen these days!" said the old man. "Take my advice, my boy, and go to the police."

The train drew to a stop. Snubby looked out casually, and then leapt to his feet suddenly, startling the old man considerably.

"Golly! This is my station! Here, Loony, wake up! Stir yourself. Good-bye, sir—and I hope you catch your locked-door thief."

"Good-bye, my boy. We've had a most interesting conversation—and take my advice, go to . . ."

But his words were lost in the whistling of the engine and the slamming of the door. Snubby was gone and so was Loony. The old man sank back in his seat. Well, well, well—what was the world coming to? To think that even a young boy could be mixed up in such extraordinary plots. Most alarming.

"Nobody's safe these days!" thought the old man gloomily. "It's all *most* alarming."

CHAPTER 3

AN UNEXPECTED MEETING

SNUBBY arrived on the platform very hurriedly, fell over Loony and sat down with a bump. A squeal of laughter greeted him.

"Oh, Snubby!" cried Diana's voice. "You *always* fall out of a train! Hallo, Loony!"

Loony flung himself on Diana in a mad bound, almost knocking her over. He barked and yelped, pawing her ecstatically. She had to push him off at last.

"No, Loony, no more. Get *down*. Snubby, tell him. He's just as loony as ever, isn't he? I say, Roger's sorry he couldn't come and meet you, but he's gone to the next station to meet Great-uncle Robert. Why you couldn't both come to the same station, I don't know! I suppose Great-uncle thought the next one was nearer to us."

"Who's Great-uncle?" asked Snubby in surprise. "I've never heard of him before. Surely he's not coming to stay?"

"Yes, he is. Maddening, isn't it, considering it's our hols," said Diana as they walked out of the station. "He's not a bad old thing, only awfully pompous and polite. Mother didn't know till yesterday that he was coming. We've had to put you in Roger's room."

"Oooh, good," said Snubby. "Loony will like that."

"Does he still take every brush he can find?" asked Diana. "He was awful last summer hols."

"Yes, he's still pretty bad about brushes," said Snubby. "And mats. And cats too. I say—you've got a cat now, haven't you?"

"Yes. A big black one called Sardine," said Diana. "She's almost a year old, so she's still pretty idiotic at times. I don't know how she'll get on with Loony."

"It'll be a lively household," said Snubby, pleased. "Cats and dogs flying all over the place, and us three, and your old Great-great-uncle."

"Only *one* Great," said Diana. "He's Daddy's uncle. Well, there's our house. Loony remembers it, look! He's rushing in at the gate. My word, he'll startle old Sardine —she's basking on the wall!"

Snubby ran after Loony. Loony had already discovered Sardine, and was chasing her madly round the front garden, yelping in excitement. Sardine flew into the house, Loony raced after her, and Snubby tore after them both.

Mrs. Lynton was amazed to see Sardine flash past her head and land on top of the bookcase. She was even more amazed to see Loony coming in like a streak of black lightning, followed by a shouting Snubby.

208

"Oh! It's *you* arriving, Snubby. I might have guessed," she said. "There's really not much difference between you and a tornado. How are you, dear?"

"Hallo, Aunt Susan!" said Snubby. "Come here, Loony. Oh, good—Sardine's gone out of the window now. Gosh, so has Loony."

He disappeared at top speed, and Mrs. Lynton sat down again with a sigh. Peace always vanished when Snubby arrived. There were loud cries from the garden, and finally a scream from Diana.

"Mother! Here's Great-uncle in a taxi with Roger."

Mrs. Lynton got up hurriedly. She wondered what Uncle Robert would say when he found the front garden full of yells and yelps, howls and yowls, and screaming children.

She went into the garden, and hissed at Snubby. "Catch Loony at once. Take him away. Go and wash your hands or something!"

Snubby gave her a startled glance. How cross she sounded! He gave a piercing whistle and Loony responded at once. He arrived like a cannon-ball at Snubby's heels, and the two disappeared indoors just as Great-uncle Robert opened the front gate. Diana smoothed back her hair and went to welcome him too.

"So nice to be here at last, my dear Susan," said the old fellow. "Such a peaceful place—far from thieves, and wars and spies!"

Mrs. Lynton felt astonished. "Oh, we're peaceful enough here, out in the country," she said. "Come along up to your room. You will like a wash, I expect."

"Thank you, my dear, thank you," said Uncle Robert, and followed his niece up the stairs. She took him to the guest-room and put his bag down for him.

"Very nice room," said Uncle Robert. "Very nice view too. Beautiful. Ah—who's this?"

It was Loony. He came nosing into the bedroom, having smelt somebody new. He stood at the door, wagging his black stump of a tail, his long ears drooping like a judge's wig at each side of his head. Uncle Robert looked at him.

"Most peculiar," he said. "There was a dog in the train, in my carriage, *exactly* like that!'

"Oh, well—black cockers are very much alike," said Mrs. Lynton. "Now you wash, Uncle Robert, and then come down to lunch. You must be hungry."

She went to a cupboard on the landing to put some things away. Snubby was whistling in Roger's room, brushing his wiry hair and making it stand up straighter than ever. He suddenly missed Loony.

"Hey, Loony! Where have you got to?" he said. He went to find him. Ah, there he was, standing in the doorway of the room next but one. He went to get him. Somebody came walking out at the same moment, stepping carefully over Loony, who didn't attempt to move out of the way. He never did if people were stupid enough to walk round or over him.

Snubby stopped in the utmost amazement when he saw Great-uncle Robert. He stared as if he couldn't believe his eyes.

Great-uncle Robert stared too.

"Incredible!" he muttered, taking a step backwards and nearly falling over Loony. "You again! What are you doing here?"

"I'm staying with my cousins," said Snubby, horrified to see that the old man in the train had suddenly become Great-uncle Robert. Gosh, this was frightful. That awful story he had told him—about the gang called Green Hands! Suppose he told Aunt Susan about it, what in the world would she say? She wouldn't understand at all. She would be furious!

"So you ran away here," began Uncle Robert. "Do your cousins know why?"

"Sh!" said Snubby desperately. "Don't say a word to anyone. Remember the Green Hands! They'll get you too if you split."

"Split?" repeated Uncle Robert faintly, not understanding the word.

"Blab. Spill the beans. Give the game away," said Snubby urgently. "Don't say a word. Just remember the Green Hands!"

The gong in the hall suddenly sounded for lunch, and both Uncle Robert and Snubby jumped violently.

"Sh!" said Snubby again, and looked all round him as if he were being hunted.

"I'll remember the Green Hands," said Uncle Robert in a stronger voice. "But be careful, my boy, do be careful."

He went downstairs, wiping his broad forehead with his silk handkerchief. He had escaped from one house where thieves made their way through locked doors—only to come to another place where there was a boy hunted by the Green Hands. Where should he go next? Incredible, quite incredible.

Up on the landing, half-hidden by the open cupboard door, was a most astonished Mrs. Lynton. She had overheard the extraordinary conversation and couldn't understand a word of it. What was all this talk of Green Hands and all the shushings and warnings she had heard? She was filled with amazement.

"What's Snubby up to now? And how does he know Uncle Robert? And what *is* this talk of Green Hands?" she thought, shutting the cupboard door impatiently. An agonised yowl made her jump. She opened the door hurriedly and Sardine jumped out.

"Silly cat! Why put your tail in the door when you know I'm going to shut it?" said Mrs. Lynton. "You're always doing things like that. There now, I'm sorry I hurt your tail. And just look out for Loony, because I don't want you streaking across the dining-table as soon as you see him!"

Loony was downstairs with the others He had attached himself to Great-uncle Robert, much to Diana's surprise. He was sniffing round his feet and pawing at his legs in a most friendly manner.

"He's acting just as if he's met you before," said Diana.

"Er—is he?" said Uncle Robert, not knowing quite what to say. "Snubby—call him off, will you? I don't particularly want his fleas, you know."

"How do you know he's got fleas?" asked Roger, surprised. "Has he, Snubby?"

It looked as if the conversation was now going to be awkward. Snubby pulled Loony away and shoved him firmly under the table.

"Of course he hasn't got fleas," he said. "You'd jolly well know if he had. Why, a chap at school had a dog that had about three hun . . ."

Mrs. Lynton came in, still looking puzzled. "What are you talking about?" she asked, sitting down at the head of the table.

Nobody told her. She didn't encourage subjects of that sort at meal-times. Uncle Robert took his place gingerly, looking under the table to see exactly where Loony was.

"What's that noise?" inquired Mrs. Lynton, hearing a thump-thump-thump on the floor under the table.

"Oh, just Loony scratching himself," said Diana.

"Oh dear, Snubby—and I hope you haven't brought Loony here with . . ." began Mrs. Lynton.

"No Aunt Susan, I haven't," said Snubby hurriedly. "I say—is that chops—and chip potatoes—and ONIONS! Golly, how smashing!"

The subject was safely changed. Mrs. Lynton served the meal, still wondering about such curious things as Green Hands. She glanced at Uncle Robert. He seemed such a nice, harmless old fellow. What *did* he mean, whispering about running away and Green Hands up on the landing with Snubby?

It was really most extraordinary!

CHAPTER 4

GREAT-UNCLE TELLS HIS STORY

AFTER the meal Snubby escaped into the garden with
Roger and Diana, Loony at their heels. They all went into
the little summer-house, which faced south and was very
warm in the April sun.

"Gosh! It's as hot as summer," said Roger. "I'll really
have to take off my coat. I say—Great-uncle is rather an
old stick, isn't he? We'll have to mind our manners a bit

213

now, or he'll get going on the 'good old days when children knew their manners, and were seen and not heard,' and all the rest of it."

"I've got something to tell you," said Snubby, rather awkwardly. "About Great-uncle."

"Go on then—out with it. What have you been doing? Using his hair-lotion for Loony or something?" asked Roger.

"Don't try and be funny," said Snubby. "It doesn't suit you. Listen—I came in the train with him, and I got off at the North Station and he went on to South, where you met him. We had quite a lot of—er—conversation."

The other two looked at him in surprise. "You did?" said Diana. "Well—why ever didn't you say so then? Why keep it such a deep, dark secret?"

"Well, you see—it's like this—he told me a silly story about running away from somewhere he'd been staying, because thieves had got through locked doors and stolen papers and things," said Snubby. "Lord Somebody's letters and Lady Somebody's recipes—a lot of awful nonsense. And—well—*I* told him a story too. I thought to myself, well, two can play at this game, and I sort of let myself go."

"Do you mean you went and stuffed him up with some frightful fairy tale?" said Roger. "Whatever did you tell him?"

Snubby related the story he had told to Great-uncle Robert, ending with his running away from a gang called Green Hands, who always wore green gloves. Diana and Roger listened in astonishment that ended in giggles.

"Gosh, Snubby—you really are the biggest fathead that ever lived!" said Roger at last. "What in the world did you go and stuff Great-uncle up with that for?"

"Well, how was I to know he was your Great-uncle?" demanded Snubby. "I didn't know you'd even got one. And I certainly didn't know he was coming to stay with you. I got a shock, I can tell you, when I saw him in the guest-room. I nearly passed out."

214

"You'll get another when he tells Dad the rigmarole you told him," said Roger. "Dad doesn't like fairy tales of that sort. He doesn't understand that kind of joke."

"I know," said Snubby dismally. "I've warned Great-uncle not to say a word. He really believes it all, you see. I expect he's terrified of the Green Hands Gang now— just as terrified as he is of the thieves that walked through the locked doors at the house where he was staying."

"Well, he must be a mutt if he believes a word you say," said Diana. "Oh dear, Snubby—you always bring trouble with you. Now don't you go frightening the old man with sinister notes, or drawings of green hands or anything."

"Oooh—that's an idea," said Snubby, sitting up. "Oooh, I say—wouldn't he have a fit! "

"Yes, he would—and the first thing he'd do would be to tell Dad, and you'd get a whacking," said Roger.

"That's no go then," said Snubby, who had quite clear memories of one of Uncle Richard's whackings. "I don't want to go too far with Uncle Richard."

"You'd better not," said Roger. "He's not in a very good mood so far these hols—because Great-uncle has come to stay, I think—and what with that, and us, and you and Loony, life seems pretty grim to him at the moment."

"Poor Dad," said Diana. "We'd better keep out of his way."

"It's an idea," said Snubby, making up his mind not to obtrude himself on his Uncle Richard any more than could be helped. "I say—I wonder if Great-uncle will tell his thief-story to Uncle and Aunt."

He did, that very night. They were all sitting in the lounge together, the children playing a game, Mrs. Lynton sewing, her husband reading, and Loony having one of his lengthy rolls all over the floor.

Great-uncle filled his pipe and then spoke to Mrs. Lynton. "It's really very kind of you, Susan, to have me here at such short notice," he said. "But to tell you the truth I was at my wits' end. I simply *had* to leave the Manor House."

215

"Did you, Uncle Robert? Why? Weren't you comfortable?" asked Mrs. Lynton.

"Oh yes, quite. Very warm, comfortable house, the Manor House at Chelie," said Uncle Robert. "But there were such extraordinary goings-on, you know."

Mrs. Lynton looked rather startled. The children nudged one another and laid down their cards. "Now it's coming," whispered Snubby.

Mr. Lynton put down the evening paper. "What extraordinary goings-on?" he asked. "Surely not much can happen in a house like that, that's more a museum than anything else."

"It's a place of great treasures," said Great-uncle reprovingly. "It belongs to Sir John Huberry, as you know, a man who collects rarities of many kinds—in particular old papers, letters and documents."

"Er—hasn't he got some of Lord Macaulay's letters?" said Snubby innocently, remembering what Great-uncle had mentioned in the train.

There was a surprised silence, during which Loony could be heard scratching himself vigorously.

"Shut up, Loony," said Snubby, and poked him with his toe. Loony stopped.

"Well, it's the first time I've ever heard you make an intelligent remark," said Mr. Lynton in surprise. "I shouldn't have thought you had ever *heard* of Lord Macaulay's name"

"Er—Snubby is quite right," said Great-uncle hastily. "There were some of Macaulay's letters, they were among the stolen articles. Richard, it was the most extraordinary theft. Doors were locked. Windows were fastened tightly. There was no skylight or other way into the room where these papers were kept. And yet one night thieves got in, took the whole lot, and vanished the way they came—through locked doors or fastened windows! What do you think of that?"

"I think it's rather foolish to make a statement like

216

that," said Mr. Lynton. "Thieves can't get through locked doors unless they have a key."

"Well, they hadn't a key," said Great-uncle. "The keys are kept on Sir John's key-ring in his pocket. There are no duplicates in existence. What is more—the doors showed no fingerprints of any sort."

"The thieves wore gloves," said Mrs. Lynton.

"*Green* gloves," said Snubby before he could stop himself.

Great-uncle looked extremely startled. Mrs. Lynton stared at Snubby, puzzled. First it was Green Hands, now it was Green Gloves. What did he mean?

Mr. Lynton took no notice of Snubby's remark. He just put it down to Snubby's usual silliness.

"Well, Uncle Robert," he said, picking up his paper again, "all I can say is, if that's what you ran away from —the idea of thieves going through locked doors—it wasn't very sensible of you. You should have stayed to try and find out who stole the papers. Why, if your hosts didn't know you well, they might think it was you, as you ran away."

"I hardly think so," said Great-uncle, on his high horse at once. "No, my dear Richard, that is quite unthinkable. Quite."

"I expect it was gypsies or tramps," said Mrs. Lynton soothingly.

Great-uncle gave a most unexpected snort. He looked scornfully at Mrs. Lynton. "My dear Susan! *Do* you think a gipsy or a tramp would know what papers were valuable and what were not? This thief knew exactly what to take."

"Well, I've no doubt the mystery will be solved sooner or later," said Mr. Lynton, opening his paper again. "I imagine if the thief is as clever as you say, he'll try his hand somewhere else."

"He's already tried it three times," said Great-uncle. "Sir John told me. He thinks it must be the same thieves because each time they apparently passed through locked doors quite easily."

217

"Well, I'll believe somebody can go through locked doors when I see them," said Mr. Lynton dryly.

"Great-uncle—do you think the thief will steal papers again somewhere?" asked Diana. "I'd like to read about it, if he does. Would it be in the papers?"

"Oh yes," said Great-uncle. "It's always in the paper. I think I've got a report of the last theft in my bag. You can go and get it, if you like."

Roger sped upstairs with Loony at his heels. Loony always went upstairs with everybody if he could, and then tried to get in their way going down again, either by getting between their legs, or hurling himself on top of them as they went down. There was a thunderous noise after a minute or two, and then a crash and a yelp.

"Oh dear," said Mrs. Lynton. "Are you hurt, Roger?"

Roger came limping in, followed by a saddened Loony. "I've smacked him," he explained to Snubby. "He did his cannon-ball act at me and sent me flying down the stairs. He's loonier than ever. I've got the paper. Where's the burglary reported, Great-uncle?"

Great-uncle found the report. It wasn't much more than a few lines. The children read them eagerly.

Then Diana noticed an advertisement nearby and pointed to it.

"Look," she said. "There's a notice about a fair held in the same town. I wonder if Barney and Miranda were there."

"Is this the Barney you told me about—the boy with the monkey that had the adventure with you last summer holidays?" asked his mother. Roger nodded.

"Yes. He's awfully nice, Mother. He leads a peculiar sort of life, you know—going from fair to circus and circus to fair, earning his living with Miranda, his monkey. She's a darling."

Mrs. Lynton looked doubtful. "Well, I don't like monkeys," she said. "But from all you have told me, Barney seems a nice boy, though a queer, roving kind of character."

"I wonder if he's at the fair advertised here," said Diana, looking at the notice again. "Look, Roger—it gives all the performers—the main ones, anyway—Vosta and his two chimpanzees, Hurly and Burly—what lovely names; Tonnerre and his elephants. Shooting gallery in charge of the famous cracksman, Billy Tell . . ."

"Short for William Tell, I suppose," grinned Snubby. "Go on."

"Hoopla stalls, roundabouts, swing-boats—no, it doesn't say anything about a boy with a monkey," said Diana, disappointed. "Though perhaps they wouldn't mention him, really—he wouldn't be one of the chief performers."

"Anyone got his address?" asked Snubby. Nobody had. Barney was a very bad letter-writer, and the children had not heard from him since Christmas.

"Come on let's finish our game," said Roger, losing interest in the paper. "No, you can't get on my knee, Loony. Go and play with Sardine—a nice little game of Spit-and-Hiss, or Growl-and-Snap. You'll like that!"

CHAPTER 5

DIANA HAS AN IDEA

A DAY or two went by. Great-uncle tried to settle down and
go on writing what he called his "Memoirs," which Roger
said were another name for "Nodding over a Pipe." Snubby
had settled in at once, as usual. He was perfectly at home,
and Roger's usually neat bedroom now always looked
exactly as if a whirlwind had just passed by.

"If Snubby doesn't mess it about, Loony does," Roger
complained. "I'm tired of keeping my shoes and the bedroom slippers and hair-brushes in a drawer so that Loony
can't get them."

"So am I," said Diana. "And I do wish he wouldn't
drag all the mats in a heap and leave them on the landing
or in the hall for people to fall over. I nearly broke my
ankle twice yesterday. As for poor Great-uncle, he's so
scared of falling over mats or brushes left about that he
walks like a cat on hot bricks—lifting up his feet very
gingerly indeed."

Roger laughed. "Oh dear—that lunatic dog put half a
dozen brushes into the pond this morning, and two of them
were Great-uncle's. Snubby told him he supposed Mother
was washing the brushes in pond-water because it was good
for them—and he believed him!"

"There's Looney now—barking at Sardine, I suppose,"
said Diana. She leaned out of the window. "Loony, Loony!
Shut up! Haven't you learnt by now that once Sardine is
up on the wall you can't get her off. SHUT UP!"

Her mother's voice came floating up from the garden. "Diana! Stop yelling out of the window like that. Your Great-uncle is trying to work."

"That means Loony's woken him up from a doze," said Diana, pulling her head in. She put it out again. "Mother! Mother! Shall I do the flowers this morning?"

"Will you *stop* shouting out of the window?" called back her mother, whilst Great-uncle Robert flung down his pipe in exasperation and stood up. He would go for a walk! What with dogs barking, and children yelling, and now his niece yelling too, the house was unbearable. Yes, he would go for a walk!

But at the sight of him appearing in coat and hat with a stick in his hand, Loony flung himself on him in delight. A walk! People with hats and coats on meant only one thing—a WALK! Loony snuffled round Great-uncle's ankles, thrilled, and then rolled over on his back, doing what Snubby called his "bicycling act," riding an imaginary bicycle upside down!

"You are *not* coming with me," said Great-uncle firmly. "I don't like you. You can only do two things well, and I don't like either of them. You can bark louder than any dog I know, and you can scratch yourself more vigorously."

But Loony meant to come with him. He kept so close to Great-uncle's ankles all the way to the gate that he almost tripped him up. "Home!" said Great-uncle sternly. "HOME."

"Woof," said Loony, and sat down expectantly, exactly as if Great-uncle had said "Bone," not "Home." The old man tried to open the gate quickly and slip out without Loony—but Loony was up to that game. He was out in the road with Great-uncle at once, dancing round him maddeningly.

The old man lost his temper. "Snubby!" he yelled. "Call this dog of yours. CALL HIM, I say. Do you hear me, boy?"

A woman opposite came over to Great-uncle. "I'm so sorry," she said, "but may I ask you not to shout and not
221

to let your dog bark so much? Your shouting and his barking have kept my baby awake half the morning."

Great-uncle was really exasperated. He walked off down the road, thumping the pavement with his stick.

"*I* kept her baby awake. What rubbish! And calling Loony *my* dog! I wouldn't own him for a hundred pounds."

But it certainly looked as if he did, because Loony kept faithfully with him during the whole of the walk, occasionally half-disappearing down a rabbit-hole, but always coming back. Poor Great-uncle.

He bought himself a paper and came back, reading it as he walked. He suddenly stood still and gave an exclamation. Loony sat down beside him and looked at him. What was this old gentleman up to now? Loony hadn't any use for him really, except to snatch a walk with him now and again.

"Look at that!" said Great-uncle. "Another robbery—same kind of thing—and same way of going about it. Locked doors again! Extraordinary!"

He showed the report of the new theft to Mrs. Lynton when he got back. The children crowded round in interest.

"See?" said Great-uncle, pointing to the paragraphs with a beautifully clean and polished nail. "Another robbery. Rare and valuable papers again. And not a trace of the thieves. Doors locked and windows bolted. And yet the things are gone. There's something queer about all this."

"Green Hands," whispered Roger mischievously behind him. Great-uncle turned sharply, but Roger's face was innocent.

"Can I borrow the paper, please?" asked Diana. "Thanks awfully."

She took it to the summer-house and the three of them pored over it. Diana looked rather pleased with herself.

"I've discovered something," she announced to the others. "Have you?"

Roger considered. "No. What?" he asked.

"Well, you know the first paper we saw, the one Great-uncle brought with him and let us read?" said Diana. "Do you remember the bit about the Fair?"

"Yes. What about it?" said Roger. "There's nothing about a Fair in this paper."

"I know. I've looked," said Diana. "But did you notice what the first paper said about the Fair—where it was going to next? It said it was going to *Pilbury*. Pilbury. Does that ring a bell?"

"Gosh, yes," said Roger at once. "*This* theft is at Pilbury. I see what you're getting at. Either the Fair goes to places where there are rare papers to be stolen—or somebody in the Fair makes inquiries at each place they go to, to see if there are any in the neighbourhood worth stealing."

"That's what I meant," said Diana. "Let's find out if the Fair was actually at Pilbury when the papers disappeared, shall we?"

"Yes. Though I must say we're rather jumping to conclusions," said Roger. "It's probably sheer coincidence."

"I bet it is!" said Snubby. "Just like Diana to think she's spotted something clever!"

Diana gave him a push. "Get out of the summer-house if you're going to talk like that. Go on! If you're not interested, you needn't be."

"I *am* interested," protested Snubby. "And don't shove me like that. If you want a shoving match you know who'll win. You won't anyway. And all I said was . . ."

"If you say it again, out you go," said Diana, getting angry. "I'm tired of you to-day, Snubby. You've hidden my gloves, I know you have, and you left my bedroom door open so that Loony could take my mats again. And *now* just look at Loony. He's got somebody's brush again. It's Great-uncle's hairbrush this time."

Snubby ran to get the brush away from Loony, who at once regarded this as a wonderful game and danced away down the garden, flinging the brush up into the air and catching it in his mouth.

Diana turned to Roger. "Roger, there mayn't be any-

223

thing in my idea at all. Let's find out first whether the Fair *is* at Pilbury. And then let's try and find out where it's going to next—and see if a theft of rare papers is reported from there too."

"It's quite an idea, Di," said Roger. "We'll bike over this afternoon—it's not more than ten miles away. We'll leave Snubby behind. I'm getting tired of him."

So they said nothing of their plans to Snubby, but got out their bicycles without his seeing and had a look to see if the tyres were all right. Yes, they were.

They set off after lunch, creeping off whilst Snubby was arguing with their mother about some missing shoes which she was perfectly certain Loony knew something about. They mounted their bicycles and rode gleefully off down the road. "Sucks to Snubby!" said Roger. "Won't he be wild? He'll hunt all over the place for us!"

It was a long way to Pilbury, farther than they thought, but they got there at last. They rode all through it but could see no Fair. Diana felt a little dampened.

"We'll ask someone," said Roger, and he got off his bicycle. He called to a small boy nearby.

"Hey, Sonny! Is there a Fair in Pilbury, do you know?"

"There *was*!" called back the boy. "But it's gone. Went yesterday—to Ricklesham, I heard."

"Thanks!" said Roger, and beamed at Diana. "Well, it *was* here—and now it's at Ricklesham. We'll just see if there's a robbery there next. Then we'll KNOW your idea's got something in it. I say—this is rather exciting, isn't it!"

CHAPTER 6

SNUBBY SAYS SOMETHING SILLY

SNUBBY was most annoyed with the other two when they came back. "Where have you been? You beasts, you've been for a bike ride and didn't tell me!"

"Well, you were so jolly unbelieving in the summer-house we thought we'd go off alone," said Diana. "Sucks to you, Snubby!"

"Whatever's the matter with Loony?" asked Roger, staring at the spaniel in surprise. "Why is he looking so dismal? He didn't even come rushing to meet us."

"He's in trouble," said Snubby. "So's Sardine. They chased your mother's ball of wool all round the lounge and didn't have the sense to see it was joined to a jersey she's knitting. They undid the ball for about a mile of wool, rolled it out to the kitchen, and almost into the pond. Aunt Susan's awfully cross. She smacked poor old Loony so hard that he went under the sofa for half an hour, and she tried to smack Sardine but she escaped."

"Just like a cat!" said Roger. "Poor old Loony."

"You go and eat up Sardine's dinner," said Diana encouragingly to Loony.

"He wouldn't touch sardines if he were starving," said Snubby. "Where have you been, you two?"

They told him. "So you see, the Fair's gone to Rickles-ham now," said Roger. "And now we'll just wait and see if any burglary occurs there."

"I wish we could hear from Barney," said Diana. "He

might know some of the people in the Fair. He's been all over the country now in fairs and circuses and shows."

"I'd like to *see* old Barney again—and dear little Miranda," said Snubby, who had a very soft spot for the small monkey belonging to Barney. "Is it any good writing to Barney's last address?"

"We did that," said Roger. "No answer came at all. We'll have to wait till he writes to us himself."

A strange dog ventured into the garden. It went out again at top speed as Loony hurled himself at it, yelping madly. "He's feeling better now," said Snubby, looking at Loony. "His tail's got a wag again."

Loony disappeared into the house, his little tail wagging. He came out again with the brush from the sitting-room fireplace.

"Look at that!" said Roger, exasperated. "I'm always carrying brushes about now—putting them back in their places. Loony, your dippy."

He and Diana went in with the brush. Snubby went off to the summer-house with a book. But Great-uncle was there, smoking his pipe.

"Oh, sorry, sir," said Snubby, and began hastily to retreat.

"Quite all right, my boy. Come along in," said Great-uncle. "There's plenty of room for two. I want to talk to you."

Snubby never liked to hear that a grownup wanted to talk to him. It usually meant a ticking-off of some sort. He sat down with a sigh.

"About this gang of yours," said Great-uncle in his rather pompous voice. "This—er—Green Hands Gang— wasn't that what you called it? Have you heard anything more about them? Or was it possibly a little make-up of yours?"

Snubby considered. He didn't really want to give up his lovely idea of a Green Hands Gang that wore green gloves. On the other hand, it wouldn't do to work up Great-uncle about it, because he might be foolish enough to say something to Uncle Richard. Then the fat would be in the fire. Uncle Richard wouldn't see that a silly pretend didn't matter. He would call it a lie, and treat it as such. And Snubby wouldn't be let off lightly.

"I think the gang have lost track of me," said Snubby at last, deciding that would be the safest thing to say. "I haven't heard a word from them since I've been here," he added truthfully.

"Really?" said Great-uncle, eyeing Snubby in a way he didn't much like. "Er—perhaps you think the gang have bigger fish to fry? Other things that are more important than you?"

Snubby blinked. Was Great-uncle getting at him. A sudden thought flashed into his mind and was out in words before he could stop it.

"Yes, I think you're right, sir—and I think you'll hear of their actitivies next at Ricklesham!"

"Ricklesham!" said Great-uncle, surprised. "Why Ricklesham?"

Snubby now wished he hadn't spoken so quickly. He fidgeted uncomfortably on the wooden seat.

"Don't know, sir. Just a hunch. You see, if you knew that gang as well as I do, you'd sort of know where they were going to—to—operate next."

"Bless us all!" said Great-uncle, staring at Snubby. "I don't know what to make of you. Talking of gangs and how they operate—and looking just a dirty, untidy boy with the most disgusting fingernails I ever saw."

That was a nasty jab. Snubby took a hurried look at his nails. Everybody was always worrying him about them. Why couldn't they mind their own business? He didn't sneer at their clean nails—why should they sneer at his dirty ones? He got up.

"I'll go and clean my nails, sir," he said, pleased at having thought of such a good excuse to get away before Great-uncle asked more searching questions about the gang!

"A very good idea," said Great-uncle. "And while

you're about it, wash behind your ears and see if you can possibly reach the back of your neck."

Snubby fled. Nasty sarcastic old man! Snubby brushed his nails hard with the nail-brush and thought darkly that it would be rather nice to have a real gang to frighten people like Great-uncle.

Diana called to him from her room. "Snubby, is that you? Come here a minute."

He went into Diana's room. She and Roger were sitting on her bed with a map spread out between them.

"Whats' that?" asked Snubby.

"It's a map with Ricklesham on it," said Diana. "We thought we might as well see exactly where it is in case we want to go over to the Fair. It's about six miles off. We'll take you with us next time if you behave yourself."

"Gosh—look at Snubby's nails! He's cleaned them!" said Roger, astonished. "You turning over a new leaf, Snubby?"

"Shut up," said Snubby, feeling quite ashamed of his spotless nails. "Great-uncle's been on at me about them. I say—I said rather a silly thing to him."

"Well, that's nothing new," said Roger. "What did you say this time?"

"He began asking me in a sneering sort of voice about the Green Hands Gang," said Snubby. "And when I said I hadn't heard a word from them, he said in a horrid scornful voice, 'I suppose they've got bigger fish to fry!' And I said yes—they might be operating next at Ricklesham."

There was a moment's silence. Diana and Roger stared at Snubby in dismay.

"Well! You're a bigger idiot than I thought you were," said Roger at last. "Suppose there *is* a robbery at Ricklesham, what's Great-uncle going to think? That it *is* your silly Green Hands Gang, and you *are* mixed up in it. And he'll most certainly split on you and tell Dad."

"I know," said poor Snubby, looking very downcast. "I thought of all that afterwards."

"You're crazy," said Diana. "Here we are on the track

of something exciting—and you go and blab about it to Great-uncle, and mix it up with your idiotic fairy tale."

"Perhaps there won't be a burglary at Ricklesham," suggested Snubby hopefully. But that didn't find favour with the others either.

"That's right. Pour cold water on our ideas now," said Diana. "Tell us we're wrong. Make out it's silly to . . ."

"I'm not, Diana, I'm not!" cried poor Snubby, feeling that whatever he said would be wrong. "I'll believe anything you tell me, really I will."

"Shall we let him go with us if we go to Ricklesham, or not?" said Roger grimly to Diana.

"We'll see," said Diana. "Any more fat-headedness on his part, and we don't tell him a thing."

Snubby departed to find Loony, feeling very subdued. He fell over on the stairs, and Roger and Diana heard him rolling down, yelling.

They grinned. "That's Sardine again," said Diana. "She always lies in wait for Snubby on the stairs."

"Do you really think there'll be a burglary at Ricklesham?" asked Roger, folding up the map.

"Well—not really," said Diana. "I did feel it was a sort of hunch, you know—but it's a bit far-fetched, actually, isn't it? I don't suppose anything will happen there at all."

"We'll watch the papers," said Roger. "And what a thrill it will be if we see Ricklesham in the news!"

CHAPTER 7

SNUBBY IN DIFFICULTIES

THREE or four days went by. Each morning the three children took the paper after the grown-ups had finished with it, and pored over it.

But Ricklesham was never in the news. It was most disappointing. And then suddenly it was!

Mr. Lynton was glancing down the paper one morning, when something caught his eye. He read it quickly and then spoke to Great-uncle Robert.

"Uncle," he said, "here's a bit of news for you. Didn't you have something to do with the arranging of some old seventeenth-century letters or documents—I've forgotten what they were—for the Forbes-King Collection?"

"Yes. Yes, I did," said Great-uncle. "A very fine collection that was—most interesting old letters. Why, what does it say about them?"

"They've been stolen!" said Mr. Lynton, and the three children sat up at once in excitement.

"*Stolen!*" echoed Great-uncle. "No—have they really? Where from?"

"They were on loan to a Mr. Curtice-Knowles at Ricklesham House," said Mr. Lynton. Diana gave an exclamation. Roger kicked her under the table. Snubby looked anxiously at Great-uncle.

"Ricklesham House! *Ricklesham*, did you say?" said Great-uncle in a faint voice. "Good heavens! *Ricklesham!*"

He looked at Snubby. Snubby had said that the Green Hands Gang might operate at Ricklesham next—and lo and behold, what it had done but steal valuable old documents there? Great-uncle did some rapid thinking. Then that meant—yes, it must mean—that the Green Hands Gang that Snubby was afraid of was the same one that was mixed up with the continual theft of precious documents!

"It must have been that very gang that came into Chelie Manor House when I was there, and stole all those papers," thought Great-uncle Robert. "Fancy that boy being mixed up with them. Most extraordinary. I'll have to have a long talk with him about all this. Really, the police should be told."

Snubby wouldn't look at Great-uncle. He was terrified that he would suddenly ask him awkward questions. Fortunately Mrs. Lynton plunged into the matter, and asked several questions.

"But, Richard! Do you think that it's the same thieves who went to Chelie Manor House when Uncle Robert was there? Does it say anything about locked doors? Did the thieves go through fastened windows and locked doors again?"

"Yes. Apparently it is just as mysterious a theft as the others," said her husband. "There is a small room set apart at Ricklesham House for these old and rare papers, and they are displayed under glass cases. The door to this room was locked, of course. The windows are not only safely fastened, but also barred, so the paper says."

"And yet the things were stolen!" said Mrs. Lynton. "Well, it certainly sounds very mysterious. The police must be very puzzled."

Great-uncle took the paper and read the report very carefully. There was no mention of a Green Hands Gang. How on earth did Snubby know that there was going to be a crime committed at Ricklesham? He lifted his head to have another look at Snubby. But Snubby had gone.

He had mentioned to his aunt in a low voice that he didn't want any more breakfast. Could he go please?

"Don't you feel well, dear?" began Mrs. Lynton, but seeing that Snubby's cheeks were the same fiery red as usual, she felt there was nothing serious wrong. So she nodded, and Snubby slipped away, thankful that Great-uncle was buried in the paper.

There was an excited meeting in the summer-house that morning. Snubby, Diana and Roger rushed there as soon as their jobs were done. Loony rushed too, sensing the excitement.

"Roger—Great-uncle kept on and on looking at me at breakfast-time," said Snubby, as soon as they were safely in the wooden house. "I know he's going to ask me awkward questions. I don't want to meet him at all. Say you don't know where I am, if he asks you."

"Well, we can't tell a lie, if we *do* know where you are," said Diana. "But we'll do our best not to give you away. It serves you right for talking too much. Now, of course, Great-uncle will believe in your silly Green Hands Gang all over again, because of this upset at Ricklesham."

"I know," groaned Snubby. "Loony, go and sit outside on guard. *On guard*, do you hear? And you jolly well know what that means. Bark if you see anyone coming!"

Loony thumped his little tail on the ground, as he sat himself down in the sunshine. He knew what "On guard" meant all right. Of course he did. He barked loudly at once, and Snubby, in a great flurry, squeezed himself under the seat in the summer-house, while Diana and Roger sat just above, their legs hiding him.

But it was only Sardine arriving. She had seen Loony and wanted to have a game. So she came walking up the path, waving her tail in the air as usual, black and sleek and purring.

Loony knew now that her purr meant "Pax! Don't chase me!" just as she knew that when he wagged his tail, it meant the same.

Still, he had to bark, as he was on guard, and Sardine paused in surprise. She sat down a good way from Loony and began to wash herself. Loony could never imagine

232

why cats washed themselves so much. They were always doing it.

"It's all right, Snubby—it's only Sardine," said Diana, peering out of the summer-house. "Shut up, Loony. You're on guard for people, not cats! Shush!"

Loony stopped barking. Sardine strolled right up to him, purring very loudly. He wagged his stump of a tail. Sardine lay down, stretched herself out on the path and patted his nose with her paw. Loony gave the tiniest bark. It meant "Sorry, I can't play now, but I'm on guard."

So Sardine went to sleep, leaving a crack of one eye open, just in case. Loony also settled down, shutting both his eyes, but listening with his long, droopy ears.

Snubby came out from under the seat, draped with cobwebs and powdered with dust. "That idiot of a Loony," he grumbled. "Look at me—I'm in a frightful mess!"

"I can't see that you look much worse than usual," said Diana, looking at him. "Come on, sit down again. We really have got something to discuss."

They talked and talked about the affair. They had all read the bit in the paper now. They knew that once again valuable letters had been stolen, and that once again the thief had apparently passed through locked doors or barred windows.

And, more important still, they knew that once again the Fair had been in the same district as the burglary. That couldn't be sheer coincidence—it couldn't be chance. The Fair—or somebody *in* the Fair—must be connected with these strange thefts. And that somebody must be clever enough to know about rare documents, where they were, and how to get them.

"The two things don't seem to go together, somehow," said Roger thoughtfully. "I mean—you don't associate show people with a knowledge of that kind of thing. You have to be a person like—well, like Uncle Robert—to know about historical documents. You have to have a lot of specialised learning."

"You mean, you have to be an antiquarian," said Diana,

233

showing off a little. "That's what people of that kind are called. Uncle Robert told me."

"Gosh—I always thought an anti—anti-whatever-you-said, was somebody who was against keeping aquariums," said Snubby, surprised.

Roger laughed. "You would! Anyway, it's not anti-aquarium, idiot, it's antiquarian."

"Sounds just the same to me," said Snubby. "I say—are we going to Ricklesham? Do say we are!"

Roger looked at Diana, and they both nodded solemnly.

"Yes," said Roger. "We'll go to the Fair, and we'll snoop round and see if we can find out anyone there who's an antiquarian. Then we might be on the track!"

"That's an awfully good idea," said Snubby. "We can put the police on to him at once."

"It won't be as easy as that!" said Diana scornfully. "We . . ."

Loony set up a tremendous barking again. Snubby dived beneath the wooden seat once more, and Roger and Diana sat close to hide him.

"It's Great-uncle this time all right," said Roger. "Keep still, Snubby. We'll do our best for you."

Great-uncle came to the entrance of the summer-house. He looked in.

"Ah," he said. "I thought I should find you here. I want to talk to Snubby."

"We'll tell him, Great-uncle," said Roger politely.

"Your mother said he was here," said Great-uncle.

"Did she?" said Diana. "Is she busy, Great-uncle? Does she want me yet?"

("That was a quick change of subject!" thought Snubby admiringly from behind her legs.)

"No. She didn't say she wanted any of you," said Great-uncle. "Do you know where Snubby is?"

"He's not far off," said Roger truthfully. "Loony's never very far from him, you know."

Loony wagged his tail at his name. He was most aston-ished to see Snubby under the seat, and would have liked

234

to go to him, but every time he went near either Roger or Diana pushed him off with a determined foot.

"Do you think he'd hear me if I called him?" asked Great-uncle. "I really do want to speak to him. It's important."

"You could try shouting," said Diana.

Great-uncle shouted, "Snubby! SNUBBY! I want you! SNUBBY!"

There was no answer, of course, except that Loony barked, and Sardine fled up to the wall.

"Do you think he heard me?" said Great-uncle.

"Er—if he's near enough, he would certainly hear you," said Roger cautiously. "Never mind, Great-uncle. I'll tell him you want him next time I speak to him."

Great-uncle called again, feeling somehow certain that Snubby was not very far away, otherwise why was Loony there?

"SNUBBY! I WANT YOU!"

"Great-uncle! That woman with her baby in the house opposite is looking out of the window," said Diana. "I hope her baby isn't asleep."

"Bless us all! I forgot the baby," said Great-uncle. "The mother will be after me again. Well, you tell Snubby I've been looking for him, will you?"

He went off down the path, and Roger and Diana heaved sighs of relief. "You can come out now, Snubby," said Roger. "He's gone."

Snubby came out, dirtier than ever. "You did jolly well," he said admiringly. "Never told a lie at all, and didn't give me away either. Thanks awfully."

"I don't know how you're going to manage to avoid Great-uncle all day long," said Diana. "It'll be difficult!"

"It won't," said Snubby, beaming. "Let's bike over to Ricklesham for the day—take our lunch and everything."

"Right! That's a fine idea," said Roger. "I'll go and ask Mother now. Come on, Di. Stay here, Snubby, and we'll fetch you when we're ready. So long!"

CHAPTER 8

OFF TO THE FAIR

MRS. LYNTON thought it would be a very good idea for the three to go off for a picnic. It would be a change to have a nice quiet house for once. Uncle Robert would like it too.

"Where's Snubby," she said. "Your Great-uncle has been calling all over the place for him. Has he got into trouble with him?"

"I don't think so," said Roger. "Mother, I suppose we couldn't have hard-boiled eggs, could we, and tomato sandwiches? And I suppose there aren't any jam tarts left over from yesterday, are there?"

"You're doing quite a lot of supposing," said his mother. "Suppose you go and ask Cook what she's got? She happens to be pleased with you because you took the trouble to fetch the fish for her yesterday, so I've no doubt she will look favourably on all your supposing."

Cook did. She willingly did them hard-boiled eggs, put salt and pepper into a screw of paper, made tomato and lettuce sandwiches by the dozen, added plain bread and butter for the eggs, nine jam tarts and enormous slices of ginger cake.

"Oooh I say! Can you really spare us some of that?" said Roger. "You only made it yesterday. It's chockful of bits of ginger and some chopped up cherries. It's a heavenly cake."

Great-uncle appeared in the doorway. "Oh! I thought I heard you here. Have you seen Snubby?"

Roger turned to Cook. "Have *you* seen Snubby?" he asked innocently.

Cook shook her head. "Hasn't been near the kitchen this morning," she said. "And *that's* unusual. I never did see a boy that came snooping round for titbits so often. No, nor a dog either."

"It's funny I can't find him," said Great-uncle irritably. "He's always about when he's not wanted, and never here when he is. Now I've got someone coming to see me in a few minutes."

He went. Diana winked at Roger. "Did you hear that? He's got someone coming to see him—so we'll just be able to slip off nicely with Snubby. Let's get some bottles of ginger beer to take with us and we'll be ready."

In five minutes' time they were ready. The lunch was packed into two neat parcels. Roger and Diana carried the food and drink to the bicycle shed. "I'll just pop round to the study and see if Great-uncle's got his visitor yet," said Roger. He came back immediately.

"Yes, he has. Come on, get the bikes. I'll wheel Snubby's. Hurry!"

They hurried. They put the lunch into the baskets, and strapped a big oblong box on to Snubby's back mudguard. They put a small rug inside. That was for Loony if he got tired of running beside them. He was very good at sitting in the box and going along like that.

They wheeled the bikes to the summer-house. Loony ran to meet them in delight, barking madly. Bikes meant a long, long run! No time for rabbit-holes alas—but still a lovely long run.

Snubby peered out. He could hear them ringing their bicycle bells to tell him he was safe.

"Got everything? Oh *good!*" he said. "Where's Great-uncle?"

"He's seeing somebody," said Diana. "We've got the lunch basket and some ginger beer. We've strapped on Loony's carrier too. Let's go while the going's good."

So they went. They cycled down the path and round by

the window. Great-uncle saw them, and stared after Snubby in exasperation.

"There he is! I thought he'd turn up just when I couldn't see him!"

Loony ran along by Snubby's bicycle, his red tongue hanging out, feeling very happy indeed. He knew the children would not go too fast for him. If he got tired Snubby would be the first to notice and stop. Then he would be lifted into the carrier box, and be taken along like a lord in a carriage. How Loony looked down his long black nose at other dogs then!

"We'll picnic at the Fair or near it," said Roger. "We shall have plenty of time to look at everyone then, if we're sitting down in the Fair field."

"Got any money?" said Snubby, jingling his in his pocket. "I like a Fair. I shall go on the roundabout and on the swings and have a go at hoopla. I threw a ring over a super toreh last time."

"I've got plenty of holiday money left," said Roger. "So has Diana. More than I have. We'll be all right."

"We'll buy some ice-creams too," said Diana. "You'll have to remember not to take Loony on the roundabout, Snubby. He was awfully sick last time."

"Yes. He wasted a perfectly good dinner," said Snubby. "Didn't you, Loony? Are we going too fast?"

Loony was too out of breath to answer with a bark. He didn't look tired. He loped along on his silky black legs, his long ears flap-flap-flapping as he went.

They stopped and put him into the carrier-box after about three miles. That was as much as he could do at a run. He sat in the box panting, his tongue hanging out looking as long as his ears!

"Now, hold tight, Loony," said Snubby, getting on again. "Here we go!"

Loony kept his balance perfectly, and enjoyed his ride enormously. Snubby didn't enjoy it quite so much because Loony was rather heavy! Still, it was better than leaving him behind.

They came to Ricklesham at last. They had a look at the house from which the valuable papers had been stolen. There was a policeman on guard at the gate. That impressed the three children very much. They got off their bicycles and looked in at the big gateway.

"No one allowed in without a pass," said the policeman. "Not even a dog!"

The children grinned. "Do they know who the thief was yet?" asked Roger.

"Not a clue," said the policeman. "You on the job too?"

The children laughed and rode off. "He little knew we *were* on the job, more or less!" said Diana. "Now let's ask where the Fair is."

They asked a woman. "Over in Longlands Field the other side of the wood," she said, pointing.

They thanked her and rode off, Loony in the carrier again because of the traffic. They skirted the wood and came to open country. At the edge of it, in a big field, was the Fair.

"Here we are!" said Roger, coming to a standstill, and leaning against the fence on his bicycle. "Looks pretty good to me. Quite a big Fair."

There were round and oblong tents with flags flying. There were caravans of all colours and shapes round the field. There were horses grazing nearby, and at the far end, tied to a tree, were two enormous elephants.

The roundabout was not going. It stood there, gay but silent, set all round with wooden animals and birds, lions, tigers, giraffes, swans, cats, dogs, bears and what looked like a chimpanzee. Swingboats were there too, but no one was using them.

"It's dinner-time, I expect," said Roger, looking at his watch. "Yes. It's a quarter to one. I expect everything will be going strong this afternoon."

"There's a shooting range over there," said Snubby. "I'll have a shot afterwards. I was pretty good last time I shot at a Fair."

"Well, tell me when you're going to shoot and I'll get a

mile away," said Diana. "I say—what a big Fair this is—
heaps of stalls and tents and things. And there's nobody
that looks in the least like an anti . . ."

"Shut up," said Roger. "Hedges and fences have ears as
much as walls. Come on—let's go through the gate and ask
if we can picnic in the field. We'll say we're going to spend
money at the Fair afterwards."

They went through the gate, and a shock-headed boy
shouted to them. "Hey, you—you're not allowed in till two
o'clock."

"We're coming to the Fair all afternoon," called back
Roger. "We only want to have our picnic here now. Do
you mind?"

"Okay," shouted the boy. He was a strange-looking fellow, with his shock of yellow hair, ears that stuck out at
each side of his head, and very wide grin. He was small
too, smaller than Snubby, and yet he looked about fifteen.

"Wonder what *he* does in the Fair," said Roger getting
the lunch packet out of his bicycle basket. "Di, you've got
the drinks. Loony's biscuits are in *your* basket, Snubby.
Better keep him by us, or he'll be eaten up by that pack of
mongrels over there."

Loony had no intention of wandering away if there was
any lunch going. Nor did he like the look of the lean,
hungry-looking dogs that were sitting down at a distance,
watching. He growled at them just to tell them who he
was.

It was a lovely picnic. The hard-boiled eggs went down
well, and so did the sandwiches. Loony got one or two,
but not many, because the children were so terribly hungry.
He got no jam tart or cake, but managed to beg two pieces
of bread and butter from Diana.

"What's the time? Is it two o'clock yet?" said Snubby.
"I can see some people wandering along up to the gate. I
expect the roundabout will start going soon."

The Fair people were on the move too. Some shutters
were being taken down from the stalls. A man went over
to the swing-boats and idly swung one. The shock-headed

boy went to the shooting-range and handled a few guns, whistling shrilly.

An elephant trumpeted and made Loony jump. People came out of caravans, and hastened to various tents. The Fair was opening!

The children cleared up the litter. Even Snubby was good about that. Never a scrap of paper was left lying about the grass when they had finished any picnic. Loony snuffled about for crumbs.

"Look—what's that coming along?" said Diana suddenly. "Golly—it's a *monkey*, isn't it—all dressed up. Oh, how sweet. She's coming over here to us. She's rather like Miranda, isn't she?"

The little creature came right up to them and took a flying leap to Snubby's shoulder. She whispered excitedly in his ear, and pulled his hair. The others watched intently.

"Roger—Roger, it *is* Miranda, I know it is!" cried Diana suddenly. And when she heard her name the tiny creature bounded up on to Diana's shoulder and put her little paw down the girl's neck—just as Miranda always used to do!

"Well, if Miranda's here, Barney is too!" cried Snubby. "Come on—let's look for him. Fancy that—*Barney*!"

CHAPTER 9

GOOD OLD BARNEY AGAIN!

THEY passed the shooting-range, where the shock-headed boy was still polishing the guns and whistling.

"Is there a boy in the Fair called Barney?" asked Roger.

"Yep. That monkey's his," said the boy, with his wide grin. "Lovaduck! Fancy Miranda going to you like that—fussing you up good and proper, isn't she?"

"Barney *is* here!" said Diana joyfully, and the three

smiled at one another. "What a bit of luck—and what a surprise too!"

Loony was jumping up, trying to reach Miranda. He knew her all right! She suddenly dropped down on his back, and rode him like a little horse, as she used to do. But he knew how to deal with that! He promptly rolled over and off she went.

She bounded chattering on to Snubby's shoulder. She was dressed in a tiny red skirt and a little blue coat with silver buttons down it. She looked too amusing for words.

"Dear little Miranda!" said Roger, patting the tiny monkey paw. "You saw us first, didn't you—you recognised us all right and came along straightaway!"

"You'll find Barney up by the Hoopla Stall!" called the shock-headed boy. "He runs it."

They hurried to the stall he was pointing at. A boy stood there with his back to them, arranging the goods neatly on the round stall, so that people might throw hoops at them, and try to ring a prize.

"That's Barney!" cried Diana. As he heard his name the boy swung round—and sure enough, it *was* Barney— Barney with his corn-coloured hair, his brown-as-a-berry face, his strange blue eyes set so far apart—and his wide, engaging grin.

"Well, *here's* a go!" he cried in amazement. "You kids —all three of you. Hiya, Roger, Diana! Hiya, Snubby and Loony. Still the same mad dog, I see!"

Loony, of course, had recognised Barney immediately and had hurled himself at him in his usual lunatic way, barking and whining, licking and nuzzling, doing all he could to tell Barney how pleased he was to see his friend once more.

Miranda leapt to Barney's shoulder, chattering excitedly.

"Miranda found us first," said Diana. "She came over the field to us. We didn't recognise her at first because she's wearing clothes now and she didn't before. Oh, isn't she sweet, Barney?"

"It's grand to see you, *grand*," said Barney, his blue

eyes brilliant with pleasure. "I've been thinking of you a lot—wanting to see you all again. What are you doing here? You didn't know I was here, did you?"

"No, of course not," said Roger. "We came over for a certain reason—we'll tell you about it some time when we're alone—and we never really hoped to see *you*, of course! "

"You might have told us you were so near us, Barney," said Diana reproachfully. "We only live a few miles away, you know."

"Is that so?" said Barney, surprised. His geography was not at all good. He never had much idea where he was, as he wandered round. "Well, to think of that! I'm not much good at writing letters, anyway. Still, you're here. You on holiday or something?"

"Yes. We're home for the Easter hols," said Snubby. "We've got about three more weeks, Barney. How long are you going to be here?"

"We're here a week," said Barney. "Excuse for a bit— I've got to get this show going. I'm in charge of the hoopla, you know. It's not my own stall, of course. I run it for the owner. You watch Miranda, and see what she does! She's a scream! "

He handed out some rings and received money in return. The customer stood by the bar that separated her from the stall, and took aim with a wooden ring.

"Got your eye on the alarm clock, Miss?" called Barney. "Now then, steady does it! "

The ring bounced on the stall, touched the clock and lay still, half on the clock, half off. The woman tried again and yet again, using her last ring.

"Hard luck, Miss," said Barney sympathetically. "You nearly did it. Miranda, get busy! "

And Miranda got busy! She leapt to the stall, gathered up the rings deftly in her tiny paws, and handed them back to Barney. The children laughed in delight.

"Oh, Barney! Isn't she clever! "

"You watch her now," said Barney, as more people came up to the stall. "Go on, Miranda, do your job."

Miranda looked at him inquiringly. She made a little chattering noise and picked up a dozen or two of the wooden hoopla rings. She slipped them over her left arm. She held out her paw for the pennies the people presented, and gave each one three rings!

The customers were amused and delighted. They called their children to watch Miranda, and soon there was a great crowd round the hoopla stand.

"She can't count more than three," said Barney, "so it's lucky we only have to give out three rings! Anyway, if she makes a mistake and gives two, the customer always points it out to her!"

"She really is wonderful," said Diana. "Barney, you must do awfully well at this stall with Miranda to attract attention like this."

"We do," said Barney. "I've made more money at the stall than anyone else ever has. I don't get the money, of course. I give it to Tonnerre, who owns the Fair, and takes it about."

"Tonnerre! What a queer name!" said Diana. "Is he French?"

"Yes, he is," said Barney, looking surprised. "How do you know?"

"Well, 'tonnerre' is French for thunder," explained Diana.

"Is it really?" said Barney. "Well, I never knew he had such a good name. It suits him fine!"

"Why?" asked Snubby, watching Miranda giving out rings again, and taking the money to give to Barney.

"Well, he's got a thunderous voice, and he's enormous, and he stamps about all the time," said Barney. "He's got a fearful temper, and he's an old miser—under-pays everyone and kicks them out if they don't do well enough for him. There he is, over there, look—the elephants are his."

The children looked where Barney pointed. They saw

245

the two elephants having their ropes undone from the tree, in order to take children for rides. The man with them was a giant-like fellow, with legs like tree-trunks, enormous feet, and great shoulders. He was shouting at the patient elephants, and his voice carried right over the field.

"It sounds as if somebody's turned the wireless on as full as as can be!" said Roger with a grin. "What a voice! Tonnerre is a good name for him. He looks as black as thunder too."

"He always does," said Barney. "He's not a pleasant fellow to work with. There are about twenty people who go with the Fair wherever it goes—the rest of them join it here and there, leave it, others come in their place, and so it goes on. I've been with it about four months—we've been all over the place."

"I don't like the sound of Mister Thunder," said Diana. "Is there a Mrs. Lightning, by any chance?"

Barney laughed his uproarious laugh, that made everyone want to laugh with him.

"No. He's not married. If anyone could be called Mrs. Lightning, it's old Ma over there—by that caravan, see? My word, her tongue's sharp as a knife. If she flashes out at anyone, they just shrivel up. Even Tonnerre goes off hurriedly if she begins to scold him!"

Ma was a peculiar-looking old woman. She looked more like a witch than anything else, as she stood stirring something in a big iron pot over a fire just outside her caravan. She had a shock of perfectly white hair, brown monkey eyes, and a chin and nose that almost met. She stood over her pot, muttering.

"I'm sure she's making a spell of some kind!" said Diana with a giggle.

"There's plenty of us show-folk that think the same," said Barney. "I don't. But lots do. They're scared stiff of Old Ma. There's only one person can do anything with her, and that's Young 'Un. He's the kid in charge of the shooting-range, see—over there!"

"Oh—the shock-headed boy," said Snubby. "Yes, we've

246

seen him. He's a bit like a hobgoblin, with ears sticking right out of his head—a nice hobgoblin, though. He got hair just like Ma's, only a different colour, of course—it sticks up straight like hers."

"She's his grandma," said Barney. "He gets round the old lady all right. But nobody else does. Don't you go near her—she'll fly at you like a cat!"

"Could we see the two chimpanzees?" asked Diana. "We saw them advertised in a paper. They were called Hurly and Burly."

"Oh yes—they belong to Mr. Vosta," said Barney. "You'll like him. Full of fun, and will do anything for you—too much sometimes. Can't say no to anyone! He's been with the Fair for years, and slaves for Tonnerre day and night. I can't understand it myself. *I* shan't stay with this Fair for long being kicked around by that bad-tempered Tonnerre!"

The Fair sounded a fascinating place, with its loud-voiced Tonnerre, its sharp-tongued Old Ma, the shock-headed Young 'Un, Vosta and his chimpanzees—and Barney and Miranda, of course. The three children stood by the hoopla stall and looked round the Fair eagerly, wondering which of all these people would be the most likely to be the thief who could get through locked doors and fastened windows.

They hadn't told Barney about that yet. There hadn't been a chance, with customers coming and going. It would be best not to say anything till they were quite alone with him.

"You go on round the Fair and have a look-see for yourselves," said Barney. "I *could* leave Miranda here to look after the stall—she's as good at it as I am—but if Tonnerre sees I'm gone he'll yell the place down."

"Right, we'll come back later. My word, it *was* a fine surprise to see you, Barney! Best surprise we've had these hols!"

CHAPTER 10

AN INTERESTING AFTERNOON

THEY went round the Fair, looking at everything and trying everything too. They went on the roundabouts and on
the swings, they rode on the elephants and they paid to go
in and see the wonderful chimpanzees. They didn't miss
a thing!

"Make the roundabout go as fast as you can," Snubby
asked the boy in charge of it.

"Hold on tight then," said the boy with a grin. "What
about your dog?"

"No. He's sick if he goes on," said Snubby. "He'll sit
by you and wait. Sit, Loony, sit! "

He chose the chimpanzee, and the others chose lions.
The wooden animals went up and down as well as round
and round. The music began to play, and the roundabout
moved off.

The boy kept his word and ran the machinery as fast as
it would go. The children had to cling tightly to the animals or they would have been thrown off. Diana began to
feel sick. The other three riders began to yell at the boy.

He slowed down and grinned again. "That all right for
you?" he asked Snubby, who was now looking slightly
green, and found that he couldn't walk straight. Nor could
the others.

"It was wizard," said Snubby. "Faster than I've ever
been. It was worth double fare! "

Not only the roundabout had gone fast, but the music

too—and Tonnerre had heard it, of course. His face went purple, and he yelled at the roundabout boy. But the music was so loud that the boy didn't hear the yells. It was only when the roundabout had stopped, and Tonnerre had parked his elephants for a minute, shouting all the while, that the poor boy knew what he was in for!

"You! You, boy! You toad of a boy!" yelled Mr. Tonnerre in his thunderous voice. "What you think you do, eh? You want to make people sick? You want to break my machine? Ar-rr-r-r-r-r-r!"

He finished off with a noise so like the growl of a giant dog that Loony was astonished, and leapt to his feet. Biff! Tonnerre boxed the roundabout boy's ear with a resounding slap.

Snubby stepped forward. "Mr. Tonnerre! It was my fault. I paid him double fare to go fast."

It looked as if Mr. Tonnerre was about to box his ears too. Then he turned to the roundabout boy. "Ah! Aha! Double fare. Where is the money? You think to keep it for yourself! Give me all the money you have got. Queeek, queeek!"

"Queeek, queeek!" apparently meant "Quick, quick." Mr. Tonnerre had a peculiar accent, English and French mixed up with American and Cockney. He towered over everyone, as elephantine as his two elephants.

He turned to Snubby next. "You come to ride on my elephants, no, yes? For double fare I make them trit-trot like horses. Yes!"

"No, thanks," said Snubby. "I mean—yes, I'd *like* to ride on your elephants, but no trit-trotting, thank you. I don't feel as if I could bear a trotting elephant."

So they rode on the great elephants, and swayed from side to side in a most alarming manner. Loony refused to get up with Snubby. He retired behind a tree, very much afraid of the enormous creatures that appeared to have tails in front as well as behind.

"Now you go watch Mr. Billy Tell," said Mr. Tonnerre in his enormous voice, as he helped them off the elephants.

"He very, very clever man. Crick-crack, his gun goes, and off goes the apple on Young 'Un's head."

"Billy Tell does the same act as William Tell, who was probably his great-great-great-great-great-uncle," remarked Roger, as they made their way to a tent marked in enormous red letters, "BILLY TELL."

Old Ma shambled over to look after the shooting-range when Young 'Un went to stand inside Billy Tell's tent with an apple perched high on his shock of hair. He grinned as the children came in to watch.

"Hiya!" he said. "Come to watch my hair being singed?"

Billy Tell was dressed in a redskin suit, and looked rather grand. He would have looked grander if he hadn't been quite so dirty. There was a long wait until enough people had paid to come into the tent.

Billy Tell sat looking bored, with his gun across his knee. Young 'Un cleverly walked about balancing the apple on his head all the time, collecting the entrance money.

The news had got round that it was Snubby who had paid double fare to the roundabout boy to make the roundabout go fast. Young 'Un came up to him grinning.

"Sure you haven't paid double to see Billy shoot off the tips of my ears?" he asked Snubby.

Snubby liked him. "You bet I have," he said. "So look out!"

He hadn't, of course, and Young 'Un knew it. He stood with his back to a steel sheet, the apple on his head. Billy Tell stood up at last and walked to the other end of the tent.

He took aim casually. "BANG!" The apple was split into a hundred bits and pieces, and Young 'Un wiped some out of his eyes.

He set another on his head. Billy Tell put his head between his legs and took aim from there. "BANG!" Again the apple split into tiny pieces. Everyone applauded loudly. Loony crouched against Snubby's legs, frightened at the bangs so near to him.

Young 'Un wiped his face again and walked over to the children. "Good shooting!" he said. "I'm a good shot too—a jolly good one. I shot a weather-cock off a steeple once."

"Garn!" said Billy Tell's drawling voice. "You and your tales! Here, take my gun and clean it. And tell Old Ma I'll have sausages for my supper to-night."

"Yes, Dad," said Young 'Un, and somehow the children felt surprised. So Billy Tell was his father—and Old Ma was his grandmother. What an interesting family to have!

"Have you got a mother?" asked Snubby.

"Naw! One woman in the family is enough for me to manage!" said Young 'Un, winking towards Old Ma, as she stood at her shooting-range.

"Say, Ma," he said to her as they came up. "Billy Tell says please to give him sausages to-night."

"Sausages!" squealed the old lady. "What does he think I am? Sausages cost money, you tell him, the varmint, and rabbits and hares don't cost nothing at all if they're shot—and what's his gun for, I'd like to know? Think he's got it just for shooting apples off your turnip head! Where is he? I'll give him sausages, so I will!"

"Well, Ma, that's all he *asked* you to give him— sausages!" yelled Young 'Un cheekily, and put his hands behind his sticking-out ears the better to hear all the rude names Old Ma called him as she went back to her caravan.

Snubby had a turn with a gun, trying his hardest to shoot one of the ping-pong balls that bobbed up and down on the top of the little fountain of water spouting continually at the back of the range. But he couldn't shoot one.

Young 'Un took a quick glance to see if Billy Tell, Old Ma or Tonnerre were anywhere near. Then he took a gun, aimed it—and bang went one ping-pong ball, bang went another, bang went a third! There was no doubt about it, Young 'Un was a very good shot. Snubby quite believed he had once shot a weather-cock down!

"Now you choose a prize," he said to Snubby. "Go on— I like you. Choose one of these here prizes."

"But *I* didn't shoot the balls off the water," said Snubby in astonishment.

"Don't matter. I did, and nobody's to know that," said Young 'Un. "I like you, see—no stuck-up nonsense about you or your dog. Go on, quick—take a prize. What about them there toffees. They're good."

It took Snubby quite a long time to convince Young 'Un that he thought it wrong to take a prize he hadn't won. Young 'Un gave way at last, but he didn't understand in the least. He didn't seem to know what honesty meant where that kind of thing was concerned.

"It's awfully *nice* of you," poor Snubby kept saying, "but it isn't *right*."

"Aw shucks," said Young 'Un, and gave in. "You better go with the others now. They're yelling to you to have a swing. Choose the boat at the end. It's best and you can make it go high."

What with roundabout riding, elephant riding, shooting, going in swing-boats, and sampling all kinds of other things, the children hadn't much money left by the end of the day! They had bought themselves enormous sticky buns in the bun-tent, and slices of cake, and lemonade, and had carried a good share over to Barney, who was still in charge of the hoopla, and doing very well; partly, of course, because of Miranda's amusing antics.

"When do you get off?" asked Diana. "We shall have to be going soon. Couldn't you come back to supper with us?"

"I'd like to do that," said Barney, his eyes shining with delight at the invitation. "I'll get Young 'Un to take over from me. Old Ma always takes over from him about now. If I give him sixpence, he'll come to my stall. I'm due for an evening off, so Tonnerre can't say anything if I go. Sure your mother won't mind me coming?"

"She won't mind—she wants to meet you," said Roger. "We've told her all about you—how we met you last summer and had that adventure at Rockingdown. How can you get to our place? We biked."

"Oh, I can borrow a bike," said Barney. "Miranda can either ride on my shoulder or on the handle-bars, she doesn't mind which."

"She can ride in the carrier-box with Loony if she likes!" said Snubby. But she didn't like. She preferred to ride in the middle of Barney's handle-bars, her soft monkey-hair streaming backwards in the wind, and her funny little skirt flapping hard.

They left the Fair behind. It was gay and noisy and crowded now. The stall-keepers were shouting, people were laughing, the roundabout was playing its harsh music. Snubby wished he could stay.

"Come on," said Roger, as he lingered behind. "We'll be late. And don't forget we've got to tell Barney our secret—we'll have to make time for that!"

Yes—their secret. Barney might be able to help them over that. How surprised he would be when they told him!

CHAPTER 11

BARNEY COMES TO SUPPER

"I SHALL have to be careful not to give Great-uncle a chance to nab me and ask me awkward questions," said Snubby as they rode off.

"It will be easy to get out of that if we've got a guest with us," said Roger. "Look where you're going, Snubby, you idiot—you rode over that hole and nearly tipped poor Loony out of his box."

"Sorry, Loony!" called back Snubby.

Barney had tried to clean himself up a little in order to meet Mrs. Lynton. He put on clean flannel trousers, and a clean, or nearly clean, sweater. His shoes were bad, but he could do nothing about those because he had on his only pair! His toes poked out of one, and Roger wondered if he had a pair that would fit Barney; but it looked as if Barney's feet were bigger than his.

They arrived home tired and hungry. Loony leapt thankfully out of the basket and ran straight to the kitchen to beg for a bone. Cook wasn't there. But there was a dish of sardine put down for the cat. Loony went over and sniffed at it. Should he take a bit? He was so hungry. No —it smelt nasty. Let Sardine the cat have it!

Sardine came in and spat at him. He ran at her and she fled out of the kitchen, up the passage and up the stairs. Into Roger's room she went, and leapt up on the chest of drawers.

Somebody else was sitting there! It was Miranda the monkey, waiting for the boys. Sardine got the shock of her life She had never seen a monkey before.

She went off like a firework, fizzing and hissing and spitting, her tail three times its size. Miranda looked at her in horror. Whatever was this explosive animal?

In a fright, Miranda leapt down to the floor, scampered on all fours across the room, out on to the landing, and into Great-uncle Roberts' room. He was there, brushing his mane of silver hair. He was startled to see a monkey leap on to his bed. Then came Sardine, and after Sardine came an excited Loony. The three of them rushed round the room twice and then disappeared.

Great-uncle sat down suddenly. What a household! A monkey! Had he seen right? Really, his bedroom was becoming a menagerie. He would have to speak to his niece, Susan, about it. No guest could be expected to put up with hordes of monkeys, cats and dogs running in circles round his bedroom.

Roger was trying out his shoes on Barney. They were

255

too small. Roger remembered what a lot of shoes Great-uncle had. Surely he could spare a pair. He went along and knocked at the door.

"Who is it now?" asked Great-uncle pettishly, as if he half-expected some more animals.

"It's me, Roger," said Roger. "Great-uncle, have you an old pair of shoes you could give me?"

"What's come over this household?" said Great-uncle. "First my bedroom's full of . . . oh, well, never mind. What on earth do you want a pair of my shoes for? They won't fit you!"

"It's for a friend of mine who's come to supper," explained Roger.

"Did he come without shoes then?" asked Great-uncle. "Good heavens, there's that monkey again! If I can find out who's brought a monkey to this house and let it loose, I'll . . . I'll . . . I'll . . ."

Roger departed hurriedly. If Great-uncle knew it was the owner of the monkey who wanted the shoes he wouldn't lend them or give them, that was certain. "Come on, Miranda, you little wretch!" he said to the excited monkey. "Don't rush all over the place. You'll give my mother a fit if she meets you on the stairs."

He rummaged in the hall cupboard and found an old pair of tennis shoes belonging to his father. At least Barney's toes wouldn't stick out of those. Barney put them on gratefully.

"Do I look too awful to come to supper with you?" he asked Diana anxiously, when she came to see if the boys were ready.

"No, you're quite all right," she said, hoping that her mother would think so too—and even more, her father. "I've told Mother you're here. She is looking forward to meeting you."

Barney was nervous. He had seldom been in a big house, and he was afraid his manners were bad. But he needn't have worried. He had naturally good manners, and a pleasant voice. When Mrs. Lynton saw his strange blue eyes, set so wide, and noticed the anxious expression in them, she gave him an even warmer welcome than she had planned.

"So you're Barney! I've heard all about you. Richard, this is Barney, the boy who went through those hair-raising adventures with our three last summer."

Mr. Lynton looked up. He expected to see a gipsy-looking boy, sly and shrewd. Instead he saw Barney, with his bright, corn-coloured hair brushed back, his honest eyes, and straight, fearless look. He held out his hand.

"You're welcome, Barney," he said. "Any friend of Roger's is a friend of mine."

Roger's heart warmed to his father. Good old Dad! He might be hot-tempered and strict and all the rest of it—but he had the right thoughts and feelings every time. Barney blushed with relief and pleasure. What nice parents Roger and Diana had—and how lucky they were!

"Mother—do you *mind* Miranda?" asked Diana anxiously, as she saw her mother's eyes stray in the monkey's direction for the first time. Miranda was sitting demurely on the back of a chair, looking most amusing in her little skirt and coat. Diana had given her a doll's bonnet and she was wearing that too.

"Oh dear!" said her mother, and began to laugh helplessly. "Richard—do look at that. I don't think I shall mind her, Diana, if she doesn't come too near me. I really *don't* like monkeys, you know."

"Shall I take her out?" asked Barney at once.

"No, no," said Mrs. Lynton. "If I can put up willingly with Sardine and Loony, I can surely put up with a harmless little creature like this. But what your Great-uncle will say I cannot imagine."

Great-uncle was a little late for the meal. Loony had hidden his evening shoes and it took him a long time to find them. When he came down at last, it was to find the family very friendly indeed with Barney and Miranda. It would have been difficult for him to make any trouble about them.

257

Barney thoroughly enjoyed himself. He loved the well-cooked food, the chatter, the laughter, the spotless mats, the flowers on the table, in fact, everything. Mrs. Lynton liked him very much. How could this boy be a circus boy, a boy who wandered about with Fairs, who probably hardly ever had a bath—and yet was nice enough to make a good friend for her son?

Mr. Lynton liked Barney too. "Have you no parents?" he asked.

"My mother died some while ago," answered Barney. "I never knew my father. He doesn't know anything about me, I'm afraid. All I know is that he's an actor, sir—and used to act in Shakespeare's plays. I've been looking for him all over the place, but I haven't found him yet."

"Do you know the name he plays under?" asked Mr. Lynton, thinking that surely any father would like to have a son like this turning up to claim him.

Barney shook his head. "No, I don't even know what he looks like. I don't know his right name either, sir, because my mother was in the circus, and took her name always, not her married name. I'm afraid I'll never find him."

"It seems doubtful, I must say," said Mr. Lynton. "Well, —you seem to have done quite well on your own."

After supper the four children went out into the garden. It was about half-past eight, and still light. They went into the summer-house and put Loony on guard again.

Miranda came too, of course. She had been on her very best behaviour at supper-time, and had sat on Barney's shoulder all the time, accepting pieces of tomato from him, and a few apricot slices from the pudding dish. Now she sat on Snubby's shoulder, and tucked her little paws into his collar to keep them warm. He loved her. Loony was jealous and tried to get up on Snubby's knee.

"Now—what was it you wanted to tell me?" Barney asked, when Loony had been sent outside on guard.

"Well," said Roger, hardly knowing how to begin. "It's

a peculiar story really—our Great-uncle is mixed up in it too. It's like this . . ."

He told the whole tale, with the others joining in occasionally.

"So you see," he ended, "we did just wonder if the Fair has got anything to do with robberies—whether somebody in the Fair knows enough about old papers and documents to steal them when the show goes near a museum, or near any other place where it's known that valuable papers are kept."

"And we want to find out how the thief can go through locked doors," said Diana. "It's a bit like magic. You'd want a spell to do that!"

"Perhaps it's Old Ma!" said Snubby, remembering how witch-like she looked, bent over her iron pot.

Everyone laughed. Barney sat in silence, considering. "I don't know anyone in the Fair who's interested in old things except Tonnerre," he said at last. "Tonnerre collects tiny carved ivory statues—but I've never heard of him collecting old papers. I shouldn't have thought he was educated enough to know whether they were valuable or not —or even where to go for them."

"And surely *he* couldn't go through locked doors!" said Diana, remembering how enormous Tonnerre was.

"No, he couldn't," said Barney.

There was a silence. "Who decides the places where the Fair is to go?" asked Diana suddenly. "Well—Tonnerre, I suppose, as he owns the Fair," said Barney. "Why? Oh— I see what you mean. Somebody knows where rare papers can be got—and that somebody decides to take the Fair there, in order to steal them. Yes—well, as far as I know Tonnerre always decides. He gives the orders anyway."

"Does anyone else in the Fair collect anything?" asked Snubby, playing with Miranda's tail.

"No—only Burly, one of the chimps!" said Barney with a laugh. "He collects toy animals—didn't you know? If you'll only give him a toy animal he'll be your slave for life! Odd, isn't it?"

259

"Very odd," said Diana, and laughed. "What does Hurly collect?"

"Sweets! But they don't last long!" said Barney. "You have to be careful of your pockets with Hurly. If you've got any sweets or chocolates there he'll pick your pockets as quickly as anything."

"We must really make friends with them," said Diana. "We hardly spoke to them to-day, there were so many things to see. Well, Barney—you can't really help us much, can you, about the probable thief in the Fair—except—that it is more likely to be Tonnerre than anyone else."

"There's Vosta," said Barney thoughtfully. "And there's Billy Tell. Both artful as can be. But somehow I can't see either of them knowing about rare papers. Why, I don't believe Billy Tell can read!"

"Oh well—perhaps it really is just chance that the burglaries occur when the Fair is in the district," said Diana. "I wonder where it's going to next."

"Didn't I tell you? It's coming near *here*," said Barney. "About a mile away, I think. On Dolling Hill over at Rilloby."

"How *smashing*!" said Snubby "How absolutely super. We'll see you every single day then—and I'll tell you what—we'll take it in turns to watch old Tonnerre! I BET he's the one. I've a feeling in my bones!"

CHAPTER 12

PLANS!

THE four children talked for a long while that night in the summer-house. Now that Barney, too, seemed to think that Diana's "hunch" might have something in it, they were keener than ever to solve the mystery.

Snubby had an unexpectedly good idea. "I say—I wonder if there's any place at Rilloby or near there that has a museum or rare collections of any kind," he said.

"Now *that's* a brainwave of yours," said Diana warmly. "You don't often have a brainwave—but that really is an idea."

"Yes. If we find out any place like that near the Fair—or within a mile or two—we could perhaps watch it," suggested Roger.

"Gosh, yes—watch it and see if Tonnerre came wandering round it to snoop about," said Snubby.

"We couldn't help seeing him if he did, he's so enormous! " said Diana.

"And if we did see him wandering about we could go to the place at night and see if we could catch him getting in," went on Snubby excitedly. "We might learn a thing or two about locked doors and how to get through them then?"

Everyone began suddenly to feel very thrilled. Could they really do all this? Well, perhaps they couldn't—but it would be very exciting to try.

"The thing to do first—is to find out whether there is a museum or anything near Rilloby," said Roger.

"How can we do that?" asked Diana. "I've never heard of one—and we've lived here for years."

"It might not be a museum," said Roger. "It might be a private collection of some sort—like the one Great-uncle was arranging at Chelie Manor House. Gosh, *I* know how to find out!"

"How?" said everyone.

"Well, ask Great-uncle, of course!" said Roger triumphantly. "He'd know. I do believe he knows where every single valuable letter, map, plan, chronicle and all the rest of it is in the whole of Great Britain. He really is very learned, you know. These antiquarians are."

"Anti what?" inquired Barney, who had never heard the word before. Diana explained.

Barney listened solemnly. He always liked to pick up any bit of knowledge that he could.

"Well, now—who's to ask Great-uncle about this?" said Roger.

"Not me," said Snubby promptly. "He'd think I was getting the information out of him to hand to the Green Hands Gang!"

"Don't be an idiot," said Diana.

"He *would*," said Snubby firmly. "He may be learned and all the rest of it, but he believes anything you tell him. I mean, he swallowed all about the Green Hands Gang and the rest of it absolutely whole! You should have seen his hair stand on end when I told him."

"Don't exaggerate," said Roger. "Anyway, we wouldn't dream of *you* asking him anything. You'd only make a mess of it, and say something silly."

Snubby subsided. Diana considered the question. "*I'll* ask him," she said. "I'll take my autograph book to him for his autograph—he'll like that—and then I'll get him talking about collections of signatures or something like that—and from that I'll get to other collections of papers

262

—and I can ask him what I want to know quite casually. He won't suspect a thing."

"That's well worked out, Di," said Roger approvingly "You do that to-morrow. Snubby had better still keep out of Great-uncle's way, in case he's asked too many awkward questions about how he knew there was to be a robbery at Ricklesham. You really were an idiot over that, Snubby."

"All right, all right, tell me again," said Snubby sulkily. "Always going on at me—and yet *I* thought of the best idea this evening."

"Yes, it *was* a good idea," said Roger. "We'll let it cancel out that mistake of yours! I say, isn't it getting dark!"

"Mother will be after us in a minute, saying it's bedtime," said Diana.

"Then I'd better go," said Barney, and he got up. "This has been a lovely evening for me. Thanks an awful lot. Are you coming over to the Fair to-morrow?"

"Of course," said Diana. "We'll see you every day till we go back to school, Barney. I'm glad Mother likes you. You can come here often now."

"Dad likes him too," said Roger. "Well, see you to-morrow, Barney, Is Miranda asleep? She's been awfully quiet."

"Sound asleep," said Barney. "She's inside my shirt. Feel her—warm as toast. She works hard at that hoopla stall with me, you know. Loony's been quiet too. I suppose he's tired out with his long run."

He was! He was stretched out on the step of the summer-house sound asleep too.

"He wouldn't have been much good as a watchdog this evening!" said Roger, poking him with his foot. "Here, wake up, you sleepy hound! Didn't you know you were on guard?"

"Woof," said Loony and sat up very suddenly.

"Good-bye, Barney," said Diana. "I'm awfully glad we've found you again. Don't forget to keep an eye on Tonnerre."

263

"I'll remember," said Barney with a laugh. "His caravan stands near to ours. I'll keep an ear open all night now to hear if he creeps out of his van—and I'll watch to see if he puts his light on in the middle of the night."

"And if he creeps out, follow him," said Roger.

Barney slipped away to his bicycle. Mrs. Lynton's voice could be heard calling the children. It was quite dark now, but the evening was very warm for April.

"I like the smell of those wallflowers," said Snubby, sniffing hard as they walked down the path. "Now, if I were a dog I'd go round sniffing at all the nice-smelling flowers—they'd just be the right height for sniffing."

"Look—there's Great-uncle standing by Mother," said Diana, clutching Snubby. "I bet he's waiting to have a few quiet words with you, Snubby."

"Gosh," said Snubby, and stopped.

"Go to bed quickly," said Roger. "Go in the back way and slip up the stairs. Don't undress. Get into bed at once, so that if Great-uncle comes up to find you, you'll look fast asleep. Quick!"

Snubby slipped round to the back door, ran through the kitchen, much to the astonishment of Cook and Anna, and disappeared upstairs, Loony at his heels. He fell over Sardine on the way, of course, and Loony took the opportunity of getting in a little nip as he passed. Aha! That would teach Sardine to lie in wait on the stairs. An explosive spitting noise followed Loony as he bounded off.

Snubby ran into his bedroom, slipped off his shoes without unlacing them, and flung himself under the sheets. He left out just the top of his shock of red hair.

"Where's Snubby?" said Mrs. Lynton, when the others appeared at the door. "Great-uncle wants a word with him."

"Oh dear. I think he's gone to bed," said Diana.

"*Has* he?" said her mother, astonished to hear that he had gone before he was sent. It was usually quite a job to get Snubby off to bed. "He must be very tired."

"Well, we went a long bike-ride to-day," said Roger.

"I'll say good-night too, Mother. I'm half asleep already. Did you like Barney?"

"Very much," said his mother. "Ask him here whenever you like. And—if you can tell him without offending him—say to him that he can have a hot bath whenever he'd like one. I'm sure there are never any hot baths at a Fair."

"Oh, Mother—you *would* think of that!" said Roger with a laugh. He gave her a hug. "I'm so glad you liked him. Good-night and sweet dreams. Good-night, Great-uncle."

"Good-night," said Great-uncle. "Er—I'll just come up with you and see if Snubby's asleep. I really do want a word with him."

He went up with them. Mrs. Lynton went too, rather puzzled. Why did Uncle Robert keep wanting to talk to Snubby? What could Snubby have done?

Nothing was to be seen of Snubby but a tuft of red hair, and a small mound under the bed-clothes. Loony was lying on his feet.

"Fast asleep!" said Mrs. Lynton. "Don't disturb him, Uncle Robert. He's tired out. Oh dear—look at Loony on the bed. I don't like to take him off in case I wake Snubby."

Snubby gave a gentle little snore. "Idiot!" thought Roger. "Now he's going to overdo things as usual."

"Well—I'll talk to him to-morrow," said Great-uncle, and he and Mrs. Lynton went out.

"Snubby, they've gone," said Roger and pulled the clothes down. But Snubby didn't move. He *was* fast asleep! In all his clothes too.

"What a boy!" said Diana. "Let him be. He's really tired out. So's Loony—not a flicker in him! Good-night, Roger. We'll have some fun now we've found old Barney again!"

CHAPTER 13

DIANA DOES HER BIT

MOST fortunately for Snubby, Great-uncle Robert had one of his bad nights that night, and asked to have his breakfast in bed the next day.

Snubby was full of glee. "I thought I'd have to get down early to breakfast, gulp a bit of porridge and make that do," he said, "so as to be away from the table when Great-uncle came down. But now I shall be able to have a proper breakfast. Goodo!"

"We'll go over to the Fair after dinner to-day," said Diana. "I've got to help Mother do all the flowers and turn out some of my cupboards. We could take tea over to Ricklesham and have it with Barney. We'll take enough for him too."

"And that will give you a chance to get on to Great-uncle about any museum or private collection," said Roger. "Snubby, you'd better spend the morning doing errands for Cook. Then you'll be out of the way."

"Oh," said Snubby, who was never very keen on doing errands. "All right. I'll see if Cook wants anything. She said something about somebody fetching a new roller for the wringer. I'd have to go to Rilloby for that."

"Well, that would take you out of Great-uncle's way for ages," said Diana. "You can go mooching round the toy shops, and have a few ice-creams at the dairy, and forget where you've left your bike, and take ages finding it again, and . . ."

"Don't try and be funny, Diana," said Snubby, giving her a push. "You'll be an old nagger when you grow up if you don't look out. Like Old Ma!"

"I shan't—and don't push me like that," said Diana, shoving back. "Why do little boys give people pushes and shoves when they get annoyed?"

"Same reason as big girls do, I expect," said Snubby, and went off pleased with himself.

He went to the kitchen and asked Cook if there were any errands she wanted done. She stared at him in surprise.

"What's come over you? Want me to make you meringues or something for dinner?"

"Oh no—I mean yes—well, no, I didn't ask you for *that* reason," said Snubby, getting into a muddle. "What I mean is—meringues didn't enter my head—but if they're in yours and you want to make them for dinner, well, all I can say is, you go ahead!"

"You're after something, *I* know!" said Cook. "Well, I'll think about the meringues. And seeing you are suddenly so helpful, yes, I'd be glad if you could get the new roller for my wringer. I keep on and on about it but nobody fetches it."

"*I'll* fetch it, Cookie," said Snubby. "Anything else?"

"Well, bless me, you can't be feeling yourself to come and *ask* for jobs," said Cook. "Still, I may as well take advantage of it! You can bring back the kippers with you —and seeing that you're going all the way to Rilloby, would you leave a note at my sister's house to say I'll be over on Wednesday? And if you could call at the cobbler's and get me my best shoes, and . . ."

"Here! Wait a minute! I haven't got all day to spare," said Snubby, suddenly feeling that he was taking on more than he had bargained for.

"I was just about to finish and say I'd be making meringues for your dinner," said Cook with a twinkle.

"You'd better write all those things down while I get my bike," said Snubby. "I'll be back in half a jiffy."

He came back and took the list from Cook. She had added one or two things. It was a real chance to get everything brought back, with Snubby in such a rare obliging mood!

"I'll just give you a jam tart to munch before you go," said Cook, and went to the larder. "Oh, by the way, your Great-uncle was in here a minute ago asking for you."

Snubby vanished at once, without even waiting for the jam tart. Cook was most surprised.

Great-uncle marched into the lounge, where Mrs. Lynton was doing the flowers. "I'm looking for Snubby," he said.

Mrs. Lynton leaned out of the window and called to Diana, who was picking daffodils for the vases. "Diana! Where's Snubby? Great-uncle wants him."

"Oh, Mother—he's just gone to Rilloby on his bike," said Diana, coming to the window. "He told me he's fetching the new roller for Cook's wringer, and he's bringing back the kippers, and fetching some mended shoes, and . . ."

268

Mrs. Lynton couldn't believe her ears. "*Snubby* is doing all that—on his own?" she asked disbelievingly. "What's come over him?"

"Oh, he can be helpful when he likes," said Diana, and turned away to hide a smile. "I'm afraid he won't be back for ages, Great-uncle."

"A nuisance this," grumbled Great-uncle crossly. "Slippery as an eel, that boy. Anyone would think he was avoiding me."

"Oh, no, Uncle Robert," said Mrs. Lynton. "Of course he's not. Why should he?"

"I shan't be in to lunch, my dear," said Great-uncle, not bothering to answer her. "I'm going up to London to see an old friend of mine."

"Oh, Great-uncle—before you go will you sign my autograph album?" called Diana suddenly. Dear me, she mustn't let him slip off without asking him a few important questions!

"Ask your Great-uncle another time, dear," said her mother exasperatingly. "He's off to catch a train."

"Oh, I'm not going just yet," said Great-uncle, beaming at Diana. "I'll sign Diana's album. I've got an old sixteenth-century proverb I once found in an old document that I'll write in for her—and I'll write it exactly as I saw it, in the old printing."

"Oh, thank you," said Diana. "I'll get my album now. I'll bring it into the study, Great-uncle. I expect you'll be in there."

"I will, my dear, I will," said Great-uncle. So Diana took her album there, and the old man painstakingly printed in old letters the sixteenth-century proverb he had once found.

"There! " he said. "Can you read that?"

"When ye thunder-clouds come, think on the Storm-cock bird—he sings," Diana read with difficulty, for the shape of the letters and the spelling of the words were strange.

"Very nice, isn't it," said Great-uncle. "We haven't a saying like that in these modern times."

269

"Well, we have, really," said Diana. "You know—'When you're up to your neck in hot water, think of the kettle—and sing!' "

"Ah—h'm!" said Great-uncle, surprised. "I've not heard that. Typical of these times—flippant, my dear, flippant, where the other proverb is beautiful."

Diana wasn't sure what flippant meant. It somehow reminded her of tiddley-winks. Yes—you *flipped* the counters—so they were probably flippant. She decided not to enter into that question, but to push on with what she wanted to know.

"Great-uncle, you know an awful lot about old things, don't you?" she said.

"Yes, my dear. It's always been my great interest—delving into the past, spreading my net there, and seeing what I can bring up," said Great-uncle.

"You've brought up some wonderful old things, haven't you?" said Diana.

"Well—*you* probably wouldn't think they were wonderful," said Great-uncle. "I'm interested really in old writings, you know—particularly old letters, which give us a vivid picture of the times in which they were written."

"I suppose you know every collection in the country?" said Diana in an awed voice.

Great-uncle was flattered at Diana's interest. "No, no," he said. "I know the most famous ones, of course—and many of the minor ones—but not all, my dear, no, not all!"

"Are there any interesting collections near here, Great-uncle?" asked Diana, bringing out her important question quite airily. She was pleased with herself! "Any near Rilloby, for instance?"

"Now let me see," said Great-uncle, considering. "Well—there's Marloes Castle, of course—but there's only a very *small* collection there. Lord Marloes was more interested in animals and birds than old documents. He's got a fine collection of those, so I hear—began to stuff them himself as a boy."

"Are the documents valuable—very valuable?" asked Diana.

"Yes—yes, I suppose they are," said Great-uncle. "I know some Americans were after them last year, so Marloes told me. He wouldn't sell, though. They're all family letters and historical documents relating to his own estate —he'd never part with them. He wouldn't part with his stuffed animals either! Now—I wonder—I believe I can get in touch with him in town—would you and the others like to go and see his collection of animals, if I can get you permission?"

"Oh, yes, *please*, Great-uncle," said Diana, delighted. This was a bit of luck. They could have a good look round the collections, and see the lie of the land—then if there happened to be a burglary there they would be able to picture the rooms and everything.

"Well, I'll telephone Marloes and see if he's back in town," said Great-uncle. "I'll take you over to the old castle myself, and you can look at the stuffed animals and I'll have another look at the documents. It'll be quite a day out, won't it, my dear?"

"Oh *yes*," said Diana. "Thanks awfully, Great-uncle. We'd all love to come."

"Dear, dear, look at the time!" said Great-uncle, getting up in a hurry. "I shall miss that train."

He went off, and Diana shut up her album thoughtfully. She considered she had done very well indeed. She had found out where valuable papers were—in Marloes Castle —and it was possible that Great-uncle would take her and the others there—and they would be able to do a good snoop round. Wonderful!

She went out to find Roger. "Roger! Roger! Where are you? Quick, I've got good news."

Mrs. Lynton heard her calling, and saw her talking excitedly to Roger. What could the "good news" be, she wondered. How surprised she would have been if she had known!

CHAPTER 14

AT THE FAIR AGAIN

SNUBBY arrived home complete with everything Cook had asked for. She beamed at him. "There are two meringues for each of you," she told him, "and there's one over. I'll tell your aunt I made it specially for you. So you can have three."

"Smashing!" said Snubby, pleased. "I say, this roller thing was frightfully heavy. I shall think twice before I say I'll fetch one again."

"Oh, we shan't want one for years," said Cook. "Loony, come out of the larder. Bless us all, if I leave that larder door open for so much as half a moment that dog's in there."

"LOONY!" yelled Snubby, and Loony backed out hurriedly. Oh, the smells in a larder! It was a far, far better place than the biggest, smelliest rabbit-hole.

Roger and Diana went to tell Snubby the news about Marloes Castle. He was excited.

"Gosh! That's a bit of luck. You're clever, Di, to manage all that. How did you wangle it?"

"Easy," said Diana. "Great-uncle just gobbled down all I said."

"I told you he'd swallow anything," said Snubby. "Now you can see why he swallowed my Green Hands Gang yarn."

"Well, if he really does get permission to take us over the collection, and there's a burglary some time, we'll be able to picture how it's done," said Roger. "We'll make a plan of the rooms where the collections are—or anyway of the room where the papers are. The thief won't be interested in the stuffed animals."

They had a very good lunch indeed, and enjoyed Cook's meringues immensely. They wished there were far, far more.

"Can't you go shopping for Cook every single morning?" said Diana to Snubby.

"No, I can't," said Snubby decidedly. "If you want meringues again, *you* go shopping for her. I've done my bit. My bike almost broke down with all the weight it had to carry. Poor Loony had to run all the way back. I couldn't possibly carry him as well. Anyway, the carrier-box was full of shoes and things."

"Are you going to see Barney to-day?" said Mrs. Lynton after dinner. "If so, take him this shirt, will you? It's one that's too small for your father, and it would do for him nicely."

"Right, Mother. He'll be pleased," said Roger. "We're just off now. Cook's packed us up some tea. It'll be nice for you to have an afternoon without us *or* Great-uncle, won't it! "

They were off at last, and Mrs. Lynton sank down thankfully on the sofa with a book. Now for peace!

They arrived at the Fair after it had opened and heard the roundabout music a long way away. Barney was on the lookout for them. He waved cheerily as they came up. Young 'Un waved too, and so did the roundabout boy. Now that it was known that they were Barney's friends they were welcome any time, whether they had money to spend or not.

There was no one at the hoopla stall just then, Hurly and Burly, the two chimpanzees, were giving their show in Vosta's tent and most people had gone to see them.

They were able to tell Barney their news about Marloes Castle.

"Jolly good," grinned Barney. "I've got no news, I'm

273

afraid. I've kept an eye on Tonnerre, but he's done nothing suspicious. All I've heard is that we move to Rilloby to-morrow."

"I saw the notices this morning," said Snubby. "There were posters advertising Rilloby Fair all over the place."

"It'll be easier for you to see me when we're there," said Barney. "Nearer for you."

"Where's Miranda?" asked Snubby, missing the little monkey suddenly.

"Gone to watch Hurly and Burly do their tricks," said Barney. "They love her, you know. Hold her and nurse her like a baby—especially Burly, the one that likes toy animals."

"Could we go and peep in at Hurly and Burly?" asked Diana. "Have they finished yet?"

"Almost," said Barney. "I'll take you over. There's no-body likely to come to the hoopla stall till the chimps' show is over. Look out for Old Ma to-day. She's in one of her tempers. Even Tonnerre is keeping away from her."

They kept an eye open for Old Ma, but they didn't see her. They heard her though, muttering loudly in her cara-van. Young 'Un saw them as they went by and winked.

"Have to go and give Old Ma a spanking soon," he grinned. "Getting above herself, she is!"

Barney took them to Vosta's tent. He nodded to the attendant and let them peep inside. Hurly and Burly were just finishing their performance. Burly was riding a bi-cycle made specially for him, and Hurly was standing on the handle-bars, turning somersaults as the bicycle went round and round the small ring of grass. He landed neatly back on the handle-bars each time.

"Good, aren't they?" said Barney.

Hurly did one last somersault and landed on Burly's head. Burly leaped off the bicycle. He bowed to the audi-ence and Hurly fell off. Everyone laughed and clapped. Burly ran to Vosta and put his hairy arms round him. Vosta patted the big chimpanzee and gave him an apple.

Hurly got over-excited at the shouting and clapping and

274

began to turn somersaults at a terrific rate round the ring, making peculiar noises. Then he scampered round on all fours.

Something landed on his back. It was Miranda, seeing a chance for a ride! Burly snatched her off Hurly's back and began to nurse her in his arms, making little crooning noises.

"Ladies and gentlemen, the show is now over! " shouted Vosta, seeing that nobody made a move. Nobody wanted to, because the chimpanzees and Miranda were so funny!

But the tent was cleared at last and Vosta came up to the children, carrying Miranda. He was very fond of her too. She was busy pulling his tie undone, chattering without stopping.

"Hallo, folks," said Vosta. "What do you think of my chimps?"

"They're champs—absolutely champion," said Snubby, making one of his frightful jokes."

"And you're a *chump*, a champion chump," said Roger, joining in. "I say, Mr. Vosta, how did you teach your chimps to ride a bike?"

"Didn't have to teach them." said Vosta. "They saw me riding mine one day, and when I put it down Hurly got on it and rode off straightaway. Then Burly had a go. Like to have tea with us this afternoon?"

"Oh *yes*," said all three. Diana turned to Barney. "What about you? Can you, Barney?"

"Yes. I'll get Young 'Un to come across again," said Barney. "Well, I must be getting back to my stall. Going on the roundabout, Snubby? Don't you get Jimmy to run it too fast again, or you'll get into trouble. I can see old Tonnerre's got his eye on you to-day."

Tonnerre was with his elephants, watching the children and Loony. He shouted to them in his enormous voice.

"You come to ride on my fine elephants, yes, no?"

But they didn't ride on the elephants. "I'd rather go on the roundabout," said Snubby. "It's not so sway-about as the elephants. Come on, Loony."

They spent a pleasant afternoon, and went to every stall. They saw Brilliant the Juggler, they watched the hoopla, with Miranda gathering up the rings so deftly, they went to the skittles and threw balls to knock them down for prizes.

Diana was the only one who managed to knock down three skittles and win a prize. The boy in charge of the skittles waved his hand towards a pile of prizes.

"Take what you like, Miss. Nice to see a girl beat her brothers. Shouldn't have thought it!"

That made Roger and Snubby immediately pay to throw some more balls, of course, just as the boy had meant them to. He winked at Diana.

"Not as good as you yet, see, Miss? Only knocked one skittle down between them. Poor shots, aren't they?"

Diana looked at the pile of prizes. She chose a small toy dog, much to the boys' surprise. Roger teased her about it.

"Baby! Fancy choosing that! Why didn't you take that little blue vase?"

"I've chosen it for a purpose," said Diana. "You wait and see!"

"Pity there's nothing for Loony to go in for," said Snubby. "I bet he'd win like anything."

"He'd win a rabbit-hole scratching competition," said Roger. "I never did see a dog scratch so fast at a rabbit-hole as he does."

"Or with so little result!" said Diana. "What he'd do if he really came upon a rabbit in a hole I can't imagine. Probably back out in a frightful hurry!"

"Woof," said Loony, knowing they were talking about him. Snubby patted his silky head.

"They're saying horrid things about you," he said. "Never mind. You're the best dog ever! A super dog, a real smasher."

"There's Mr. Vosta calling us," said Diana. "He says he's going to have tea. Get the things out of the bike-

276

baskets, Roger—we'll share them. And I'll tell Barney to come along now if he can."

They all went to Vosta's caravan. Inside was a small table spread with a marvellous tea—and sitting at it already were Hurly and Burly, wearing feeders!

"Get up, chaps, and bow!" said Vosta, and the two chimps rose and bowed politely.

"This is going to be fun!" said Diana, and she was right!

CHAPTER 15

A NICE AFTERNOON—AND A SUDDEN ENDING

IT WAS rather a hilarious tea-party, because Miranda and
Loony were there too. Miranda behaved really badly—
like a spoilt child. She snatched at this and that, she took
things off Burly's plate, and she teased Loony unmerci-
fully.

"Miranda! I'll give you to Tonnerre to deal with if I
have any more nonsense!" said Barney sternly.

"Oh, let her do what she wants to," said Snubby, delighted. "She's frightfully funny like this. Look—she's picking all the cherries out of the cake now."

Hurly reached out a hairy paw and smacked Miranda sharply. He liked cherries too! Miranda made little crying noises and Burly reached out his paws and picked her up, cradling her against his red-striped jersey. Hurly at once pulled her tail, which lay across his plate.

Burly then punched Hurly, and Vosta hammered on the table. "Behave yourselves! Don't you know how to behave when visitors are here?"

The chimpanzees looked ashamed. Hurly took off his sailor hat and hid his face behind it. The children squealed with laughter.

The tea was fine—a peculiar mixture, but very appetising.

"It's the sort of tea I like," said Snubby, pleased. "Potted meat and bread and butter, and tinned pineapple and cream, and cherry cake and biscuits, and our own tomato sandwiches and jam tarts."

"And there's ham here too, if you'd like it," said Vosta hospitably.

Snubby did. It was amazing what he could put away when he really liked a meal. The others did their best but he outdid them all. Vosta grinned to see him munching away happily. He liked Snubby, and he loved Loony.

Loony lay with his head on Vosta's foot. Snubby felt quite jealous! It wasn't often Loony did that with anyone.

"Vosta's a magician with animals," said Barney. "He's better with Tonnerre's elephants than Tonnerre is himself."

"Ho, Tonnerre! Br-r-r-r-r-r!" said Vosta unexpectedly. "All these years I have worked for him and still he shouts at me. Br-r-r-r-r-r!"

Hurly imitated him. "Br-r-r-r-r-r!" Then he bent down and looked under the table. Loony was near him, his head still on Vosta's foot. Burly made crooning noises to Loony, who lifted his head and looked astonished.

Burly suddenly disappeared below the table, and put his arms round the surprised spaniel. He tried to lift him up. Loony yelped and snapped, but he did not bite. Snubby rescued him.

"It's all right," said Barney. "Burly is cracked on monkeys and dogs and cats—he's got a nurse-maid idea of himself, I think—wants to nurse them all. Vosta, show us Burly's collection of toy animals."

Vosta opened a cupboard. Inside were a good number of toy animals—a teddy bear, a tiny monkey, two pink cats, a golliwog, and a few others. Burly made a grab at them.

He set them out on the tea-table, his eyes watchful in case anyone tried to take them from him. But nobody did. They were his toys, precious to him. They watched him arrange them to his liking.

Then Miranda snatched the teddy bear and was off to the top of the caravan with it at once, sitting by the chimney, chattering. Burly leapt up, growling queerly. Vosta forced him back.

"Stop it now. Silly of me to have let him have his toys out with Miranda there. Barney, can you get the bear back before there's trouble?"

Barney went out of the caravan and called sternly to Miranda, who was still hugging the chimney, looking very comical in her little skirt and coat.

Burly made a miserable, howling noise. Diana felt sorry for him. She remembered something she had brought for him and felt in her pockets for the little toy dog she had won for a prize at the skittle match. She held it out to Burly.

He looked at it in surprise. He sat up and reached out a paw for it. He took it very gently and set it down on the table, still keeping hold of it. He stroked it with his other paw and crooned to it. He was a queer chimpanzee!

He forgot about the bear that Miranda had taken. He gave his whole attention to the little toy dog.

"He loves it," said Vosta. "That was nice of you, Miss Diana. He's all right now—forgotten about the bear. Good thing too. I thought he was going to turn nasty for a minute."

Burly took up the toy dog and looked at Vosta, making a deep chattering noise as if he were talking. Vosta understood.

"Yes, it's yours, Burly," he said. "Yours. You can put it with your other toys."

Burly gathered all the toys up and put them back in the cupboard. Barney came in at that moment with the teddy bear. Burly took it, and put that in the cupboard too. He placed the little dog in the very front.

Vosta shut the cupboard and rubbed Burly affectionately on the head. "Funny fellow, ain't you? Isn't this a nice girl to bring you a present like that?"

Burly understood. He put out a big paw and stroked Diana gently on the arm, making a funny crooning sound as he did so.

"He's thanking you," said Vosta. "And now look at poor old Hurly—he feels left out of all this! "

Hurly was stretching out both hands as if to say, "What about me? I haven't had anything! "

"I've brought him some sweets," said Snubby, remembering, and felt in his pocket. Roger began to feel in his too. "I got him some chocolate," he said.

But neither of the boys found the sweets or chocolate. They were puzzled. "I've lost the sweets," said Snubby. "Blow! "

Barney smiled his wide smile. "I guess Mr. Vosta can find them for you. Watch! "

Vosta spoke sternly to Hurly. "Hurly! Turn out your pockets. Go on, you heard what I said—your pockets! "

Hurly made a whimpering sound and stood up. He pulled at his pockets. Vosta slipped his hand in, and out came a bag of sweets and a bar of chocolate!

"He's a pick-pocket when there's any sweets around," said Vosta. "Can't blame him. He's only a chimp and he doesn't really know right from wrong when it comes to things like honesty. Bad boy, Hurly! Very bad!"

Hurly took off his hat and hid his face behind it again. But he peeped over it, his bright eyes looking at Vosta.

"Give them back to him, Mr. Vosta," said Snubby. "He's an awful dear. They both are. Gosh, I wish I had a couple of chimps of my own. It's the first thing I shall buy when I'm grown up."

"It will be fine to see three chimps walking together down the road," said Vosta solemnly, and laughed to see Snubby's indignant face.

"Hallo—Tonnerre's taken his elephants off somewhere," said Barney, when the tea-party was over and the little company climbed down the steps of the caravan to the grassy field.

"He's probably taken them to Rilloby," said Vosta. "That's where we go to-morrow. He sometimes takes his elephants the day before we leave. They are so slow in their walking."

Snubby pricked up his ears. If Tonnerre had gone for the evening, it would be a good idea to snoop round his caravan a bit—look in at the window, or at the door—see if there was a safe there that valuable papers could be kept in, perhaps.

He didn't say anything to the others. He wanted to snoop by himself—and anyway three or four people would be noticed at once round a caravan. He waited till Roger and Diana had gone on the roundabout again and then he set off to Tonnerre's big caravan.

Loony went with him, puzzled by the sudden "hists" and "pssts" that Snubby suddenly addressed to him. He trotted at his heels obediently. He liked the Fair. It was full of astonishing smells, and amazing animals. He didn't much like the mongrel dogs though, and kept strictly to himself where they were concerned.

Snubby came to Tonnerre's caravan. No one seemed to

be about. He looked underneath it. It was hung with all kinds of things below—but then, so were all the other caravans. The underneath of a van was a convenient place to put a lot of things not wanted for a time.

He stood on a wheel and peeped in at a window; but the curtain was drawn and he couldn't see inside. He went to the other side of the van. Ah—the curtain was not drawn across there. He could see in quite well.

Snubby took a good, long look. It seemed a fairly ordinary caravan really—a bunk for a bed—a table that folded down—a stove in one corner for heating—a chair and a stool.

But what was that under the bunk? Snubby could see something sticking out a little. It looked like a black box—a good big one.

Would precious papers be kept in there? The more he looked at that box the more he felt certain that it was full of stolen papers!

He decided to go round to the door and see if it had been left unlatched. But it hadn't, of course. It was locked. Snubby bent to peep through the keyhole to see if he could get another view of that big black box.

Three things happened at exactly the same moment! Loony gave a terrific growl . Somebody gave a tremendous yell that almost deafened Snubby—and a hand descended on a very tender part of him with a terrific whack!

Snubby yelled and fell off the caravan steps. Loony yelped too, as the hand dealt him a slap as well. Snubby caught sight of a giant-like figure about to whack him again, and he rolled over quickly, jumped up and fled.

An enormous voice came after him. "YOU! COME HERE! I'LL TEACH YOU TO PRY! YES!"

It was Tonnerre. He had only taken his elephants for a little walk down the lane and back—and had just caught Snubby nicely.

He tore after Snubby and Loony, shouting. Everyone stared. Roger and Diana saw Snubby shoot past like a bullet out of a gun, with Loony at his heels. After them

283

came Tonnerre, black as thunder, yelling for all he was worth.

"Gosh—we'd better go," said Roger. "Come on, Di—slip round to the back of the stall, and we'll get behind the vans and creep down to the gate. What in the world has that idiot of a Snubby done? See you at Rilloby tomorrow, Barney—I *hope!*"

CHAPTER 16

A MORNING AT THE CASTLE

SNUBBY had a bad time from the others that evening. "Messing things up! Putting Tonnerre against us! Even perhaps putting him on his guard!" raged Roger on the way home. "What do you want to go snooping round his caravan like that for?"

"It's just the sort of crazy thing that Snubby *would* do," said Diana. Making everyone stare. I don't feel as if I want to go to the Fair any more."

"Oh, shut up," said Snubby, angry with the others and angry with himself too. "Going on and on at me. I tell you I thought Tonnerre had gone off to Rilloby with his elephants. Anyway, I wasn't doing any harm."

"Harm! You keep *on* doing harm!" said Roger. "What with your silly Green Hands Gang, and your blabbing about the possibility of a theft at Ricklesham, and now this snooping round Tonnerre's caravan."

There was a silence as the three rode on down the road. Snubby was really very much upset about it all. "He went off like a crack of thunder," he said at last. "And I got a frightful whack."

"Not nearly frightful enough," said Roger at once, and Snubby gave up trying to make peace. Let them be as cross as they liked! He still had old Loony. Loony never raged at him or nagged him or thought badly of him. Never.

Great-uncle Robert was not back from town when they arrived home. Snubby was glad. Now he wouldn't have to go dodging about all evening to avoid him. They had their supper with their mother and father, and then Snubby wandered off alone with Loony. The others still looked annoyed with him.

Great-uncle came back about half-past nine. Snubby, bored, had retired to bed. Roger and Diana were just about to go.

"Had a good day, Uncle Robert?" said Mrs. Lynton, taking his coat and scarf from him.

"Yes. Most interesting, my dear, most interesting," said Uncle Robert. "And I've got a nice bit of news for the children. Where are they?"

They were in the lounge, clearing up their things. "Well, my dears," said Great-uncle, beaming at them. "I managed to get into touch with Lord Marloes this morning. And he's given me permission to take you to his castle—and see his collection of rare papers and interesting animals. We'll go to-morrow, if you like."

"Oh, thanks, Great-uncle! That's fine!" said Diana. Roger beamed too. Now they would be able to have a look round before the thief came—if he meant to come!

"I thought you'd be pleased," said Great-uncle. "I'm pleased myself. I haven't seen his collection for years. It will refresh my memory nicely."

Mrs. Lynton looked slightly astonished. She went out into the hall with Diana and Roger when they left the room to go up to bed.

"Do you really want to go looking at dull old papers?" she said. "Because you *will* find them terribly dull, you know—and dear old Uncle Robert can be a bit of a bore when he's explaining them. I know because he often took me with him when I was a girl."

"It's all right, Mother—we shall love it," Diana assured her. "It's really the stuffed animals we want to see. There's quite a good collection of them there."

"Oh well—you go if you like," said her mother. "It will please your Great-uncle tremendously."

It certainly did! He set off with them at ten o'clock the

286

next morning in a specially hired car, smiling all over his face. He was so pleased about the little expedition that he quite forgot that for the last two days he had wanted to talk to Snubby about something important!

Loony, alas, was not allowed to come. "I'm sorry, but no dogs are allowed in the castle," said Great-uncle, quite determined in no circumstance to take Loony. Loony had only to see Great-uncle to take it into his head to sit down and scratch himself violently—and the old man wasn't going to have him indulging in a prolonged scratch in the car!

They arrived at the castle. It was not really a very large one, more like a big mansion in fact. The big iron gates at the entrance to the drive were opened by the lodge-keeper, who came out of his little lodge nearby.

"Your pass, please, sir," he said, and Great-uncle gave it to him.

"That's all right, sir," said the man. "Quite busy this morning, we are! Yours is the third pass I've checked today. Well, we've got a nice little museum up there, sir—and be sure to look at the albino badger, sir. I caught him myself! His lordship was right down pleased with me."

"We'll look at it, my man," said Great-uncle, and the car went on up the drive to a large front door. A butler opened it, and the pass was shown once more.

"This way, sir," said the butler, in a voice as pompous as Great-uncle's. Snubby nudged Diana and she smiled. She knew what Snubby was thinking.

The man took them down a stone-floored hall, and up a vast flight of marble stairs that swept round in a magnificent curve to the floor above.

They went up to another floor, and the man led the way to a small wing built off from the main part of the house. He unlocked a big wooden door that led into a dark stone passage. Another door stood at the end. He unlocked that too.

It led into a big room that was lined with books from ceiling to floor.

On they went, through the room to the other side, where a small, stout door was let into the wall. This was unlocked by two different keys!

"You keep the place well locked," said Roger. "Two locked doors, and now a third one, double-locked! You don't mean burglars to get in! "

"No, sir," said the butler. "His lordship prizes his collection greatly. Here you will find the stuffed animals, sir, and beyond, on those shelves, are the papers. Before you leave, sir, I must ask you to wait whilst Mr. Johns, the custodian, checks up the collection. We have to do that, sir, otherwise it would be easy for people to put something valuable in their pockets—there are plenty of dishonest people about these days! "

"That's all right," said Great-uncle. "Check all you like. It's good to see such care taken of a valuable collection. There have been so many thefts lately."

"Yes, sir," said the butler and locked them into the room!

"We're locked in! " said Diana, half-alarmed.

"That's quite usual," said Great-uncle. "It's just a sensible precaution. We have to ring that bell when we are ready to go. Hallo—there's somebody else here."

There were two people—one an old, old man who was so bent that it was quite impossible to see his face. The other was a younger man with a beard and very bushy eyebrows indeed. He had a moustache, and was altogether a most hairy-looking person.

"He's even got hairs growing out of his ears! " whispered Snubby to Diana. "Like eyebrows! "

"Sh! He'll hear you," said Diana crossly. Snubby's whispers were always much too loud.

The two men were examining the various papers set out and labelled on the shelves. The bearded man glanced round at the newcomers and then lost interest in them. He turned the pages of a manuscript carefully over and over, as the children wandered round.

"Di! You go and listen to Great-uncle Robert and we'll

have a look round," whispered Roger. "I'll make a rough plan of the room—just in case, you know!"

Diana went with Great-uncle and began to ask him questions. The old man began a lengthy explanation of this manuscript and that one. Diana was very bored. She hardly understood a word. She looked round for the boys. They were walking all round, looking here and there. They were not really very thrilled with the stuffed animals, which were a poor, mangy-looking lot, some with the moth in their furry coats.

The white badger was there, looking extremely dirty. There were two foxes with a litter of cubs, all stuffed and standing together, looking very unnatural. There was a pole-cat with one eye. The other had apparently dropped out at some time and had not been put back. There were two squirrels, red ones, outside what was supposed to be their nest. The very moth-eaten head of a young squirrel peeped over the edge of the dusty nest.

"I don't think much of these," said Snubby, disgusted. "They must be animals Lord Marloes stuffed when he was a boy, and was so proud of them that he couldn't bear to part with them. They're horrible."

"What's that fellow doing?" whispered Roger suddenly to Snubby, nudging him. Snubby looked at the man with the beard. He was laying something down on one of the manuscripts, moving it up and down the page.

"It's only a magnifying-glass, idiot," said Snubby. "You've seen Great-uncle using one on his old papers. Don't be so suspicious!"

Roger looked a bit crestfallen. He turned to look at the bent old man. How could anyone be so bent! It must be dreadful. Even when he walked from shelf to shelf he was so bent that he was forced to look down at the floor all the time.

Roger was glad when the two men rang the bell and went. The custodian, a wrinkled old man, came in, shut the door, and went rapidly through the papers on the shelves to make sure they were all there. He didn't even glance at the animals!

"I expect he hopes somebody *will* steal them some day, the horrible moth-eaten things," said Snubby, as the two men went out with the custodian. The door was once more double-locked.

"Now I'm going to make a sketch of the room," said Roger. "Just in case!"

"Put in the other two locked doors leading to the room," said Snubby, watching Roger beginning to draw. "Oh, you're doing it awfully well. What are those—windows?"

"Yes. They're well and truly fastened. Did you notice?" said Roger. "And they've got bars outside too. Nobody could get in there."

He looked up to see if there was a skylight, but there wasn't. He sketched in where the shelves were put and put dots for the stuffed animals on the floor. He marked where the chairs were, a desk, the fireplace, and a small table on which stood some kind of plant.

It really was quite a good drawing. Roger felt rather pleased. Snubby admired it whole-heartedly.

They glanced at poor Diana. She was looking rather pale, having been standing beside Great-uncle for about an hour, listening wearily to a lecture she didn't understand and didn't like.

"Poor old Di!" said Roger under his breath to Snubby. "She looks fed up. Shall we go and take her place?"

"No," said Snubby firmly. "You can if you want to. I'm not going to. I should be sick."

"Well, go and be sick," said Roger. "Great-uncle would take us all out then. You couldn't be sick in here."

Snubby caught sight of something on the broad mantelpiece. It was a clock. The hands pointed to half-past eleven. Snubby tiptoed over to it, opened the front of the clock and turned the hands till they said half-past twelve. Roger gave a snort of laughter, which he hurriedly turned into a sneeze.

Snubby went up to Great-uncle Robert. "Er—Great-uncle—I just hate to interrupt you—but do you think it's time to go? The clock on the mantelpiece says half-past twelve."

"Bless us all! How the time flies!" said Great-uncle in amazement, and rang the bell for the custodian. "Incredible! Quite incredible!"

CHAPTER 17

THE FAIR MOVES TO RILLOBY

THEY went home in the car, Roger longing to show Diana his really excellent drawing. Great-uncle rambled on, unable to stop. The children listened, bored, wishing they were home.

"Thanks awfully, Great-uncle," said Roger politely. "We've had a wizard morning."

"A *what* morning?" asked Great-uncle, puzzled.

"Wizard. Smashing. Super," explained Snubby. "Thanks a lot."

"I'm very glad, very glad," beamed Great-uncle, thinking what nice interesting children they were all of a sudden. He really must take them to some other collection some time. "Now you'd better go and get tidy for dinner," he said. "Dear me—I hope your mother won't think I've brought you back too late."

Considering that it was only ten to twelve, and not ten to one, as Great-uncle thought, Mrs. Lynton thought they were back very early, not late. As for Great-uncle, he was simply amazed to find what a long time there was before the dinner-gong went! He couldn't understand it at all.

Roger showed his map to Diana. "Now," he said, "if there's a burglary we shall have a map of the whole place. It may be very, very useful."

Loony was so pleased to see them again that he had one of his mad fits, rushing up and down the stairs at top speed, in and out of all the bedrooms, sending mats flying this way and that. Sardine was scared out of her life and fled to the top of the grandfather clock, where she sat swinging her tail like a pendulum till Loony's madness had exhausted itself.

Great-uncle locked himself into his bedroom when he realised that Loony was having a mad fit. That dog! If he wasn't barking, he was scratching, and if he wasn't scratching, he was going mad. The only really satisfactory dogs were stuffed ones, Great-uncle thought. At least they didn't scratch!

The children didn't go to see Barney that day, partly because Mr. Lynton was at home and told them all to come out into the garden and help him with some trees he was chopping down; and partly because they knew the Fair was moving to Rilloby, and they thought that Barney might be too busy to want them that day.

Snubby had a third reason. He was still smarting from the enormous whack Tonnerre had given him, and he thought it would be wise to allow him to forget what had happened. He meant to give Tonnerre a very wide berth in future!

Barney turned up himself that evening with Miranda on his shoulder. He waited in the garden till he saw Roger Then he whistled his low clear whistle.

Roger turned. "That you, Barney?" he called. "Oh, good! Had any supper? We've had ours, but we can easily ask Cook for something for you."

"I wouldn't mind a bit of cake," said Barney, who had had very little to eat that day in the move to Rilloby.

"Come to the back door. We'll ask Cook for something," said Roger. They appeared at the back door and Cook gave a shriek to see Miranda.

"Land sakes! Is it a monkey? Don't you dare to let it come into my kitchen. Whatever next!"

However, she calmed down enough to cut poor hungry Barney some sandwiches and gave him a big chunk of treacle tart. He held up a sandwich to Miranda and she

293

delicately took out a bit of tomato from the middle and ate it.

"A monkey now! What next!" said Cook.

"You come to Rilloby Fair and you'll see a couple of chimpanzees," said Roger. "You should see them ride their bicycles."

"Now that I *don't* believe," said Cook. "All right, I'll come and if I see two chimpanzees riding bicycles, well, I'll eat my best Sunday hat."

"You look out—you'll have to go to church in your *second* best hat now—you'll have eaten your best one," grinned Roger.

Barney hadn't any news except that they had moved the Fair successfully to Dolling Hill at Rilloby, and that Tonnerre seemed to have recovered his temper and had spent a happy afternoon spring-cleaning his two elephants.

"Spring-cleaning them! What do you mean?" said Diana, who had joined them with Snubby.

"Oh, he gets a step-ladder, and a can of oil, and a brush —and he oils the creases in their skins and rubs them all over," said Barney, eating the sandwiches very fast indeed. "He loves that job. It's put him into quite a good temper."

"He gave me an awful whack," said Snubby. "I can hardly sit down."

"Serves you right," said Diana. "If you always got what you always deserve, you'd always never be able to sit down."

"I don't like that remark," said Snubby, having worked it out bit by bit. But by that time Roger was showing Barney his map of the room in the castle and nobody took any notice of him.

"How are Hurly and Burly?" asked Diana. "Do they get upset with a move?"

"Not a bit," said Barney, giving Miranda a tiny piece of treacle tart. "Oh, you little nuisance—you've dropped it down my neck!"

"What—the treacle?" said Diana sympathetically. "How awful."

That reminded Roger of something. "Would you like a bath?" he asked Barney. "Mother says you can have one any time."

Barney hesitated. "Well—I'd awfully like one now if she really means it. I'm filthy with all the moving to-day. I just can't seem to get clean in cold water, and that's all I get."

So Barney was escorted to the bathroom, where he stared at the great, cream-coloured bath, quite overcome. Diana brought him a thick, cream-coloured towel, a very big one.

"What's this?" he asked, thinking it was a bed-quilt or something. He was astonished when she told him it was only a towel. His towel was usually a very dirty rag of a handkerchief. How he enjoyed that hot bath! Miranda sat on the cold tap and looked on in amazement. What *could* Barney be doing in water that smoked? She put one small foot down into it and curled it up with a squeal.

"Did it bite you?" asked Barney, soaping himself all over, and replacing the soap in its dish. Miranda took it up and smelt it. She nibbled it and flung the soap into the water in disgust. She spat out the bit she had nibbled.

"Miranda, that's not nice behaviour in a bathroom like this," said Barney. "Now where's the soap gone?"

He hunted in the water for it and then lay peacefully in the warmth. Loony scratched at the door .

"Sorry. The bathroom's engaged, Loony," murmured Barney, half asleep. Then he heard the voices of the others outside in the garden and he sat up, reaching for the wonderful towel.

It was a lovely night, and the children walked back to the Fair with Barney in the moonlight. Miranda couldn't understand Barney's sweet-scented smell. It didn't seem like Barney! She sat on Snubby's shoulder all the way, hoping Barney's nice Barney-smell would come back to him.

As they came to the gate of the field where the Fair was

being held, someone came out. It was Tonnerre, all by himself. Snubby recognised him at once and hid quickly in the hedge. The others walked boldly on.

"'Evening, sir," said Barney politely. Tonnerre peered at him.

"Oh, it's you. Give an eye to my elephants, will you, when you get in? Young 'Un's with them now, but they're restless—they don't like a move."

"Yes, sir," said Barney. "Will you be long, sir?"

"No. Just one hour," said Tonnerre. "Going down the road and back."

Roger pulled Barney to him. "Where's he *really* going? You go on into the field. I'll follow him and see where he's going. You never know!"

Barney nodded and went through the gate. Snubby detached himself from the hedge. He had heard Roger's whisper.

"I say—are we really going to follow Tonnerre?" he asked excitedly. "Loony would be awfully good at following his track if we lost it."

"He won't follow it because he's jolly well not coming," said Roger. "Nor are you. You take Di home. I'll do the tracking! Go on now, Snubby. I must get after him, or I'll lose him."

He left the other two and ran down the lane. Where was Tonnerre going? Was he really only going down the road and back?

He came to a fork and saw Tonnerre's figure in the distance, enormous in the moonlight.

"Oho!" said Roger to himself. "He's taken the turning to Marloes Castle. Now what do you think of *that*?"

CHAPTER 18

SNUBBY ENJOYS HIMSELF

TONNERRE strode on down the road, right in the very middle of it, his shadow black behind him. Roger followed. Marloes Castle was, by the signpost, half a mile away—not very far from Rilloby Fair! Roger kept close to the hedge, not wanting Tonnerre to see him.

He felt excited. What was Tonnerre going to do? Surely he wasn't going to commit any kind of robbery at that time of night? It was early, surely, for thieves!

"If I see him shin up over the wall, or do any other funny business, I shall call the police somehow or other," thought Roger. "I'd better notice if there's any house on the way that has telephone wires running to it—because I could go and ask to use their telephone. Gosh, this is exciting!"

He thought of the room in the little separate wing of the castle—protected by two locked doors and a third one double-locked. Windows fastened and barred. Well, well, if Tonnerre could go through all those, leaving them still locked and fastened, he was a very clever man indeed!

Tonnerre walked on and on. Roger kept well back in the shadows at the side of the lane. Tonnerre did not turn to see if anyone was following him. He simply walked straight on.

Marloes Castle loomed up in the distance. It had a high wall all round it. Its windows gleamed in the moonlight. Roger tried to see the barred window of the room where

297

the stuffed animals and valuable old papers were kept. He spotted it at last. How on earth could a great fellow like Tonnerre climb up a sheer, straight wall, and get through barred windows?

Tonnerre did nothing of the sort, of course. He came to the big iron gates, and there he stopped for the first time. He peered through at Marloes Castle, his great arms holding on to the gates as he looked this way and that.

Roger held his breath. What was going to happen now?

It was all very disappointing. Nothing happened at all. Tonnerre simply went on walking round the walls of the grounds, went all the way round, followed by Roger, and finally arrived at the iron gates again, and went back by the way he had come!

"Well!" thought Roger, "what a long walk I've had for nothing! All the same, perhaps Tonnerre was looking to see how he could get in some other night. Making his plans. Yes, that's it, I expect. He means to come back some other night and get in. But *how* does he mean to do it? It beats me!"

Roger saw Tonnerre safely back to the Fair field, and then went home. Mrs. Lynton was cross with him for being so late. "The others have been in for a long time," she said, "and have gone up to bed. Do you know it's ten o'clock? I'm surprised at you, Roger. I suppose you've been with Barney—but do remember that although I like him very much, I shall not allow you to keep the hours he does."

"Sorry, Mother," said Roger, and said no more. He couldn't possibly explain about Tonnerre.

The others were very disappointed when they heard that all that Tonnerre had done was to peer through the gates of the castle and walk round the walls.

"Still, I think you're right when you say he was looking round and laying his plans," said Diana. "Good night! We'll talk about it again to-morrow."

They all went to the Fair again the next day, after it had opened. They saw Cook there, having an afternoon off. Snubby went over to her.

"Got your best Sunday hat out, ready to eat?" he said. "You'll see the two chimps riding their bicycles this afternoon. Come on— I'll buy your ticket. I've never seen anybody eat their hat, and I'd just love to see you gobble yours."

"Go on with you now," said Cook. She went with all of them into the tent where Hurly and Burly gave their performances. Vosta nodded to them, and gave Cook a front seat. She was very pleased.

Her eyes nearly fell out of her head when she saw Hurly and Burly doing their tricks, and when they rode the bicycle round and round the grass ring, Burly on the pedals first, with Hurly on the bars, and then the other way about, she exclaimed in wonder.

"Well, I never did! Well, I never did in all my life! Well, who would have thought of that now! Well, of all the extraordinary things!"

Snubby grinned. "You'll have to eat your words as well as your hat. When can I come and see you at your meal, Cook? And do you eat your hat with a knife and fork, or just chew it?"

"Get away with your nonsense now," said Cook in a daze, watching the chimpanzees going head-over-heels without stopping. "It fair makes me dizzy watching them do that."

"Yes, but what about your Sunday hat?" persisted Snubby. "You can't go back on your word, you know."

Cook began to feel uncomfortable. "Go on now, you know a hat can't be eaten," she said. "You let me off, you little pest, and I'll make you some more meringues. Oh, my goodness, what are the creatures doing now? Tell this one to go away—I don't like its hairy face!"

Hurly had come up to Snubby, grinning all over his funny face. He patted Snubby, and then, as Cook appeared to be Snubby's friend, he patted her to. She rose from her chair and fled out of the tent, scared and trembling.

"Well, there now, I never did in all my life!" she kept saying to herself. "I never did!"

299

Snubby wondered what it was she never did. He followed her and reminded her of her bargain.

"Remember—either you eat your hat or I eat your meringues!"

"You're a caution, you are," said Cook. "You keep away from me now. I want to enjoy myself. You and your hats and meringues!"

Snubby kept carefully out of Tonnerre's sight. He kept as far from his caravan as possible too. He didn't want another whack! He saw the others by the hoopla stall and went to have a word with them. "Cook's not going to eat her best Sunday hat—she'll make us some meringues instead."

"Good work!" said Roger. "Hallo—here comes Old Ma. Wonder what she wants."

Old Ma came up to the hoopla stall. Her bright-bird-like eyes darted all round. She spoke to Barney.

"You seen Young 'Un anywhere, Barney? I want him to come and watch my pot for me. I got to do some washing and I can't do both."

"He's gone to help with the elephants," said Barney. "There's such a lot of people here to-day that Mr. Tonnerre can't cope with everyone that wants rides. There he is, look. Billy Tell's got the shooting-range."

"Never anyone to help Old Ma," muttered the old woman, and turned to go.

"I'll come along and stir up your pot," said Snubby, thinking it might be interesting to talk to the old woman.

"You! The only thing you'll ever stir up is trouble!" said Old Ma, and went off into a cackle of laughter. "All right—you come along then—and you can get me some water from the stream. I've not got enough."

Snubby found that he had taken on more than he bargained for. He had to fetch various pails of water from the stream first of all, then he had to fetch more wood for the fire, and then stand and stir the big iron pot with a long iron spoon whose handle got hotter and hotter.

300

"What's in here?" asked Snubby, peering into the bubbling liquid.

"Ah, don't you ask no questions and you won't get no lies," answered the old woman, now busy washing clothes in a tub. Snubby grinned. By the smell it seemed as if rabbit, hare, a chicken or two and possibly a duck were all in the big pot. Snubby felt that he wouldn't at all mind having a plateful of the delicious-smelling concoction.

Ma began to talk as she washed. Snubby listened, fascinated. She talked about Billy Tell and Vosta and many others he didn't know—Presto the conjurer, Sticky Stanley the clown, Mr. Volla and his bear, Madame Petronella and her parrots—people in other circuses and fairs, people she had known and had never forgotten. Out came the names in a never-ending stream, all with some story attached to them.

"What about Mr. Tonnerre?" ventured Snubby. "Have you known him long?"

"Long! Too long! Ah, that man's temper. It doesn't bear thinking about," said Old Ma, rinsing a peculiar-looking garment in her tub. "Always he had a temper, always he was shouting, always he was big—but what a wonderful acrobat! Ah, to see him on the tight-rope—why, he could dance better on that than most men on a dance floor."

Snubby was amazed. Tonnerre an acrobat! How very extraordinary. He didn't look a bit like one. He was so big and heavy—and yet, when Snubby thought of it, he walked very lightly and softly when he wanted to—as he must have walked when he caught Snubby snooping round his caravan!

Snubby remembered how easily and lightly he leapt up to the necks of his elephants when he wanted to, too. Yes —he must have been a fine acrobat.

"Does he do any—er—acrobating—now?" asked Snubby.

"Who? Tonnerre?" Old Ma gave a squeal of laughter. "That fat old man! He is nothing but an elephant now— but still he can walk the tight-rope, and he can leap his own height from the ground. But the strongest thing about Tonnerre now is his temper. He is afraid of nothing, that one—nothing but one thing."

"And that's you, isn't it, Old Ma?" said Snubby with a grin. "I say, how long have I got to stir this stuff. The smell is so super that I can't stand it much longer unless I keep licking the spoon."

Old Ma cackled again. She liked Snubby and his cheek. "You stay and have dinner with Old Ma," she said. "Just you and that dog of yours. What's his name now? Snubby, isn't it? And yours is Loony. Well, well—whoever named *you* was a clever one!"

"Here, Ma—you've got it all wrong," protested Snubby, leaping out of the way as Old Ma emptied her tub of soapy water much too near him.

"Mind out, Loony," she said to him, and both dog and boy minded out. "Now you set yourself down and wait a minute—and I'll give you the best meal you've ever tasted in your life. Old Ma knows how to cook, she does!"

CHAPTER 19

MORE DOINGS OF SNUBBY

THE others were quite jealous when they saw Old Ma ladling out an enormous plateful from her iron pot and presenting it to Snubby.

"Look at that now," said Barney in amazement and envy. "Never seen Old Ma so generous before. How does Snubby do it? Getting supper from Old Ma and meringues out of your cook, and . . ."

"Just pure cheek," said Roger. "Gosh, look, Old Ma's putting a plate down for Loony too. How wild all those mongrels look, sitting in a ring there, watching!"

Snubby came over to the others at last, looking very satisfied with himself and his supper. Loony looked more than satisfied. He looked extremely fat and developed a fit of hiccups at once.

"Stop it," said Snubby severely. "Hiccups mean you've been over-eating. Don't give yourself away like that, Loony!"

Loony did another hiccup and looked surprised. Sneezes and hiccups always surprised him. They were so sudden and seemed to belong to him in some mysterious way that he couldn't understand. He sat down and began to nod, feeling full and comfortable.

Snubby suddenly got the hiccups too, and retired to get over them, annoyed at the laughter and remarks of the others. He decided to buy some sweets for Hurly and Burly. He could see Vosta walking them round the field, holding them by their paws, one on each side of him. They loved a walk like that, when there were plenty of people to see.

Vosta brought them over to the hoopla stall. Miranda chattered to the two chimpanzees, showing them the row of wooden rings she had pushed up her left arm ready to hand out to customers. Hurly held out a hand for some.

"No, you don't," said Barney swiftly.

"Why not?" asked Roger.

"Well, he rings everything in sight," said Barney. "Never misses. And then he makes such a clamour for the things he's ringed. He's as cute as can be."

"Oh, do let's see him!" begged Diana. Snubby came up and joined in too. He had a pocketful of cheap sweets for the chimpanzees, and some better ones for himself and the others.

"Go on—let him throw," said Snubby. "I'll pay for the rings for him."

"I'll let him have them for nothing," said Barney. "But

don't you let him grab the things he rings like he did last time, Mr. Vosta. He smashed one of my clocks."

Hurly threw a ring. It fell exactly over a small doll. He chattered excitedly. Everyone clapped him. He threw another, and that slid beautifully over a little green vase. The third one fell round a packet of cigarettes without touching it. It really was good throwing.

Miranda deftly gathered up the rings and slipped them back on her arm. She held out her hand to Hurly for the penny he should have given her for them.

"It's all right. He's not paying," said Barney. "And he's not having the things he ringed either. Take your great paws away, Hurly!"

Hurly was longing to get the things he had ringed. Snubby felt quite sorry for him. It did seem a shame to throw so well and not have any reward. He remembered the sweets he had bought.

He put his hand into his pocket to get the ones he had bought for them—and they were not there, of course!

"Hurly! You've pinched the sweets I bought for you!" he cried, and pulled at the chimpanzee's hairy arm. Hurly at once put it round him and hugged him affectionately.

"No. You're a wicked pick-pocket," said Snubby severely. "Mr. Vosta, I bought some sweets for them both, and they're gone!"

"Hurly. Turn out your pockets!" said Mr. Vosta sternly. Hurly whimpered and pulled at one of his pockets. Out came a bag of sweets!

"Bad boy! Naughty boy!" said Vosta, smacking him hard. "No more rings for you! No more sweets either!"

"Keep the sweets and give them to Hurly and Burly later on," said Snubby. "I bought them for them. I say, can't you let Burly throw rings too?"

"Yes. But he goes wild after a bit and throws them at everybody," said Vosta. "So we don't encourage him to begin. Come along, Hurly and Burly. We'll go and see Mr. Tonnerre and say goodnight to him and his elephants."

The chimpanzees loved the two elephants and went willingly to see them. Snubby roared to see one of the elephants put his trunk round Burly and lift him right to the top of his great head. There sat Burly, swinging himself to and fro, chattering excitedly.

"I wish I belonged to a fair," said Snubby enviously. "Gosh wouldn't I like to have a couple of chimps like that —I'd have a string of monkeys too—and some elephants— and I wouldn't mind a bear or two."

"I think we ought to be going home to supper," said Roger, looking at his watch. "I suppose you can't come too, Barney, to-night?"

"I'd love to," said Barney, "but there's no one to take over my stall, and as you can see, we're pretty busy to-night. Young 'Un can't take it—he's still with the elephants."

"Bad luck. Come on, Snubby—we shan't get any supper if we don't go now," said Roger.

"I can't face supper to-night," said Snubby dolefully. "Not after Old Ma's helping out of her pot. I just can't face it. I say, Barney—*could* I take over the hoopla stall for you—and you go and have supper with the others?"

"What will Tonnerre say?" said Barney doubtfully. "I daren't go and ask him. He'll probably run you out of the field if he sees you at the stall."

"I'll go and ask Old Ma," said Snubby suddenly. "Tonnerre's afraid of her. If she says I can, I will."

He went off to where she was hanging out clothes on a line she had put up from caravan to caravan. "Ma," he began, "I'm afraid of asking Mr. Tonnerre—so can I ask you instead? Barney wants to go off for a bit. May I take over his stall? I'll do it properly."

"'Course you can, Loony," said Old Ma, with a twinkle. "You and your dog Snubby can surely look after a stall for an hour or two. I'll manage Tonnerre if he starts shouting around."

"What's she call you Loony for?" asked Roger, who had followed him. "All right—you needn't tell me. I can guess. it's quite a good idea on her part!"

Snubby scowled. Then he cheered up. He was to have the hoopla stall to himself—that was fine! He'd make a terrific lot of money and show Barney what he could do!

"Shall I leave Miranda to help you?" asked Barney.

"No thanks. I can manage with Loony," said Snubby. "Go on, all of you. Leave me to it. I shall do fine."

They went off and left him, all feeling very hungry. Snubby must indeed have eaten a magnificent meal not to be able to manage two suppers!

Snubby had a good time with the stall. He really let himself go. He tried out the loudest voice he possessed and it really was a pretty good one.

"Walk-up, walk-up, WALK-UP! Walk-up, walk-up, WALK-UP!" he bellowed. "Finest stall in the Fair. Clocks, cigs, chocs, bowls, spoons, brooches, pins, ring anything you like! Try your skill, try your SKILL! Mothers, come and beat the fathers, sisters, come and beat your brothers, choose what you like and ring it. Walk-up, walk-up, WALK-UP!"

People listened in amusement, surprised to see such a small boy in charge of the stall. Snubby was only twelve, and with his snub nose, red hair and masses of freckles, to say nothing of his cheeky grin, he made people smile whenever they looked at him.

They drifted over to the hoopla stall and soon he was doing a brisk business. Loony was very useful. He kept watch for any rings that fell to the ground and picked them up at once.

"You're as good as Miranda," Snubby told him, and Loony wagged his stump of a tail, pleased.

Tonnerre soon spotted that it was not Barney in charge of the stall, and he wandered over to see what was up. When he saw Snubby, his face took on its look of black thunder. Snubby saw him and was petrified.

But Old Ma was there at once. "You let him be!" she cried shrilly. "He's doing fine! You lay a finger on him, Tonnerre, and I'll tell you some of the things you did when you were a lad. Yes, and I put you across my knee many a time, and you yelled like . . ."

But Tonnerre was gone. He was no match for Old Ma's tongue and he knew it. Anyway, the boy was doing well and taking money. There was no need to interfere. Plenty of time later on to take it out of that snooping little rogue if he wanted to.

Snubby stayed there till Barney came back. The others weren't with him. "You're aunt says you're to go straight back," he told Snubby. "I don't think I ought to have left you here, really. She didn't seem very pleased. Thanks a lot. I *say*—did you take all that money?"

"Yes. It was easy," boasted Snubby. "And you should have seen Tonnerre turn green when he came up and saw me raking in all that money—more than he's taken all night with his elephants, I bet. He just faded away, and didn't say a word to me. I just looked him in the eye, and . . ."

"Go on—you didn't do anything of the sort," said Barney, who knew Snubby's little ways very well indeed, by now. "But anyway, thanks very much. I enjoyed my supper and going to your home again."

Snubby remembered the sweets he had bought for himself and the others. He felt hungry and thought he would like a few. He could give some to Barney too. He put his hand into his pocket—and gosh, the sweets weren't there! Blow—that tiresome Hurly must have taken them at the same time as he had taken the other bag. Snubby felt annoyed. Really, Hurly might have been content with just *one* bag! He wasn't only dishonest, he was greedy too!

"I'm just going over to Vosta's caravan to see if Hurly's got some more sweets of mine," said Snubby. "I'll be back."

He went over to the van. It was in darkness except for a very small oil-lamp burning on a shelf with a safety-ledge. Snubby knocked.

A chattering noise greeted him, and he heard the creaking of bunks. Hurly and Burly slept in the same van as

Vosta. He would never be separated from them, even at night.

"Are you there, Mr. Vosta?" asked Snubby. But Vosta was not there. Only the chimps were there, curled up in their blankets on the small bunks they had. Hurly came to the door and opened it. Both chimpanzees could do ordinary things like that.

"Hurly! Did you take my sweets?" said Snubby severely. "Turn out your pockets!"

But Hurly had no clothes on! He always had to undress at night, and he stood there dressed only in his hairy coat. Loony sniffed at his legs. With a bound Burly was beside them, trying to lift Loony up in his arms.

"Oh, Burly, don't—Loony doesn't like it," said Snubby, trying to rescue poor Loony. "Get back to bed. Go on. Do you HEAR me?"

To Snubby's surprise, the chimpanzees obeyed him. They got back under their blankets, making a few peculiar noises to one another. Snubby saw their clothes on the floor nearby. He saw that there was a bulge in one of the pockets, and he slipped his hand into it. He pulled out his paper bag of sweets.

"Bad Hurly!" he scolded. "Go to sleep, both of you. I shan't buy you sweets again if you behave like this. Good-night, you couple of scamps!"

CHAPTER 20

A MOST EXCITING FIND

SNUBBY went over to Barney again, but Barney didn't want any sweets. He had had such a fine supper, he said!

"Do go home," he begged Snubby. "Your aunt will be so annoyed. She'll never ask me to supper again. Do go, Snubby."

Snubby went. Very fortunately for him, his aunt was telephoning to somebody, so he simply crept behind her, gave her a kiss and rushed upstairs before she could turn and scold him.

"You're frightfully late, Snubby," said Roger's sleepy voice. "I say, Mother wasn't at all pleased at us leaving you there with the hoopla stall."

Snubby yawned. He suddenly found that he was really very tired. He said a few words to Roger, and fell into bed after a very short wash and a rub-over of his teeth.

It was the next morning that he discovered something that excited the three of them so tremendously that they could hardly do their morning tasks!

Snubby overslept. He rushed down late to breakfast, got a scolding from his uncle, and decided that he had better go straight upstairs and make his bed as soon after breakfast as possible, to get out of any further scolding from his aunt.

He stripped his bed. Under the pillow was the bag of sweets he had rescued from Hurly's pocket the night before.

He picked them up, wishing that toffees didn't ooze out and make everything sticky.

Stuck to the bag was a bit of torn paper. Snubby pulled it away without thinking.

There was something written on it, but first he didn't even bother to read it. Then a word caught his eye.

"Castle."

That rang a bell in Snubby's mind immediately, of course, and he smoothed out the dirty, sticky bit of paper at once. Part of two words were there, and the whole of one.

This is what Snubby read:

He stared in excitement. He gave such a whistle of surprise that Roger came over and looked at the paper too.

"What's this?" he said. "Where did you get it? Why the excitement?"

"Roger! Hurly stole a bag of sweets last night—and I went to get it out of his pocket in his van—and stuck to the bag was this torn bit of paper. It must have been part of a note," said Snubby, his face red with excitement. "See what it says?"

Roger looked at it a lot more carefully. He took it from Snubby, and his face went red too.

"Gosh, yes—'oes'—that's the end of Marloes, I suppose. 'Marloes Castle. Midnight.' That last word must surely be part of 'midnight.' I say, Snubby—we're on to something now!"

The two stared at one another, thrilled. Loony whined and scraped at Snubby's leg. What was up?

"Let's tell Di," said Snubby, and they called her. She was as excited as they were.

"Let's work it out," said Roger. "How did this bit of paper get into Hurly's pocket with the sweets to begin with?"

"Well, you know what Hurly is—he picks up anything he sees on the ground," said Snubby. "Or he takes things out of people's pockets. He may have got this from anywhere! Somebody must have torn it up, that's plain—and probably thrown it away on the field. This is just one of the bits."

"Who handed the note out—and who *got* the note?" wondered Diana. "Or did a messenger come and give it to somebody in the Fair? Or did it come by post to somebody, who read it, noted what it said, and tore it up? We can't tell."

"The only thing we do know is that *somebody* got the note—and *somebody* is going to Marloes Castle at midnight—and we can jolly well guess why!" said Snubby. "I say—isn't this thrilling—absolutely super."

"Smashing," agreed Roger. "I wonder who *got* the note. Do you suppose the one who got it is to meet the one who sent it?"

"There's only one way of finding out," said Snubby, his eyes shining, and his voice solemn. "Only *one* way. We'll have to go there at midnight ourselves and watch."

There was a silence. "I say—what a thrill!" said Roger. "But—we don't know what night. The note only says 'Midnight'—it doesn't say Monday, Tuesday, Wednesday —though the whole note must have, of course."

"Well, we'll go *every* night then!" said Snubby.

There was another silence. "Anyone know how long the Fair's going to be at Rilloby?" said Diana at last.

"Barney says till Wednesday," said Snubby. "And to-day is Thursday. Five more nights till they go—and on one of them we know there's a robbery going to take place."

"Had we better tell the police, do you think?" asked Diana. The boys looked at her scornfully.

"What! When we're nicely on the track now! Don't be a spoil-sport!" said Roger. "Besides—what exactly can we tell the police? About Diana's hunch—our suspicion of Tonnerre—and this torn note? They'd laugh at us."

"'Course they would," said Snubby, who couldn't bear the thought of handing over this mystery to anyone else. "Just like a girl to think of the police."

"All right, all right. *I* don't want to," said Diana. "But I don't see how we can go on watching Marloes Castle for five nights running. We'll be so sleepy we won't be able to do a thing the next day."

"Di—the note says *midnight*," said Roger, exasperated. "That means the robbery will be done then—and we can go home and go to sleep."

"Pooh—as if we'd any of us go to sleep after seeing a robbery done," said Diana. "All right, I'm not really making difficulties. I'm just seeing what's the best thing to do."

It really was a most exciting thing to discuss. Mrs. Lynton couldn't imagine what was the matter with the children that morning—no beds made, no jobs done, even Loony not brushed!

"What mischief are you planning, I should like to know," she said. "Diana, the *beds*! If they are not made in the next twenty minutes I shall be REALLY CROSS."

Of course, Barney had to be told. They streaked over to Rilloby Fair as soon as ever they could, and got him into a corner where nobody could possibly hear them, or see the torn bit of paper they handed him.

Barney was amazed. "Well, think of that!" he said. "Diana was right. There *is* somebody in this Fair who's got something to do with the robberies."

"We saw Tonnerre going off to the castle the other night," said Diana. "But the thing is—I can't picture him

313

doing any acrobatics—climbing up walls and so on. He's so big."

Snubby remembered what Old Ma had told him. "He *was* a very fine acrobat," he told the others. "And Old Ma says he can still walk tight-ropes and do things like that although he's so enormous."

"How do you suppose he goes through locked doors?" asked Diana.

"Perhaps he has skeleton keys, or whatever you call them," said Snubby. "Or perhaps he can wiggle the locks with a wire like some burglars can. Or perhaps . . ."

"It's all perhaps, perhaps," said Diana impatiently. "If only we could find out something solid—it's impossible to think of Tonnerre doing the robbery—and yet he went off to the castle the other night—and we know he's the one who decides where the Fair's to go—and it *always* seems to go to a place where there is some valuable collection of papers."

"It's a good old mystery," said Snubby. "And we're going to solve it. We've only got to hide somewhere in the grounds of the castle some time before midnight and watch who comes, and what he does. Easy! "

"Oh, *very* easy! " said Diana mockingly. "And how do you suppose you're going to get into the grounds—can *you* walk through a locked gate—or through a high wall?"

"It's easy enough to get into the grounds," said Barney. "There are spikes at the top of the wall. We can chuck up a rope-ladder, let it catch on the spikes, and climb up."

"Well, I'm not sitting on any spikes, thank you," said Diana promptly.

"Diana's not very helpful, is she?" said Snubby, getting annoyed with her. "Let's leave her out of it."

"No," said Barney. "She's in it all right. Of course she doesn't want to sit on spikes. Nobody does. But we'll just take half a dozen sacks, fold them, and pop them over the spikes. We can climb over easily enough then."

"And hide somewhere where we can watch the windows

314

of that wing," said Snubby. "Gosh—we'll go to-night, won't we? All of us! What an adventure!"

"Yes—to-night," said Barney. "We'll meet at eleven o'clock, near the gate. And for goodness' sake, keep quiet —just in case somebody else is hiding there too."

CHAPTER 21

MIDNIGHT AT THE CASTLE

SNUBBY could hardly contain himself all day. He whistled and sang and was altogether so noisy and restless that Great-uncle Robert nearly went mad. Wherever he was he could hear Snubby making a noise. What was the matter with that boy?

The evening came at last. To Mrs. Lynton's surprise, Snubby didn't seem to be hungry for his dinner. Nor Diana. Roger ate stolidly as usual. He wasn't so excitable as the other two.

"Do you feel quite well, Snubby?" asked Mrs. Lynton anxiously when he refused a second helping. "And you too, Diana?"

"I'm all right," said Snubby, and Mrs. Lynton, looking at his bright red cheeks and shining eyes, had no more doubts of his health.

"I suppose you've been stuffing yourself up with sweets and ice-creams again," she said. "Well, I shall think twice about getting you a nice supper if you do that."

They all went to bed at the usual time but they didn't undress. Roger fell asleep and had to be awakened at half-past ten.

"Are Mother and Dad in bed yet?" whispered Roger.

"Yes. They went early, thank goodness. There isn't a light anywhere except in Great-uncle's room," said Diana. "He's reading in bed, I expect."

They crept downstairs, warning each other to look out

for Sardine. But Sardine was away on business of her own that night. Loony crept down with them, his tail-stump wagging. What was up?

They went into the moonlit garden, and out of the gate. Then they made off across the fields to Marloes Castle. There was a short-cut to it which didn't take very long.

They came to the big iron gates, and then disappeared into the hedge on the other side. Diana gave a sudden little scream.

"Shut up, idiot!" said Roger fiercely in a low tone. Diana pulled away from him, shaking.

"There's somebody there already!" she whispered. "Oh, Roger!"

So there was. But it was only Barney and Miranda, who had got there first, and happened to choose just the bit of hedge that Diana had pushed herself into! Barney came out grinning.

"Sorry I scared you, Diana. You scared me too. You were all so quiet I didn't hear you. I got an awful fright when you pushed against me in the hedge."

"Have you seen anything or anyone?" asked Roger.

"Not a thing," said Barney. "Come on. We'll choose a place to get over the wall. I've got a rough rope-ladder and a few thick sacks. Carry the sacks, Roger and Snubby, and I'll take the rope."

With Miranda on his shoulder, and Loony at his heels, Barney led the way, keeping to the shadows of the hedge. They came at last to a place where the wall curved round, and the spikes did not seem to be quite so thick.

"This'll do," said Barney in a low voice. "Snubby, will Loony growl if he hears anyone, and warn us?"

"Yes, of course," said Snubby. "Loony, do you hear? You're on guard. On guard!"

"Woof," said Loony, understanding at once, and he sat down, ears, eyes and nose all on guard together.

The four of them got busy. Barney deftly threw the rope-ladder up to the spikes. The first time it slithered back again. The second time the spikes held one of the rungs.

Barney pulled. It was quite tight. Up he went like a cat, his feet treading the wooden rungs lightly. "Chuck up the sacks," he whispered down. Roger and Snubby threw them up one by one.

Barney put them in a neat pile over a dozen or so of the sharp, pointed spikes. Then, sitting on the sacks, he pulled at the rope-ladder till he had got a lot of loose slack up—enough to let half the ladder down the other side into the grounds!

"That's jolly clever!" thought Roger admiringly. "A ladder up to the top—and a ladder down the other side—and a pile of sacks in the middle to protect him against the spikes! I should never have thought of all that."

"Come on up," whispered Barney.

Diana went up first. Barney helped her over and she sat on the sacks beside him. He then helped her down the other side. Then came Roger. Then Snubby, hauling up Loony with great difficulty, helped by Barney.

"No good leaving him outside the wall," gasped Snubby. "He'd bark the place down. Gosh, Loony, you're an awful lump. Whoa there—you're falling! I say, he's gone down the other side at top speed. He'll break his legs!"

There was a thud and a yelp. Diana called up softly. "It's all right. He's not hurt. He's like Sardine, always falls on his feet!"

Barney pulled up the ladder so that no one could climb up it from the road. The place he had chosen to climb over the wall was in deep shadow, and nobody could see the pile of sacks on the spikes from the road. Barney slipped down and joined the others.

"Where shall we hide?" whispered Roger, excited.

Barney stood a moment or two to get his bearings. "There are the barred windows up there," he whispered. "Let's make our way to that clump of trees. We can watch the windows easily from there."

They crept from tree to tree and shrub to shrub until they were under the clump that Barney had decided on. From there they could easily see the barred windows. Now, if any thief were going to enter from outside, they couldn't possibly help seeing him!

They found a dry place under a bush and huddled together, parting the branches to keep a good lookout on the windows. From somewhere not far off a church clock began to strike. It chimed first—and then the deep clanging sounds came through the moonlight night.

"One, two, three," counted Snubby under his breath. "It's going to strike twelve. It's midnight! We must watch out. Lie down, Loony. Not a whimper from you! On guard, old fellow. On guard!"

There wasn't a sound anywhere. Then a nightingale began to sing. But it didn't sing for long—just tried out its notes and stopped. Not for a week or two would it sing all night long.

Not even an owl hooted. The children watched the moon move slowly along the sky, and waited patiently. Loony listened with both his ears. Diana always thought he would be able to hear much better if his ear-holes were not covered up by such long, drooping ears. But, drooping ears or not, he still heard twice as well as they did.

The church clock chimed the quarter and then the half-hour. Snubby yawned. Diana felt cold. Miranda cuddled inside Barney's shirt and went to sleep.

The clock chimed the three-quarters. Still there was no sound. There was not even a tiny breeze blowing that night, and no mouse or rat or rabbit was to be seen or heard.

"I say—I don't think the thief's coming to-night," whispered Barney. "It's long past midnight. This can't be the night. We'd better go."

Nobody minded! They were cold and tired. The excitement had fizzled out and they all thought longingly of nice warm beds. Loony gave a sigh of relief when he felt them on the move once more.

"Come on, then," said Diana thankfully. "We've had enough for to-night. We'll try again to-morrow."

They made their way to the wall, still keeping well in the shadows, just in case anyone was about.

Over the wall they went and down the other side. Barney sat on the sacks beside the rope, unhitched it from the spikes, and threw it down to Roger.

"Have to leave the sacks here and hope no one notices them," he said, taking a flying leap to the ground. He landed on hands and knees and rolled over, quite unhurt. He sat up.

"Don't you think the sacks will be noticed by anyone coming down the lane?" asked Diana anxiously.

"No. This bit of the wall is well hidden by trees, and unless anyone is actually walking just below, looking up, I don't think they'd be noticed," said Barney. "We'll stuff the rope-ladder under this bush. Save us carrying it to and fro."

They were silent and disappointed as they went off down the lane. They said good-night at the fork, and Barney went one way and they another, taking the short-cut across the fields.

"Better luck next time," said Roger to Diana rather gloomily, when he said good-night. "Gosh, I'm sleepy."

They all over-slept the next morning, of course, and Mr. Lynton told them wrathfully that they would have to go to bed an hour earlier that night.

But alas, when the evening came, Barney, Roger and Diana were all feeling ill! Diana and the two boys had gone over to see Barney at Rilloby Fair, and Roger had bought some sausage sandwiches. Snubby refused them, and bought himself some tomato sandwiches, of which he was very fond.

As he was the only one who didn't feel very sick that night, everyone felt that the sausage sandwiches must be to blame! Barney put Young 'Un in charge of the hoopla stall and staggered off to the caravan he shared with somebody else, feeling very ill. Roger and Diana got home somehow, and promptly collapsed in the hall, groaning.

Snubby rushed to tell Mrs. Lynton. "It's the sausage

sandwiches," he explained. "There must have been something wrong with them. They feel awfully sick."

They were, poor things. Mrs. Lynton got them into bed and dosed them well. Snubby looked in on them and was quite shocked to see them looking so green.

"Oh, I say—what about to-night?" he asked in a loud whisper. "Will you be able to go and watch?"

Roger groaned. "Of course not. I don't feel as if I shall ever be able to get up again."

Diana didn't even answer when he asked her. She felt really ill. Snubby tiptoed out with a most surprised Loony, and fell over Sardine on the stairs.

"Oh, Snubby—*don't* do that," said Mrs. Lynton crossly, looking out of the lounge door. "Can't you possibly be quiet when people are feeling ill?"

"Well, I like *that*!" said Snubby indignantly. "How did I know Sardine was lying in wait for me? It's Sardine you want to nag at, not me."

"Now, Snubby, don't you talk to me like that," began Mrs. Lynton, advancing on him. But Snubby fled.

What about to-night? *Some*body ought to watch, surely? All right—Snubby would watch all alone!

CHAPTER 22

A NIGHT OUT FOR SNUBBY

SNUBBY went to bed very early, for two reasons. One was that Mrs. Lynton was worried about the other two, and was inclined to be very cross with Snubby. He thought it best to get out of her way. The other was that he had quite made up his mind to go and watch in the castlegrounds by himself that night, and he wanted to get a little sleep before he went.

So he popped off to bed immediately after supper and took an alarm clock with him, set for a quarter-past eleven. He put it under his pillow, wrapped in a scarf so that it would be heard only by him. He hoped Roger wouldn't hear it.

Roger was sound asleep, exhausted by his bouts of sickness. Snubby didn't undress. He just got into bed and shut his eyes. Immediately he was asleep, and slept peacefully till the alarm went off. Loony, who was on his bed, leapt up in fright, barking.

"Shut up, you silly, crazy idiot!" said Snubby fiercely, and Loony shut up. Snubby lay and listened for a moment, after he had shut off the alarm. Had anyone heard?

Apparently not. Roger muttered something in his sleep, but that was all. Nobody else seemed to be stirring. Good! Snubby got cautiously out of bed, and felt for his clothes, remembered with agreeable surprise that he was fully dressed, and got his coat out of the cupboard. He had been cold the night before, and Snubby didn't like feeling cold!

"Come on, Loony—and if you fall over Sardine on the

stairs I'll drown you," Snubby threatened. They got downstairs safely, and were soon running over the fields, Loony surprised but pleased at this second unusual excursion.

They came to the castle walls as the church clock struck the three-quarters. "A quarter to midnight," thought Snubby, feeling feverishly about in the bush for the rope-ladder. "Blow it—where's the ladder? Is this the right bush?"

It wasn't. Loony knew the right bush and dragged out the ladder for Snubby. Then followed an agonised five minutes with Snubby trying to throw the ladder up to the spikes.

It wasn't as easy as it had looked when Barney did it. Snubby grew extremely hot and agitated.

"Go up and stick, you beast of a ladder!" he muttered. And miraculously, the ladder did stick on a spike or two, and held.

Up went Snubby joyfully, pleased to find that the ladder was fairly close to the pile of sacks that Barney had left on the spikes. He lifted them off and pulled them to the rope-ladder. Soon he was sitting on them, the spikes beneath him blunted by the sacking. He hauled up the ladder in the way that Barney had done, and soon half was on one side of the wall and half on the other. Snubby felt really proud of himself.

As he climbed down the other side, into the grounds, the church clock struck midnight. "Dong, dong, dong," it began. A whine reached Snubby, and he stopped short.

"Blow! I've forgotten Loony. I don't see how I'm going to get him up without help. He'll have to stay on the other side. I'll put him on guard."

He climbed up to the top again, and whispered to Loony. "It's all right, old fellow. I shan't be long. You're on guard, see? On guard."

Loony settled down with a whimper. All right, he would be on guard—but he thought it was very mean of Snubby to go off without him.

Snubby crept over to the clump of trees where he and

323

the others had stood the night before. It was a moonlight night again—but with much more cloud about. There were periods of brilliant light and then periods of darkness when the moon went behind clouds. Snubby settled down under a bush and waited.

He felt extremely pleased with himself. He had been the only one sensible enough not to take the sausage sandwiches. He had actually got over the wall by himself—and he didn't feel a scrap scared. Not a scrap. He hadn't even got Loony with him and he felt as brave as a lion. Yes, Snubby felt very pleased with himself indeed, ready for anything that might happen.

The moon went in. Everywhere became dark—and in the darkness Snubby thought he heard a little noise. He didn't know if it was near him or not. He listened, and thought he heard another small noise. No, it wasn't near him—it was over by the castle, he thought. He waited impatiently for the moon to come out again.

When it came out Snubby got a terrific shock. A black shadow seemed to be climbing up the side of the castle walls! Up it went, and up, lithe and confident. Snubby strained his eyes. Who was it? It was too far away to see. Was it Tonnerre? No, surely it wasn't nearly big enough for him—but the moonlight played tricks with your eyes.

It looked as if the black figure was climbing up a pipe, leaping on to window-sills, climbing up again—now scrambling up ivy. This was the thief all right! No doubt about that!

But how was he going to get through the barred windows? Snubby held his breath to see. The bars were so close together. Oh *blow* the moon—it had gone behind a cloud again.

When it came sailing out one more there was no sign of the climbing figure. It had vanished. Snubby suddenly began to feel very scared indeed. His hair gradually rose up from his head with a horrid prickly sensation. Shivers went down his spine. He longed for Loony.

His eyes began to play tricks with him. Was that a figure

standing at the bottom of the castle walls, far below the barred windows? Or was it a shadow? Was that a figure half-way up the walls? No, no, that was the outline of a small window. Was that a figure up on the roof by the chimney? No, no, of course not, it was a shadow, just the shadow of the chimney. And was that a . . . ?

Snubby groaned and shut his eyes. He was scared stiff. Why had he come? Why had he thought he was so brave? He daren't look anywhere because he thought he saw sinister figures creeping, climbing, running. Oh, Loony, Loony, if only you weren't on the other side of the wall!

There was a noise near him. Somebody was panting not far off. Snubby turned quite cold with fear. He stayed absolutely still, hoping that whoever or whatever it was would go away.

But it didn't. It came nearer and nearer. There was the crack of twigs, the rustle of dead leaves under the bushes.

Snubby nearly died of fright.

And then, worse than ever, something stuck itself into his back and snuffled there. Snubby was absolutely petrified. WHAT was it?

A tiny whimper came to him, and Snubby felt so relieved that he could have wept. It was LOONY!

He got the spaniel's head in his hands and let the delighted Loony lick his face till it was wet all over. "Loony!" he whispered. "It's really *you*! How did you get here? You couldn't climb that ladder! Oh, Loony, I was never so glad to see you in all my life!"

Loony was simply delighted at his welcome. Having been left on guard, he had been afraid that Snubby would be very angry to see him. But it was all right. Snubby was pleased, very, very pleased. It didn't matter that Loony had left the place he had to guard, had found a convenient hole by the wall, and had enlarged it to go underneath it with terrific squeezings and struggling.

Everything was all right. He had found his master, and what a welcome he had got!

Snubby recovered completely from his fright. He sat

325

with his arm round Loony and squeezed him, telling him in whispers what he had seen. Then he stiffened again as Loony growled softly, his hackles rising at the back of his neck.

"What is it? What's the matter? Is it the thief coming back?" whispered Snubby. But it was quite impossible to see anything because the moon was now behind a very big cloud indeed. Loony went on growling softly. Snubby didn't dare to move. He thought he heard noises from the direction of the castle and longed for the moon to come out again.

It came out for a fleeting instant and Snubby thought he saw a black figure descending the walls again, but he couldn't be sure. Anyway he was sure of one thing—he wasn't going to move from his hiding-place for a very long while! He didn't want to bump up against that terrifying robber.

He cuddled up to Loony, and put his head on the dog's warm, silky-coated body. Loony licked him lovingly.

Most surprisingly, Snubby went to sleep. When he awoke he couldn't at first think where he was. Then with a twinge of fright, he remembered. Good gracious—how long had he been asleep? He waited till the church clock struck again, and found with relief that he hadn't slept for more than half an hour. How could he have gone to sleep like that? Anyway it should be safe to go home again now. Surely the thief would have gone long since. My word, what a tale he had to tell the others!

Feeling a good deal braver with Loony at his heels, Snubby pushed his way cautiously out of the bush. The moon came out and lighted up the castle brilliantly. Nothing was to be seen of any climbing, creeping figure. With a sigh of relief, Snubby made his way to the wall.

Somehow he missed his way and wandered too far to the left, towards the iron gates. And then he got a really dreadful shock!

He came through a little copse of trees and found himself looking into a small dell—and from the dell many pairs of gleaming eyes looked up at him! He could see small shadowy bodies behind—but it was the eyes that frightened him. The moon sent its beams into the little dell and picked out the glassy, staring eyes that seemed to watch Snubby warily.

Loony growled and then barked, his hackles rising again. He backed away and began to whimper. Then Snubby knew that poor Loony too was scared, and he turned and fled. How he ran, stumbling through bushes and shrubs, tearing his coat, scratching his legs, away, away from those gleaming eyes that waited for him in the dell.

How he found the ladder he never knew. He climbed up it, pulled it up behind him, loosened it from the spikes and sent it down to the ground. He left the sacks and flung himself to the ground. He wasn't as clever as Barney at this kind of thing, and fell far too heavily, twisting one ankle, and bruising and grazing his knees badly.

Loony ran to find his hole. He squeezed through with difficulty and raced up to Snubby. Snubby was trembling, almost in tears. He flung his arms round Loony's neck.

"Keep with me, Loony. Let's go home. There's something queer about and I don't like it. Keep near me."

Loony had every intention of doing so. He wasn't feeling too happy himself. He kept as close to Snubby's feet as he could, almost tripping him up at times. The two of them took the short-cut across the fields and got home at last.

Roger was sound asleep. So was Diana. Snubby longed to wake them up and tell them everything, but he hadn't the heart to. They had both been so very, very sick.

But he woke them up early in the morning and told them! He shook Roger and woke up Diana. He made Roger go into Diana's room, and then he told them both.

"I had an adventure last night," he said. "You'll never believe it. Listen!"

CHAPTER 23

IT'S ALL IN THE PAPERS!

ROGER and Diana still felt a little weak from their upset of the day before. They were not too pleased at being awakened so early. But they soon pricked up their ears when they heard Snubby's story.

He exaggerated, of course, which was a pity. He related how he had gone to the wall and got over it, how he had waited without Loony, and how he had suddenly seen the black figure climbing up the wall.

"Up and up," said Snubby, "jumping from window-sill to window-sill, climbing up the ivy, using pipes—gosh, you should have seen him. Talk about an acrobat!"

"Was it Tonnerre?" asked Roger excitedly.

"Might have been," said Snubby. "I was too far away to see. And there was a figure at the foot of the walls too —and one on the roof—and . . ."

By the time Snubby had finished it sounded as if the castle grounds had been swarming with thieves!

"I saw something else too," went on Snubby. "Both of us saw them, Loony too. And Loony was really scared."

"I bet you were too," said Diana.

"I was as brave as could be!" said Snubby most untruthfully, having completely forgotten his terror. "Do listen. Well, we came to a little kind of dell—and there lying in wait for us were all kinds of things with gleaming eyes!"

"And I suppose you did what any sensible person would have done—you took to your heels and fled?" said Roger.

"Well—I didn't stay long," admitted Snubby. "Nor would you."

"You bet I wouldn't!" said Roger. "What did they do? Snarl? Growl? Call out?"'

"Oh—a kind of mixture of all the lot," said Snubby, exaggerating wildly again. "And one or two took a step forward as if they were going for Loony and me."

Diana and Roger couldn't help being impressed by all this. "Could you take us to see this field?" asked Roger.

"In the daytime, not at night," said Snubby promptly. "We'll go this morning."

But they didn't. When Snubby got down to breakfast, late as usual, but forgiven because he offered to take up breakfast trays to Roger and Diana, he found everyone exclaiming over the morning paper.

"What's up?" asked Snubby, and suddenly he knew. Of course—the robbery! It would be in the paper!

So it was—with big headlines.

STRANGE ROBBERY LAST NIGHT
AT MARLOES CASTLE

STUFFED ANIMALS TAKEN AND LEFT IN

GROUNDS

IS THIEF A MADMAN?

HOW DID HE GET IN THROUGH FASTENED

WINDOWS AND LOCKED DOORS?

Snubby looked over the shoulders of the grown-ups and read the report. There it all was. Somebody had mysteriously got into the locked room and had taken—dear me, how queer—taken all the smaller animals, but apparently nothing else!

Snubby felt himself blushing. Gosh,—those gleaming eyes—they must have been the eyes of the stuffed animals that the thief had put together in that little dell. Why had he said anything about the creatures making noises—and moving towards him? Oh, gosh, the others would rag him like anything!

Snubby ate his breakfast very soberly. He didn't say a word about what he knew. He would let the grown-ups discuss it, and wondered what to say to Roger and Diana upstairs. He was very puzzled. Why had the thief stolen worthless animals? Why hadn't he taken the valuable papers there? It didn't make sense. Was the thief really a madman? Then he must be a different thief from the one that so sensibly took rare papers!

And anyway how did even a madman get into that room? Snubby had seen him climbing the wall—but according to the papers the windows were still fastened and the bars unbroken.

Great-uncle Robert suddenly gave a loud exclamation and made everyone jump.

"Listen to this. It's in the stop-press news. They've found a clue to the thief."

"What?" Mr. and Mrs. Lynton and Snubby chorussed.

Great-uncle Robert lowered the paper and spoke in a very peculiar kind of voice.

"The clue they've found, out in the grounds, is—a *green glove*!"

He stared hard at Snubby. Snubby went pale. Gosh— how extraordinary. Why ever had he made up that fool story of the Green Hands Gang that wore green gloves. It was going to haunt him for the rest of his life.

"I think," said Great-uncle ominously, "I think it must be the Green Hands Gang. What do *you* think, Snubby?"

Mr. and Mrs. Lynton stared at Great-uncle and Snubby in bewilderment. Snubby swallowed down his last bit of toast, nearly choked, and got up.

"I—er—I don't know anything about a Green Hands Gang," he said. "Nothing at all. Aunt Susan, I'll go and get Roger's tray and Diana's."

Mr. Lynton turned to Great-uncle when Snubby had gone. "What *is* all this?" he said. "It sounds like a film plot or something—Green Hands Gang! Absurd!"

"The time has come for me to tell you what I know," said Great-uncle solemnly. "It isn't much. I dismissed it, the last few days, as Snubby's silly make-up—but now that a green glove has been found, things look different."

Whereupon he told them the fairy tale that Snubby had told him in the train, about the gang that had its hold on Snubby because of his stumbling on their plot, his running away, and how he had told Great-uncle that the gang, called the Green Hands Gang because they wore green gloves, would be operating at Ricklesham—stealing valuable papers.

"And bless us all, so they did," said Uncle Robert.

"And here's a theft again—and a green glove is dropped!"

"Snubby's been pulling your leg, Uncle Robert," said Mrs. Lynton soothingly. "I'll speak to him about this."

"Yes—but the *green glove!*" said Uncle Robert. "The boy couldn't have made that up. There actually *is* a clue of a green glove."

"Coincidence—sheer chance," said Mr. Lynton impatiently. "Snubby doesn't know a thing. He wants a good whacking and I'll see he gets it."

"No, no—don't do that," said Uncle Robert in alarm. "I really do think Snubby knows something. Give him a chance Richard. I wouldn't have given him away if I'd known you would whip him."

"Oh, it's been coming to him for some long time," said Mr. Lynton, gathering up his letters. "You can tell him from me that he's going to get a whacking—unless, of course, he really *does* know something and can produce a member if this wonderful gang who actually *does* wear green gloves. Pah!"

Out he went. Great-uncle Robert sighed. He was getting mixed up in a lot of things. Dear dear—to think Marloes Castle was burgled—and not one of those precious papers taken—only the stuffed animals. Extraordinary!

Snubby tiptoed into the room where only Great-uncle was left there.

"What did you tell them?" he demanded. "Uncle Richard's furious. I can tell by the way he went out."

"My boy, I told them what you had told me—and they not only disbelieved your whole tale—in *spite* of the green gloves," said Great-uncle solemnly, "but your uncle, I very much regret to say, is going to give you a beating—unless you can—er—produce one of the green glove thieves."

"You shouldn't have given me away," said poor Snubby, feeling very sorry for himself indeed. "Didn't I twist my ankle last night, and bruise and cut my knees—look—and now I'm to have a whacking. It isn't fair. Especially as I know more than anyone else about the burglary!"

"Do you?" said Great-uncle, startled. "Or is that just

another of your tales?" he asked more cautiously. "Tell me."

"I'm not telling you or anybody else a single thing," declared Snubby, almost in tears. "Sneaking and blabbing like that! Getting me a whacking. It's not fair. I wish there *was* a Green Hands Gang—I'd jolly well set them on to everyone in this house, and be glad to!"

He went out and slammed the door. Great-uncle was upset and worried. He also felt extremely muddled. Dear, dear, Snubby was a most unreliable and really extraordinary boy!

CHAPTER 24

THE POLICE ARRIVE

Suddenly quite a lot of things began to happen. The first one was the arrival of the police!

"I say—there's Inspector Williams coming up the front path—and somebody in plain clothes with him—a detective, I should think!" called Roger in excitement.

"Why should they come here?" said Diana. Snubby began to shake at the knees. Had Great-uncle said anything to the police about the Green Hands Gang? Surely not!

Poor Snubby crept into the boxroom and shut the door. He was absolutely certain that the police had come to question him about his idiotic Green Hands story.

"I'll never make up a tale again, never," vowed poor Snubby. "This one has followed me and followed me—and however much I say I made it up, no one will believe me now that a green glove has been found."

The Inspector asked for Great-uncle Robert. He and his colleague were shown into the study.

"Mr. Robert Lynton?" asked the Inspector. "I've come in connection with this queer Marloes Castle case, sir. Lord Marloes asked us to come and have a word with you. He is thinking of placing all his papers somewhere in safety now that a thief has actually been able to get into the room where he keeps them. Funny business that, sir—taking the animals and leaving the papers. Must be mad, I should think."

"Very strange indeed," agreed Great-uncle. "Er—does

Lord Marloes want me to do anything about the papers for him?"

"Yes, sir. He wondered if you would go up to the castle and advise the custodian how to pack them, and in what order they should be packed, and so on," said the Inspector.

"I'd be pleased to," said Great-uncle.

"There's another thing," said the Inspector. "When you went there with the children the other day, sir, did you notice two other men there?' '

"Yes, I did," said Great-uncle. "Why?"

"Well, sir, anyone visiting the Marloes Collection has to have a pass on which is written his name and address," said the Inspector. He gave Great-uncle three passes. "That's yours, sir, with the names of the three children on. That's another visitor's, a Professor Cummings, very, very bent old fellow. And here's another—name of Alfred James Smith, address given 38 Thurlow Crescent, Leeds. Well, we've checked yours, of course, and Professor Cummings—addresses given, correct. But in the case of this third one, sir . . ."

"It's false, I suppose?" said Great-uncle, getting excited. "But why? And what's the connection between a man with a false name and address coming to look at the papers, and another man, presumably mad, coming to steal the stuffed animals. It doesn't make sense."

"You're right, it doesn't," agreed the Inspector, and the plain-clothes man nodded his head. "But it may be there *is* a connection, and we want to find out all we can about this fellow with the false name and address. Can you give us an exact description, sir?"

"Well, no, I can't. I hardly noticed him," said Great-uncle. "But why not ask the three children? They're as sharp as needles, all of them. They'll give you a full description."

"Good idea. Can you get them for us, sir?" said the Inspector. Great-uncle rose and went out. He called loudly.

"Roger! The police want to have a word with you three. Come down, will you?"

Roger felt excited. What was up? He went to fetch Diana. "Where's Snubby? Snubby! I say, SNUBBY! Where are you? The police want to talk to you."

Snubby's heart went cold inside him. He clutched at the trunk he was sitting on. Now what would happen to him?

"SNUBBY! Where *are* you?" yelled Roger. He opened the boxroom door. "Gosh, what do you think you're doing in here, all alone with Loony? Didn't you hear me calling you? Come on down. The police want a word with us."

Snubby rose and with shaking knees went down the stairs. Roger and Diana skipped down, thrilled.

"Good morning, youngsters," said the Inspector with a very nice smile. "I want a word with you. Now did any of you notice the two men who were in the room with you at Marloes Castle, when you went to see the animals and the papers?"

Snubby's heart lightened a little. Perhaps the police hadn't come for him after all?

Roger nodded. "Yes, I remember them quite well. One was very old and bent—he bent so far forward that we couldn't see his face."

"And the other one was so hairy you couldn't see *his* face either! " said Diana.

The plain-clothes man, who had been writing in a little norcbook, looked up at this description.

"How hairy was he?" he asked.

"Well," said Diana, "he had very thick hair on his head, thick shaggy eyebrows, a thick moustache and a beard. You couldn't tell what he was really like at all, because he was all hair! "

"Was he big?" asked the detective.

"Yes," said Diana, "a heavy sort of man. Why, do you know him?"

The detective was turning back some pages of his notebook. "Your description happens to fit men who were known to visit two collections of rare documents, some of which were stolen recently," he said. "It fits exactly, in fact."

The children digested this in silence.

"Then do you think that's the man that stole the other papers—and stole the animals from Marloes Castle too?" asked Rover at last. "Why should he take those moth-eaten animals?"

"Ask me another!" said the detective. "Now—would you know this hairy man again if you saw him?"

"Yes—if he was still hairy," said Roger. "But I should think most of the hair was false!"

"You're probably right," said the Inspector. "Er—did you see the man's hands, by any chance?"

The children frowned, trying to remember. "I saw him using a magnifying glass, sliding it up and down the pages," said Roger. "And as far as I can remember he had quite ordinary hands—I didn't notice that they were very hairy, now I come to think of it—and perhaps they should have been as he was such a hairy man. Great-uncle Robert's got an awful lot of hair—and his hands are hairy on the back—look."

Everyone gazed at Great-uncle's hairy hands. He looked rather uncomfortable, and put them in his pockets as soon as he could.

"Would you say that the hairy man could wear this glove?" said the Inspector, producing a green glove from his pocket.

The children gazed at the glove. Loony went over to it and sniffed it excitedly. He pawed at it and whined.

"Why—he knows who wore that glove!" said Snubby, astonished. "That's the way he always acts if you show him anything that smells of a person he knows."

"Aha—now we're *getting* somewhere!" said the detective, sitting up suddenly. "You sure your dog knows the owner of that glove? Quite sure? Then that narrows things down considerably. The owner of the glove must be somebody you children know."

"Gosh!" said Roger, his thoughts flying to Tonnerre at

337

once. He looked closely at the glove. It was a small one, made of the very softest, finest leather imaginable. No—he didn't think it would fit Tonnerre. As far as he remembered, Tonnerre had very large hands—or had he? Perhaps he hadn't—perhaps Roger only thought that because Tonnerre was enormous and therefore it seemed right for him to have large hands.

Snubby took the glove and looked at it. Loony stood on his hind legs, still sniffing and whining. If only he could speak—what name would he say?

"Who wears this glove, Loony?" asked Snubby.

"Woof!" said Loony at once. The detective took the glove from Snubby and tossed it to the Inspector. He didn't want Loony to nibble their biggest clue.

"You haven't answered my question," said the Inspector, pocketing the glove. "I asked you if you thought the hairy man could have worn a glove as small as this."

The children thought hard.

"Yes, he might," said Roger.

"I don't remember," said Diana.

"He couldn't possibly," said Snubby.

"Hmm—very helpful!" said the Ispector with a laugh. "Well thanks, children. That's all I want to ask you. Keep your eyes open for the hairy man, will you? It's just possible he might tell us a few interesting things if we can find him."

Snubby escaped thankfully, throwing a grateful glance at Great-uncle Robert.

Loony tore after the children. Roger stopped to pat him. "So you know who the owner of the green glove is, do you?" he said. "Who wore that glove so as not to leave fingerprints, Loony? And where's the other glove of the pair? Can't you find it? Can't you tell us anything?"

"Woof-woof!" said Loony joyfully, enjoying this earnest conversation, and leaping round Roger excitedly.

"It's funny about that hairy man, isn't it?" said Diana. "What was he doing there that day, if he was the thief?"

338

Looking to see if there were any papers worth stealing—
or what?"

"Goodness knows," said Roger. "It's all a muddle—
the hairy man—the green glove—the stolen animals—and
Loony knowing who it is! It's really very, very peculiar."

CHAPTER 25

QUITE A LOT OF TALK!

ROGER and Diana felt quite themselves again, and suggested going over to see Barney to see if he had got over his sick attack too. They had a tremendous lot to tell him!

"Yes, you go and see him," said Mrs. Lynton. "A walk on this sunny morning will do you good after that nasty attack you had yesterday. Be careful what you buy at the Fair, *please*. You'd be wise not to buy any food there at all, after your horrid experience."

They went off together, Loony wild with delight at the thought of a walk. He capered ahead, putting his head down every hole they came to, sniffing for rabbits.

Barney was quite all right again. He had felt very sick and ill all night, but had at last gone to sleep and slept soundly till ten o'clock that morning. Now he was up and about, whistling, giving his hoopla stall a really good clean down.

"It's Saturday," he explained. "We always get most people that day, so I like to have everything looking spick and span. Hey, Miranda, leave Loony alone. If you pull his long ears, he'll pull your long tail!"

But that's just what Loony couldn't do because Miranda aggravatingly went and sat up on top of the round roof of the stall, swinging her tail well out of poor Loony's reach!

"Barney—have you seen the paper?" said Roger urgently.

"No," said Barney, surprised. "What's up? Gosh—you don't mean to say there's been a robbery—at the castle! Blow! We've missed it. We were ill and didn't go to watch."

"Sh!" said Diana warningly. "We've *heaps* to tell you, Barney. Can you come into some safe place for half an hour where no one can hear us?"

"Let me finish cleaning my stall and I'll come," said Barney, looking thrilled. "I'll be another ten minutes. Go and talk to the chimps. They seem rather down in the mouth this morning."

So they were. They sat together, their arms twined round one another, looking very mournful. "Have they had sausage sandwiches too?" asked Snubby of Vosta. But Vosta seemed cross and answered him shortly.

"Don't be silly. I'd never give them that kind of food. They're all right. Tonnerre's been at them, that's all. They can't bear his shouting."

"Nor can I," said Roger, putting his hand to his ears. He could hear Tonnerre yelling loudly. Somebody else was

341

getting into trouble too. It was Young 'Un. He came along howling, holding one side of his head.

"Whacked me for nothing," he wailed, and showed the children his red and swollen ear. "Said I'd kept some of his elephant-ride money for myself. I didn't. But I will next time."

"No, you mustn't," said Diana, shocked.

"Why not?" asked poor Young 'Un. "Look, he's boxed my ears for something I didn't do. All right, I'll go and do it then, to earn my punishment. I'll be straight with him then."

"Straight with him and crooked with yourself," said Roger. "Don't do anything wrong, Young 'Un. You'll be sorry."

Young 'Un didn't think so. He'd get even with Tonnerre, see if he wouldn't. He went off muttering.

The children left the bad-tempered Vosta, and his mournful chimps with their arms still round one another, and went to see if Barney was ready. He was.

They went off to the caravan Barney shared with another boy. "We'll be all right here, if we talk quietly," said Barney. "Now—what's in the paper? What's happened?"

They had bought a paper on the way and they showed it to Barney. His face was a study as he read about the curious robbery.

"Stuffed animals! Are they valuable?" he asked.

"Not these," said Roger. "They're the ones we saw ourselves, up in the castle—moth-eaten, badly-stuffed things."

"And *I* saw them in the castle grounds last night, where the thief had put them—and where the police found them this morning," put in Snubby. Barney's eyes nearly fell out of his head.

"*What?*" he said. "Did you go last night? All by yourself, to watch? My, but you're a brave one!"

Snubby swelled with pride at this. He told his story to Barney, who listened with intense interest.

"Barney—do you know anyone who wears green gloves —small ones?" asked Diana eagerly. "Especially an acrobatic man—one who could climb up steep walls and jump from sill to sill and all that?"

"Does Tonnerre wear green gloves ever?" asked Snubby in a whisper.

"Never seen him wear any gloves at all. Never seen anyone in the Fair wear gloves," said Barney. "Why, they'd laugh at it!"

"Is there anyone in the Fair who's an acrobat and has small hands?" asked Diana. "Anyone at all?"

Barney thought hard. "There's Vosta," he said at last. "He's a fine acrobat, you know, though training chimps is his job here. And he's got small hands, almost like a woman's."

Vosta! Could it be Vosta?

"Did the figure you saw climbing up the wall look anything like Vosta?" Roger asked Snubby. Snubby considered.

"Well—it's difficult to say, because I really couldn't see him clearly. All I know is he seemed absolutely certain and confident in all his movements," said Snubby. "As if he was quite used to such amazing climbing and leaping."

"It can't be Vosta," said Barney. "He wouldn't be such an idiot as to steal the wrong things. The one who steals the papers and things must either know them himself or be told in great detail which to take. Vosta wouldn't be such an idiot. Something went wrong last night."

Roger got out his map—the map he had made of the room in the castle.

"We mustn't forget that once again the thief apparently got in through fastened and locked windows," he said. "The paper says he didn't go through the locked doors because there's a burglar alarm set there, which rings if a door is opened at night. And the alarm didn't ring, so the doors weren't opened."

They looked at the map, poring over it. It was obvious that the thief meant to get in through the windows, as he climbed the outside walls. But how did he unfasten windows that were locked on the inside? And how in the world did he squeeze through the narrow bars?

"Give it up!" said Roger. "Unless by any chance he was Santa Claus and came down the chimney! Now that's an idea—would the thief be Santa Claus, do you suppose? Snubby, did it look like Santa climbing up the walls?"

"Don't be daft," said Snubby. "All the same—I *did* think I saw a figure up on the roof, by the chimney."

"You saw figures everywhere, according to you," said Diana disbelievingly. "The trouble with you, Snubby, is that we never know how much you are exaggerating."

"You don't suppose the thief could come down the chimney, do you?" asked Roger suddenly. "Joking apart, I mean. Look, I've marked where the fireplace is in this map. There was only one chimney up on the roof of that wing, because I expect all the fireplaces in the wing are under one another, in each room, and one chimney serves for all."

"These old houses have very wide chimneys," said Diana. "Big enough for a man to come down them quite easily, I should think."

"That fireplace didn't look awfully big, though," said Snubby, remembering. "*I* could have got down, perhaps—but I'm pretty certain that a fellow as big as Tonnerre couldn't."

"Then we'll have to rule the chimney out too," said Roger. "It's queer, you know. It's impossible for anyone to have gone through the burglar-alarm doors—it's impossible for anyone to have unfastened the windows from outside—and we're agreed that the chimney and fireplace are too small for anyone to get down those. All these impossibilities—and yet *somebody* found it possible to enter that room, and take from it a dozen or so stuffed animals!"

"He couldn't have taken them all at once," said Snubby. "There were too many. He must have made a good many journeys. I suppose he did all his climbing up and down whilst I popped off to sleep for half an hour."

"Well! You didn't tell us that before!" said Diana.

"I didn't think about it," said Snubby.

Footsteps came up the caravan steps at that moment and the door was flung open. Tonnerre stood there, black as thunder.

"So! This is where you idle with your fine friends, Barney!" he roared. "Reading the newspapers, too, when you should be doing your work!"

He snatched the paper from Barney and tore it across. Snubby began to tremble. He really was scared of Tonnerre.

"Get back to your work," he roared to Barney. "And you! You clear out of my field!" he shouted at the others. "Not this boy, though. Aha, it is the little snooper again. I will take him to my caravan and teach him a few things. Come, my little snooper."

Poor Snubby was hauled off before the others could do anything. Roger and Barney ran off after the angry Tonnerre, but they might as well have been dogs barking at a bull for all the notice he took of them. He really was in a towering rage!

Barney ran to Old Ma. "Old Ma—can you go after Mr. Tonnerre and make him let Snubby go? He hasn't done anything."

But even Old Ma was afraid of Tonnerre that day. "A black-hearted man he is," she said, staring after him as he dragged poor Snubby to his van. "I can't do nothing with him in one of his black moods."

But Loony wasn't afraid of anyone if they were hurting his beloved Snubby. He flew at Tonnerre, snapping and growling. He snapped at his ankles all the way up the steps of Tonnerre's caravan, he tore his trousers as he went in, and he bit his leg so hard, at last, that Tonnerre dropped Snubby with a yell and turned on the dog.

Loony shot out of his way under the bunk-beds. Snubby took his chance and leapt down the caravan steps, taking them all in one bound. Tonnerre leapt after him, also taking the steps in one bound.

Loony was scrabbling under the bunk. He came out with something in his mouth, and shot down the steps with it. He dropped it on the ground and went after Tonnerre again at top speed.

Diana, standing nearby, quite petrified by all this, looked to see what Loony had dropped. She stared in the greatest amazement.

It was a green glove—partner to the one that the police had shown the children that morning!

CHAPTER 26

THE SECOND GREEN GLOVE

DIANA picked up the glove at once. She stuffed it into the pocket of her dress. She didn't know why she did that—she just felt that it was important that she should.

Snubby was now outside the field gate. Loony was worrying Tonnerre's ankles, and the giant-like man was kicking out at him, shouting. All the people in the Fair ground were watching, most of them silent.

Barney sidled up to Roger. "Take Diana and go. Go through the gate at the opposite end of the field. Snubby's all right now—he'll race home. Don't come back here. I shall leave this Fair to-day. Tonnerre's got his knife into me, and I won't work for him any more. I'll come to your home and tell you what's happened as soon as I can. Go quickly now."

"Will you be all right, Barney?" asked Diana anxiously, as Roger pulled her away to the gate Barney had pointed to.

Barney nodded. "I know how to look after myself. Tonnerre's had some bad luck—something's gone wrong with him. He's always like this then—a dangerous fellow. Did you notice his hands? Enormous! *He* couldn't have worn that green glove!"

Diana had no time to tell him about the other glove. She was being dragged out of the gate at top speed by Roger. They set off to skirt the field, and join poor Snubby.

They found him sitting on a fence by the roadside,

Loony licking his ankles. He looked rather pale, and gave them a watery grin.

"Hallo," he said. "So you escaped all right. Gosh—I'm scared stiff of Tonnerre. I shall dream about him all night."

"Come on home, quick. I've got something to show you," said Diana.

They went home together, Loony at their heels, occasionally looking back to see if Tonnerre was by any chance stalking them. But he wasn't, of course. He was probably giving poor Barney a bad time now!

Diana could hardly contain herself. She was bursting to produce the glove! "Come into the summer-house quickly," she said. "Come on!"

They all went in and sat down, Sardine strolled in to join them. Loony wagged his tail, feeling so pleased with himself for biting Tonnerre that he couldn't even find it in him to chase Sardine.

Diana put her hand in her pocket and took out the green glove. The boys stared at it.

"Where did you get it?" asked Roger. "Did the police leave it somewhere?"

"No—it's not the glove they brought. It's the other glove!" said Diana. "What *do* you think of that?"

Roger snatched it up with a loud exclamation. "Good gracious! Where *did* you get it?"

"*I* didn't get it," said Diana. "Loony did. When Tonnerre took Snubby into his caravan, Loony followed, snapping and snarling. And when he came out he had this green glove in his mouth! He must have picked it up from the floor of the van."

Both boys stared at the glove, and Roger fingered it and turned it over in his hands. "What exactly does that mean then!" he said. "As far as I can see, it means that although Tonnerre himself can't wear these, he lends them to someone who does—in other words, he lends them to the thief!"

"That's right," said Snubby. He bent down and held the

348

glove to Loony's nose. The spaniel at once whined and sniffed excitedly.

"See? He knows the owner of *this* glove too—it's the same owner as the glove he sniffed this morning. It's somebody at the Fair," said Snubby.

"It's Vosta then," said Roger. "I noticed he had quite small hands this morning."

Diana slipped the glove on to her own hand. It fitted her perfectly. She laughed. She put on a mysterious, sinister voice.

"I belong to the Green Hands Gang," she said in a deep, hollow voice. "See my green glove!"

Great-uncle Robert was coming up to the summer-house with a book when he suddenly heard these words spoken in a very peculiar voice indeed. He stopped, alarmed.

Who was that speaking? What a queer voice! And good gracious, was that a green-gloved hand appearing out of the door of the summer-house?

It was. Diana was now doing a weird dance in the little house, and waving her green-gloved hand about.

Great-uncle Robert was very surprised indeed. He suddenly walked determinedly up to the summer-house and looked in, expecting to see something extraordinary.

All he saw was the three children and Loony, very startled by his sudden appearance. Diana put her green-gloved hand behind her back at once.

"What *is* the meaning of this?" Great-uncle asked irritably. "Diana, where did you get that glove. Tell me at once."

There was silence. Diana glanced desperately at the boys.

"Well?" said Great-uncle in quite a nasty voice. "Are you going to tell me—or would you rather I called your parents? Diana, I am quite sure you children know something that *we* ought to know—that maybe even the police ought to know."

"We'd better tell him," said Roger to the others. "Any-

349

way, I think it's got a bit beyond us now we've found this glove. All right, Great-uncle, we'll tell you all we know— and really, it's quite a lot."

"But first you'll have to believe that Snubby's tale of the Green Hands Gang was all a lot of nonsense," said Diana. "Or else you'll get muddled. It's just chance that a pair of green gloves has come into this."

"Will you please begin to tell me all you know," said Great-uncle impatiently, and sat himself down on the wooden seat in the summer-house.

Roger began the tale. Diana and Snubby added bits to it that he forgot. It was a long tale and an extraordinary one, especially the bit where Snubby had come across the gleaming-eyed creatures in the dell the night before. Great-uncle grunted.

"Hmm. An alarming experience. I hope it taught you a lesson! Tut-tut! What a story! And now what about this glove? It seems to me that this fellow Tonnerre had better be handed over to the police for questioning."

Snubby thought that was an awfully good idea. Aha! He'd get a bit of his own back on Tonnerre then! Yes, Snubby certainly thought that was a very good idea.

"Give me the glove," said Great-uncle importantly. "And understand this—the matter is out of your hands *entirely* now—you've nothing to do with it, and you must keep your noses out of it, or you'll get into trouble. This is for grown-ups to solve, not children."

But alas, not even Great-uncle, or Mr. and Mrs. Lynton, or even the police seemed to be able to solve the mystery of Rilloby Fair and the thefts at the castle.

Mr. Tonnerre said he didn't know anything at all about the green glove. Somebody must have put it into his caravan. He had never, never seen it before. Why should he have a green glove so small? See his enormous hands! It would fit his thumb and no more.

"Did you lend them to the thief to wear, in order that he might leave no fingerprints?" asked the Ispector patiently

350

for the twentieth time. But Tonnerre shook his great head impatiently.

"What have I to do with thieves who steal stuffed animals? I, who have live ones of my own. I tell you, I know nothing, of this pest of a green glove. NOTHING AT ALL."

And so the police had to let him go, because they certainly could not prove that he had lent the gloves to anyone, or that he even knew the thief. He went back to his van grumbling loudly, and everyone kept well out of his way.

Then the police called on Vosta. What did *he* know about the gloves? Were they his? Had he ever worn them? Could he climb walls? Would he please put them on?

He did so—and certainly they seemed rather small for him, although his hands were not very large for a man.

The two chimpanzees watched the policemen when they went to Vosta's tent to interview him. They still seemed rather subdued, especially Burly, and sat quietly with their arms round one another's necks.

They were interested to see the gloves. They got up and peered at them and patted them.

"Anything new interests them," said Vosta, pushing the chimps away. "Go and sit down, you two. Look out for your handkerchief, sir, if you've got one in your pocket. They'll be after it, especially Hurly, who's a real pick-pocket."

It was impossible to get anything helpful out of Vosta at all.

He just said he didn't know, he didn't know whose the gloves were, he didn't know who the thief was, he didn't know anything.

The Inspector put the gloves into his pocket impatiently. He felt that both Tonnerre and Vosta *did* know something—but he was up against a blank wall. He could ask no more questions, go no further.

He went off with the detective. Vosta made a grimace

after them. He watched them go all the way across the field.

He didn't see Hurly show Burly something. He didn't see Burly hold out his paw for it. He didn't see the chimps tuck their find under the blankets in their bunk.

Hurly had picked the Inspector's pocket as he turned to go. He had got the pair of green gloves—and now they were well hidden under the blankets!

The gloves excited Burly. He wanted to put them on. He must wait till Vosta wasn't there, because Vosta would take them away.

CHAPTER 27

SUNDAY—AND MONDAY

THE next day came. It was Sunday. It seemed very peaceful and quiet after all the excitement of the day before.

Barney turned up in the morning with Miranda. He saw Roger at the window and waved. Roger opened the window and shouted to him. "The others are in the summer-house. I'm just coming."

Barney went to the summer-house, and found Diana and Snubby there with Loony. Loony gave Barney and Miranda a tremendous welcome.

"I say!" said Barney, looking at Diana in awe. "You going to a party or something? You're all dressed up. And Snubby looks awfully *clean*."

"No, we're not going to a party," said Diana, surprised. "It's Sunday, and we've just been to church, that's all. Don't you ever go?"

"No. But I'd like to," said Barney. He wanted to do everything these friends of his did, if he could. "Hallo, Roger!"

Roger walked in, also looking very clean and spruce. "Hallo, Barney," he said. "Have you left the Fair?"

"No. Tonnerre won't let me go till the Fair leaves Rillo-by," said Barney. "But he's better now. Not nearly so fierce. I really think the visit of the police gave him a fright. I came to see if you'd got any more news. Solved the mystery yet?"

"No. I don't think it ever *will* be solved," said Roger.

"It's just a list of impossible things—things that can't happen and yet did—with a pair of green gloves complicating everything still more."

"Listen," said Barney, "I shan't be able to see you to-morrow. Vosta's having the day off, goodness knows why—and I'm to see to the chimps. Young 'Un is taking the hoop-la stall. You mustn't come to the Fair again, of course. You'd be like a red rag to a bull if Tonnerre caught sight of you."

"Well, can't you spend the day with us to-day?" said Diana at once. "The Fair doesn't open on Sundays. Wouldn't you like to be with us?"

"Well, yes, of course I would," said Barney, his blue eyes shining. "I love your home. But would your mother mind? And what about your father? He's home to-day, isn't he?"

"They won't mind if we keep out of their way," said Diana. "They do like us to be quiet on Sundays, of course. But we can always talk and read."

"You lend me another book of Shakespeare's," said Barney. "I'll be quiet enough then! "

The others laughed. It always amused them to see Barney labouring through a play of Shakespeare—determined to understand it, so that if ever he did come across his unknown father who had once acted in so many of Shakespeare's plays, he would at least have *something* in common with him.

"I'll lend you *Hamlet*," said Roger. "You'll like that. There's a super ghost in it."

Mrs. Lynton was very willing for Barney to spend the day. Great-uncle Robert was not too pleased to see yet another child, complete with monkey, added to the riotous trio.

"How I'm ever going to get my Memoirs written, I don't know," he complained to Mrs. Lynton. "Children and dogs and cats and monkeys everywhere I go! "

"You go and have your little nap in the study and I'll

send the children out-of-doors this glorious day," said Mrs. Lynton.

"I said 'my Memoirs,' not a nap," said Great-uncle with dignity, and retired to the study. He carefully put out paper, fountain pen and notes on the table, headed a page "Chapter Five," and then promptly settled down in an arm-chair and went to sleep.

"Now don't you dare to disturb your Great-uncle," Mrs. Lynton warned the children. "Don't let Miranda leap in at the window on to him—and don't let Loony bark—and see that Sardine doesn't get into the study and jump up on Great-uncle's knee."

"Right, Mother," said Roger. "And I'll tell that loud-voice thrush to pipe down, and shoo all the bees out of the garden, and as for that earwig I saw stamping about this morning, I'll . . ."

"Now, now, Roger!" said his mother, smiling. "Don't be ridiculous. Go along to the summer-house and don't let me hear a sound from any of you!"

Sunday was very peaceful. Barney enjoyed it more than anyone. It was heaven to him to be in a family, in a home, to belong, even for only one day, to a little company of people who liked him and accepted him as one of them-selves.

"They can't understand what it's like not to have any people of your own, not to have a home you can always go to—no, not even Snubby understands, although he's got no parents. He belongs here. I don't belong anywhere," thought Barney soberly. "Perhaps if I ever find my father, I shall have a home with him, and belong there."

The children talked a lot about the green gloves, Ton-nerre, Vosta, the castle and the rest. They went over and over everything again and again. What a mystery!

"The Mystery of Rilloby Fair!" said Diana. "It would be exciting if we could solve it."

Barney went back to the Fair reluctantly that evening. Miranda had enjoyed her day as much as he had. "Good-bye," he said. "I'll see you on Tuesday—if I can get over here. The Fair leaves on Wednesday, you know, and I certainly shan't go with it. I don't want to work for Tonnerre."

"What will you do then, Barney?" asked Diana.

"Oh, I'll get another job somewhere," said Barney. "But I'll keep in touch with you. I'll send you a card telling you where I am always. And perhaps I shall be able to get a job somewhere near here when the summer holidays come."

He went off. The children all went to bed, feeling tired. "Though I can't imagine why," said Snubby. "We simply haven't done a thing to-day—not even taken poor old Loony for a walk."

"Woof," said Loony hopefully. But there was no walk that night!

The next day Great-uncle announced that he was going to Marloes Castle to arrange and pack up the valuable papers there, in order that they might be locked away in safety.

"I shall go about three o'clock," he said. "And seeing that Diana here has such an interest in old documents, I'd be glad to take her with me. She would be a help, I'm sure."

Diana was horrified. What, spend ages listening to dry information about centuries-old papers that she couldn't even read—all alone with Great-uncle! She gazed round at Roger and Snubby in despair.

The looked back. Poor old Diana! How awful! Then a thought came into Roger's mind. It would be rather interesting to go to that room again—and have a good look round. He might find a clue the police had missed. Anyway, it would be fun to see if there was any single place where the thief could have come in.

"It's just conceivable there might be a secret passage somewhere," thought Roger. "I never thought of that!'"

He pictured himself tapping round the wall of the room. He could have a look at the fireplace too, and see if it really was big enough for, say, Tonnerre.

"Great-uncle, I should like to come too," he said politely.

"So should I," said Snubby. "I'd awfully like to have a look round the grounds, Great-uncle. Do you think Lord Marloes would mind?"

"Dear me—so you would all like to keep me company this afternoon?" beamed Great-uncle, pleased at finding himself so popular all of a sudden. "Very well. I will certainly take you. I see no harm in your looking round the grounds, Snubby, if you behave yourself."

He said nothing about Loony and neither did Snubby. But when Snubby heard that Great-uncle was going in a car he knew there was no hope for Loony.

"I'd like a walk, Great-uncle," he said, "so if it's all right with you I'll walk across the fields and join you at the gates."

"Certainly, my boy, certainly," said Great-uncle. "Anything you like! We'll have a grand time together!"

"We shall have to be back in good time for supper," said Snubby suddenly. "There'll be meringues."

"How do you know?" asked Diana.

"Cook told me. She wouldn't eat her Sunday hat yesterday, though I begged and begged her to—so we're eating meringues to-night instead."

Mrs. Lynton looked astonished. "What's all this about Cook's Sunday hat? Oh, Snubby, you haven't been upsetting Cook finding fault with her Sunday hat, surely?"

"Aunt Susan! She's got a *marvellous* Sunday hat," said Snubby indignantly. "It's got three roses, a wreath of violets, and five carnations in it. It's wizard. I can quite well understand why she doesn't want to eat it."

"There *are* times when I think you are not quite sane, Snubby," said Mrs. Lynton. "I don't know *what* your masters at school think of you."

"Oh, they think the same as you," Snubby assured her cheerfully. "I don't mind. It's all the same to me."

That afternoon the car came for Great-uncle, and he

and Diana and Roger got into it. Snubby had already gone off with Loony. He was to meet them at the gates.

"Now for a nice happy afternoon," said Great-uncle, pleased. "Nothing I like better than browsing among old, rare papers, breathing in the air of past centuries. What a peaceful place that old room is."

It wasn't going to be. It was going to be just about the most exciting place in Rilloby that afternoon. But Great-uncle didn't know that!

CHAPTER 28

THINGS BEGIN TO HAPPEN

SNUBBY met them at the castle gates with Loony. Great-uncle eyed the spaniel with annoyance.

"I didn't say you could bring that dog!"

"You didn't say I wasn't to," pointed out Snubby in a reasonable voice. "Stop scratching, Loony. You do seem to have a bad effect on Loony, Great-uncle. It seems as if he's *got* to scratch whenever he sees you."

"You can't bring him into the castle," said Great-uncle, determined not to enter into a conversation about scratching again. "You'll have to stay out here in the grounds."

Snubby didn't mind. He meant to explore the grounds thoroughly, and see if he could find any clues. He also meant to go and find the dell again, where the stuffed animals had been, and enjoy remembering that terrifying episode. He wondered if the sacks were still up on the wall. And what about the rope-ladder? Was it still under the bush?

"I expect it's there still—and the sacks too," he thought. "The police said nothing about those. Gosh, they're not very bright. I'd have spotted those at once if I'd been one of the police on the job."

Great-uncle presented his pass. He and Diana and Roger were taken into the castle, whilst Snubby wandered off into the grounds with an excited Loony, who foresaw all kinds of rabbit adventures for himself that afternoon.

Roger was impatient to be inside the room with the

double-locked door. The butler unlocked one door—then
the second one—and finally the third one, with its two keys.
They then were in the old room, with its shelves of yellowed papers.

Roger and Diana glanced round with interest. Half the
stuffed animals were gone, of course. The police had not
brought them back. They were probably still somewhere
in the police station, staring at the policemen with their
lifeless, glassy eyes.

"All the big animals are left," said Roger. "I suppose
the thief couldn't manage them. The squirrels are gone—
and the fox-cubs but not the foxes—and the pole-cat—
and the albino badger. He wasn't very big either."

"Diana—we'll just go carefully through all the papers
before we pack them," said Great-uncle, longing to explain
pages upon pages to poor Diana. "Now this one . . ."

Diana cast a look of misery at Roger and went to listen
Roger began to look round. He examined the windows. Nobody could *possibly* undo those fastenings from outside!
And only the very smallest, thinnest person could squeeze
through the bars.

He went to the double-locked door and examined that.
No thief could come in that way without keys—and if he
had the keys, the burglar alarm would ring as soon as the
door was opened. No—that way was impossible too.

He went to the fireplace. It was an old-fashioned open
grate. As the fire was never used, there were no fire-irons
at all, but only an old fire-screen made of wrought-iron.

Roger bent down and tried to look up the chimney. It
looked decidely narrow. "I *might* be able to squeeze up,"
thought Roger. "But I doubt it—and it would be frightfully uncomfortable. I dare say it widens out a bit above
though."

He looked at the fire place itself. It was full of bits and
pieces that had fallen down the chimney. "Of course, they
might have been dislodged by somebody getting down, but
on the other hand, bits and pieces always *do* fall down
chimneys," thought Roger, feeling rather like a detective.

He went to the window and looked out. He saw something that filled him with extreme amazement! He stared intently. Then a shout came to his ears.

"I say! Look at this!" cried Roger suddenly, making Diana and Great-uncle jump violently. "What's going on down there?"

He might well ask. Snubby, down in the grounds, was also feeling extremely astonished. He had been wandering round with Loony and had come to the little dell where he had seen the stuffed animals, when he heard a sound nearby.

He had turned—and looking down at him from out of the bushes was a hairy, grinning face with shining eyes! Snubby got a frightful shock. He thought it was one of the stuffed animals come to life!

"Gosh—what is it?" he said, and took a step backwards. Loony gave a delighted bark and rushed into the bushes where the hairy face was. Snubby was amazed. Loony should have barked or growled! Instead of that he had yelped in delight and gone off with the Face!

Then Snubby heard yells, and recognised Barney's voice. "Come here, you pest, you! Do your hear? Where have you gone?"

"It's *Barney*! What's *he* doing here?" said Snubby, full of surprise. "Loony, where have you gone? Hey, Barney, where are you?"

Barney's voice came back, surprised. "That you, Snubby? What are *you* doing here? I say, have you seen Burly? He's gone completely mad, so look out."

"*Burly!*" said Snubby, more amazed than ever. "What's *he* here for? Gosh, yes, I've seen him. At least, I saw his grinning face. He's gone now, and taken Loony with him."

He made his way towards Barney's voice. Barney was on the road side of the wall. He called again.

"I'm going to see if our rope-ladder is still under the bush, and the sacks on the wall, if the police haven't found them! I'm coming over. I simply must find Burly. He's gone crackers."

He found the rope-ladder under the bush and soon had it up on the wall. He climbed it quickly and sat on the sacks. He looked all round to see if he could spot Burly.

"What happened to make Burly so mad?" asked Snubby. "Why did he come all the way here?"

"Don't ask *me*!" said Barney. "I was in Vosta's caravan with both chimps, when bless me if Hurly didn't pull out a pair of green gloves from under the blankets of his bunk."

"What—the ones we saw?" said Snubby.

"I don't know. The police had those—but I wouldn't put it past Hurly to sneak them out of the Inspector's pocket," said Barney. "I bet that's what he did! Anyway, Burly snatched them and put them on—and they fitted him marvellously. Like a glove, in fact! He kept stroking them and muttering to himself, and then he rapped at the cupboard where his toy animals are kept."

He stopped for breath, still keeping a look-out for Burly from the top of the wall.

"Well, I hadn't the key to his toy cupboard. Vosta's got that," said Barney. "So he couldn't have his little toy animals to play with. Then he just seemed to go mad! He banged himself with his arms, and yowled like anything. And then he was out of the window like a streak, haring over the Fair field!"

"Gosh!" said Snubby, enthralled with this story. "Go on!"

"Well, I followed him, of course," said Barney. "And he came straight here. I couldn't catch him up. He was up and over the wall as easy as anything—*he* didn't need a ladder. Well, I suppose he's somewhere in the grounds. What's made him come here?"

Before Snubby could answer a deep voice spoke from the other side of the wall. "I'm afraid I shall have to hold you for questioning concerning this here ladder," said the voice. Barney almost fell off the wall.

"Golly—it's a bobby," he said. "Where were you?"

"I've been hiding behind that tree ever since we found

this here ladder hidden, and the sacks atop of the wall," said the policeman. "We reckoned whoever put them there might use them again, if we didn't let on we'd found them. And seemingly we were right. You come down, and let me take you to the police station for questioning."

"No," said Barney, and scrambled down the other side as fast as he could. "I must find Burly," he said to the petrified Snubby. "And Miranda too. She scampered after him over the wall, and left me standing on the other side! Come on—take no notice of the bobby. We can easily shake him off!"

He dragged poor Snubby into the bushes, whilst the annoyed policeman began to climb slowly and painfully up the rope-ladder. "Take me to the place you saw Burly in just now," said Barney. He may still be near there."

Snubby took him to the dell—and sure enough, there was Burly, with Miranda and Loony! Burly was behaving in a peculiar fashion. His head held in his hands, he was rocking to and fro, making a little whimpering noise.

Miranda was stroking him, and Loony was licking him. It was plain that the chimpanzee was very unhappy.

He looked extremely queer in his red shorts, red-striped jersey—and *green gloves*! What was the matter with him? Why was he behaving like that?

Burly suddenly sprang up. He gave a loud howl and bounded away. Loony ran after him and Miranda ran too, whimpering. Both the animals knew that something was wrong with Burly.

Burly ran through the trees to the castle walls. Barney gave a shout. "Hey, Burly, come back! Come to old Barney!"

That was the shout that Roger had heard up in the old room on the second floor. He looked out and saw Burly tearing over to the castle, with his green gloves on, and behind him came Loony and Miranda, followed at some distance by Barney and Snubby—and behind them, good gracious, a policeman!

No wonder Roger could hardly believe his eyes. But what was to come was even more unbelievable.

Burly came to the walls of the castle. He leapt to a window-sill. He leapt to a gutter-pipe and shinned up it rapidly and easily. He leapt to another window-sill, and up another pipe. Then he climbed confidently up the thick ivy nearby, right to the roof.

"Look at that," said Snubby, awed. "What a climb. It was *Burly* I saw the other night! I'm sure it was!"

Burly was now on the roof. He ran to the one and only chimney and peered down it. He leapt into it and disappeared.

Down in the room below three startled people stared at one another. Great-uncle, Roger and Diana had tried in vain to see what was happening outside. They had lost sight of Burly when he had begun to climb up the walls—and then had caught a quick glimpse of him again as he leapt on to their window-sill and off. What in the world was he doing?

They heard a noise in the chimney. Roger ran to it. Two hairy legs appeared, and then Burly swung himself down into the fireplace, blinking. He had managed it easily.

He stood there, looking at three amazed people. Diana spoke to him. "Burly! What are you doing?"

Ah! That was the kind girl who had given him a toy dog. Burly was no longer frightened to see people staring at him. He came out into the room, looking very strange in his queer dress.

Great-uncle shrank back. He had never seen Burly before. To him the chimpanzee looked fierce and savage. He was horrified to see Diana go up and take the green-gloved paw. Suppose the creature bit her?

But Burly didn't bite. He stroked Diana's arm, and then he looked round the room. He sniffed the air. He ran to the shelves where the yellowed parchments were.

The three watched him, amazed. What was he doing now? Burly smelt each pile. He stopped at one and took out a paper. He sniffed at another lot, and took another piece of parchment. Great-uncle watched him, gaping.

Roger touched Diana's arm. "The solution of the mystery!" he said. "I see it all now. How *could* we have been so blind?"

CHAPTER 29

BURLY IS VERY CLEVER

ALL three watched the chimpanzee as he sniffed through
the papers and took one here and one there. He seemed
quite certain which to take. There was no hesitation at
all.

"How does he know which to choose?" said Great-
uncle Robert, puzzled. "He's taking one or two of the
most valuable—I can see that. But how does he know?"

"He sniffs before he pulls a paper out of its pile," said Diana. "Look, each time, he sniffs first."

"Well! Of course! *I* know how he knows which papers to take!" exclaimed Roger suddenly. "Diana—do you remember that hairy man—how we watched him sliding his magnifying-glass up and down some of the papers?"

"Yes, I remember," said Diana.

"Well, he must have had something on the base of the magnifying-glass that was rubbed off on the papers," said Roger excitedly. "And the stuff would leave a smell—and when the chimp was sent to take certain papers he knew which to take because of the smell. See him sniffing at them all now!"

"Remarkable. Most remarkable," said Great-uncle, who looked rather dazed. "I suppose he's trained to do that. Chimpanzees must be extremely clever."

"Oh, they *are*," said Roger, watching Burly take yet another paper. "But that's an old circus trick, Great-uncle, to smear papers with something that smells, so that an animal will instinctively choose those. Who trained *you*, Burly?"

Burly looked up at his name and gabbled something. His green-gloved hands worked quickly through the parchments.

"No fingerprints, you see—not even a chimp's prints left behind!" said Roger. "I wonder what made him come along here this afternoon to do the job he should really have done the other night?"

"Perhaps he saw the gloves—and they reminded him," suggested Diana. "Oh—what's he going to do now?"

Burly had caught sight of the stuffed animals. He dropped all his papers on the floor and whimpered. He ran across to the few animals left and lifted up a fox. Great-uncle quietly gathered up the papers, opened a drawer in the nearby table, and put them inside. He meant to have them examined to see exactly what gave them the smell that Burly recognised so easily.

The chimpanzee sat down on the floor and nursed the stuffed fox. Diana nudged Roger.

"I'm sure I know what happened the other night," she whispered. "He came for the papers with no other idea in his head but to do the sort of job he's often done before, and he must suddenly have seen the stuffed animals staring at him in the moonlight! You know how mad he is on toy animals—he must have thought these stuffed ones were extra big toy ones—possibly put there for *him!*"

"Yes—and he took them into the grounds, one after the other—just the little ones that he could manage easily," went on Roger. "Poor Burly. He stood them all in the dell, and for some reason left them there. But he didn't take any of the papers. He was so wrapped up in the animals."

"And I expect that's why the chimps were so miserable the next day when we saw them," said Diana. "Somebody had scolded Burly hard—and he was upset, so Hurly was upset too. Do you remember how they sat with their arms round one another, looking thoroughly miserable?"

"Who had scolded them?" wondered Roger. "Vosta, do you suppose?"

"Maybe. And probably Tonnerre too, because Vosta said he had, you remember?" said Diana. "Somehow or other Tonnerre's in this mystery, Roger. I'm sure he is!"

Burly put down the fox and picked up a stuffed dog, very moth-eaten indeed. He nursed that too. Then he got up and looked at the fireplace, evidently considering whether or not he could get up the chimney with such a large animal.

There suddenly came the sound of doors being un-locked. Voices were heard. Burly looked alarmed. He ran to Diana and crouched down beside her, chattering. She patted him gently on the head. "Don't be afraid, Burly. I won't let anyone hurt you!"

The door of the room was unlocked with its two separate keys. It opened. In poured Barney, Snubby, Miranda, Loony, the policeman, the custodian and the butler!

"Is Burly here? He went down the chimney!" cried Snubby.

"Yes—there he is!" cried Barney and ran to the chimpanzee, who took his hand trustingly. He loved Barney. Miranda leapt on to the chimpanzee's shoulder, chattering. He looked happier at once.

The policeman looked absolutely bewildered. What with cheeky boys, a spaniel and a monkey, and now a chimpanzee he didn't really know what to do. He looked with relief at Great-uncle, glad to see a responsible-looking grown-up.

"Perhaps you can help me, sir?" he said. "What's all this here about?"

"Constable—we have found the one who stole the stuffed animals," said Great-uncle solemnly. "Before our very eyes this afternoon he stole more valuable papers."

"Then I shall arrest him," said the constable at once, importantly. "Which of them is it, sir?"

"It's the chimpanzee," said Great-uncle. "Be careful how you arrest him!"

Snubby gave a chortle at the sight of the policeman's alarmed face. Loony sat down and began to scratch himself violently. Burly put down the stuffed dog he was hugging and took Miranda into his arms instead, nursing her and crooning.

"Hrrrm. I find that beast rather pathetic," said Great-uncle unexpectedly. "Can't blame him for anything he's done, Constable. Whoever trained him is responsible. That's the fellow you want—the trainer."

Heavy footsteps came down the little passage to the door, and in came the Inspector. The policeman had telephoned for him as soon as he had got into the castle, and he had jumped into his car and come along at once.

"Well," he said, looking round at the big company in amazement. "You're a mixed lot, I must say. My word— *the green gloves!* Look who's wearing them—well, well, well!"

He stared at Burly as if he couldn't believe his eyes. The

369

chimpanzee stared back. He remembered the Inspector. This was the man out of whose pocket Hurly had taken the green gloves. He took them off suddenly and flung them on the floor.

The constable began to talk to the Inspector, trying to tell him what had happened, but Barney interrupted. "I can tell you all that happened, sir," he said. "I can see it all now! I understand why the sight of the gloves sent Burly here again. I understand why . . ."

"Speak when you're spoken to," said the Inspector. He turned to Great-uncle. "Mr. Lynton, sir, perhaps *you* would say a few words first. I'm all at sea."

Somehow or other, first by this person and then by that, he was told every single thing. He listened, astonished and almost disbelieving. He was shown the fireplace where Burly had come down. He was shown the pile of papers that Burly had so carefully chosen after sniffing at them. He sniffed at them too.

"I can smell something myself," he said, sniffing again. "Yes—a very clever trick. The chimp had no other way of telling which were the valuable papers and which weren't, except by smell. There's somebody remarkably clever behind all this. Who is it?"

Everyone took a turn at sniffing at the papers. Certainly they had a faint, elusive smell, quite distinguishable.

"So that's how the other thefts were planned," said the Inspector thoughtfully. "Someone examined the collections first, and smeared the papers he wanted with something to make them smell. He must also have examined how the chimp could get in and out—a skylight sometimes, a chimney another time, a small window a third time, or maybe a ventilator—somewhere impossible for a grown man to get through. But the chimp could always manage to climb and wriggle through a tiny entrance—he's small and supple and a born acrobat."

"A most remarkable and successful plan," put in Great-uncle. "If we could only lay our hands on the hairy man who was here the other day smearing the papers with something on the base of his large magnifying-glass—you'd have the ring-leader, Inspector."

"Yes," said Barney. "But there must be two or three go-betweens, Inspector. Vosta must be one. He'd have to take Burly to whatever place had been chosen, and point out the way to go up the walls. And there must be another go-between too—the one who warns Vosta what to do—the one who received the note we found a bit of the other day —that said 'Marloes Castle. Midnight.' Who received that note?"

"Quite a lot of loose ends to tie up!" said the Inspector. "Well, we'll see if we can tie up a few to-day. We'll take this chimp back to the Fair, and find out where Vosta is—he may be back by this time."

The custodian and the butler, neither of whom had said a single word, so completely amazed and bewildered were they, let the little company out of the castle. The Inspector took the pile of papers with him that Burly had so carefully chosen. Burly went down the stairs holding Barney's hand, chattering away to him.

Two cars stood outside—the Inspector's and the one that Great-uncle had hired. "Room for everyone," said the Inspector genially. "Hop in. We'll all go to the Fair. Take the chimp, the monkey and the dog into the other car, if you don't mind. Now—are we all set? To the Fair then!"

CHAPTER 30

THE MYSTERY IS SOLVED

VOSTA was back in his tent, puzzled to find Burly gone, when they all arrived in the field. He looked frightened when he saw the Inspector. Burly ran to him and flung his arms round him.

"What have you been up to?" said Vosta to Burly. "And where have *you* been?" he said to Barney. "I told you not to leave the chimps."

"Illia Juan Vosta, I have some questions to ask you, and I must warn you that anything you say may be taken down and used in evidence against you," said the Inspector sternly. The constable took out a black notebook and licked his pencil, preparing to write.

Vosta looked extremely alarmed. "I haven't done anything," he stammered.

"You have trained this chimpanzee to steal, and to break into various buildings," went on the Inspector in a cold, calm voice. "We know that various papers are smeared with a substance that the chimpanzee can smell, and these are the papers he takes. We know further that . . ."

"I didn't have anything to do with that," cried out Vosta, turning very pale. "I've always said it was a mug's game, using the chimp. I've never had anything to do with it."

"Except that you lent your chimpanzee, which you yourself had trained to steal, and you took him each time to the place where the theft was to be committed," said the Inspector in a voice that sent a shiver down Snubby's back. "Didn't you, Vosta?"

"They're not my chimps," muttered Vosta. "And I never trained them to steal. They were trained before I had them."

"Whose were they before you had them?" rapped out the Inspector.

Vosta looked terrified. "They were Tonnerre's," he said in a low voice. "He trained them. He trained Hurly to pick pockets, and he trained Burly to do all kinds of other stealing tricks. Burly's clever. You can teach him anything."

"Why did you take on the chimpanzees from Tonnerre?" asked the Inspector.

"I was an acrobat," said Vosta, still in a low voice. "And I hurt my back. So Tonnerre offered me the chimps if I'd keep on with him in the Fair—and do one or two things he wanted."

"I see. And one of the things he wanted was that you should take Burly to whatever building he told you, and see that he got in somehow and sniffed out the papers he had marked," said the Inspector.

"*He* never marked them," said Vosta. "He didn't know a thing about old papers. I used to take them from Burly and give them to Tonnerre—and he passed them on to someone else. I don't know who—but it was the fellow who did the marking of the papers. This fellow used to tell Tonnerre where to take the Fair—we never knew where we were going."

"Quite. I imagine he chose whatever place he had marked down for his next theft," said the Inspector. "And now just tell me the name of the man at the top of all this."

"I tell you, I don't know," said Vosta obstinately. "Why don't you ask Tonnerre? Why pick on me? I'm only the cat's-paw, I am."

"It's the hairy man," said Snubby, butting in. "We do

know that—do you know a very hairy man, Vosta?"

"I'm not answering any questions from *you*," snarled Vosta. "If you kids hadn't come here, snooping and prying . . ."

"That's enough, Vosta," said the Inspector. "Constable, stay here with him. I'm going across to this fellow Tonnerre. He, too, is only a cat's-paw, it seems, but a bigger one than Vosta. Still, maybe he'll lead us to the real villain."

Barney led him to Tonnerre's caravan. The Fair folk, who had stood around in silence, watching Vosta being interviewed, moved back. Old Ma called out:

"Tonnerre's got a visitor. He's in a black mood. You've got to watch out, Mister!"

The Inspector did not deign to reply. He rapped imperiously on the door of Tonnerre's caravan.

"Get out!" yelled Tonnerre's voice. "Didn't I say I wasn't to be disturbed?"

"Open up," came the Inspector's stern voice. The door was flung open and Tonnerre stood there frowning blackly. He shut the door behind him and came down the steps.

"Say what you've got to say and go," he growled.

"Who's your visitor, Tonnerre?" asked the Inspector mildly. "Let's have a look at him."

"He's a gentleman, see? I'm not going to have him dragged into any funny business," said Tonnerre angrily. "He's a friend of mine, with nothing to do with you at all. Anyway, what's brought you here again, wasting my time and interfering?"

"Let's have a look at your visitor, Tonnerre," repeated the Inspector. "What are you hiding him away for?"

Snubby was so full of excitement and anticipation that he could hardly contain himself. His enemy had met his match! The Inspector wouldn't take no for an answer. Who *was* the visitor?

"I bet it's the hairy man, I bet it is," said Snubby to himself. "He's come to get the papers and he's wild with Tonnerre because the chimp didn't get them."

Tonnerre made no move to open the door—but it suddenly opened behind him and somebody came out on to the top step.

"What is all this disturbance?" said a cultured voice. "Tonnerre, have I come at an awkward moment? I will go."

He stepped down, but the Inspector placed himself in front of him. "Your name, sir?" he asked.

The four children gazed at the man in disappointment. He was not the hairy man. He was quite clean-shaven. He had smooth black hair tinged with grey, no moustache, no shaggy eyebrows, no beard.

"My name is Thomas Colville," said the man. "My business with Mr. Tonnerre is private—he and I are old friends. I am sorry to see he seems to be in trouble. My business with him can wait."

"You didn't happen to come and see him about some papers you wanted him to get for you, did you?" said the Inspector stolidly.

"I don't know what you are talking about, my good fellow," said the man, and pushed by the Inspector impatiently.

Snubby stared at him. No, he certainly wasn't a bit like the hairy man—though he was about the same size and build.

Snubby walked a few steps beside the man, staring at him, much to his annoyance. Then Snubby suddenly gave such a yell that Loony barked wildly and ran to him.

"I say—he *is* the man we saw looking at the papers—the hairy man. He is! I couldn't help noticing the tremendous tufts of hair he had growing out of his ears—and look, he's got them—just the same. It's him!"

Things happened all at once then. The man began to run. The constable, watching from Vosta's tent, saw him, and ran to cut him off. Young 'Un ran out and tripped him up neatly. Tonnerre went mad and tried to hit the Inspector. Loony bit him and then everyone closed in, yelling and

375

shrieking with excitement, so that the poor Inspector didn't know *what* was going on for a few minutes.

"You take your sister and brother home," he said urgently to Roger. He thought that Snubby was Roger's brother. "Go on—we may be going to have a rough time here. Telephone the police station and tell them to send up men quickly."

Roger fled with Diana, Snubby and Loony. He was sorry to go at such a time, but he knew he had to take Diana into safety in case things began to get too rough.

Outside the gate stood two cars—one was the police car, with Great-uncle Robert waiting patiently inside, rather alarmed at the excitement going on in the Fair field. The other was the taxi he had hired, complete with its driver.

"Oh, good!" said Roger, stopping. "I'd forgotten the cars—and Great-uncle. I say, Great-uncle, things are boiling up terrifically—everything's really smashing—and we've got to telephone the police station for more men. Can we bag the taxi and drive there?"

"Bless us all!" said poor Great-uncle in alarm, and clambered out of the police car as quickly as he could. He got into the taxi and in a quavering voice told the man to drive to the police station.

Great-uncle wouldn't let the car stop at the police station more than half a minute, just time enough for Roger to give his message.

"I must get home," the old man kept saying. "This isn't good for my heart. Dear, dear—little did I think I'd get mixed up with a lot of criminals and madmen and chimpanzees when I came to stay with your mother. I must go. I must leave. I can't stay a night longer!"

"But Great-uncle—it's been absolutely *wizard*," protested Snubby. "I mean—if you want a first-class mystery, well, you couldn't have a better one than the one to do with Rilloby Fair."

But Great-uncle didn't want any mysteries or adventures. "I just want to pack my things and go," he said. "That man Tonnerre's a dreadful fellow—I was glad I

376

was safely in the car when I saw him come down the caravan steps as black as—as——"

"Thunder," said Diana.

"He looked as if he might be the chief of some horrible
gang," shuddered poor Great-uncle.

"The Green Hands Gang," said Snubby, with a chortle.

CHAPTER 31

ALL'S WELL!

GREAT-UNCLE was as good as his word. As soon as he got in, he found Mrs. Lynton, announced his intention of leaving that very night, and went up to pack his bag.

Mrs. Lynton was amazed. She looked at the excited children.

"What's the matter with him? What *have* you been doing?"

"Nothing!" said Roger indignantly. "Oh, Mother, do listen—we've got the most exciting news."

"Well, here's your father—tell him too," said his mother. "And do come in to your supper. You're so dreadfully late, and Cook's made you some meringues for your pudding."

"Gosh—do you know we've never had any tea?" said Snubby in an injured voice. "Would you believe it? No wonder I feel jolly hungry."

"So many things have been happening that it's difficult to know where to begin our story," said Roger to his mother.

"Go and wash before you begin," said his mother, suddenly noticing how dirty they all looked. "Your news can wait. It can't be as important and exciting as all that."

But it was, of course—and when the three children were at last sitting down to eat an enormous meal, the two grown-ups gaped in astonishment when told the extraordinary tale.

"You should have seen the chimp going top speed up the wall!", said Snubby, waving his fork.

"You should have seen him coming down the chimney!" said Roger, getting out of the way of Snubby's fork.

"You should have seen him sniffing at the papers to see which to take!" said Diana.

It was a very disturbed evening. Great-uncle condescended to have some dinner, when he had packed his bag, and he too added his quota to the tale. The Inspector arrived to make his report. Lord Marloes telephoned to Great-uncle to ask for details of the latest excitement at the castle, and asked him to be his guest in town. Great-uncle then telephoned for a taxi.

"I'm really *very* sorry you've had such an upsetting stay," said Mrs. Lynton. "Certainly you seemed to be as much in the thick of things as anyone else, Uncle Robert. Say good-bye, children!"

The three stood at the gate and shouted good-bye. The last that Great-uncle saw of them was Snubby holding Loony in his arms, making him wave his paw violently.

"That dog!" said Great-uncle, sinking back into the taxi. "Well, thank goodness he can't sit down and scratch himself in front of me any more!"

And then Barney arrived. He whistled outside the window, standing half-hidden in the darkness.

"There's Barney!" said Snubby, almost falling from his chair in his anxiety to get to the window.

"Ask him in," said Mrs. Lynton. "We might as well hear his tale too. I never did know such a set of children for getting into all kinds of trouble!"

"Come in, Barney!" yelled Snubby, and Loony raced out of the room into the garden, barking madly. Barney came in looking rather pale and worried.

Miranda was on his shoulder as usual, and she chattered merrily when she saw the friends she knew. She leapt off Barney's shoulder on to Snubby's.

"Don't let her come too near me," said Mrs. Lynton in

alarm. "I do like her—but I really can't bear monkeys."

"I'll stick her under my shirt," said Snubby. "She's cold."

Miranda disappeared from view for a while. Loony went and sniffed at Snubby's shirt. He felt a little jealous to think Miranda was so close to his beloved master.

"What happened when we left, Barney?" asked Roger. "Did everything blow up?"

"Pretty well," said Barney. "Tonnerre's been taken off, and so has Vosta. I hear they're not coming back, so I don't know if that means they've gone to prison."

"They haven't taken Hurly and Burly to prison, have they?" asked Snubby in alarm.

"Of course not," said Barney. "Billy Tell's taking care of them. I offered to, but the show-folk say they don't want me there any more. They say I put the police on to Tonnerre and Vosta."

"But you didn't!" cried all three children indignantly. "You didn't!"

"Well, they think I did," said Barney. "So I've been chucked out. And Miranda too. The Fair's breaking up to-morrow, and everyone's going here, there and everywhere. But nobody wants me to go with them."

"What—was even Young 'Un horrid—and Old Ma?" asked Snubby, amazed.

"Youg 'Un's all right—but he's got to do what the others do," said Barney. "Show-folk don't like the police—and if they think somebody's split on them they chuck them out."

"It's not fair," said Diana, almost in tears. "It wasn't your fault that Tonnerre and Vosta and the hairy man got caught. So they should be too."

"What happened to the hairy man?" asked Roger. "Was he taken off too?"

"Yes. He's the big man behind all these planned thefts," said Barney. "He paid Tonnerre to arrange with Vosta for the chimp to steal the papers. He always went beforehand

and marked the papers he wanted. Well, I'm glad Tonnerre's gone. He was a black-hearted fellow."

"That's what Old Ma said," put in Roger. "Well, Barney, what are you going to do? Where are you going to sleep to-night?"

"It's a fine night," said Barney. "I'm sleeping in a barn not far off. The farmer said I could."

"Oh no you're not," said Mrs. Lynton suddenly, entering into the conversation.

Barney looked at her in surprise. The children stared too. They had forgotten that she was in the room, sewing.

"Great-uncle's left to-night," said Mrs. Lynton. "So we've got a guest-room again. If Diana likes to give me a hand, I'll have the bed made up for Barney. He can stay with you till you have to go back to school—and by that time perhaps we shall have found a job for him."

Barney was quite overcome. "It's very good of you," he began, but he couldn't finish because Snubby swept by him and almost knocked him over. He flung his arms round his aunt's neck and hugged her like a bear.

"Aunt Susan! I was *willing* you to say that! I was. I was! I kept saying to myself, 'Say Barney can stay!' and you said it."

"Oh, don't be so ridiculous, dear," said his aunt, "and stop strangling me. It was nothing to do with your 'willing' me—I made up my mind to ask Barney as soon as I saw your Great-uncle off in the car."

Barney's face shone. "Why—I'll be here about two weeks," he said. "Two whole weeks. But—what about Miranda? You don't like monkeys, Mrs. Lynton."

"Oh, I can put up with Miranda so long as she doesn't leap on to my shoulder," said Mrs. Lynton bravely. "I dare say I shall get used to monkeys if she comes to stay. After all, I've got used to Loony, and I really didn't think I'd *ever* do that!"

"Woof!" said Loony, hearing his name mentioned. He hadn't stopped watching the lump inside Snubby's shirt, which meant that Miranda was still curled up there.

"It will be *lovely*," said Diana, thinking of the two weeks ahead. "There'll be us four—and Miranda—and Loony . . ."

"And Sardine," said Roger, seeing the big black cat coming softly in, eyeing Loony in a way that meant she was just about to spring on him. "Yes—we'll have a super time."

"And a *peaceful* time, I hope," said Mrs. Lynton, getting up to go and make Barney's bed. "It's all been *much* too exciting for me!"

"Oh, Mother—I *loved* the Rilloby Fair Mystery!" said Roger. "Every minute of it. I'd like it all over again."

"No—another one would be better still," said Snubby, tickling Miranda under his shirt. "I'd like another mystery, as wizard as this—and we'll have one too! Won't we, Loony?"

"Woof," said Loony, and jumped up to sniff at Miranda. She put out a tiny paw and pulled his ear.

"Well, as long as you four and Miranda and Loony are together, you're sure to get into plenty of trouble!" said Mrs. Lynton. "But spare me a mystery for a little while, will you? I haven't got over this one yet!"

"Right," promised Snubby generously. "We'll give you a bit of a rest, Aunt Susan—and then whoosh, we'll be heading into another mystery—the biggest one that ever was!"

THE END

The Ring O'Bells Mystery

The Ring O' Bells Mystery was
first published in the U.K. in a single volume
in 1951 by George Newnes,
and in Armada in 1967

CHAPTER ONE

THEY COULDN'T GO BACK TO SCHOOL

" I THOUGHT those three children were going off to school to-day," said Mr. Lynton. "Why aren't they down punctually to breakfast?"

"Oh, Richard—isn't it *tiresome*—Snubby and Diana aren't well," said Mrs. Lynton. "They've both got temperatures—and I can't send Roger back in case Snubby and Diana are going to have something infectious. The school would not take him back if so."

"Good gracious!" said Mr. Lynton, exasperated.

" After four long weeks of Easter holidays, when there has been nothing but noise and racing about, and that dog Loony under my feet all the time—now we get another two or three weeks of it, I suppose! "

" Oh, well, Richard, we can't help it if they fall ill," said his wife. " Snubby really *must* be feeling bad—he can't eat even a sausage for his breakfast, and you know how fond he is of them."

" It won't hurt him to starve for a week," said Mr. Lynton hard-heartedly. " I'm not wasting any pity on Snubby. I've never known anyone eat as he does. They can't make a penny profit on Snubby at school, I'll be bound! "

He gathered up his papers and went off to catch his train, looking rather gloomy. He had been looking forward to a little peace in the house, with the three children enjoying themselves away at school. Now it looked as if they wouldn't be gone for another week or so, possibly longer.

Mrs. Lynton went up to see Snubby. He groaned when she came in. " I do feel bad, Aunt Susan. And do you think you could possibly take Loony out again? He keeps wanting me to play and I can't bear it. He's such a very *scrapey* dog this morning—scrapes the clothes off me, and scrapes the rugs off the floor, and——"

" I know, I know," said his aunt soothingly, pulling the clothes straight. " There's not much about Loony that I don't know already. Now try to get a little sleep till the doctor comes. I'm going in to see Diana."

Diana was feeling bad too. Mrs. Lynton felt her hot hands. " I think you've both got a touch of 'flu," she said. " What a pity, just at the end of the holidays! "

Roger still seemed all right, though he was in bed too, as he had just a slight temperature. He had been able to manage a little breakfast.

The doctor came at half-past ten, and tripped over Sardine, the cat, on the stairs. "I'm so sorry," said Mrs. Lynton. "I should have warned you! Sardine, if you do that again, I'll send Loony after you."

"Dear me—who's Loony?" asked the doctor, and knew immediately, as Loony came racing down the stairs after Sardine, nearly sending him to the bottom.

He was a nice, cheery doctor, and the children liked him, though Snubby and Diana could only raise rather feeble smiles when he made his jokes.

"Ha! I suppose this is all faked just to get out of going back to school!" he said, taking Diana's hand to feel her pulse. "I know these tricks! I've half a mind to order you up and about!"

"I couldn't possibly get up," said Diana weakly. "I got up in the night to get a drink and I could hardly stand."

"Well, don't worry," said the doctor cheerily. "You've only got a touch of this wretched 'flu that's going round. You'll soon be all right."

"Well, thank goodness it's only 'flu and not scarlet fever or anything like that," said Mrs. Lynton, when the doctor went downstairs with her again.

"It's a pretty nasty 'flu, though," said the doctor looking for his gloves. "Now—where did I put my gloves?"

"Loony! *You've* got them!" said Mrs. Lynton sharply to the black spaniel. "Drop them! Bad dog!"

The doctor got back his gloves at last. "Well, as I was saying," he said, "it's a pretty nasty 'flu. Keep them in bed till I say they can get up—and then, I'm afraid, they ought not to go back to school for another ten days or so. They'll feel pretty washed out afterwards. Perhaps you could get them away somewhere."

"I'll see what I can do," said Mrs. Lynton. "Well, thank you, Doctor, I'll be seeing you to-morrow then."

Roger was soon as bad as the others, and the amount of grumbling and groaning that went on was terrific. Perhaps the most miserable person in the house was Loony the spaniel. He wasn't ill, of course—but he simply couldn't understand why the three children were kept in bed and didn't appear to want his company at all!

"He's awful," complained Diana. "If I let him in, he goes mad, and I simply can't stand it, I've got such a headache—and if I don't let him in, he scrapes at the door and whines till I do. Can't Snubby have him in his room? He's Snubby's dog."

"He doesn't want him either," said Mrs. Lynton. "I'll send him out for a long walk with the baker's boy this afternoon. He's very fond of him, and would love to take him for a walk."

"I don't mind Sardine so much," said Diana. "She doesn't stamp about like Loony. But I don't like it when she sits on my tummy and kneads me carefully with her claws as if I were a bit of dough. Oh, Mummy—I do feel bad!"

"Poor old girl," said her mother. "You'll soon feel all right again. Don't worry!"

Mrs. Lynton had put Roger in a room by himself when Snubby had fallen ill, hoping that perhaps he wouldn't catch it. But now that it was certain he was in for the 'flu as well, she moved him back into his own room with his cousin Snubby. They both felt so miserable that she was sure they wouldn't get up to any tricks together just yet!

The illness ran its course, and in a few days all three were feeling decidedly better. "If only my *legs* weren't so wobbly!" said Snubby. "They feel as if they were made of jelly. Will they ever get all right again, Aunt Susan?"

"Of course. Don't be silly," said his aunt. "Anyway,

I know you're much better because you asked for a sausage for breakfast this morning. To-morrow you'll probably ask for three."

" Woof," said Loony, who always knew the word " sausage " when he heard it. He put a big black paw on Snubby's bed, and looked mournfully at his master. He hadn't understood Snubby at all for the last few days. Snubby hadn't been pleased to see him—he hadn't yelled and laughed as usual—he hadn't even been pleased when Loony brought him a half-chewed and very smelly bone.

Snubby patted Loony's smooth, silky head, and fondled the black, drooping ears. " I'm feeling better now, Loony," he said. " We'll soon be out for walkies again."

" Woof! " said Loony excitedly, and leapt with one bound on to Snubby's middle. But that was more than Snubby could yet stand, and soon Loony was being taken sternly out of the room by Mrs. Lynton.

" I think the children had better go away for a change of air," Mrs. Lynton said to her husband that night. " They are all much better, but I feel rather tired myself now. I could get Miss Pepper, my old governess, to look after them for a bit, I know. She's very fond of them all."

" Good idea," said Mr. Lynton warmly. " I know what Snubby was like after he'd had a chill once—do you remember? He appeared to be twice as full of beans, and three times as full of cheek. I don't feel I could stand that after four or five weeks of him here."

" Yes—that was the time when he managed to get up on the roof, wasn't it—and emptied a can of water down the dining-room chimney," said Mrs. Lynton. " I remember how startled I was. Well—I think I'll ring up Miss Pepper and see what she thinks about it. She's very good at handling the three. She doesn't stand any nonsense."

Miss Pepper said yes—she would take the three children off Mrs. Lynton's hands with pleasure. It was a long time since she had seen them—not since they had all stayed at Rockingdown with her, and plunged into peculiar adventures!

"You'll see that they don't get up to mischief at all, won't you?" said Mrs. Lynton anxiously. "You know what they are—so headstrong and lively and daring. They want firm handling."

"You needn't worry," said Miss Pepper. "Now where did you think of sending them? By the sea?"

"Well, no," said Mrs. Lynton. "The doctor says somewhere inland, but not too low—and somewhere fairly warm. He doesn't want them paddling or bathing or doing anything like that just yet. Can you suggest anywhere?"

There was a pause. Then Miss Pepper spoke doubtfully. "Well—I do know a place. It's got a lovely name but it's not as pretty a village as it sounds. Have you heard of Ring O' Bells Village?"

"Yes—isn't it that very old place, near the town of Lillinghame?" said Mrs. Lynton.

"That's right," said Miss Pepper. "I've a cousin who keeps a little boarding-house there—I'm sure she would be pleased to have the children."

They talked about the idea for a little while. Ring O' Bells sounded just right to Mrs. Lynton. There were riding stables nearby, where the three children could hire horses and hack round the countryside. There were walks up the hills and through the woods. Miss Pepper was sure the air would do them good .

"Right," said Mrs. Lynton, thankful to have settled everything so easily. "Will you telephone your cousin, Miss Pepper, and arrange everything? The children can travel this week, the doctor says—so I could pack them in the car, and drive over to you—and then drive down to Ring O' Bells. It really is a lovely name, and sounds so *peace*ful somehow."

"Yes," said Miss Pepper, wondering if it would be quite so peaceful when Loony and the three children got down there. Thank goodness there wouldn't be that queer circus friend of theirs there too—the boy Barney and his monkey, Miranda!

CHAPTER TWO

RING O' BELLS VILLAGE

" Ring O' Bells Village! " said Diana delightedly, when she heard the news. " Oh, Mother—it sounds lovely. I should like to go there. It sounds as if it's out of a nursery rhyme."

" Are there bells or something?" demanded Snubby, who was now up and looking more himself, though he was very pale under his thatch of red hair. Even his mass of freckles seemed to have faded. " I'd like to ring church bells—you know, pull those ropes and make them play a tune."

" It's not as easy as all that," said his aunt. " Well, I'm glad you are all pleased. You'll be able to ride, anyway, and you all like that. I believe Ring O' Bells is an interesting old village, too, with all kinds of stories and legends about it."

" Good! " said Roger. " I like places like that. You never know when you might happen on something mysterious."

" I don't want you to go smelling out any mysteries or anything," said his mother. " I just want you to get well enough to go back to school as quickly as possible, so as not to miss any more of the lovely summer term than you need."

School didn't appeal to the children very much just then. " I believe I'd faint if I had to go and sit in maths class now, Aunt Susan," said Snubby, trying to sound pathetic. He had enjoyed being fussed over by his aunt. He had no parents, and his Aunt Susan was the nearest he had known to a mother.

"It's much more likely that your maths master would faint," said his aunt unsympathetically. "He's probably thanking his stars that he hasn't had to cope with you yet this term, Snubby."

"I'm afraid I shan't get much of a report this term, Aunt Susan," said Snubby, still looking pathetic. "I mean—if I get a bad one for a change, you'll quite understand, won't you?"

"It won't be a change," said his aunt. "Have you forgotten last term's report already? Shall I quote some of it for you?"

"No," said Snubby hurriedly, suddenly remembering a few very nasty bits. He changed the subject. "When do we go? I say, it'll be fun riding again, Aunt Susan— though I don't know if I'll be able to get on a horse now. My legs still feel peculiar."

"Well, let the others ride then, and you wait till your legs let you mount," said his aunt hard-heartedly. Snubby sighed. The time of being petted and fussed and coddled was over. He could see that. Well, it had been very nice while it lasted!

They all set off one day after breakfast. The three children looked pale, but they were in high spirits. It was fun to be going away to a strange place. Diana thought pityingly of her friends, swotting away at school. It was almost worth while having that awful 'flu, to be going away unexpectedly like this.

Mrs. Lynton drove the car with Diana beside her. At the back were Roger, Snubby and, of course, Loony. Loony's great idea in a car was to stick his head as far out of the window as possible.

"Go faster, Aunt Susan," urged Snubby. "I want to see what Loony does when his ears stand out straight behind him in the wind."

"Don't talk to the driver," said Diana. "And don't let Loony hang out of the window too much. He'll get a chill."

" He won't," said Snubby. " He never gets chills. He didn't even take the 'flu from us! "

They picked up Miss Pepper on the way, and then Diana went to sit at the back of the car with the two boys. They were all pleased to see the tall, trim woman, with her eyes twinkling as usual behind her glasses. She had a very nice smile that quite altered her rather prim face with the straight grey hair brushed away from it.

" The three children are not *quite* as lively as usual," said Mrs. Lynton, " but you won't mind *that* of course. Loony, I fear, is much the same as ever—perhaps a little madder, if anything."

Loony was delighted to see Miss Pepper. He put his paws up on the back of her seat and snuffled lovingly down her neck. Then he pawed at her hat and she clutched it in haste.

" Is Loony still fond of taking brushes away and hiding them? " she asked.

" Yes! " chorused the children. " *And* towels now too, Miss Pepper."

Miss Pepper groaned and made a mental note to keep her towel in a drawer, and not hanging by her wash-basin. She liked Loony but he really was a trial. She wondered how her cousin would put up with him. Oh dear—she hadn't thought of that!

It was a long drive to Ring O' Bells Village. They had a picnic on the way, and then, in the afternoon, Diana, Roger and Snubby lolled together in the back of the car and fell asleep. They were already tired with their journey. Loony stuck his head farther and farther out of the window, then his shoulders, and enjoyed himself thoroughly.

" We're getting near the village now," said Miss Pepper, looking at the map on her lap. " See those hills? Well, Ring O' Bells is behind them, on the south side, so it's very warm, though fairly high."

They rounded the foot of the hills, and came in sight of

the sprawling old village. The houses were made of white stone, and looked very solidly built indeed. The children woke up as they came into the village, a little way up the slope of the great hill.

"We're almost there," said Miss Pepper, turning to them. "Look—that's Hubbard Cottage. When I was here as a little girl I really thought Mother Hubbard lived there. And over there is a very old show-place called Ring O' Bells Hall—it was once a mansion, built in the sixteenth century. It's now on show to the public, with a lot of the old original furniture in it. It's got a secret passage too."

"*Has* it!" said Diana in delight. "Are the public allowed to see that, too, Miss Pepper?"

"Yes, on payment of an extra sixpence," said Miss Pepper. "They make a lot of money here in the summertime, because people come from all over the place to see Ring O' Bells Village and hear its old legends. There are one or two old cottages in Ring O' Bells Wood that really might have been where Red Riding Hood lived!"

"Ring O' Bells Village—Ring O' Bells Wood," said Diana. "Mother Hubbard—Red Riding Hood—a secret passage! I say—this sounds exciting!"

"I dare say it's all quite ordinary to the people who live here," said her mother. "Look—there are the riding stables. I'm sure you'll be there more than anywhere else, helping with the horses and getting yourselves even dirtier than usual!"

The riding stables looked nice. They too seemed old, and a bit tumbledown at the back, but the horses in the paddock were spruce and well groomed. The children felt their spirits rising high.

At last the car drew up in a lane off the main road, outside an old solid-looking stone house. It was quite big, and rather rambling, as it spread away at the back into an odd wing or two and some outbuildings. Hens ran over the garden, and ducks quacked from somewhere not far off.

A dog ran barking to welcome them, its tail wagging furiously.

"A golden spaniel," said Snubby, delighted. "Hey, Loony—meet your cousin. Do you know his name, Miss Pepper?"

"Yes—it's Loopy," said Miss Pepper, with a chuckle, and everyone roared with laughter. Loony and Loopy—what a pair of names—and what a pair of dogs too!

Loopy seemed practically as mad as Loony in the way he pranced about and barked and fawned over everyone. They might all have been long lost friends of his! Miss Pepper's cousin hurried out to greet them, smiling. She was like Miss Pepper, but shorter and fatter, and her smile was not quite so wide and cheerful. Still, the children thought she looked quite jolly—and anyway she had a very nice dog, who would be good company for Loony.

Soon they were all indoors, sitting down to a fine meal of home-made bread, scones and cakes, with home-made jam, and home-made honey in dishes. Mrs. Lynton saw with approval that the three children seemed to have suddenly recovered their enormous appetites. Diana's cheeks began to glow a little and she chattered as fast as the boys.

Loony and Loopy sat impatiently beside first one child and then another, hoping for titbits. Occasionally they sniffed each other approvingly, though Loopy growled if Loony got a titbit he thought *he* ought to have.

"And now—" said Mrs. Lynton when they had all finished, "now, you three—you're to go straight to bed. You have had a long and tiring drive, and I can see that Snubby's legs are turning to jelly again."

All three protested—but not very violently. Secretly they all longed to get between the sheets and lie down in comfort. Snubby felt surprised at himself for wanting such a peculiar thing, and wondered seriously whether he wasn't suddenly turning into an old man.

It wasn't long before they were all in bed, and Diana'

eyes closed almost at once. She shared a bedroom with her mother that night, but Mrs. Lynton was going off early the next morning, to drive herself home. Then Diana would have her room to herself. The boys shared one. Loony shared it too, of course. He would never be parted from Snubby at night.

"Have you got an old rug or something to put on Snubby's bed?" Miss Pepper asked her cousin. "Just so that the dog won't spoil your nice blankets, you know. I'm afraid he *will* sleep on the boy's bed. I do hope you won't mind."

"I would have minded last year," said her cousin, producing an old rug from a chest. "But since I've had to put up with Loopy I've learnt a lot of things. I won't let him sleep on my bed—but he insists on sleeping on my couch. Here you are, Becky—take it to Snubby. What a name!"

"It's because of his snub-nose," said Miss Pepper, escaping with the rug. Snubby was already asleep. So was Diana. Roger opened his eyes just a little to say good night and then he too was asleep. His mother peeped in as Miss Pepper arranged the old rug on Snubby's bed for Loony to lie on.

"I do hope you'll all have a peaceful, restful time," she said. "I shouldn't think anything much ever happens here, does it?"

"No, nothing," said Miss Pepper. "It's a funny old dreamy, half-forgotten place. We shan't have any excitement at all!"

She shouldn't have said that. It was just *ask*ing for things to happen, of course!

CHAPTER THREE

MOTHER HUBBARD'S COTTAGE

FOR ONCE, not one of the children awoke early. Mrs. Lynton was away before even Snubby had opened his eyes! They didn't even hear her car purring down the lane, and they didn't hear the hens clucking, Loopy barking, or the rooks cawing as they sailed overhead.

Snubby only woke because Loony insisted. Loony was tired of hearing everyone awake and astir, and of being shut up in a bedroom with two sleeping boys. He scraped at the door but nobody came. He heard Loopy barking and suddenly gave a loud answering bark.

Snubby awoke with a jump, but Roger went on sleeping peacefully, his head under the clothes. Snubby sat up and looked at the time. Twenty-five-past *nine*! Good gracious! Whoever heard of such a thing? He leapt out of bed, quite forgetting to test his legs as he usually did, since they had become so curiously jelly-like. However, they behaved very well, and didn't let him down or even wobble. He went to the window, Loony licking him madly, his tail wagging nineteen to the dozen.

It was a brilliant morning in early May. Snubby's bedroom looked out on the back garden of the house, and there was plenty to see there! Dozens of hens scrabbled about. Three great geese cackled in a corner. Ducks swam on a round pond in the field just outside the garden, upending themselves in their usual ridiculous way.

A cat sat sunning itself on a wall, keeping a wary eye open for Loopy, who was always under the impression that he could leap any wall. He couldn't, but the cat was always afraid that he might. It stuck one leg up in the air and began to give itself its thorough morning wash.

" Now this is just the kind of place I *like*," said Snubby, rubbing his hands. " Plenty going on. Is that a goat I see beyond the duck-pond—and two little kids? And surely that's a grey donkey? I'll have a ride on him to-day."

" Woof," said Loony, trying his hardest to see out of the window too. Snubby lifted him up. He caught sight of Loopy down below, sniffing hard at a smell of some sort, and almost leapt out of the window in his excitement. His sudden barking awoke Roger.

" Come on, Roger, get up! " said Snubby eagerly. " It's awfully late. This is a wizard place. All kinds of animals and things. Loopy's down there, longing for Loony to join him."

" Well, let him then," said Roger, fending off Loony as he tried to cover him with licks. " Can't you teach your dog to stop washing everyone he loves? I'm dripping already. Shut up, Loony, keep your tongue in your mouth! "

Snubby opened the bedroom door, and Loony shot downstairs, taking the stairs in almost one bound. He slid across the polished hall on his four feet, neatly avoided a little table there, and gave Miss Pepper a real shock as she came in from the garden. Before she could say a word, Loony was hob-nobbing excitedly with Loopy, who at once began to show off.

" Couple of mad creatures," said Miss Pepper to herself. " I suppose that means that the children are now awake."

Judging by the thuds upstairs, they were. Miss Pepper called to her cousin, " Hannah! The children are awake at last. I'll get the milk out of the fridge for them. They do so love it icy-cold."

" Oooh," said Snubby, who in two minutes' time appeared dressed at the dining-room door, and was gazing

401

with joy at the table. "Ham and tomatoes! And what's this? Hot sausage rolls! For *breakfast*! I say—are we going to be fed up, like the doctor said? I heard him tell Aunt Susan to feed us up well."

"Yes—you're going to be fed up," said Miss Pepper, smiling. "I hope I shan't be—by the end of these few days here!"

"Ha ha—joke!" said Snubby politely. He sat down. "I don't need to wait for the others, do I? Do I begin with porridge?"

"You do," said Miss Pepper, helping him out of a dish on the food-warmer. "And take plenty of cream—plenty! Doctor's orders. You've gone skinny and I don't like you skinny."

"Gosh! Can I really take as much cream as I like?" said Snubby, reaching for the big jug with its pattern of flowers all down it. "All my life people have been telling me to go carefully with the cream!"

Hannah Pepper came in after a while to see that everything was all right. She seemed pleased to see the three children tucking in. "They won't be long putting a bit of flesh on again," she said to her cousin, who was now knitting by the window. "But don't let the dog have any cream. He's fat enough as it is."

"He's only licking a drip off my fingers," said Snubby. "Hallo, here's Loopy. Have a lick, Loopy?"

But cream was no luxury to Loopy, and he disdained it. He sniffed at Loony's mouth to smell what other food he had received. Loopy was very ready to welcome Loony, but he didn't mean him to have anything more than his fair share!

"Can we go and have a snoop round the place, Miss Pepper?" asked Diana, when they could not possibly eat any more. "You don't need to come," she added hastily, feeling that it would be nicer to snoop round by themselves. "And is there a book about Ring O' Bells we could read? A guide-book or something?"

"No. But I dare say the woman at the old mansion we passed yesterday—Ring O' Bells Hall, it's called—can tell you all you want to know," said Miss Pepper. "Can't she, Hannah?"

"Yes, she can," said her cousin, who was now clearing away the breakfast things. "It's a pity she's not a native here—she's a stranger really, who read up all about the old place, and put in for the job as caretaker and guide to Ring O' Bells Hall when it was decided to open it as a show-place. Still, she certainly knows all the history of the place, and explains it very well—better, maybe, than one of the villagers could have done it."

"We'll go and have a good look all round," said Roger, feeling the sun warm on his face, as it streamed through the window. "I'm going to enjoy this unexpected holiday. Can Loopy come with us, Miss Hannah?"

"Oh, *yes*," said Miss Hannah thankfully. "Do take him. He's under my feet all the time, and he *will* keep running off with the mats. Now just look out of the window—if he hasn't got somebody's towel too this morning!"

Snubby had a feeling that it was Loony not Loopy who was responsible for the sudden appearance of the towel. He got up in a hurry to fetch it, only to meet Loony running through the hall with another towel dragging behind him!

"Loony! This is not your home!" scolded Snubby, in a low voice. "It's somebody else's place. If you start dragging towels about, you'll be sent away. Do you hear? Then we shall play with Loopy, not with *you*!"

Loony's tail went down, and he put on his most mournful expression. Snubby put the two towels back in their places, and went downstairs. This time he met Loopy carrying a mat in his mouth, evidently taken from the

403

dining-room, where there were many rugs laid down to cover the old wooden floor.

Snubby didn't interfere with Loopy. Let him take his own rugs! It was no business of Snubby's. Anyway, the more mischief Loopy got up to, the less Loony's mischief would be noticed!

The three children set off together. They went down the sunny lane, already sweet with the scent of the first drifts of may-blossom. Cowslips danced in the nearby fields, and primroses lined the ditches by the road. The brilliant blue of the germander speedwell shone beneath the hedges. What a lovely place Ring O' Bells was!

They came to the white stone cottage that Miss Pepper had called Hubbard Cottage. The name was on the gate. The children stood there staring. They supposed Mother Hubbard must have lived *some*where when she was alive —and why not here?

The door opened and an old woman in a red shawl and printed skirt appeared, shaking a duster. She looked so exactly like a Mother Hubbard that the children gazed in delight. She smiled at them.

" You visitors here? " she said in a pleasant brogue. " You've brought the good weather with you! "

Loopy scrabbled at the gate, trying to get in. This sounded like the kind of old woman who was generous with titbits. Loony put his paws on the middle bar and looked through.

" Ah—there's Loopy," said the old woman. " I'll find him a bone—and one for the other dog too."

" She really *might* be Mother Hubbard," said Diana in excitement. " I wonder if *she's* got a dog. We'll ask her."

They opened the gate and went up the tiny stone path, edged with polyanthus and wallflowers, and stood at the little door, waiting. They peered inside the cottage. It was dim, and they could hardly make out anything.

" Come away in," cried a voice, and they went cautiously in, their eyes finding it difficult to get accustomed to the dim light after the brilliant May sunshine outside.

The front door opened straight into a little room. Mother Hubbard, as they all called her, was in a room beyond. Diana clutched Roger's arm. "Look—the cupboard!" she whispered. "She's got a cupboard!"

Mother Hubbard was at an open cupboard, that went back into the thick stone wall of the cottage. But it wasn't bare! It was filled with pans and dishes and jugs of all kinds—it was, in fact, her larder, set in the cool stone wall. She brought out two bones for the dogs.

"Did you ever have a dog?" asked Diana suddenly as the old lady came back into the sitting-room, or parlour.

"Dear me, no," said Mother Hubbard, looking surprised at the sudden question. "Not of my own, if that's what you mean. I've lived with my old grandad nearly all my life, and he don't like dogs, never did. I like them, mind you—I've always got a bone for one that comes along. Old Grandad don't mind, so long as they don't go worriting him out in the garden there."

It was astonishing to hear that this "Old Mother Hubbard" actually had a grandfather out in the garden. "Could we see him?" asked Roger. "I expect he's very interesting, isn't he? He could go a long way back in history, couldn't he?"

"Well, he says he's over a hundred years old," said Mother Hubbard. "He's asleep now, look—you come and talk to him some other time. He knows a rare lot about Ring O' Bells—more than that woman at Ring O' Bells has ever read or heard of, I can tell you *that*!"

This was interesting, and rather exciting. "We'll certainly come back!" said Roger. "And thanks most awfully for the bones!"

CHAPTER FOUR

RING O' BELLS HALL

As THE children went past the queer little " Mother Hubbard " Cottage, they peeped over the high garden wall of stone, just to see if they could spy " Old Grandad " there.

They saw a tiny old man fast asleep in a chair, propped up with cushions. A long clay-pipe dangled in one gnarled, wrinkled hand. He had a little fringe of fluffy white hair round his head, which otherwise was quite pink and bald. His nose was a mere button, but his eyebrows made up for that. They jutted out fiercely and shaggily, snow-white and thick, almost hiding his closed eyes.

" He looks fierce, except for his nose," said Diana in a low voice. " Look at his mouth, with its stuck out lower lip, and his chin with the funny bit of white beard on it. Do you suppose he really *is* a hundred years old?"

" He looks *two* hundred," said Snubby. " Get down, Loony, you ass. I warn you, Grandad won't stand any nonsense from a silly young thing like *you*. Get hold of Loopy, Di—he looks as if he's going to leap over the wall."

" We'll certainly come back and talk to him," said Roger. " A hundred years old! The things he could remember! He's a bit of living history."

They went on their way, and soon came to Ring O' Bells Hall. It was a big, grand building, but rather grim looking, built of such solid grey-white stone that it looked as if not even a bomb would disturb it.

It had two towers, one square, and one round, which seemed queer to the children. A stone-flagged path led up to the great door, which was studded with iron nails. It was open.

The children went in with the dogs. A cold voice greeted them. "Dogs not allowed inside, please. Tie them up outside."

"But they'll bark their heads off!" protested Snubby.

"Then don't come in yourselves," said the voice. At first they could not see who was speaking, because the great hall of the building was dark, lit only by a slit of a window at one end, and the dim light that came through the front door.

Then they saw that there was a table set at one side of the hall, and a woman sat there, knitting. She was dressed very neatly in plain black, and her grey hair was strained away from her white face, and put into a bun at the back. She was rather shapeless, and her hands looked very big and bony as she clicked her knitting-needles in and out.

The children didn't like her face very much. The mouth was set in what was meant to be a smile, but the small black eyes above it were hard and unsmiling as they looked over at the three children and the dogs. How old was she? She might have been any age, Diana thought.

"We thought we might see round the Hall," she said, at last. "Are we allowed to?"

"Yes, but not with dogs," said the woman. "Not allowed, as I told you. This place has some very valuable old furniture and ornaments in it, and no animals are allowed inside. They might cause great damage."

"Well, that's fair enough, I suppose," said Roger, and he took Loony and Loopy outside. They didn't in the least mind going, because neither of them liked the great cold Hall, nor the small cold woman. Roger tied them to a post, put their bones down beside them, and left them, hoping that they wouldn't begin barking.

They paid their fees to the woman. She put down her knitting, rolled up her wool, and wrote down the sums of money in her big account book, which lay open before her.

Then she got up. The children followed her round the

mansion. It felt a dead, forgotten place, and everywhere struck cold, that lovely warm May morning. Diana shivered. She didn't like any of it much.

The woman recited long strings of facts about the old place, but she didn't make them sound very interesting.

"In 1645 Hugh Dourley lived in this Hall, and it was he who first caused it to be called Ring O' Bells," she droned on.

"Why?" asked Snubby, his interest caught at last.

"He had a peal of bells put in the south tower," said the woman, beginning to gabble. "He rang them when he had anything to rejoice about. But one night they rang themselves, so it's said—and it wasn't because there was anything to rejoice about, either. His eldest son had been killed, and he didn't know. But the bells rang at the very moment of his death."

This sounded rather weird. The children were now at the bottom of the square south tower. A small spiral stairway went up, and they wondered if they might climb it.

"Yes, climb up if you want to," said the woman. "You'll see the bells hanging there, high up. They say they're still the same ones that Hugh Dourley put in, but it stands to reason they can't be."

The children climbed up the stairway. It was steep and narrow and twisted sharply, so that it was difficult to climb without slipping.

At the top of the stairway was a small platform. The children looked up, and saw, high above their heads, a cluster of bells, hanging silently on what looked like thick ropes.

Snubby stared at the bells, and his hands itched to ring them. Snubby always liked anything that made a loud noise.

"Can we ring them?" he asked, feeling, of course, perfectly certain of the answer.

The guide-woman looked shocked. " Of course not," she said. " Whatever would people think?"

" I don't know," said Snubby. " We could ring the bells and find out."

" There aren't any ropes to *ring* the bells," said Diana. Sure enough, there were no long ropes hanging down to the little platform they stood on. The bells hung high up on their own short ropes, and there was no way of ringing them at all.

" They'll never ring again," said the guide. " People say they'll ring only when enemies come to Ring O' Bells, but that's nonsense. How can bells ring if there's nothing to peal them with?"

" And what enemies could come here, to this little out-of-the-way place?" said Diana. " Roger, isn't this a queer tower, with its tiny spiral staircase, and its long-forgotten bells, unable to ring ever again."

" You sound very dismal," said Roger. " Like me to throw up a stone and make one of the bells ring?"

" Now, now," said the woman sharply. " Don't talk like that or I shall have to ask you to go."

" I'm only funning," said Roger, grinning. " What else is there to see?"

The history of the old place was full of boring recitals of this person and that person, who happened to have lived in the house. The children followed the guide about, yawning, but one piece of information made them prick up their ears.

" The Lady Paulet had a secret chamber made in the fireplace here," droned the guide, as she took them into a small room with an enormous fire-place. All the rooms had big, old-fashioned fire-places. The children had actually been able to stand upright in some of them, their heads and shoulders up the wide chimney. There was no soot, because it was years now since Ring O' Bells had been lived in.

" A secret chamber! " said Roger. " Where? " He gazed at the big fire-place, and could not imagine where any secret room could be.

" Look up the chimney," said the guide. " You will see what looks like two steps there, cut in the wall of the chimney. If you go up those steps, and then put out your hand, you will feel a cavity behind the fire-place there. It is big enough for a man to step inside and hide."

" Can we go and see? " asked Snubby, eagerly, visualising a proper little secret room, with perhaps a small table and a bench, as dark as pitch.

" If you like," said the woman, and she produced a torch, which she held out to them. Roger went first. He shone the torch up the wide chimney, and saw the two rough steps hewn there in the side. He climbed up and began to feel about for the cavity the woman had mentioned. He soon found it. It was a fairly big hole, taller than he was, and he found that he could easily step into it.

But that was all he could do! There was no room for anything except just his own body! It wasn't so much a secret room, as a secret place to hide in, just big enough to take a man—and woe betide him if there should happen to be a fire on the hearth!

" He'd be suffocated, or would be cooked," thought Roger, getting down thankfully, and handing the torch to Diana. He gave her a shove up. She didn't like the cavity at all when she felt it and shone her torch there. She wouldn't go into it.

" Ugh! It's horrid! " she said. " It feels so dirty too. Fancy hiding there! Why, it would only just about take a grown-up."

Snubby went next, and he, of course, insisted on squeezing himself right into the cavity, and feeling all round it, just in *case* there was something else to find. But there wasn't. It was just what it was meant to be—a temporary hiding-place for some man in danger. Snubby found that he could sit down in it too. The others got impatient and called to him. "Snubby! Come along! You'll get filthy."

Roger was very dirty through getting into the cavity. He hadn't realised it might be so filthy. As for Snubby, when he finally jumped down on to the big stone hearth, and appeared before the others, they could hardly believe their eyes. He looked like a sweep!

"I say—Miss Pepper's going to have something to say to you," said Diana. "Keep away from me, for goodness' sake. You look awful—and you smell awful too. Just like you to get dirtier than anyone else, Snubby. Keep *away* from me, I said!"

Snubby blew down at himself, feeling rather dismayed to see his coating of dirt. He glanced at the guide and caught a look of pleasure on her face. "Horrid old thing!" he thought. "She only encouraged us to get into that cavity because she thought we'd get black, and be rowed when we got home."

He went near to her and banged himself violently as if to get rid of the dust and soot. Some flew over her, and she started back in disgust.

"You'd better go home and clean up," she said.

"Oh, no!" said Snubby at once. "OH, no! We haven't seen the thing we want to see most—the secret passage. Where is that? We want to see it, please."

CHAPTER FIVE

THE SECRET PASSAGE

" No—you go off home and clean yourselves," said the woman crossly. " I've had enough of you. You'll mess up all the clean rooms if you go about like that now."

" Well, it was your fault," said Snubby, banging himself violently again, and making the soot fly. " You must have known that place was filthy. Come on—we paid you an extra sixpence each to show us the passage. Where is it?"

" You come back clean to-morrow and I'll show it to you," said the woman. But Snubby could be very obstinate when he wanted to.

" I'll walk all over the Ring O' Bells Hall banging off my soot, if you don't show us," he announced, and gave himself such a blow on the chest that everyone sneezed because of the soot.

The woman scowled and said no more. She went back to the hall and took a bunch of keys from a hook. She selected one and led the way to a panelled room, which she unlocked.

" The secret passage was made in the year 1748," she said. " Or so the chronicles say. This room was panelled then, and an entrance to the passage was made behind the panelling. It runs behind it for a little way, and then curves downwards into the foundations of the house."

" Does it go to the cellars?" asked Roger.

" No. It avoids those, and ends blindly," said the guide.

" What was the use of it then, if it didn't lead anywhere?" asked Snubby. " What a pity!"

"It was probably used as a hiding-place," said the guide. "More people could crowd into it than into the small cavity behind the fire-place. Now—can any of you find the secret passage?"

They looked round the panelled room. It was dark, because the windows were heavily leaded and not very large. The ivy that grew outside obscured the light even more.

Snubby began tapping over the panelling. He gave a triumphant cry at last. "It sounds awfully hollow here! Tap it, you others. Then tap this bit. Can you hear the difference?"

They could. One panel sounded hollow, the other sounded solid. The woman watched them, looking bored.

But Snubby could not find out how to enter the secret

passage. He pushed this and pulled that, but nothing happened at all. He turned to the woman at last.

"Tell us where it is exactly. It's very cleverly hidden."

"Watch," said the woman, and she went to an enormous tapestry picture over the mantelpiece. The children went with her. "But the panelling sounds solid all round here," protested Snubby. "We tapped it."

The woman said nothing. She reached up to the dim face in the old picture. The face wore a helmet, or what looked like a helmet, pushed back over its forehead. The woman pressed a stud in the helmet and then stood back.

The great picture slid silently to one side—about four inches only —but enough to show a small panel of wood that looked just a little different from the others.

The woman put her hand firmly on the small panel and pressed it to one side. It slid along under her hand, leaving a tiny space, just big enough for a hand to go into it.

"Feel inside the space," she said. They all groped there, feeling curiously excited as they did so. There was something mysterious about this—a secret planned long ago by a clever brain, a secret well hidden, and perhaps of great use more than two centuries before.

Each of them felt a knob in the space behind. "Now you—press it," said the guide, tapping Roger on the arm. He pressed the knob hard and it yielded suddenly beneath his hand. At the same moment something rattled softly behind the panelling not far off.

"That knob releases a lever which in turn enables us to press back a bigger panel," said the woman, going to the panelling from behind which the rattle had come. She pressed her hand against a big panel, and it gradually slid into the wall, sliding neatly behind the panel next to it. A hole yawned there at last, big enough for a man to squeeze into. The woman shone her torch into the hole.

"There you are," she said. "Not much to see, really. Just a passage behind the panelling. It runs along beside it for a few feet and then goes downwards to the blind end I spoke of."

" I want to go inside," said Snubby, of course, and he put one leg into the hole.

The woman pulled him back roughly. " No! " she said. " No one is allowed to go inside. Now surely you don't want to get dirtier than you are! Get back at once."

Snubby struggled away, and tried his hardest to get into the dark hole. He badly wanted to follow that secret passage. Why did it go to a blind end? Was it only a hiding-place, then, not a passage? He didn't believe it.

The woman got angry. " I shall report you," she said, still holding Snubby by his coat. " Do you want me to lose my job? Now, you just do as you're told. And listen to those dogs of yours barking! Something's up. You'd better go and see what's the matter."

Snubby heard Loony and Loopy barking and he reluctantly got back into the room. But he made up his mind about one thing—he was going to explore that secret passage before his holiday was ended!

All three rushed out into the front garden of Ring O' Bells Hall to see what was exciting the dogs. It was only another dog! He had come trotting by, and had smelt the two bones belonging to Loony and Loopy. He had also seen that the other two dogs were tied up.

He had apparently nipped up to them and taken one of the bones before either Loony or Loopy had seen him. Then he had sat himself down well out of reach and proceeded to crunch up the bone.

This, of course, made the two spaniels go nearly off their heads with rage and desperation, and if their leads had not been very strong, there is no doubt that the four-footed thief would have been chased out of the country!

As it was, all they could do was to bark madly, almost strangling themselves with their leads. Snubby ran at the thief-dog, and he tore off, leaving the bone behind him.

" Take your dogs away," called the woman from the door of Ring O' Bells Hall. " And don't come here again with them. Anyway, you've seen all there is to see."

The children went off, the dogs still on the lead, straining after the scent left behind by the other dog. Snubby got cross. " Stop it, Loony—you're almost pulling my arm out. You've got back your bone, so what's all the excitement about?"

Diana suddenly looked white. Roger noticed it and took her arm. " Come on, old girl," he said, " we'll get back. This is the first day since the 'flu that we've taken much exercise or had much excitement. You look fagged out. Lean on me and we'll go home."

They were all very glad to get back to the house. Miss Pepper was there, looking out for them. Lunch was being laid, but alas, none of them felt quite like it after their rather queer morning.

" You all look very tired," said Miss Pepper reproachfully. " Whatever have you been up to?"

" Only talking to old Mother Hubbard and getting the dogs a bone, and seeing over Ring O' Bells Hall," said Snubby, sinking down into a chair. " And examining secret hidey-holes in fire-places and secret passages behind panels and——"

" Oh, Snubby! You surely haven't been doing all that?" said Miss Pepper. " And what in the world has made you so dirty? *Look* how dirty you've made that cushion. You look as if you've been up a chimney or something."

" Good guess! " said Snubby. " Oh, Miss Pepper—*must* I go and change and have a bath and all that? I do suddenly feel so tired."

He wasn't pretending. Miss Pepper patted him kindly, and then was horrified to find a cloud of sooty dust rising into the air out of his shoulder. Dear, dear—trust Snubby to arrive home in some sort of dirty state. But she hadn't the heart to make him change even his coat.

They ate rather a poor lunch, mostly because they had had a late and very good breakfast. Then they dragged themselves off to have a rest in their beds. Snubby managed to undress himself and throw his sooty things down to Miss Pepper. Then, rolled round in his dressing-gown, he fell fast asleep.

"That 'flu really did take it out of them, poor things," said Miss Pepper to her cousin Hannah, as they sat sewing together peacefully that afternoon. There wasn't a sound to be heard from the children. Loony was on Snubby's bed, of course, and Loopy was out in the garden, making futile leaps at the cat on the wall.

"You've done enough walking for to-day," said Miss Pepper firmly, when the children came down to tea, showing signs of a healthy appetite. "Just potter about the garden after tea. You can feed the chickens for Miss Hannah and collect the eggs."

However, Loony and Loopy made up for the lack of energy on the part of the children, by indulging to the full their craze for purloining mats, towels and brushes, and when the children arrived back in the garden after feeding the hens, and looking for eggs, they found half the mats and towels in the house strewn over the grass. Somebody's hairbrush sat in the middle of a clump of polyanthus!

Loony got a spanking with the hairbrush and retired under the sofa, sulking. Loopy, who had never seen anyone spanked with a hairbrush before, rushed away in horror and didn't appear till suppertime.

"By the way," said Miss Pepper, at supper, "do you ever hear from that strange friend of yours—Barney. He was a circus boy, wasn't he—and had a monkey called Miranda."

"Yes," said Roger. "We don't *very* often hear from

him. He's been all over the place since we last saw him. We ought to hear soon, though. Good old Barney."

"Who's this?" asked Miss Hannah, with interest. "Barney? I've not heard of him before."

"Oh, he's a circus boy we made friends with," said Roger. "He's a nice chap. Mother likes him, so you can guess he's all right. He's got no mother, but he's hoping to find his father one day. He's got one somewhere—an actor, he thinks. But you should see Miranda, his monkey."

"No thank you," said Miss Hannah, with a shudder. "I can't bear the nasty little things. I hope you won't hear from your friend just yet, anyway, if he's got a monkey."

But they did hear from Barney—the very next day too.

CHAPTER SIX

NEWS FROM BARNEY

THE THREE CHILDREN didn't wake quite so late the next day. In fact, though rather on the late side, they were down for breakfast with Miss Pepper and Miss Hannah.

And by Roger's plate was a letter in Barney's characteristic handwriting—large, sprawling, slanting all over the envelope! Good, good, good!

Roger snatched it up. " I say—a letter from old Barney! Funny we should have been talking about him last night. I wonder if there's any chance of seeing him."

He tore open the envelope and read the letter aloud, with Diana and Snubby hanging on every word.

" DEAR ROGER,

Just to say I'm out of a job again after a very good one indeed. What do you think I've been doing? Looking after a troupe of monkeys in a circus! Right up my street, of course. Miranda's had a grand time—she's been cock of the walk, putting on no end of airs, and bossing all the monkeys in the troupe.

Well, I made a good bit of money, and I thought it would be nice to see you all again. The only thing is— won't you have gone back to school by now? If you have, it's no use, of course, and I'll have to try and see you all in the summer. But if you're not back yet, let me know, and I'll hitch-hike along to you, no matter how many miles it is. Can't neglect my old friends like this too long, else they'll be forgetting me!

So long—and here's hoping to see you.

BARNEY.

Miranda sends warm love."

All three looked at one another in glee. " Good old Barney! Dear old Barney! We'll have to get him along here to Ring O' Bells Village, and see him again for a bit. What a bit of luck we aren't back at school yet! " Roger rubbed his hands joyfully.

" Barney can't come here with his monkey," said Miss Hannah firmly. " I'm having no monkeys in my house. If the boy likes to ask someone to look after his monkey for him, I'd be pleased to have him here, for your sake—but no monkey. That's flat."

" Oh! " said all three. They knew perfectly well that nothing in the world would persuade Barney to leave Miranda with anyone else. It was quite unthinkable.

"He could perhaps lodge somewhere in the village," said Miss Pepper, seeing the children's disappointed faces.

"Yes. Though as it's May and so fine and warm he'd probably just as soon sleep out of doors," said Diana, remembering that Barney didn't need a roof over his head, as ordinary people did. "He'll find a barn or haystack or something."

"Very well," said Miss Hannah. "But I will not have the monkey here. Becky, you'll see that it doesn't come here, won't you?"

Miss Pepper nodded at her cousin. "Yes, Hannah. Don't worry—the monkey shan't come here—though it's not a bad little thing at all. I didn't mind it after a bit."

Miss Hannah gave a mild snort. "Well, I should never, never take to a monkey," she said. "And at my time of life I'm not going to try."

The children went out into the garden after they had made their beds and tidied up. Diana took her fountain pen, and Roger had note-paper and envelopes. Snubby, as usual, merely looked on and made unhelpful remarks about what to say to Barney.

"Dear Barney," wrote Diana:

"Thanks awfully for your letter. You'll be surprised at our address, but we've had 'flu, and we've all been sent away here for a change, Snubby and Loony too. Loony didn't have the 'flu though, of course. There's a dog here, called Loopy, who's very good company for Loony, because he's just as idiotic."

"Tell Barney how he takes all the mats out," put in Snubby.

Diana took no notice. "I wonder if I've spelt ' idiotic ' right," she said. "Yes, I think I have. I'll go on now."

She went on with the letter, with Roger and Snubby looking over her shoulder, breathing down her neck.

"We all felt pretty awful after the 'flu, and . . ." she went on writing. Snubby interrupted.

"Tell him my legs felt just like jelly," he said.

"*Do* you think that would interest him?" said Diana scornfully. "Who cares about your jelly-legs? And do stop panting down my neck. You feel like Loony."

Loony heard his name and bounced up at her, so that her pen made a deep mark across the letter. "Blow you, Loony—it was such a nice neat letter and now look what you've done. Anyway, Barney will guess it was you. Get down!"

"Go on, Di—you've just written: 'We all felt pretty awful after the 'flu,'" said Roger. "Are you going to tell him how to get here? He won't have any notion of where this place is."

"If he's going to hitch-hike, what's the good of telling him?" asked Diana. "I'll just say, 'Show this address to anyone you're hitch-hiking with, and they'll tell you if you're going in the right direction or not.'"

"Tell him about the secret passage," said Snubby. "He'll like that."

"You seem to think I'm writing a *book* or something," said Diana, exasperated. "And *will* you stop breathing down my neck. I'm going to end the letter now. It's long enough already."

She finished it. "We're here with Miss Pepper, you remember her, don't you? We're staying with her cousin, Miss Hannah, who doesn't like monkeys, so you won't be able to stay with us, worse luck. But we can arrange something when we see you. Lots of love to darling Miranda.

Your friends,

Diana, Roger and Snubby.

P.S.—Loony sends his best woof."

They all signed their names, and Diana heaved a sigh of relief. "There—that's done. I do hate writing letters, but it's nice to be able to tell Barney to come. *What* a bit of luck we're not back at school!"

They posted the letter, and speculated for some time as

o when Barney would get to them. "He'll get our letter 'o-morrow," said Roger. "And maybe he'll start straight away. If he hitch-hikes as cleverly as he usually does, he might be here any time after to-morrow."

This was very cheering. Everyone felt much better somehow, now that they could look forward to seeing Barney and Miranda.

They pictured Barney's wide-set startlingly blue eyes in his brown face, and Miranda's dear little monkey face. Yes—it really would be fine to see them both again.

On the way back from the post, they passed Mother Hubbard's Cottage. The old lady was out in the garden, picking polyanthus. She smiled at them.

"Good morning, Mother Hubbard," said Snubby, quite forgetting it wasn't her real name. Roger and Diana gave him a punch, one each side. He was taken aback. "Oh— er—I mean—well, good morning, Mam!"

The old lady laughed. "Call me Mother Hubbard if you like," she said. "It's no matter to me what I'm called. And I've certainly a cupboard, though it isn't bare."

"Is your Grandad asleep to-day?" asked Roger, remembering the old, old man with his fierce, shaggy eyebrows and fluff of white hair round his head.

"I'll see," said Mother Hubbard, and disappeared. She soon came back. "No, he's not asleep," she said. "You go out and talk to him. He's got a wonderful memory, though he repeats himself sometimes. He remembers what happened years ago, better than what happens these days. Why, he forgets what he had for dinner as soon as he's eaten it, poor old man!"

They had to leave Loony and Loopy tied up outside, of course. Old Grandad didn't like dogs. Mother Hubbard took them out of her back door into the little garden beyond. Old Grandad was there, sitting up in his cushioned chair, smoking the long clay-pipe.

423

"Good morning," said the three children, marvelling again at his immense eyebrows. They could hardly see his eyes because of them. They wondered how *he* could see. Diana secretly thought that he looked a little like an old English sheep-dog, with its shaggy hair over its eyes!

"Good morning to you all," said Old Grandad, and pointed with his clay-pipe to the ground. "Sit you down, and tell me your names and who you be. I've not set eyes on you before."

They told him their names. He chuckled when he heard Snubby's. "Ah, they call you that acause of your turn-up nose, don't they? And do you see *my* nose? Button of a thing it is—and so they used to call me Button. And Button I be now, to my pals--Button Dourley, I am, and Button Dourley I'll die. I misremember my rightful name. Mebbe it was John, mebbe it was Joe. But my nose named me, just like your nose named *you*!" And the old fellow pointed his pipe at Snubby and went off into a peculiar cackle of laughter, rather like a hen makes when she has laid an egg.

What he said interested the children very much. They sat up, all ears, when he told them his name. It wasn't the "Button" so much, it was the surname—Dourley. Where had they heard it before? It rang a bell in the mind of each of them.

Diana remembered first. "Hugh Dourley!" she said, out loud. "Of course—Hugh Dourley."

The old man heard her, and his shaggy eyebrows drew down even farther over his eyes. He pointed his pipe at Diana.

"That's my name you said just now, young lady! It was Hugh--that's right. It wasn't John or Joe—it was Hugh. How come I forgot it? But how do you know that, young lady?"

Diana was remembering how she had heard the woman at Ring O' Bells Hall telling the history of the old mansion. What was it she had said? Oh, yes! "In 1645 Hugh Dourley lived in this Hall, and it was he who first caused it to be called Ring O' Bells," she had droned.

Diana answered Old Grandad. "We heard there was a Hugh Dourley who put in the bells at Ring O' Bells Hall," she said. "It's such an unusual name—Dourley—I remembered that long-ago Hugh Dourley, when you said *your* surname was Dourley. That's all."

The old man had sunk back into his chair. His eyes were closed all but a slit.

He opened them suddenly and leaned over to the children as if he had a secret to tell. "Hugh Dourley was my Great-great-great-great-grandad," he half-whispered. "I don't know how many Greats. Yes, I'm one of the Dourleys of Ring O' Bells. I know all about that old place—I know things nobody else knows. Maybe I'll tell you a few—just a few. Shall I?"

CHAPTER SEVEN

OLD GRANDAD TALKS

THE THREE CHILDREN were thrilled beyond words. They looked at Old Grandad, and at last Diana spoke.

"Would you really tell us about Ring O'Bells Hall? It's such an old, mysterious place—full of secrets. We saw that secret chamber in the old fire-place, and——"

"Oh that," said Grandad scornfully. "That's a poor thing. I doubt if anyone ever hid up there."

"And we saw how the tapestry moved, so that the lever could be worked to free that big panel," said Snubby. "But the woman there wouldn't let us get into the secret passage behind."

"Ah, many's the time I've been in that," said Old Grandad, with a chuckle.

"What's the use of it?" asked Roger. "Was it just a hiding-place, not really a passage? Does it go to a blind end, as the woman said?"

"A blind end!" said the old man, astonished. "No, that it doesn't. Blind end indeed! What would be the good of that? No, no, young sir—that was a way of escape from the house centuries ago. Times were good and bad in those days, just like they are now—and the folks at Ring O' Bells never knew when enemies might come—or gangs of roaming thieves—or folks after revenge. Those were cruel days, so I've heard my old Grandad say."

"*Your* old Grandad!" said Diana, in amazement. "Good gracious—that must go right back into history. How old were you when your Grandad told you these tales?"

"That's getting on for a hundred years ago now," said the old man. "Victoria was on the throne, and a bonny little woman she was too. It's said she visited Ring O' Bells once, but I misremember that."

"Do go on," said Diana. "How old was your Grandad when he told you these tales?"

"Oh, he were a youngster," said the old man with a curious high chuckle. "He were only sixty mebbe, or thereabouts. But he'd heard plenty from *his* old Granny, and the tales he told you wouldn't believe!"

The children stared at him, watching his eyes go slit-like under their shaggy eyebrows as he wandered far away back into a past that seemed as near to him as the present day of May sunshine and warmth. How curious to be so old—how strange to read the pages of history in your own mind, instead of in a book!

Diana patted the gnarled old hand softly. "Are we making you tired?" she said. "Can you tell us any more? What did your Grandad's old Granny tell *him*?"

The old man began to pour out a jumble of queer tales. "In the days when there were wolves round about here," he began, and immediately they seemed to be back in Red Riding Hood's time!

"In the days when there were wolves, there came a hard winter. Ground were so hard that my old Grandad said sparks could be knocked out of it if so be you hammered it! But that's a tale, o' course. Well, one night the wolves came in a howling flock to Ring O' Bells, looking for cattle, looking for chickens, aye, and looking for humans too."

"How horrible!" said Diana, with a shudder. "Surely this must be long long ago?"

"I told you, it were in my Grandad's Granny's time," said the old man, impatient at being interrupted. "Folks were asleep, and the wolves got nearer. They got to

Mother Barlow's cottage in Ring O' Bells Wood, and they smelled the old woman. And there they stood, howling——"

Old Grandad leaned forward suddenly in his chair, making the children jump. "And what do you suppose happened?" he said, his cracked old voice rising high. "Why, them bells in Ring O' Bells Hall rang out loud and clear! They did so—loud they rang, and woke everyone up."

He sank back, and said no more. "And I suppose the people heard the wolves howling, when they awoke, and went to drive them off, and rescued poor Mother Barlow?" asked Diana, after a minute or two. She felt that she *must* hear the end of the story.

"Ay, that's it," said Old Grandad, seeming to wake up again. "But here's the queer bit, Missy—no one rang those bells—they rang theirselves!"

Diana gave a little shiver. "That's what the woman at the Hall said," she remembered. "She said the bells rang themselves when Hugh Dourley's son was killed one night —and ever since then they rang themselves when enemies came. And as the wolves were enemies of the little village, I suppose it was right for the bells to ring themselves again! How very weird!"

"Have they rung at other times?" asked Snubby, who was very thrilled by all this.

"Oh, yes—there was the time when the outlaws came creeping up at night," said Old Grandad. "And the day when soldiers came to take old Dourley off to prison— that were in my own Grandad's time. Many's the time he's told me that tale. Out rang the bells, all of a sudden, and old James Dourley escaped down the secret passage."

"The secret passage—the very one we saw yesterday!" said Roger. "It can't possibly have a blind end then."

"The soldiers went after him," went on the old man.

428

" Down the passage they went, climbing in one after another—but he got away."

" Where does the passage go to?" asked Roger, getting quite worked up with all these old stories.

" You ask Mother Barlow," said the old man, and he gave his curious high chuckle again. " She knows all right."

The children looked at one another, puzzled.

" But—you said Mother Barlow lived in the time when there were wolves," said Diana. " She's not alive now."

" But she'm there all right," said Old Grandad. " In her old cottage. *She* knows, I tell you. Ah, she knows. Old Grandad doesn't give away too many secrets."

This was most exasperating. The old man must be wandering in his mind, Diana thought. Perhaps he was tired out with all his talking, and was muddling up past and present.

" Don't *you* know where the secret passage goes to?" asked Diana, trying again. " Does it go to the cellars of Ring O' Bells Hall? Or does it go to——"

" It goes to Mother Barlow," said the old man obstinately. " That's where it went when I was a boy. Me and Jim, my brother, we went down there once—and we found some old books."

" Old books! " said Snubby excited. " I say—have you still got them?"

" Where did you find them—in the passage—or at Mother Barlow's?" asked Roger, feeling that the old man was getting muddled.

" Down in the passage," whispered the old man, as if this were a secret. " There was a little old cupboard there —hidden away—and me and Jim, we opened it. There was books and papers there—and a little old carved box— and I misremember what else."

" Did you take them?" asked Snubby, after a pause. " They weren't really yours, so I suppose you didn't."

429

The old man took another long look back into the past. He began to mumble excitedly.

"Wasn't Jim and me of the Dourley family? Wasn't we Dourleys ourselves, even though we lived in a little cottage, and not at Ring O' Bells Hall? Who knew about them old things? They weren't no value. We thought mebbe some old Dourley had hidden them there long since—and we was Dourleys too, so why shouldn't we have them?"

The children could think of many reasons why the old man and his brother should not have had them, but they said nothing. What they really wanted to know was— were these old treasures still in existence!

Diana spoke to the mumbling old fellow, who now seemed to have got quite lost in the past. She spoke very gently, as if he were a child.

"Old Grandad—don't worry yourself about all this. You took the things, and brought them back. Have you still got them?"

"Aye, we took them back," said Old Grandad, and a gleam came into his watery eyes. "Jimmy had the box and I had the books."

"What were the books about?" asked Roger.

The old fellow snorted. "How was I to know? I couldn't read. I never did have no learning, but I wasn't any the worse for that."

This was disappointing. Diana tried again.

"What happened to the books, Grandad? Have you still got them?"

"You ask my granddaughter," said Old Grandad. "She've got all my things now. But what's the use of them old books—she've burnt them long ago, no doubt!"

"Grandad, *do* tell us exactly where the secret passage goes," begged Snubby.

The old man scowled at him so ferociously that Snubby drew back in alarm.

"Me and Jim got thrashed for going there," he said. "We boasted about it, see—and Mr. Paul Dourley, who had the Hall then, he took us and he thrashed us till we yelled for mercy. He said if we told what we knew about it, he'd have us sent away from Ring O' Bells Village, sent right away to a foreign country where we'd work as slaves. So Jim and me, we held our tongues. I'm not talking no more about it. You might get summat done to me, you might. Who be you, anyways?"

His voice rose, and he half got out of his chair.

"Why—you know who we are," said Diana, scared. "We're just three children. Your granddaughter told you our names and everything. We wouldn't do anything to hurt or harm you."

But the old man was now so wrapped up in the past that he could no longer place the children in the present. He peered at them, as he sank back in his chair again.

"Who be you? Strangers come to pester me, and get my secrets! Prying and poking and worriting me!"

His voice rose high, and his granddaughter, Mother Hubbard, heard it. She came hurrying out.

"Now, now, Grandad—don't you go exciting yourself! Don't look so scared, children. He's been telling you some of his old tales, hasn't he? He always gets excited then."

"He thought we were trying to pester him and pry secrets out of him," said Diana, almost in tears. "But we were just very interested, that's all."

"Of course you were," said Mother Hubbard. "Now don't you worry. Grandad didn't always do right in his time—he's got a guilty conscience sometimes, poor old man—and when it begins to work, he gets afraid. He'll soon forget!"

She tucked the old man back into his cushions, and led the three children into the house. They looked round, wondering if they would see any old books. They didn't

431

quite like to ask just then, after having upset the old grandfather.

"I must go back to the old man," Mother Hubbard said, taking them to the little front door. "You come along again whenever you like. You'll be welcome!"

CHAPTER EIGHT

A MORNING IN THE VILLAGE

THE CHILDREN wandered off down the road, feeling rather bemused with all they had heard. They came to Ring O' Bells Hall, the two dogs racing round them in delight. They had gone nearly mad at being untied at last, though Mother Hubbard once more supplied them with bones to gnaw and keep them quiet.

They stood still and looked at the old stone mansion. " I shouldn't have liked to live there," said Diana. " Those small windows, the dim light inside, the stone floors and walls, so very cold -ugh! It must have been a very uncomfortable place to live in."

" And never knowing if the bells were going to ring out by themselves! " said Snubby. " I should have been scared stiff. How *did* the bells ring by themselves? Who rang them? I mean -bells can't *really* ring themselves."

" Don't let's talk about it," said Diana, with a shiver. " I expect it's all made-up tales, really. Things like that don't happen."

The woman who acted as guide came out to sweep down the front path, and saw the children standing there.

Loony ran up to her at once and frisked round her in his usual friendly fashion. She swept out at him crossly with her brush.

Loony never could resist a brush. He leapt at it, trying to bite it, quite thinking that the woman was playing some sort of game with him.

Loopy then thought he would join in too, and the woman got really angry, and half frightened. She hit out with the brush, and the dogs went quite mad with joy.

"Loony! Loopy! Come here!" called Roger at last. The dogs came obediently, and the woman glared at the children.

"Don't you bring them here again," she said threateningly. "I'll report you if you do."

"Who to?" asked Roger. "Do tell us! Is there a Mr. Dourley you can report us to? We'd like to meet him, if so. We want to ask him questions about that secret passage!"

The woman stopped her sweeping and looked at Roger. "That secret passage? What questions are there to ask? You've seen it, haven't you?"

"Yes—but you said it led to a blind end, and we've heard that it doesn't," said Roger.

"Well, you heard wrong, then," said the woman. "It does. I've seen it myself! It's been walled up now, so it's no longer really a passage. It just comes to a blind end."

"Oh," said Roger. That seemed all there was to say. He hadn't thought of that solution. Secret passages often were walled up when they were no longer in use. It *was* quite likely that this one would be too, especially as Ring O'Bells Hall was now a show-place and no longer lived in.

"Do you know where the passage led to?" asked Snubby.

"To nowhere," said the woman promptly. "The roof had fallen in, and it was impassable—no one could get through it."

"But where did it *once* lead to?" persisted Snubby.

"I don't think anyone knows that," said the woman, beginning to sweep again, keeping a wary eye on Loony and Loopy, who were watching her brush longingly. "It's not been used for centuries, I should think. Anyway, no one would want to explore the ruined old passage—the roof was likely to fall in at any moment, all the way along."

"It's a long passage then?" asked Roger. But the

woman didn't answer. She merely gave an impatient snort, shook the dust out of her brush, and disappeared into the dark hall behind her.

"She's a bad-tempered creature, isn't she," said Diana. "Well—I suppose she's right. The passage got dangerous, was of no use, and was walled up when the Hall was taken over as a show-place. I dare say the old house wasn't lived in for years, and everything was in an awful state. Some society or other must have bought it and opened it to show to tourists or trippers."

"It's a pretty queer place, I must say, all furnished with old, forgotten things that seem to stand and dream in the rooms," said Snubby.

The other two stared at him, surprised. "You've gone all poetical or something," said Roger.

"No, I haven't," said Snubby, blushing at the idea of being called poetical. "That old place seems to have got hold of me somehow. It's mysterious, with its hidden chambers and secret passages and bells that ring themselves. I'd just hate to spend a night there."

"Well, nobody's asked you to," said Roger. "So don't worry!"

"Look—Loony's gone into the Hall!" said Diana suddenly.

"Loony, Loony, Loony!"

Loony came tearing out with a brush in his mouth, looking very pleased with himself indeed.

"You idiot!" said Snubby, and took it from him. It was a small, hard brush, used for stair-carpets and mats.

Snubby took it cautiously back to the front door and peeped inside. There seemed to be no sign of the guide-woman so he tiptoed inside to replace the brush somewhere.

An angry voice made him jump. "Now then! I can see you, coming in to snoop round without paying! If I have any more bother with you children and your dogs,

435

I'll go straight to the police station and ask them to warn you about your behaviour! "

Snubby saw the woman at the back of the hall looking rather like an angry black witch against the light that trickled in through the slit-window there. He fled, and the others roared with laughter at him, as he came out at top speed, almost falling over the two delighted dogs.

" Heard the bells, or something?" inquired Roger. " My word—your legs must have got over their jelly-feeling, or they wouldn't have taken you so fast just then. Talk about being jet-propelled! "

" Oh, stop it! " said Snubby crossly. " Let's go and get some ice-creams or something—if they've got any in this old village! They've probably never even heard of them."

They went on down to the village. Diana began to talk about Old Grandad. " It's like turning the pages of history to hear him talk," she said. " Wasn't it queer, though, the way he mixed everything up—the past and the present—and thought we were people out of the past come to find out his old, old secrets and punish him. Poor old man."

" Fancy him going down that secret passage and finding those old books and that carved box," said Snubby. " I suppose the box has gone long ago—he said his brother took that, didn't he? But it's quite likely that the *books* are still about somewhere."

" He would probably have been scared in case anyone found out that he'd taken them," said Roger, " and he'd hide them away for years. Then he probably forgot about them, and his granddaughter found them when she kept house for the old man."

" And quite likely put them on the rubbish heap," said Diana. " Fancy the old fellow not being able to read! How tantalising to have exciting old books like that and not be able to read them! "

" I don't expect we'd be able to, either," said Roger, making his way to a small village store that appeared to sell everything. " I expect the words are in that peculiar old writing where all the letter s's are f's."

" Or maybe in Latin," said Diana. " Well, Snubby could translate that all right, couldn't you, Snubby? You're good at Latin, aren't you?"

Snubby gave her a punch. Everyone knew that the remarks about Latin on Snubby's report were most sarcastic. Latin was not Snubby's best subject.

They sat down and had ice-creams. They were very good ones too, made of real cream. After that they had glasses of orangeade, and felt much better.

" I'm almost forgetting we've had 'flu now," said Snubby, sucking up his orangeade through a long straw. " I feel much more myself."

" What a pity," said Roger. " A little of you goes a long way, Snubby. Too far."

" Don't be funny," said Snubby. " I don't feel well enough yet to punch your head when you make one of your fat-headed remarks—but I soon shall! "

" Woof," said Loony, putting a paw on Snubby's knee. Snubby looked down. " What do you want? You don't like orangeade."

" Maybe he's thirsty," said the shopwoman, and she put down a dish of water for the dogs. They lapped noisily.

" Oh, thanks! " said Snubby. " That's nice of you! "

The shop-bell rang and somebody came in. Diana nudged Roger.

" Somebody out of a fairy-tale," she whispered. It was a little old woman in an old red cloak. A ragged hood hung down her back.

" Red Riding Hood grown old," whispered back Roger. Diana nodded in delight. Yes—Red Riding Hood grown old—and maybe still living in the same cottage as in her

437

childhood. It wasn't possible of course—but it pleased Diana to fancy it!

"A pound of butter, please—and an ounce of black pepper—and a bag of flour—and a jar of your own honey," said the cloaked customer, in a small clear voice. She turned to look at the children as she stood waiting.

She had curious eyes—almost green, Diana thought. Her mouth was the mouth of an old woman, fallen in and toothless, but her eyes were still very bright. Her hair was snow-white and still curly, and she smiled and nodded at the children.

"Good morning," she said, in her small, rather child-like voice. "Are you visiting here?"

"Yes," said Diana politely. "We're staying with Miss Hannah Pepper. We've had 'flu so that's why we're not back at school yet. Do you know Miss Pepper?"

"Oh yes," said the old woman. "I worked for her mother years ago. You tell her you've seen me—she'll remember me all right."

"I will," said Diana. "What is your name?"

"Barlow," said the old lady. "Naomi Barlow, and I live out in Ring O' Bells Wood."

"Barlow!" said all three children at once. They had immediately remembered what Old Grandad had said. "Ask Mother Barlow!" Could this old woman be the same Mother Barlow he was thinking of?

Before they could make up their minds to ask her, the old lady was away out of the shop with her bag of goods. Diana turned to the shopwoman.

"Er—we've heard to-day of a Mother Barlow," she said. "I suppose—I suppose *that* wasn't Mother Barlow, was it?"

The shopwoman laughed. "Dear me, no—Mother Barlow lived long ago—before my time! She lived where old Naomi lives now—in Ring O' Bells Cottage away out in the wood."

CHAPTER NINE

TALK AT TEA-TIME

THE CHILDREN paid their bill and walked slowly back to Hannah Pepper's. " Ring O' Bells Cottage away out in the wood! " repeated Diana two or three times. " This is all getting more like a nursery rhyme place than ever—or a fairy tale! "

" Did you notice the curious greenish eyes that Naomi Barlow had?" asked Roger rather sheepishly. " Witches have green eyes—or they were supposed to."

"Don't be silly," said Snubby. "*She* wasn't anything like a witch—she was a nice old thing, I thought."

"I didn't say she was a witch, or even *like* one," said Roger. "I just pointed out that she had queer eyes. I'm not idiot enough to believe in witches nowadays."

"*I* thought she looked exactly what Red Riding Hood would look like when she grew old," said Diana. "With that old red cloak and ragged hood. You could imagine Red Riding Hood keeping the cloak for years and years and years."

"She'd probably grow out of it," said Snubby, getting rather tired of this conversation about green eyes and witches and cloaks. "Let's get home quickly. I'm *just* beginning to feel my legs going a bit wobbly again."

"You and your legs," said Diana. "There doesn't look anything wrong with them to me."

Miss Pepper insisted on their having a rest again that afternoon, though Snubby, whose legs seemed to have made a miraculous recovery, wanted to go and hire a horse for riding over the countryside.

"Well, you can't," said Miss Pepper. "You're to have a rest."

"Couldn't I just have a quarter of an hour's rest and then take Loony for a walk?" asked Snubby. "He's awfully fat. He *needs* a long walk this afternoon."

"I agree with you," said Miss Pepper. "He's much too fat—and he does need a long walk. I'll take him myself this afternoon, with Loopy—though my name will probably be Dotty, when I come back—I shall certainly be driven crazy with two mad dogs capering round me."

"Ha ha—joke," said Snubby automatically. He didn't think much of Miss Pepper's jokes. "No, Miss Pepper— I'd rather have Loony on my bed with me, thank you. You can take Loopy."

"Thank you very much," said Miss Pepper. "Now *will* you go upstairs at once and do as you're told? I warn

440

you that if you start being awkward, I shall go back to an old punishment of mine, and you won't like it."

"What's that?" asked Snubby, with great interest. "I'm sure I shouldn't mind your punishments very much, Miss Pepper."

"Right," said Miss Pepper. "We'll try this one then —no jam or cake at tea—only bread and butter."

This didn't sound so good. Snubby hastily went up the stairs, with Loony at his heels. He felt sure he would be far too hungry at tea-time to relish a silly punishment like that.

He was more tired than he knew, and slept solidly till tea-time, with Loony stretched over his legs, sleeping too. Loopy could not imagine where Loony disappeared to in the afternoons and, after hunting vainly for him in all kinds of unlikely places, including the coal-hole, he went off happily with Miss Pepper for a walk.

Snubby was very glad that Miss Pepper said nothing about his having no jam or cake at tea, when he sat down at tea-time, feeling extraordinarily hungry after his long sleep.

"Hot scones!" he said, touching the warm dish. "Goody! Home-made butter and home-made honey! Couldn't be better. And what's that over there? New currant-bread? Oh, I say—whatever shall I begin on first?"

"Don't sound so greedy, Snubby," said Diana, helping herself to a scone. "And don't gobble. You've got plenty of time before you reach the cake stage."

"Shut up," said Snubby. "*You* can teach me about gobbling any time!"

Miss Hannah looked across at Miss Pepper, and gave her a small smile. "They're rapidly recovering from the 'flu," she said.

"They are," said Miss Pepper. "Snubby, will you tell Loony to remove himself from my feet. I think he's under

441

the impression that he's sitting on yours, and he's really very heavy."

Loony removed himself, and Loopy immediately took his place. Miss Pepper put up with it. She didn't like to ask Hannah to tell Loopy to remove *him*self. The dogs always seemed to play this kind of " musical chairs " at meal-times.

" I wonder if old Barney will come quickly," said Snubby. " I wonder if he's got our letter yet."

" Of course he hasn't," said Diana. " We only posted it this morning."

" Did we really?" said Snubby, astonished. " You know, this holiday's beginning to act like all holidays—time seems to get all muddled up—and then, whoosh—the whole holiday's gone before you've even got it by the tail."

" Don't talk such nonsense, Snubby," said Miss Pepper —but Diana and Roger knew exactly what Snubby meant.

" Miss Hannah," said Diana, remembering the green-eyed old woman in the village shop, " do you know an old lady called Naomi Barlow?"

" Dear me, yes," said Miss Hannah. " She worked for my dear old mother years ago—and a very good worker she was too. I remember her from when I was a small girl. She must be quite old now."

" She lives in Ring O' Bells Cottage," said Roger.

" Yes," said Miss Pepper suddenly. " That's the little cottage in the woods—the one I always thought must belong to Red Riding Hood."

" Old Naomi Barlow has a red cloak and hood," said Diana. " She probably had them when she was much younger and you might have seen her, Miss Pepper. I expect that's what made you think of Red Riding Hood Cottage."

" Do you know anything about old Mother Barlow who used to live in the same cottage years and years ago?' asked Roger.

"No," said Miss Hannah. "I've just heard the name somewhere, that's all. How did you hear about her?"

"We talked to Old Grandad this morning," said Diana. "You know—Mother Hubbard's grandfather."

"Mother Hubbard?" said Miss Hannah, surprised. "Whoever is she?"

"Well, that mayn't be her right name," said Roger, "but she lives at Hubbard Cottage and she *looks* exactly like Mother Hubbard. She's got a very old grandfather—he says he's over a hundred years old—but he looks more like two hundred to me."

"Don't be absurd, Roger," said Miss Pepper. "I know who you mean, of course. I don't know his real name—everyone calls him Old Grandad."

"His real name is Hugh Dourley and he's related in some way to the old Dourleys who used to live in Ring O' Bells Hall," said Diana. "*He* told us about Mother Barlow. He said she knew all about the secret passage under Ring O' Bells Hall."

Miss Pepper looked bewildered—but her cousin followed what Diana meant. "What a lot you seem to have found out in a day or two!" she said. "I do remember a bit more about old Mother Barlow now. She must have lived about eighty or ninety years ago—when Old Grandad was a bit of a boy."

"He *could* have known her then," said Diana. "Oh, what a pity she's not alive now—she could have told us all the secrets of Ring O' Bells Hall. Perhaps she even knew who it is that rings the bells to warn the village of danger!"

"Oh, that's an old, old story, almost a legend," said Miss Hannah. "The bells haven't rung during *my* lifetime! And you may be sure that if ever they did ring, they were rung by human hands. It was people like old Mother Barlow who put about these queer old stories. She was supposed to be a witch."

"Was she *really*?" asked Diana. "Oh, Miss Hannah!

443

Then no wonder Naomi Barlow's got green eyes—she takes after Mother Barlow, the witch!"

"Don't take all this too seriously," said Miss Pepper. "These are only old tales and legends, with possibly no truth in them at all. Mother Barlow was probably a kindly old woman, who knew a good bit about herbs and the roots of plants, and could make medicines and ointments to cure all kinds of ills. That would be quite enough to make her a witch in the eyes of the ignorant village people!"

"I do like this place," said Diana. "I really do like places that are old and full of long-ago tales. Bits of real history are wrapped up in them, and it's so exciting to unwrap them and discover what they are."

"As for Old Grandad, he's like a real live history book," said Roger. "Why, he even told us a tale about wolves coming to Ring O' Bells Village!"

"That may be quite true," said Miss Hannah. "There is a place outside the village called Wolfwick—only a glen now with a cottage or two—where the wolves were supposed to gather in winter time."

"I wish we could wake up one morning and find ourselves back in the past," sighed Diana. "Just to see what it was like. We might see Mother Barlow going by the window on her way to work."

"And we'd see a sprightly youth with his brother, capering by to go to work in the fields," said Roger with a grin.

"Who would they be?" asked Diana.

"Old Grandad and his brother Jim," said Roger. "I know it's impossible to think of Old Grandad ever being young, but he must have been."

"And we might hear the bells ringing in Ring O' Bells Hall one night," said Snubby. "And if we could see into the old place, it would be full of the old Dourleys who lived there—children like us, but dressed differently."

"And their dogs," said Roger. "Spaniels like Loony and Loopy, I expect. They were used a lot for country sport."

Loony and Loopy had got up immediately on hearing their names. They came from under the table, wagging their tails eagerly, putting heavy paws up on Snubby and Roger.

"Are you tired of this silly conversation?" said Snubby, pulling Loony's long ears.

"We seem to have sat here a long time," said Miss Pepper, pushing her chair back. "Have you all finished?"

"Well, there's nothing left to eat," said Snubby. And he was right. Every plate was empty, the whole of the currant-loaf was gone, and the big new fruitcake had disappeared too.

"I should think you'll be able to last till breakfast-time now," said Miss Pepper hard-heartedly, and was quite surprised at the chorus of, "No, Miss Pepper, no!"

CHAPTER TEN

BARNEY STARTS ON A JOURNEY

NEXT DAY the children went off to the riding stables and asked for horses to hack round the countryside. The owner was a youngish woman with a face so like a horse that it quite astonished the children.

She wore her hair tied down at the back of her neck like a horse's tail, and had a laugh like the whinny of a horse. But she was very nice indeed, and soon sized up the children's ability.

"You can have Tom Tit Tot," she said to Snubby, who wasn't as big as the other two. "And let me warn you, he stands no nonsense, so don't play the fool with him."

He was a good little pony, sturdy, with white socks and a star on his forehead. Snubby liked him.

Diana had a quiet horse called Lady, and Roger had a fine-looking one called Heyho. The children had put on jodhpurs, yellow jerseys and riding-coats—but they were far too hot, and left their coats hanging up on nails in the stables.

They walked their horses through the gate and into the road. "Take the road up the hill and down through Ring O' Bells Wood," said the riding-mistress, when she saw them off. "It's a beautiful ride, and good going for the horses."

It was a most magnificent day. Birds sang joyously, lambs, fat and frisky, leapt about the hillside, the hawthorn was out everywhere like snow-drifts on the hedges. The trees were in new leaf, tender and green, and daisies sprinkled the grass all around.

> " Oh Maytime, fold thy fleeting wing,
>   And let it be forever spring! "

sang Diana, as she cantered over a daisy-strewn path,
away up the hill.

They had a good gallop that morning. The horses were
fresh and happy, and the children were good horsemen.
They went almost to the top of the hill, which was long,
but not very steep and enjoyed the magnificent view
below.

" There's Ring O' Bells Village," said Diana, pointing
with her whip. " And look—aren't those the towers of
Ring O' Bells Hall—one square and one round, peeping
above the trees?"

" Yes—and there's the church," said Snubby. " Its
spire is sticking right up, not far from the Hall. Can we
see Miss Hannah's house from here?"

They couldn't. The wood stretched between them and
the house and hid it. It was a big wood, full of beech and
oak, some of the trees very tall and spreading.

" Look—there's a thin thread of blue smoke rising up
from that corner of the wood over there," said Snubby
pointing. " There must be a house in the wood."

" Well, we know there is," said Roger. " Ring O'
Bells Cottage is there—where Naomi Barlow lives."

" Oh, of course! " said Snubby. " It's really not very
far from Ring O' Bells Hall, is it, tucked away in that
corner of the wood?"

" It's much farther than it looks," said Diana. " Can't
you picture old Mother Barlow down there in the cottage,
perhaps a hundred years ago, bending over her black
iron pot, boiling up all kinds of herbs and roots and
things? Perhaps the people of Ring O' Bells Hall bought
their physics from her—their ointments and medicines and
lotions."

" A green-eyed witch," said Roger. " All the books

say that witches or anyone distantly related to the Little Folk have green eyes. I'm sure Naomi's old grandmother, or whoever she was, was a witch, and that's why Naomi has green eyes."

The horses stamped impatiently, and Loony and Loopy appeared from the rabbit-holes they had been excitedly examining.

"Come on," said Snubby. "We sound a bit cracked when we talk like this. We none of us really believe it!"

But in their secret hearts they wondered if there *was* some truth in the old, old stories, and if bits of that truth were not still hidden here and there in this beautiful, ancient countryside. Diana, especially, wanted to believe it—it was romantic and exciting and mysterious.

They rode back through Ring O' Bells Wood. The path was broad, and the horses knew it well. Occasionally the children had to dodge twigs and low branches by bending this way and that. The wood was rather silent, and although sunshine came in here and there through the branches of the trees, their way seemed dim and shadowy.

"I wonder if we pass Ring O' Bells Cottage," said Diana. "It must be somewhere near here."

"I can see smoke from a chimney, anyway," said Snubby. "It must be quite near. We shall pass it!"

But they didn't. A little path ran off the main path, and wound away between the trees. That must be the way to the cottage. Diana glanced at her watch.

"We oughtn't to stop and have a look at the cottage to-day," she said regretfully. "It's getting so late and we promised to have the horses back by half-past twelve. Anyway, it's a very narrow path for horses. We'd better bring the dogs up here for a walk one day, and have a good look at the old place."

"Right," said Roger, turning his horse down the broad path. "Come on. There's a good clearing there—we'll gallop!"

It was a good ride, and all three enjoyed it very much. The horses enjoyed it too, and the two dogs trotted home happily their long pink tongues curling out of their mouths.

What a lunch the children ate! Miss Hannah looked on, quite dismayed, as they demolished a huge stew and an even huger treacle pudding.

" Becky, we can't let them go riding every morning if this is how it makes them eat! " she said comically.

" You can always do plenty more potatoes," said Diana.

" I did you four each as it was," said Miss Hannah. " Well, well—you'll certainly feel better after to-day! "

They were tired that night, though. They only had a very short rest that afternoon, and by the time eight o'clock came not one of them could keep his eyes open. Even the dogs, tired out by their long walk, lay motionless on the hearth-rug, Loopy's head resting on Loony's black body. They were very fond of one another.

As they undressed, the two boys wondered about Barney. Had he got their letter yet? Would he, by any chance, arrive the next day? What fun if he did!

" Di! " called Snubby through the door. " We're talking about Barney. He might come to-morrow, if he's got our letter."

" Well, that's the very earliest he could arrive! " said Diana, getting into bed. " We'll look out for him. Good old Barney. I wonder what Loopy will say to Miranda. He's never seen her. I should think old Loony will go mad with joy."

Barney *was* on his way! He had got Diana's letter that very morning, and had read it with delight. He had no idea where Ring O' Bells Village was, of course. He had been sleeping in a caravan lent to him by one of the men he knew, and all he had to do was to tidy it up, and return the key to the owner. Then he was ready to leave.

Barney travelled light. All his possessions were in a big red handkerchief, tied up in a knot, and either slung over his shoulder on the end of a stick, or carried knotted about his arm.

Miranda, of course, travelled on one or other of his shoulders! She sat there, a little bright-eyed creature, with an old, wizened-looking face, and a host of youthful ways. She was as mad and playful as a kitten.

"Now, Miranda, we're off on our travels again," Barney said to her, as they set off together. "You've had a mighty fine time lately—bossing all the other monkeys and pretending you're Princess Miranda, too high and mighty to do any performing in the ring!"

Miranda chattered back at him gaily. Barney listened seriously as if he understood every word. He certainly answered her as if he had!

"Well, I'm glad to hear you enjoyed yourself so much. Now who do you think we're going to see? Guess!"

Miranda bounced up and down on his shoulder, chattering again.

"Quite right, Miranda! We *are* going to see Diana, Roger and Snubby," said Barney. "And don't forget Loony!"

Most excited this time, Miranda gave another bounce or two. She recognised Loony's name, and a picture of the little black spaniel flashed into her monkey mind. She chattered excitedly, and nibbled Barney's ear.

"Now then, now then," said Barney. "Careful with that ear. You've already taken the edge off it."

People turned and smiled as they saw the big, loose-limbed boy walking down the road, with the little monkey on his shoulder. Barney was very striking to look at, with his brilliant blue eyes set in his brown face. His hair was thick, the colour of ripe corn, and he looked the picture of health.

He took Diana's letter from his pocket, and looked at

the address. He thought he had better try and make for the big town of Lillinghame, rather than for the village of Ring O' Bells. It wasn't likely that any lorry or van would be going to that little village, but one might go to Lillinghame, or near it.

He stood by the roadside, with Miranda on his shoulder, thumbing passing lorries. At last one stopped and the man beckoned him up to the seat beside him.

" That a monkey?" he said. " Is she tame?"

" Oh yes," said Barney. " Salute this kind gentleman, Miranda."

Miranda saluted smartly, bringing her tiny paw up to her forehead and down again. The man laughed.

" Well, I've given many people a lift, but never a monkey. This will be something to tell my little boy at home to-night. Where do you want to go to, mate?"

" Do you know Lillinghame?" asked Barney.

" Never heard of it," said the driver disappointingly. " Where is it?"

" It's in the county of Somerset," said Barney, looking at Diana's letter. The man whistled.

" That's a long way, chum. You won't get there before to-morrow, unless you're lucky. I'm going about fifty miles on your way, then I turn off. You'll have to pick up another lorry then, going in your direction."

" Right. Thanks," said Barney, and off they went on the first stage of his long journey to Ring O' Bells.

CHAPTER ELEVEN

HITCH-HIKING ALL THE WAY

BARNEY AND MIRANDA enjoyed the ride. They both liked
the fresh air in their faces, and Miranda enjoyed the fussing and petting she got whenever the lorry stopped, and
the driver had a minute to spare. He was very proud when
she actually went to sit on his shoulder whilst he drove.

" She's got her paw down my neck, under my collar," he
said to Barney. " I say—I suppose you wouldn't sell her,
would you?"

"No, I wouldn't," said Barney at once. "For one thing I'm too fond of her—and for another she'd pine away and die if she left me."

He hopped down after they had gone about fifty miles, and the driver rattled on, waving good-bye to him and Miranda, quite sorry to part from them both. Barney went to a roadside café to get something to eat, and to ask where was the best place to wait for lorries to thumb.

"Wait here, mate," said the café owner, polishing his cups till they shone. "This is a good pull-up for lorries—there'll be a lot along presently. Where do you want to go?"

"To Lillinghame in Somerset," said Barney.

"You're a long way from there," said the man. "Let's see now—you want to take the Biddlington road—and get a lorry to drop you off at Biddlington. Then, if you're lucky you'll get a ride right into Somerset, and be able to pick up another lorry to Lillinghame."

Lorries drove in soon after that, and the men got down for snacks and a cup of coffee. The café owner introduced Barney and Miranda, and inquired whether anyone could take them on their way.

"I'm going that way," volunteered a middle-aged driver, "but I don't know as I can do with monkeys sitting beside me. I never did take to them."

"Can I sit at the back then, out of your way?" asked Barney, anxious not to lose the lift. So it was agreed that he should sit at the back among the crates that the lorry was carrying.

It was very uncomfortable indeed. The floor of the van was hard, and the crates were even harder, the van shook as it rattled over the roads at a good speed, and poor Barney began to feel very bruised indeed. He was thankful when the van slowed down and the driver yelled to him.

"Better get down here, lad. I'll be taking you out of your way if you go any farther with me."

Barney shouted his thanks and jumped down quickly with Miranda. The van rattled away, leaving him standing on a broad deserted road.

His luck was not so good after that. Not many lorries came by, and only a few private cars, which took no notice of him. Nobody wanted a monkey in a car!

Barney trudged on, mile after mile, thumbing each lorry or van that passed. He came to a small town and had something to eat, for he was getting very hungry. He bought Miranda a banana and some raisins. She loved raisins and spent a most enjoyable time picking the pips out of each before eating them.

The only thing was that she took it into her head to poke the pips down Barney's neck! Stop it!" said Barney in disgust. "Miranda, I'm surprised at you—nasty, sticky, messy pips like that! I'll take your raisins away if you do that any more."

Miranda stopped putting the pips down his neck, and spat them into the road instead. Barney laughed and went to stand at a good corner for thumbing traffic.

Nobody stopped for him until an enormous removal van came slowly by. Barney thumbed it hopefully. The two men sitting in front took no notice, but then one of them suddenly caught sight of Miranda on Barney's shoulder.

He nudged his companion, and the big van stopped.

"That a monkey you've got, mate?" yelled the driver.

"Yes!" yelled back Barney, and went to the front of the van.

"You go at the back of the van then, and tell Alf," said the driver, with a broad grin. "He's daft on monkeys. He'll let you go into the van and sit with him, if you'll let him play with your monkey."

This was a bit of luck. Barney ran to the back of the van. A small man, with moustache rather like a walrus's was already looking out to see why the removal van had stopped so suddenly. When he saw Barney with Miranda he grinned in delight.

"They told you to come along and look for me, didn't they?" he said, nodding his head towards the front of the van. "They know I'm cracked about monkeys. Come along in, lad, and make yourself comfortable. Where do you want to go to?"

Barney told him. The little man took down a map and had a look at it. He put a dirty fingernail on a certain spot and handed it to Barney. He held out his arms to Miranda, and the little creature leapt straight into them. Barney was surprised.

"They all know me," said the small man, winking at Barney. "I go to the Zoo whenever I'm back in London, and you should see the monkeys when they spot me coming along. They all crowd to one side of the cage, the nearest they can get to me, and put their tiny hands through the bars for their titbits. Talk about dogs! Give me a monkey every time! As for cats, you can have the lot. Now a monkey is——"

He went on chattering without a pause, and soon Miranda began chattering too. Barney looked up in amusement. The two of them looked distinctly alike! The van-man had a little wizened face, with monkey eyes, and his moustache looked like thick whiskers. He was enjoying himself thoroughly.

Barney had a much more comfortable journey this time. The van was full of furniture, and he and the little man reclined at their ease in big soft arm-chairs whose springs gave to every bump on the road. Barney felt as if he could go to sleep at any moment!

He had looked at the map, which he didn't understand at all. He knew all he needed to know—that he had to get off at the third big town, and then see whether he could get a lift from there to Lillinghame. He could walk after that.

The little monkey-faced man was almost in tears at having to part with Miranda when the van drew up at the town where Barney had to get out. Miranda clung to him as if she too hated to part with him, but when she saw Barney stepping down from the van, she was on his shoulder with one enormous bound. She waved to the disconsolate little vanman.

"Well, you certainly gave him a treat, and got us a welcome lift," said Barney to Miranda, as he waited at the corner for another lorry to come by. It was getting rather dark by this time. Barney began to wonder if he would get to Ring O' Bells Village in time to see the children.

It was quite dark when a small, closed van came by. As it passed a lamp-post Barney saw the name on it. "PIGGOTT, ELECTRICIAN." He stepped out and thumbed it.

It accelerated at once, swerved past him and went on. Barney was used to this sort of thing and stepped back to the pavement. Then he saw that the van had stopped some way down the road. He wondered why. Perhaps it had stopped for him, after all?

He went to see. He soon saw that the van had a puncture in one of the front wheels. The driver was already out of his seat and looking at it.

"Bad luck, mate," said Barney, going up. "Want any help? That was a pretty sudden puncture."

"This wheel's been a bit of a nuisance lately," said the man. He was short and plump, but that was all that Barney could make out in the dark. "Do you know anything about changing a wheel? I don't want to get my hands filthy, and all the garages will be shut by now. I'll make it worth your while if you can change this wheel for me."

"Yes—I know how to change wheels," said Barney.

456

"And if you'd give me a lift to Lillinghame, if you're going there, sir, that'd be payment enough. I just want a lift, that's all."

The man hesitated. He struck a match and looked at Barney as if he wondered whether he might be taking on a rogue or a ruffian for a lift. When he saw that Barney was only a boy, he looked relieved. "Right," he said. "You change my wheel and I'll take you to Lillinghame. I go right through it."

Barney was pleased. He set to work, whilst Miranda sat on the roof of the van and watched. She disappeared after a while, and the man looked round for her.

"Where's that monkey of yours?" he asked. "I don't want her in my van."

"Miranda!" called Barney. There was a scuffle from inside the van, and then Miranda's face appeared at a small open window in front of the van, just by the driver's seat.

"She went inside!" exclaimed the man. "Get her out quick!"

"She won't do any harm to anything, sir," said Barney. Miranda had now disappeared again inside the van. She was very inquisitive and liked to explore and examine any strange place as thoroughly as possible.

Suddenly there was an agonised shriek from her inside the van. Barney snatched up a torch the man had lent him, and thrust it inside the opening in the front of the van. He was just in time to see something white moving quickly at the bottom of the van. Miranda was crouched at the back, squealing in fright.

Barney watched to see if the moving white thing appeared again, but he could see nothing but boxes and sacks. Then he felt himself roughly pulled away and the torch snatched from his hand.

The driver shouted at him. "Come away from there, you and your monkey. Don't mess about with my goods."

"All right, all right," said Barney, surprised at all the excitement. "Here, Miranda, what's frightened you?"

The monkey had now climbed out, and had scrambled on to Barney's shoulder, trembling. Something had obviously given her a fright.

"Shall I finish changing the wheel, sir?" asked Barney. "Sorry my monkey got inside. She's always so inquisitive."

The man hesitated, then spoke roughly. "All right—finish the wheel, but buck up about it. I don't want to be all night on the road!"

CHAPTER TWELVE

JOURNEY'S END

BARNEY finished changing the wheel in silence, with Miranda clinging tightly to his shoulder, still very scared. The boy was remembering the white moving thing he had seen in the van. What was it? It was something that had frightened Miranda very much, that was plain. Was it something alive, or what?

"Thanks," said the man, when Barney had finished. "Here's some money. I won't give you a lift after all. I've changed my mind."

"Oh no, you haven't," said Barney, and he slipped quickly into the seat beside the driver. "A bargain is a bargain. I don't want money. I want a lift. Now don't try to turn me off my seat, or my monkey will fly at you. She can bite hard."

The man said something under his breath, stood still for a moment and then climbed up into his own seat. He let in the clutch, and away they went into the night, the van's strong lights raking the road in front of them.

Neither Barney nor the man said a word. Miranda made no sound, but clung to Barney tightly. She didn't like this man beside him.

"Here's Lillinghame," said the man at last, and stopped. He said no more at all, but watched Barney get down. Barney looked up in the darkness into the white blur of the man's face.

"Thanks," he said. "Tell me one thing before I go. What have you got in your van that frightened my monkey so much?"

"Pah!" said the man, fiercely and angrily, and drove

off so suddenly that Barney almost fell to the ground. He laughed and patted Miranda.

" Whatever's in that van is a mystery," he said. " And if you could talk really *properly*, Miranda, you could tell me what it was. Nasty little fellow, wasn't he?"

Barney walked on until he came to a signpost. He heaved a sigh of relief, because on it, lighted now by the moon which had sailed out from behind a cloud, was the name he wanted—RING O' BELLS!

" Good," said Barney. " I haven't done so badly to come all the way here in one day. The thing is—it's too late to find where Roger and the others are now—so we'll just walk into Ring O' Bells, Miranda, and see if we can find somewhere to sleep."

As he walked down the road, the moon sailed into great black clouds that were coming up from the west. Soon rain fell, and Barney pulled up his coat-collar. He debated whether to shelter under a hedge or not, but decided to go on. The rain might not last long.

He trudged on, with Miranda now tucked under his coat. She hated the rain. He came to another signpost at a fork in the road. " RING O' BELLS two miles."

That didn't seem far to Barney. The rain was now only a drizzle, so on he went, whistling very softly. To-morrow he would see his friends. He hadn't seen them for weeks and weeks. It would be good to meet them all again.

He walked down the road and along lanes, past small cottages and one or two farm-houses. Then after passing into Ring O' Bells Village, which was now silent and dark with not a light to be seen, Barney stood still and debated with himself.

Where now? The rain had begun to pour again, and he didn't somehow fancy a night under a hedge. He might find a haystack and burrow into that. So on he went, bending his head to the pelting rain.

He came to a great building, its black shadow making

460

the night even darker. He wondered what it was. If it was a church, perhaps he could creep into the porch and sleep there out of the rain. He walked cautiously up the flagged path, and then stopped.

He could hear voices—low voices. Where were they? Barney slipped into the shadow of a bush. He waited. Then he heard a door closing very quietly, and some one came up the flagged path in soft-soled shoes. Then some-one went to the gate—and then, to Barney's amazement, he heard a car starting up outside!

He hadn't noticed any car outside. It must have been driven well into the shadow of the hedge, or he would surely have seen it. He ran on tiptoe to the gate. Some-one stood there, lighting a cigarette, unaware that there was anyone watching nearby. As the match flared up, Barney recognised him!

" It's the man who gave me a lift to Lillinghame—the man whose wheel I changed for him! " he thought. " Short and plump—and with very black eyebrows and jutting chin. I caught sight of his face when we passed a lamp-post during the drive. I wish I'd taken more notice of him now. What's he up to?"

Barney watched the little van disappear up the road, its red light getting fainter and fainter. He wondered if he ought to have taken the number, but the rear light was far too dim to allow him to read anything on the back of the car.

He turned back to the building behind him and won-dered what it was. It couldn't be a church, he thought. Was it a private house?

The rain stopped. The moon came out again, and Barney stepped quickly into shadow. Then he caught sight of a big notice set up near the front door. He went on tiptoe towards it.

He read it carefully. Well! After all, the building was only an old show-place—a museum or something, Barney

thought. He wondered if he could shelter inside somewhere. He was wet, and would like to take off his coat.

There must be someone inside, surely, because he had
heard voices—and yet, only one man had gone to the car.
So perhaps he had better not try to get in. He might be
arrested as a thief, if he were found.

Barney had no sooner thought this than he heard the
sound of cautious footsteps inside the front door, near the
noticeboard. He slipped round to the side of the house.
He heard the door open, and then it was shut very quietly.
Someone came down the flagged path, keeping to the
shadowed side.

The someone gave a little cough, and Barney stiffened
in surprise. That was a woman's cough! Whatever could
a *woman* be doing wandering about in the darkness like
this? The figure soon disappeared into the shadows of the
lane, and then there was silence.

Barney went to the front door and tried it. Locked, of
course. He went all round the place, but found every
window locked or shuttered.

The moon shone down through one window as he peered
inside. " Gracious! It's all furnished—it's not empty, or
full of cases and things like museums usually are," said
Barney, in surprise. " I wish I could get into *this* room—
I could sleep very comfortably on that old sofa! "

Ivy grew very thickly indeed on one wall. Barney looked
up at the thick green screen and noticed a window on the
first floor. It *looked* as if it might be open.

He tried his weight on the ivy stems. They were as
thick as small trunks, and held his weight easily. So up
he went like a cat, testing each ivy stem as he climbed.
Miranda climbed beside him, flinging herself up and down
the ivy in a way that Barney very much envied.

He got to the window and found that he was right. It
was a small casement window, and because the fastening
was broken, it could not be shut. It had swung open and

Barney saw that he could easily get inside, once he had got astride the windowsill.

He pulled himself up. Miranda shot up to his shoulder at once. She had seen the half-open window and had guessed Barney was going to enter there. It wasn't long before they were both in the old room behind the open window.

The moon went in and Barney stood still in the darkness. He waited till the moon came out again and then saw that he was in an old-fashioned bedroom. An enormous four-poster bed stood in the middle of the room, almost shut in by side-hangings that were slightly pulled back with tarnished gilt girdles.

Barney tiptoed to the door and opened it. He found himself on a gallery that ran round a great room below, overlooking it. All was silence. Not even a mouse pattered across the floor.

Barney found the stairs and went down. They were shallow stairs that swept down in a curve, right into the big room below. Smaller rooms opened off it. Barney peeped cautiously into each, but there was nobody there, and not a sound to be heard. It did seem quite safe to sleep upstairs in that great four-poster!

A screech made him jump, and Miranda gibbered in fright. But it was only a barn-owl outside, screeching to frighten the field-mice into sudden movement, so that it could see them and pounce.

Barney decided to go upstairs again. He was damp and very tired. He didn't think it would matter if he slept on that great bed. He would take off his shoes and his wet coat. Perhaps there would be something up there that he could wrap himself in.

He went up the wide stairs, and came to the gallery again. He found the bedroom through whose window he had climbed. He looked around in the moonlight for something to wrap round himself.

There was an old table in one corner, covered by a table-cloth of some kind. Barney couldn't see what colour it was or what it was made of. He fingered it, and it felt thick and warm. He pulled it off, took off his coat, and wrapped himself round in the table-cloth. It certainly was nice and cosy!

Miranda tucked herself into its folds, glad to think they were going to bed. She was tired out with her long and exciting day.

Barney slid his shoes off his feet. He felt his socks. Blow, they had holes in them already—just as he wanted to visit his friends too. Well, perhaps he had better wear shoes and no socks, then the holes wouldn't be noticed!

He got on to the bed. It was high, rather hard, and not really very comfortable, but it was bliss to poor, tired Barney. Dragging the table-cloth closely round him, he put his head on the pillow and immediately fell asleep.

Not very far away, at Miss Hannah's house, Diana was lying awake, wondering if Barney would come the next day. Little did she know that at that very moment he was fast asleep in the middle of the old four-poster bed in the best bedroom of Ring O' Bells Hall!

Yes—Ring O' Bells Hall. That was where Barney had ended up for the night. Wake up early, Barney or you'll be discovered—and then what trouble you'll be getting into!

CHAPTER THIRTEEN

UP IN THE BELL-TOWER

FORTUNATELY for Barney he did awake quite early the next morning. The sun shone directly into the window, and a bright beam rested on his face. It woke him, and he sat up blinking in the yellow sunlight, wondering wherever in the world he was.

He soon remembered. Yes—he was in some old building—some kind of show-place. He had better get out quickly! He woke up Miranda, who was fast asleep in the rug, her tiny face hidden in her paws. She opened her eyes, and made a little chattering noise.

She ran up Barney's chest, as he sat up on the bed, and sat cuddled into his shoulder, pulling at one of his ears, and putting her monkey face against his cheek. He fondled her lovingly.

"You're the best little companion in the world!" he said, and tickled her. "Aren't you, Miranda? Say—do you know who you're going to see to-day?"

Miranda chattered back eagerly, and Barney nodded solemnly. "Quite right—we're visiting our friends. Now we'd better think about going. Better not shin down the ivy this time, in case someone sees us. Let's go and see if there's a back door we can open. We could slip out cautiously then."

Barney replaced the table-cloth on the table. It looked very crumpled but he couldn't do anything about that. He put on his shoes, but stuffed his holey, rolled-up socks into his pocket. He felt his coat. It was quite dry, so he pulled that on too. There was a mirror on the wall, and he looked into it.

"Just look at that scarecrow in there, Miranda!" he said to the listening monkey. "You might not guess it, but it's me! I wonder if there's anywhere I can wash here —or didn't these old places run to a bathroom? I guess not."

He took a comb from his pocket and combed back his bright hair. Then he straightened the covers of the big four-poster bed, and went into the gallery that ran outside the room, over-looking the enormous room below.

He walked quietly, but there was no one about. Miranda leapt about from table to chair, from chair to chest, chattering and excited. Any strange place always pleased her.

Barney was not very interested in the old building. It meant very little to him, for he didn't know much of history. He thought some of the big wooden chairs looked extremely uncomfortable, and marvelled at the suits of armour that stood here and there round the wall. He stood and looked at one.

" Pretty small, isn't it, Miranda?" he said to the monkey. " I could just about get into it, but only just. I reckon the old-time men couldn't have been as big as we are— tiddley little things they must have been. And fancy walking about in that, clanking all the time! "

He came to the back door, which was a massive affair, though not as enormous as the front door. He looked round for Miranda. " Come on," he said. " We'll slip out here."

There was no chattering in reply, and Miranda didn't come flying on to his shoulder. Barney looked round the room he was in. It was a huge kitchen, furnished just as it might have been two or three hundred years back. Where on earth was Miranda?

Miranda was off on a little exploration of her own. She hadn't realised that Barney was looking for a way out. She thought he was exploring too. She had completely disappeared.

" Miranda! " called Barney softly. " Blow you, Miranda! Where have you got to?"

He heard a little noise somewhere and went quickly in its direction. He came to the foot of the big square tower, though at first he had no idea what it was.

All he could see was the little spiral staircase going up. Up to where? Perhaps another bedroom, Barney thought. He stood and listened. Surely that tiresome little monkey hadn't gone up the stairway? A noise from above made him certain that she had.

And then another noise made him jump. Somebody was unlocking a door! " It's the big front door! " thought Barney, scared. " Somebody's coming in. I shall be caught."

He glanced round. There seemed no sensible place t
467

hide—and anyway he must get hold of Miranda and keep her quiet, or she would certainly give the game away.

He began to climb the little spiral staircase quickly, his rubber shoes making no sound on the stone. Up and up he went, and at last came to the little platform at the top. He gazed up and saw the silent bells hanging far above his head.

And up there, looking down at him cheekily, was Miranda! She was playing hide and seek with him! He had taught her that—but now she had chosen a most unfortunate time to play it!

" Miranda! " he said, in a whisper. " Come on down! Quick! "

Miranda immediately disappeared. Barney craned his neck. Where could she be? And how had she got up so high. It was too far for her to leap.

He was in the tower. Barney could hardly see anything except the bells high up, gleaming and silent. He felt up the wall with his hand and at last came to something he had guessed must be there.

There was a row of footholds in the stone wall of the tower on the south side. The stone was hollowed out at set places, so that a foot or hand could be inserted for climbing up. Barney slipped his hand into one hold and found that it was hollowed in such a way that his fingers could grip quite well.

He gave a little groan. Now he would have to climb all the way up in this half-darkness to get Miranda! Once she was playing hide and seek she wouldn't come to him unless he found her and cornered her. He stood on tiptoe and felt for the handholds above his head. He slipped his hands in, and then put his toes into the ones below.

He felt for the next holds and put his hands there, clutching hard with his strong fingers. It was not a very pleasant way of climbing up the steep walls of a stone tower—but Barney was used to acrobatic feats of all kinds, and he didn't really find it very difficult.

As for Miranda, she must have discovered the footholds at once and climbed up easily, with glee. Barney went steadily up, slipping first his hand into the stone hollows, and then his feet. At last he was up to the bells. Now—where was Miranda?

He couldn't see her anywhere, nor hear her either. He looked cautiously round in the dim light. The bells, looking remarkably big and bright now that he was so near them, hung near his head, held by their ropes. He strained his eyes to see beyond them.

He caught sight of a pair of gleaming green eyes looking down at him. Miranda! "You little scamp!" muttered Barney, exasperated. "How did you get beyond the bells?"

He felt about for another handhold and found it. Then his hand found the end of a thick rope. He felt it cautiously. It didn't seem to be loose. It seemed to be fastened tightly. Was it to help a climber to go up above the bells?

Barney pulled at the rope, and it felt very firm and safe. He swarmed up it, through what looked like a hole in the roof of the tower—and found himself in a most curious place!

It was a small square room above the bells. It would have been completely dark if it hadn't been for a slit-like window set in the south side, that let in a bright ray of sunlight. Now Barney understood why the bells had gleamed so queerly when he was standing below them. This beam of sun had penetrated into the queer square room, and a little piece of it had pierced through the hole of the floor, and fallen on the upper surface of the bells.

"So that's why they shone so curiously!" thought Barney, looking round the little stone room. There was a

469

low bench there, very small, and a heap of what looked like rags. There was an old wooden candle-stick with the remains of wax still in the bottom.

" This must have been a hidey-hole long ago," thought Barney, kicking the rags which looked as if they had once been a rug or blanket of some kind. Miranda at once ran over to them and cuddled herself up, peeping out comically.

" I'm not too pleased with you, Miranda," said Barney severely. " Making me climb up all that way to get you. And now we've got to climb down again—but this time you'll be on my shoulder, and keep there—see?"

He looked out through the slit-like window. The whole countryside lay before him, smiling in the bright May sunshine. Not a cloud was in the blue sky. It made Barney long to be out there.

He suddenly felt very hungry indeed. " Come on, Miranda," he said. " We'll go and find Snubby and the others, and get some breakfast."

Miranda knew the words breakfast, dinner, tea and supper very well indeed. She leapt on to Barney's shoulder and held on to his collar.

He let himself down through the hole in the floor, found the guide-rope, and then felt for the first footholds in the stone wall of the tower. It was easy to climb down, and soon he was standing far below the gleaming bells, on the little platform at the top of the spiral staircase.

He listened. He could hear what sounded like someone beating a mat. Perhaps the caretaker of the building was at her morning work. He might be able to slip out past her.

He went down the stone stairway very silently and carefully. He peered out at the bottom. No one was to be seen. He made his way to the front door. He caught sight of a woman in one of the rooms, dusting the old furniture. She had her back to him, so Barney took his chance and fled to the open front door. He was out in the sunshine in a trice, rejoicing to feel the warmth on his head and shoulders.

He saw the name of the old building on the gate, Ring O' Bells Hall. " So that's where I slept for the night," he thought. " Ring O' Bells Hall, in Ring O' Bells Village. Very nice too! "

He debated how to find his three friends—but his difficulty didn't last long. Up the road came Roger, Diana, Snubby and the two dogs!

Barney yelled loudly. " Ahoy there! Here we are! "

CHAPTER FOURTEEN

A HAPPY MEETING

Shouts, squeals, laughter, barks, chattering, back-slapping
—what an excitement and scurry there was, as all the
friends rushed together once more!

"Barney! Dear old Barney! We did hope you'd come
to-day!"

"Miranda! You're just as sweet as ever! Oh, she's
leapt on to my shoulder!"

"It's grand to see you all—Diana, you've grown.
Snubby hasn't. Hallo, Roger—it's good to see you."

"Woof, woof, woof!"

"Barney, you're a bit taller—and as brown as ever!
Oh, do listen to Miranda chattering! I know exactly what
she's saying!"

"When did you come? How did you get here?"

"Where did you spend the night? Oh, I say—the dogs
have both gone mad."

" Woof, woof, WOOF! "

It certainly seemed as if both the dogs had gone completely off their heads. Loony recognised Barney and Miranda at once, of course, but Loopy didn't know them, as he had never seen them before. But when he saw what a tremendous welcome the excited Loony gave them, Loopy felt he must certainly join in.

He almost outdid Loony in his excitement. He leapt up and barked and licked and wagged and rolled over, and altogether behaved like two Loonies rolled into one. Loony himself got rather annoyed with him at last. These were *his* friends, not Loopy's. What did Loopy mean by behaving like this?

Loony gave the surprised Loopy a sharp nip as if to say, " Keep off! This is *my* welcome, not yours! "

Miranda leapt from one shoulder to another, delighted and so excited that she hardly knew what she was doing. She suddenly dropped down on Loony's back, and rode him as she always used to do. Loopy seeing this, got the surprise of his life. He backed away at once.

Miranda sprang from Loony's back on to Loopy's, and the golden spaniel ran for his life, with the cheeky little monkey jigging up and down on his back. He whined in panic.

" Woof, woof, woof! Roll over, woof! " barked Loony, runnning after him. So Loopy rolled over on his back, which, of course, was a sure way of dislodging Miranda. Before either dog could pounce on her she was up on Barney's shoulder again, chattering for all she was worth.

The children's excitement died down at last. They linked arms with Barney and strolled back to Miss Pepper's, quite forgetting that Miss Hannah had said she would not welcome any monkey to her house. Barney mentioned that he hadn't yet had any breakfast, and was hungry.

" Could we stop and buy some food somewhere?" he

asked. " And I'd like to buy some socks. Mine have got holes in them. I don't want to appear with holey socks."

" You *have* got particular! " said Diana. " You never used to mind things like that."

" No," said Barney, and didn't like to say that he was so proud of his friends that he wanted to be like them, and look decent if he could.

" Better come to Miss Hannah's and we'll ask her for something for you," said Roger. " Look at those dogs and Miranda! What a time she'll have with them! "

Miranda was sitting on a wall, holding a long twig, and was poking this at the dogs every time they tried to leap up at her. Loopy by now had decided that she was a very peculiar kind of cat, and he meant to have some fun with her.

Miss Pepper was in the front garden, picking flowers. She was delighted to see Barney. " Just the same startlingly blue eyes and brown face! " she thought to herself, as she went to meet him. " What a striking boy he is! "

" Miss Pepper," said Roger when the greetings were over, " Barney hasn't had breakfast. Can we get him some?"

" Of course! " cried Miss Pepper, and took them all inside. Miranda came too. Miss Hannah came out of the kitchen, when she heard all the excited voices—and stopped dead when she saw Miranda on Barney's shoulder. She gave a piercing scream and ran back to the kitchen, slamming the door behind her. Barney felt astonished. The others, of course, guessed at once what the matter was.

" Oh—of course—she hates monkeys! " said Roger. " Blow—we all forgot. Miss Hannah—it's all right. I'll take Barney back to the garden, and the monkey too."

So poor Barney was ushered back to the garden and given a deck-chair to sit in, whilst the rest went back to pacify Miss Hannah and get a meal of some kind for Barney.

474

Loony and Loopy remained with Barney. Loony had already given him about five hundred licks, but he still had plenty to spare, and Barney had to wipe his face with his handkerchief every minute or so.

Then Loopy began to show off to Miranda. He rushed indoors, got a mat from the hall and dragged it out at top speed, falling over whenever his hind legs got caught on it. He placed it in front of Miranda, who promptly dropped down on it and sat there.

Loony watched jealously. He also disappeared into the house, and when he came back he held a large bath-towel between his teeth. He deposited it on the rug. Miranda at once took it and draped herself round in it with a very naughty air indeed.

"Woof," said Loony to Loopy and disappeared again. He brought back somebody's hairbrush, and Miranda brushed her fur vigorously with it. Barney roared with laughter. Off went Loopy for another mat.

When Roger and the others appeared with food for Barney the grass looked very queer, strewn with mats and rugs and towels, a hairbrush and a broom, which Loony with much trouble had managed to drag out by the head.

"Good gracious," said Miss Pepper. "Just look what those dogs have done! Are they showing off to that little Miranda?"

Diana collected everything and took mats, brushes and towels back into the house, laughing. Those two dogs! Nothing was safe from them when they took it into their heads to be silly.

The three children exchanged all their news with Barney. Barney told them of the jobs he had had since he had last seen them. They sounded remarkable to the children, even though they were used to their circus friend's doings.

"I told you I managed a troupe of monkeys—with Miranda's help," said Barney, munching away at bread and ham. "My word, she *did* boss those monkeys! Before

475

that I had charge of an elephant. He was grand, that elephant."

"What was his name?" asked Diana.

"Mr. Little," said Barney with a grin. "He was enormous, but very gentle and deft. You wouldn't believe it, but if you put cups and saucers down in rows in front of him, he'd walk among them without even touching a cup!"

"What else did you do?" asked Snubby.

"I took a job with a man who owned two roundabouts," said Barney. "That was a messy job, though. I had to oil them and see to the works. I didn't do that long. The man was mean and bad-tempered. I went to a good little job after that."

"What was it?" said Roger.

"It was in a little theatre," said Barney. "Not much more than a shed, really. Different travelling companies hired it for their shows. It was my job to manage the lights and the scenery."

"I know why you took that job," said Diana suddenly. "It was in case your father might come there and act!"

Barney nodded. He was always on the look-out for anyone who might be his father. He felt sure he would know him, though how, he didn't know. He didn't feel so bad about not having a father or mother now, though, because he had three good friends, and had even shared a little of their home-life at times. A home and people meant a great deal to Barney, who had none. Still, he had Miranda—she was all the world to him!

The children told him their news too—how they had had the 'flu, and had been sent away for a change and they told him about the queer Ring O' Bells Hall, and the secret passage and legend of the bells.

"My word! Those must be the very bells I climbed past when I went to hunt for Miranda in the tower!" said Barney, and told them about the little room above the bells. Then he remembered the queer episode of the night before, when he had seen once again the man who had given him a lift, and had heard him talking to someone in Ring O' Bells Hall.

"What was he up to, do you think, at that time of night?" asked Barney, eating the very last bit of cheese, and feeling pleasantly full. He drank his glass of milk, and got out his hanky to wipe his mouth. Before he had made friends with the children he had always wiped his mouth with the back of his hand!

"Goodness knows what anyone would be up to in this old village!" said Roger, puzzled. "And Ring O' Bells Hall is always shut up and locked at night. Nobody is there!"

"Well, someone was definitely there late last night," said Barney. "And, as I say, I know who one person was, because it so happens he was the man who gave me the lift! I said I wanted to go to Lillinghame, never dreaming anyone would be going to Ring O' Bells itself. But apparently he was. He must have gone in his car, and I followed painfully on foot, not knowing he was away in front of me!"

"It's queer," said Diana. "And you say you heard a woman cough too—well, I should think that must have been the bad-tempered woman who guides people round the old place, and gives lectures on it. The one who showed us the secret passage but wouldn't let us go down it."

"Perhaps she's got something down there she doesn't want anyone to see," said Barney idly. "After all, she's the caretaker, she can forbid people to snoop down there—what's to prevent her from hiding away anything she likes!"

"Do you mean that, Barney?" asked Diana, after a pause. It suddenly seemed to fit in with their idea of the woman, and with her behaviour.

"No—not really," said Barney, giving Miranda a piece

477

of an orange. "I just said it. Why? You seem to have gone all serious about it."

"You know—I think we ought to examine that secret passage," said Roger. "Just to make sure there *isn't* something queer going on down there!"

CHAPTER FIFTEEN

A WONDERFUL DAY

MISS PEPPER came out and interrupted this most interesting conversation. " Barney, have you had enough?" she asked. " Sure? Well, listen. My cousin Miss Hannah really *is* scared of monkeys, she's so scared she's quite likely to faint if Miranda comes near her. It's a pity, but there it is. So I thought as it's such fine weather you could all go off for the day together, and take your meals with you."

" Wizard! " said Snubby and Roger at once, and Diana's face shone. Barney got up politely and smiled.

" Nothing I should like better," he said. " And I quite understand about your cousin, Miss Pepper. I won't come farther than the front gate in future."

" It's very nice of you not to mind, Barney," said Miss Pepper. " Hannah is very sorry about it—and she's packing up a most exciting lunch and tea for you to take with you, just to make up to you for her unfortunate dislike of monkeys."

" Goody! " said Diana, pleased. " Where shall we go? I know! Let's go through Ring O' Bells Wood, and walk through the bridle path all the way to the top of the hill where we rode to yesterday. It would be heavenly."

" Woof," said Loony approvingly. He had heard the word " walk," which always seemed to him to be one of the most sensible words in the language of humans. " Bone " was another and " Dinner " was a third. A conversation made up of those three words, with perhaps " Biscuit " and " Chocolate " and " Rats " and " Rabbits " thrown in occasionally would have interested Loony very much.

"Let's go and see old Red Riding Hood in Ring O' Bells Cottage on our way," suggested Snubby. Barney looked surprised.

"Who's she? I never heard of an *old* Red Riding Hood before," he said. "All the ones I've seen in panto-mimes have been young."

"Well, wait till you see ours," grinned Snubby. "And wait till you see her green eyes! We think she's the grand-daughter of a witch."

"Don't be idiotic, Snubby," said Roger. "Di, hadn't you better go and see if Miss Hannah wants a bit of help with the sandwich-packing? There's a lot to cut up and pack, I should think!"

Diana went. Miss Hannah was pleased to see her, and let her arrange slices of tongue on the bread cut for sand-wiches. There seemed quite a mound of cut slices! "Have I cut enough?" asked Miss Hannah anxiously. "My cousin said you all ate twice as much out of doors as in, and that scared me a bit. I don't want you to go hungry."

"We shan't," said Diana, eyeing the loaded table. Sandwiches, sausage rolls, hard-boiled eggs, bread and butter to go with them, tomatoes, lettuce, slices of thick, solid fruit cake, biscuits in a packet, bars of chocolate— good gracious, what a picnic it would be!

She gave Miss Hannah a sudden hug. "You're awfully nice," she said. "As nice as Miss Pepper. Thank you very much."

Miss Hannah went red with pleasure, and put an extra lot of butter on the bit of bread she was buttering. She liked these children, noisy though they were, and quite mad at times. But they had nice ways and good manners and were always ready to help. You just couldn't help liking them, even that monkey of a Snubby. That re-minded Miss Hannah of Miranda and she gave a shudder.

480

" Do see that the monkey doesn't come anywhere near me, won't you, Diana?" she said beseechingly. " Why, the very thought makes my legs turn to water! "

Diana glanced with interest at Miss Hannah's legs, but they seemed just the same as usual—not even wobbly as Snubby's had been. She finished putting the tongue in the very last sandwich.

There was so much food and drink that Miss Hannah had to find three satchels to put it in, for the boys to carry. Snubby didn't see why Diana shouldn't take her share of the carrying and said so.

" I'm *going* to take my share of the load, Snubby," said Diana. " But you might at least let Miss Hannah go on thinking you're a perfect little gentleman—though how anyone can think that, I really——"

She had to stop and laugh, because Snubby picked up a cushion to smother her. Anyway, who could quarrel or bicker on such a day, when they had got Barney and Miranda back with them, and a whole day's picnicking in front of them!

" I hope you won't be lonely, Miss Pepper," called Snubby kindly as they set off down the front path.

" Oh, it'll be quite a *nice* loneliness! " called back Miss Hannah. " Don't you worry about us. We shall get on quite well without you."

Miranda was on Barney's shoulder as usual. The two dogs, their tails wagging furiously, capered round and round, getting in everyone's way. They knew by the satchels on the boys' backs that this was to be a long, long walk!

It certainly was a wonderful day. The four children and the animals went up through Ring O' Bells Wood, and when they came to the little path that led off to Ring O' Bells Cottage, they debated whether or not to go and have a look at it, or to call on their way back.

" On our way back," decided Roger. " Old Red Riding

Hood might give us a glass of milk or something then. We shall probably be thirsty on our way home."

"All right," said Diana. "Come on—up the broad path we go. Loony, that's not a rabbit-hole—that's where a tree has been uprooted."

They walked through the wood, which was dim and cool on this hot May day. Bluebells were coming out everywhere, and lay like pools of shimmering amethyst among the trees. The children sniffed the sweet smell, with just as much enjoyment as the two dogs sniffed rabbit-smells.

"Look at those wind-flowers—there are hundreds of them!" said Diana. Barney stood with her and watched the pretty, star-like flowers dancing in the wind. Barney didn't know many flower-names, and he liked to learn them. Diana knew such a lot! She enjoyed teaching Barney. He was a very willing pupil, with an excellent memory.

They had their lunch on the very top of the hill, overlooking the valley. Far away in the distance they could see the gleam of the Bristol Channel, thrusting up from the sea. It was dazzling silver in the sun, though it would turn blue later in the day.

"This is a most magnificent lunch," said Barney, biting into a hard-boiled egg. "Where's the salt? Anyone remember it?"

"I did," said Diana, and gave him the screw of paper with the salt inside. "Look out—don't let the wind blow it all away."

The four children worked their way through most of the food. They left very little for their tea. "We really ought to stop eating," said Diana, examining what was left. "We're sure to be hungry for tea, and we've eaten nearly everything."

"Perhaps old Red Riding Hood will offer us tea," suggested Snubby.

" Why should she?" said Diana. " I should think she'd be scared of four like us. We've got frightful appetites. Everyone says so."

" Snubby only said that because he'd like to finish everything now," said Roger, and gave Snubby a poke in his fat middle.

" *Don't*! " said Snubby, in alarm. " I've eaten too much to be jabbed in the middle."

This was the kind of silly, friendly talk that Barney enjoyed, and got nowhere else in his life. Most of the circus children he knew were rough and cheeky, and the adults he had lived with had no use for simple friendly talk like this. Barney listened to every word and enjoyed it. How nice to be a family and know each other so well! He thought he was very lucky to be friendly with this one.

The dogs had their share of the food, and Miranda ate a banana daintily, peeling it herself. She threw the skin on the grass. " Now then, Miranda, manners! " said Barney sternly. " Pick that up at once. We don't leave litter about."

Miranda picked up the banana skin and hopped on to Roger's shoulder. She suddenly stuffed it down his neck, and leapt away chattering with glee at his yell of dismay. He put it into the bag of bits of pieces that was to go into one of the satchels and be taken home to be burnt.

It was a long lazy day, and by the time three o'clock came they were red-brown with the hot sun, all except Barney, who was already so brown that he couldn't possibly get any browner!

" It's time we went back," said Roger lazily. " Where are those dogs? It's a good thing rabbit-holes aren't any bigger, or both of them would be wandering lost for ever in a maze of warrens! "

" They never learn they can't get down," said Diana. " If I were a rabbit I'd sit a little way down the hole, where

483

I could see Loony's black face poking down at me, and laugh my head off at him."

"That's just what rabbits probably do," said Snubby. "I've often wondered what it is that makes Loony go so dippy about digging out rabbit-holes—he's probably feeling furious with a grinning rabbit sitting a little way down."

The dogs came back at last, their noses sandy, and their tongues hanging almost to the ground! They flopped down beside the children.

"Up you get," said Roger, getting up himself. "We're starting back on the way home. We're making a call on the way, Loony, on Red Riding Hood. Look out for the wolf! "

They walked leisurely down the long slope of the hill, and reached the wood. The bluebells were a deeper blue now, and the wind-flowers no longer danced because there was no breeze. It was very hot indeed.

"I could do with a drink of water," said Roger. "If I had a tongue long enough it would be hanging out on my chest! "

"Here's the little path that leads to Red Riding Hood's Cottage," said Diana at last, and they turned down it and walked till they came in sight of the little house.

"Honestly, it's a fairy-tale house! " said Diana, as they came near. She was right. It was. It looked as crooked and tumble-down as a cottage in a tale, its chimneys were surprisingly tall, its windows small and diamond-paned. Bluebells grew right up to the little wall that surrounded it.

"There's an old well in the garden," said Diana, pointing. "I say—isn't it an adorable place. I do hope old Red Riding Hood is in! "

CHAPTER SIXTEEN

RING O' BELLS COTTAGE

THEY OPENED the little white gate and walked up a tiny flagged path to the front door. It was painted blue, as were the shutters outside the windows. Diana knocked.

" Come in! " said a voice, and Diana opened the door. Inside was a small room, perfectly square, with a big fire-place at one end. The uneven floor was of stone. Old Riding Hood was standing over the fire, stirring something in a pot.

But she wasn't wearing her old red cloak and hood, so

she didn't look like Red Riding Hood any more. The cloak hung on a nail nearby.

Naomi Barlow looked out of her green-grey eyes at the children. They were disappointed to see that her eyes didn't seem nearly so green as they had imagined. Still, she looked a bit of a fairy-tale person still, with her white apron, red shawl, and snow-white hair.

"Well! If it isn't Miss Hannah's visitors!" she said. "Sit you down, and I'll get you some home-made biscuits. I'm sorry I've no milk to offer you, for you must be rarely thirsty this hot day. Would you like some ice-cold water out of my well?"

This sounded good. "Yes, please," said Roger at once. "Can I go and get some? Is there a bucket on a chain, and a handle that winds?"

"Yes," said Naomi. Then she suddenly caught sight of Miranda on Barney's shoulder. "Why, the little mite!" she said, and left her pot and came over to Barney. "I once had a monkey of my own. It was left for dead by a circus that once came to Ring O' Bells. I took it and nursed it and it lived with me many a year."

She fussed over Miranda, which made Loony and Loopy jealous. She seemed quite at home with children, dogs and monkey. They all liked her.

Roger went out with Barney to get the water. They took a large white jug that Naomi had given them.

"What an enormous well for such a small place," said Roger, in surprise. "I bet it's deep."

It was. It was so very deep that neither of the boys could see the water. Roger took a stone and dropped it down. It was quite a time before he heard the splash. He peered down.

"It's a nice well," he said. "It's got ferns and things growing all the way down the sides. I bet the water's cold!"

He and Barney wound the bucket down till it reached

486

the water. Then they wound it up again, the chain making quite a noise. They took the bucket off and emptied the water into the big jug. "Feel it," said Barney. "Absolutely icy-cold!"

They all enjoyed drinking the crystal-clear cold water, and eating Naomi's home-made biscuits. They tasted of cinnamon, and were very spicy indeed. She put some into a bag for them.

The children asked to see round the cottage. "There's not much to see," said old Naomi. "Just three tiny rooms! This is my parlour-kitchen, where I cook and sit. And this is my bedroom."

The bedroom was even smaller than the kitchen. The children looked at the flat stone floor, and thought how cold it must be in the winter. The kitchen was the same, set with big, solid, white flags, a little uneven here and there.

"And this is my store-room," said Naomi, opening a door off the kitchen, and showing them a cupboard of a room. She had made it into a store-room, and there were jars of pickles, jam, honey, spices, and all kinds of things. It too had a cold stone floor, and even on that hot May day, it seemed chilly to the children.

"That was my bedroom when I was a girl," said Naomi. "I slept there for years. Then when my old Dad died and Ma followed him, I made it into a store-room. Barlows have lived here for years upon years—four hundred years, so I've heard tell. But there won't be a Barlow here after me, more's the pity."

It was a quaint, queer, uncomfortable old cottage, too dark with its too-small, leaded windows, and probably far too cold, with its solid stone floor, in the winter. But, as Diana said afterwards, "it had a lovely *feeling* about it, it was full of old thoughts and old doings, and past and gone days."

"Mother Barlow must have lived there too," said

487

Snubby, as they went home. " I'd like to have known her.
I do wonder why Old Grandad kept saying, " Ask Mother
Barlow, ask Mother Barlow," the other day, when we
wanted to know where the secret passage went. Why
should *she* know so much about it?"

" Because she probably used it, and caught him!" said
Roger. " I say—what about Barney's lodging to-night? I
was thinking he'd be coming home with us, but of course
he can't. We'd better ask in the village if there's anywhere
for him to sleep!"

So they asked, first at the village stores, and then at the
various addresses that the woman there gave them.

But although many would have been willing to take
Barney, nobody wanted Miranda. In vain Barney and the
others sang her praises, said she was quite harmless, and
very sweet and good-mannered—nobody would have
Miranda!

" She'd bring fleas," said one.

" She'd bite my baby," said another.

" I don't hold with monkeys," said a third.

And so it went on—no, no, no, till the children got quite
desperate.

Barney, of course, didn't mind. He was used to sleeping
anywhere, in a caravan, in a tent, under a hedge or a haystack.

" Don't you bother about me," he kept saying, but the
children did. Diana pointed out that great clouds had
rolled up again and threatened the same downpour of rain
as the night before.

" You simply *must* be under cover," she said.

" All right," said Barney. " What's the matter with me
sleeping in the Ring O' Bells Hall again? Nobody sleeps
there, and I shan't do any harm."

" Well, you could," said Roger. " I can't see what it
would really matter. What's the time? I believe it would
still be open. Let's go and see. If it is, we'll pay and go in,

and find a better place for you to sleep than the four-poster bed you spoke about. We can leave you there! "

The woman looked sourly at them when they arrived in the hall, having tied up the two dogs securely. " It's just upon closing time," she said.

" There's five minutes to go," said Roger firmly, and he placed the money on the table. " We want to show our friend round."

The woman caught sight of the monkey. " Not with that monkey! " she said. But the children had already marched on down the hall.

" Show me the room where that secret passage is," said Barney suddenly. " I'd like to see that."

" Right," said Roger. " But we can't look at the passage because you have to pay extra for that, and I don't want to go back to that bad-tempered woman! Now let's see—which room was it?"

They went into two or three and then found the little room into which the secret passage opened. Roger showed Barney the big tapestry picture which could be moved to one side in order to open the tiny panel that had to be used to move the lever that freed the big panel.

" Sounds like the House-that-Jack-Built to me! " said Barney, with a grin. " Move the picture to open the panel to move the lever to free the panel, to——"

" It does sound a bit complicated," said Roger. " I tell you what—we'll come one day and explore that passage all by ourselves. Though how we're going to do it without that woman suspecting, I don't know."

" Have to come one night then," said Barney. Diana shivered.

" I only hope the bells don't ring then! " she said.

" They wouldn't. We're not enemies! " said Snubby. " I say—that would be a bit of an adventure, wouldn't it— to explore a secret passage one night! "

" I think I'll sleep in the little room here for the night," said Barney, looking round. "There's a big couch with cushions—though they look pretty hard—and I could take that cloth off the table over there to put round me. You wouldn't believe how warm the table-cloth was last night! I shall be very comfortable here."

A voice came sharply from the hall. "I'm just closing the place. Will you please come, or you'll be locked in!"

"She doesn't guess that one of us *wants* to be locked in!" whispered Snubby in glee. "So long, Barney. Sleep well. See you in the morning."

"Take old Red Riding Hood's biscuits for your supper," said Diana, pushing the paper-bag into Barney's hand. "And here's the rest of the chocolate. Come up to Miss Hannah's in the morning and wait outside the gate. We'll bring you breakfast."

"Thanks," said Barney, gratefully. The others went quickly out of the room and looked round the hall. The woman could be heard locking up somewhere at the back. Now was their time to go, before she realised that only three were departing instead of four!

"Good night!" called Roger, in a stentorian voice and Snubby and Diana joined in. There might have been a dozen of them, not three!

The woman made no answer. The children went out quickly, grinning at one another. It was easy! They untied the impatient dogs and went off up the road to Miss Hannah's rambling old house.

"Barney will be all right in that little room," said Roger, glancing up at the overcast sky. "Here comes the first big drops. Hurry!"

They hurried, glad to think that Barney and Miranda wouldn't have to sleep under a hedge. They ran in at the gate, and were welcomed by Miss Pepper.

"*Just* in time!" she said. "I was afraid you'd be caught by the storm. Did you have a good day?"

" Wonderful! " said Diana. " Where's Miss Hannah? We want to tell her that the food was absolutely super! "

" Wizard," said the boys, together. " We ate it all! "

" What have you done with Barney and Miranda?" asked Miss Pepper, as they went indoors. " I hope you found him lodgings of some kind."

Roger grinned. " Yes—we did. He'll be quite comfortable, Miss Pepper. He's got a *very* nice little room of his own, with nobody to disturb him at all! "

CHAPTER SEVENTEEN

IN THE MIDDLE OF THE NIGHT

BARNEY certainly had a nice little room of his own! He felt quite glad to be there, too, when he heard the thunder crashing and the rain pelting down. The caretaker-woman had gone slamming the front door behind her. He was quite alone, except for Miranda.

Barney waited for the slamming of the front door, and then he stood up. He didn't want to go to bed yet! He wondered if there were any books about that he might read.

He had crouched by a chest waiting for the caretaker to go, ready to open the lid and slip inside, if she came near. But she didn't. She apparently thought that all the children had gone, and that the place was quite empty.

" And now I'm master of Ring O' Bells Hall," said Barney, out loud, as he wandered through the great mansion. He went into the kitchen and marvelled at the enormous cooking stoves there. What meals they must have cooked in the old days here! He went idly to the tap over the great wide sink and turned it on, not expecting any water to come out.

But a stream of cold water splashed at once into the sink. Barney found an old tankard on a shelf and filled it. He drank deeply, for the night was hot and he was really very thirsty He rinsed out the tankard and put it back. He supposed that water was laid on for the caretaker to use. Well, that was lucky for *him*!

He found some books in a panelled room that looked like a library. In fact, he found about two thousand books. They lined the shelves from floor to ceiling, most of them leather-bound. Their colours were old and faded now, and they looked as if nobody had ever read them.

Barney took one or two down. They were printed in old-time lettering and he found them too difficult to understand. He put them back carefully, noting that they were very dusty. The caretaker-woman needed to take her duster round a bit more, he thought!

It was dull all by himself, and he was glad when he felt sleepy. He ate all the biscuits and the chocolate that Diana had given him, and then got another drink of water. He gave Miranda a drink too, and a few raisins to eat.

" And don't you put the pips down my neck this time, and don't you spit them out, either! " he said. " Put them into your paw and give them to me."

So for once in a way Miranda was very polite, and spat each pip into her tiny brown paw, and handed them solemnly to Barney, who just as solemnly put them into an ash-tray on one of the tables.

When it was almost dark, he took the table-cloth off the table and carried it to the big couch. He arranged the cushions for his head and then lay down. He pulled the big cloth over him. It was heavy and warm—too warm after a while, and Barney had to push it partly off him.

Miranda cuddled into his jacket, putting her little paws inside his shirt. He liked to feel them there. He blew softly on the top of her head.

" Good night, Miranda. Sleep well, and we won't wake up before morning! "

But he was wrong—they did!

Miranda woke first, and lay cuddled against Barney, her ears twitching. What had awakened her? She lay listening, and then settled down again. But before she had fallen asleep once more, her ears twitched again. This time she scrambled out of Barney's coat and sat on the head of the couch. She chattered a little in a very small voice indeed.

She awoke Barney, and he sat up, feeling for Miranda.

Where had she gone? He heard her low chattering nearby and put out a hand to touch her. She nestled into his arms at once.

What woke you, Miranda?" Barney whispered. "Something disturbed you. What was it. It's the middle of the night. Did you hear a mouse or a rat?"

On the night air came the sound of the church clock striking some distance away. Dong—dong—dong.

"Three o'clock," said Barney. "There's still a lot of the night left, Miranda. Go to sleep."

And then he too heard a noise. At first he thought he must be mistaken. Then it came again. Where was it? Surely it wasn't in the room? It was a curious noise, and it came and went in spasms. What did it sound like?

Barney decided that the noise certainly *wasn't* in the room. He felt in his pocket for the torch that Roger had lent him. He switched it on. The beam flashed round the room. It was quite empty. There was nobody and nothing there.

The noise could not be heard outside the little room where he had been sleeping. He soon made certain of that. He then went carefully round the room, stopping and listening at various points.

He came to one place where the noise sounded loudest. He flashed his torch on the spot. It was the panel which Roger had pointed out to him as the one that opened into the secret passage. He pressed his ear to it.

Now he could hear the noise much better, when it came. It was a curious, spasmodic noise, fairly regular, but too far away to make out whether it was made by a machine, or by a human being or animal, or by water—in fact Barney couldn't make it out at all. It came spasmodically, but it was always the same when it did come—a series of quick sounds more or less regularly spaced. Barney guessed they came up from the secret passage, and were altered considerably before they reached him because of the distance and the hollowness of the secret passage.

He didn't know how to open the secret passage, so he couldn't find out anything. He went back to lie down on the couch, with Miranda beside him.

" Might as well go to sleep," he told the little monkey. " We're not likely to find out anything by just listening to those sounds for hours. But—I think we certainly ought to examine that secret passage, Miranda. What do you suppose is down there?"

Miranda hadn't the faintest idea. She cuddled down again and went to sleep. So did Barney. Whether the noises went on again or not, he didn't know and he didn't care.

Barney awoke in good time in the morning and got up cautiously, in case the caretaker had come early. But the whole building was silent. There was not even the mysterious sound he had heard in the middle of the night.

He wondered if he could have dreamt it. No, he couldn't, he remembered it too well. He stole into the kitchen to put his face under the tap and to get a drink.

Miranda pretended to hold her paws out to the tap, but she didn't get wet. She wasn't fond of water!

" You're a fraud," said Barney, drying himself on his big red handkerchief. " No, I'm not going to dry your paws when they're not even wet. You wash your hands properly then I will."

He went back to the little room where he had slept and made it tidy, draping the table-cloth over the table again. He wondered if the caretaker would notice how crumpled it was, and be puzzled. He didn't think she noticed much though, judging by the layers of dust she had left here and there.

He went into the hall to watch for her coming. He didn't like to go out of the back door, leaving it unlocked, in case she was suspicious.

He hid behind a big chest and waited. She should be coming soon now. In a little while he heard her footsteps coming down the path outside, then she slid the big key into the door and opened it.

As soon as she had disappeared into one of the rooms Barney slipped out with Miranda. Nobody saw him. He made his way to Miss Hannah's house and stood by the front gate, waiting.

Snubby rushed out to him. "Barney! I've been watching for you. We're in the middle of breakfast and I'll bring a tray out for you here. You can sit in the garden, Miss Hannah says, if you'll promise not to let Miranda off your shoulder."

When the others came out after breakfast Barney told them of his peculiar experience in the middle of the night. "I can't imagine what it was," he said. "It was a silly sort of noise. I can't place it, and yet I feel I know it and have heard it many times. But, of course the hollowness of the passage must make it sound very different from what it really is."

The others listened, amazed and thrilled. "Did it *really* come from behind the panelling, Barney?" asked Roger. "What's down there then? That woman says the passage is walled-up, so whatever is there can't be very far down!"

"It sounded a good way down," said Barney. "Are you all game to explore it?"

They were—though Diana sounded a bit quavery. Snubby felt very brave sitting out there in the bright sunshine, discussing weird noises that happened in the night—but he couldn't help wondering if he would feel quite so brave in the dead of night!

"That woman would never let us go down in the daytime, that's certain," said Roger. "So it means we must explore after she's gone home. But we can't very well slip out before supper, or Miss Pepper would want to know

496

what we're up to with you. We'd better come after we're supposed to be in bed."

They debated it solemnly, and decided it would be best to go then. Miss Pepper and Miss Hannah went to bed very early, about nine o'clock. The children could easily dress and slip out. Nobody would know.

"Right," said Barney, finishing his breakfast. "That's settled then. To-night about half-past nine. We'll do the 'This is the-House-that-Jack-Built' business—move the picture that slides the panel that works the lever that frees the panel that opens the passage that lets us go down, that brings us to——"

"What?" cried the other three eagerly. But Barney shook his head. "That's as far as I can get," he said. "We'll know the rest of our little story to-night, I hope. Now if you've got to do some jobs for Miss Hannah, I'll take the two dogs for a walk. They're pawing at me as if they want to get my jacket off! All right, all right, Loony and Loopy. I'll take you for a walkie-walk and get some of your fat off!"

He went off with the two dogs, whistling his lovely clear whistle. The others went back to help with the various jobs.

"To-night—at half-past nine!" thought Diana, with a little shiver. "It's exciting—but I do feel a little bit scared!"

CHAPTER EIGHTEEN

DOWN THE SECRET PASSAGE

AT HALF-PAST NINE that night Miss Pepper and Miss
Hannah were both in bed, and Miss Hannah was fast
asleep. The children were ready to go and were debating
whether to take Loony or not.

"Will he bark the place down if we don't take him?"
whispered Diana.

"Yes," whispered back Snubby. "We'd better let him
come. I'll carry him downstairs so that his great paws
don't make a noise."

So Loony was carried downstairs, puzzled but very good
and quiet. Loopy slept on a couch in Miss Hannah's
room, which was fortunately in another wing of the house,
so he heard nothing.

They all heaved a sigh of relief when they were safely
out on the road, walking softly in the moonlight. They
soon arrived at Ring O' Bells Hall, and Barney let them
in at the front door. He closed it quietly.

"Have you heard those noises again?" asked Snubby.
Barney shook his head.

"No. Not to-night. Not a sound. Come on, let's go
to the little room and get going."

They went to the room where Barney had slept the night
before, and where the entrance of the secret passage was.
All of them had torches, and they shone them on the big
tapestry picture on the wall.

"See that face with a helmet pushed back on the forehead?" said Roger in a low voice. "Well, watch—I press
it just *here*—and see what happens!"

The picture slid quietly to one side, exposing the small
panel. Roger pressed on it and the panel slid aside in its
turn. He put in his hand and felt for the knob. He pressed
that too, and at the same moment a small rattling noise
came from behind another panel some distance away on
the wall.

Barney looked startled. "That's the lever freeing the
other panel, so that we can push it to one side," whispered
Diana. They went to the second panel which was large.
Roger pushed against it hard, and to Barney's surprise it
slid to one side, passing neatly under the panel next to it,
disclosing the yawning hole that was the entrance to the
secret passage.

Loony gave a tiny yelp. He couldn't understand all
these curious happenings by the light of torches. "Shut

up," said Snubby, tapping the dog's head. "Don't say a word, Loony."

Roger thrust his torch inside the panelling and tried to see the passage. But all he could make out was a dark and narrow way behind the panelling.

"Shall we get in and follow the passage now?" whispered Roger. "It's all quiet—nothing to be heard at all!"

"Right—you go first, Roger, then Diana can go, then Snubby and I'll follow with Loony," said Barney. "It's so narrow we'll have to go in single file."

Roger got in, lifting his leg over the panelling. He stood in the passage, which smelt dusty and musty. He moved along a little way and one by one all the others got into it too. Loony was lifted in by Snubby.

He was surprised and very subdued. He thought this was a most peculiar evening!

"Where's Miranda?" whispered Snubby.

"She wouldn't come into the hole," whispered back Barney. "She was scared. She'll be all right in that room. She'll wait for us."

The passage was indeed dark and narrow. It went behind the panelling of the room for about twelve feet and then turned abruptly to the left. It then went downwards by means of very shallow steps, down and down and down.

Roger was in front, keeping his torch level so that its light flashed on what was before him. Once he stopped, and the whole line bumped into one another.

"What's up, Roger?" asked Diana anxiously.

"Look," said Roger, and flashed his torch on two tiny wooden doors set in a hole in the wall at one side of the passage. "A cupboard! Perhaps the very cupboard where Old Grandad found those books and the carved box!"

He opened the doors, expecting the cupboard to be

500

empty. But it wasn't. What it held was rather surprising. Nothing old, but something very new and modern. There were torch batteries, candles, a little tin of paraffin oil, and a dozen boxes of matches.

"What queer things to store here," said Diana, looking at them. "I suppose they've been left here ever since the passage was walled up—maybe they were useful for exploring it before the roof fell in and they closed it."

"That was a long time ago," said Roger. He shut the cupboard doors thoughtfully and went on once more, picking his way slowly. The passage was much wider once it left the panelling. Roger reckoned that it was really a tunnel now, going underground. Possibly it had left the house behind and was no longer underneath it. The caretaker-woman had told them that it avoided the cellars, which, presumably, spread themselves under the house.

He suddenly stopped again, with a short exclamation. The others did their usual bumping. Loony whined.

"You might give us warning when you're going to stop so suddenly," grumbled Snubby under his breath. "What's up now?"

Roger was flashing his torch on what looked like a brick wall in front of him. It stretched from ground to roof. "Here's the wall that woman told us of," he said. "The passage *is* bricked up then! Look at that! We can't go any farther!"

This was bitterly disappointing. None of the children had really believed in their hearts that the woman had spoken the truth. But she had. There was the wall! If there was any more of the secret passage it must be on the other side of the wall, and she had said that the roof had fallen in there.

"What a swizz!" said Snubby.

"What about the noises Barney heard? We haven't come across anything that could make them," whispered Roger. This was passed back to Barney.

"Funny," said Barney. "Where could they have come from then?"

"Let's go back," said Diana. "I don't like the smell down here."

So back they went, turning themselves round and having Barney for leader this time. They passed the queer little cupboard but didn't open it again. Then they were up behind the panelling, and in a moment or two were climbing out of the passage and into the room beyond.

Roger pressed the panel back into place. A rattling noise came as it slid back. That was the lever moving back against the panel to prevent anyone opening it unless they pressed the hidden knob behind the picture. Roger then slid back the little panel, and wondered how to move back the picture into place. He couldn't find out, so it had to be left out of place.

"Perhaps that woman will think she left it out of place herself, if she notices it to-morrow," said Diana. "I say—what a disappointment. I don't quite know what I expected to find, but I expected *some*thing. But we didn't even hear one of Barney's noises!"

"Sh!" said Barney, suddenly. "I believe I did hear it again—just then. Hush, everyone!"

They all stiffened, and listened hard. Yes, there *was* a noise—a few quick, regular sounds, far away and hollow-sounding. It *did* seem as if it came up the secret passage, muffled and distant.

"There you are," said Barney. "I began to think I'd dreamt it—but I hadn't."

And then they suddenly heard another noise—quite a different noise, that made them go tense and clutch one another.

It was only a small sound—a tiny jangle of a noise—as if—as if one of the bells up in the tower had moved, and its clapper had bumped against it!

"That was a bell-noise," breathed Diana. "And it

502

came from the tower. Oh, don't say the bells are going to ring themselves! "

And then it happened. The bells rang out, jingled and jangled, clashed and rang away up in the tower! Diana clutched Roger so tightly that her nails went into the flesh of his arm. Loony howled dismally.

The bells suddenly stopped. The echo of the clanging died away, and Diana sank down on the couch, trembling. Snubby was petrified and couldn't move. Barney and Roger spoke together softly.

" Who rang them? There's nobody here but ourselves."

" And anyway there are no ropes to pull. Why did they suddenly ring?"

" In the old days it was said that they rang because enemies were coming. Surely the bells don't count us as enemies! They couldn't have rung against *us*! "

" Bells can't ring themselves," said Roger, trying to convince himself that they couldn't. But they *had* rung themselves! The children had heard them.

A little scared, whimpering noise made them all jump. " Oh—*poor* little Miranda! " said Diana, picking the tiny monkey up. " Did the bells scare you too? Never mind. It's all right now."

" Do you think we dare to go and look in the square tower, just to see if anyone has rigged up ropes to peal the bells?" asked Roger, after a time. They were now all sitting close together on the couch, trying to recover from their fright.

" I'm not going," said Snubby promptly. " They might begin to ring again and I'd have a double fit! "

" I'm going to see," said Barney and walked off. Roger followed him rather reluctantly.

They soon came back. " No ropes at all," said Barney. " The bells are all quite still. There's nothing to be seen. Well—I don't know who the enemies are—but *I* can't see or hear any. The bells made a mistake *this* time! "

" *Listen*," said Diana urgently. " I can hear something. I can really—out in the hall there."

They listened tensely. They heard a key being thrust into the front door, and somebody opened it. There were voices—footsteps! The door closed softly.

" The bells were right! " whispered Snubby. " These must be the enemies! "

CHAPTER NINETEEN

ALL VERY PECULIAR

" WE MUST HIDE! " said Barney. " They may come in here." Fortunately the footsteps went into the kitchen, and the children could hear water running. They looked round the little room desperately. They didn't dare to leave it in case they were seen.

A great chest stood in one corner, and a smaller one in another. Barney lifted up the lid of the large one. " Get in," he whispered to the others. " There's room for three of you. I'll get into the other with Miranda."

They got in hurriedly, making as little noise as possible. Snubby dragged poor Loony in, tapping him fiercely on the head every time he showed an inclination to growl. Barney slipped inside the other chest. But Miranda refused to come! She shot away from him in the darkness. She hated being shut up anywhere.

Barney gave a little groan. He hoped Miranda would keep out of of the way of the " enemy " whoever they were. What in the world were people doing here at this time of night?

They had only just hidden themselves in time. Footsteps—two pairs—came into the room where they were hidden.

" Where is he?" said a man's voice.

" I'll take you to him." It was a woman's voice that answered—the caretaker! Barney lifted up the lid of his chest a fraction and listened.

He heard the now familiar rattle behind the panelling as the lever fell back to release the larger panel. Ah— they were going down the secret passage then. Why?

There was nothing there. It was bricked up not very far down. Barney was puzzled. The woman had apparently not noticed that the big picture was out of place, which was a relief.

He saw her by the light of the man's torch. He couldn't see the man very well, but noticed that he had a bag, a small attaché case of some kind. His voice was deep and rough. He didn't sound at all pleased.

Loony growled suddenly—a deep, blood-curdling noise from the depths of the large chest. The woman and the man stood still, as if transfixed.

"What in the name of goodness was that?" said the man at last. "What a fearful noise!"

From above his head came a small gibbering sound. That was Miranda, of course, telling Loony to be quiet! It made the man and woman jump violently. The man swung his torch upwards, but Miranda had gone. She gibbered from the opposite side of the room now.

Loony growled again, and was immediately stifled by Snubby.

"There's that frightful noise again,"—said the man. "It's enough to give anyone the creeps. What's the matter with this place?"

"Nothing," said the woman, in a trembling voice. "I've never heard these noises before. But it can't be anything—just—just owls or something."

"Owls don't make blood-curdling noises like that," said the man, switching his torch into the yawning hole in the panelling. "Well, come on—do we really have to get in here?"

The woman gave a sudden scream, and Barney almost dropped the lid of the chest in surprise. Now what was happening?

Miranda had sat herself on a shelf near the woman's head, and had pulled at her hair. No wonder she screamed.

She made the man jump, and he became angry. "Stop it!" he growled. "We're getting nerves or something. What's the matter now?"

"S-s-s-something pulled my hair," the woman quavered.

"And so will I if you don't stop all this play-acting," said the man. He gave the woman a shove and she went into the secret passage more quickly than she had intended to. He followed. Barney could hear their steps going along behind the panelling, and then down the shallow steps underground. He opened the lid wide and jumped out, padding across the floor to the opening in the panelling. He put his head in and listened.

But except for a scraping kind of noise which he couldn't make out, he heard no more. All was silence. Where had the two gone?

He ran lightly to the other chest and opened it. "Come on," he said. "Now's our chance to go. They've gone down the secret passage, goodness knows where or why. We'd better clear out. I don't like this much."

The others gladly scrambled out. They shut the lid down and ran quietly in their rubber-soled shoes to the door. They sidled into the dark hall and made for the front door, which they knew was directly opposite. Barney thought it would be safe to switch on his torch for half a second.

They came to the front door and Barney opened it quietly. He would have to leave it open because he couldn't risk making a noise when he closed it. He suddenly put out a warning hand to the others.

"Be careful. There may be a car waiting somewhere," he said. "We don't want to be seen."

He looked sharply out to the road, and made out a dim red light—the rear light of a car!

"We'll go round the house to the back," he whispered. "We can squeeze through a hedge and into the lane farther up. Come on. Don't make a sound!"

They all breathed more freely when at last they were some way up the lane, having squeezed through the hedge half-way down the garden of Ring O' Bells Hall. Loony was completely bewildered. What kind of game was this, played so late at night? He was tired of being tapped on the head by Snubby when he wanted to growl.

"Don't say anything till we get back to Miss Pepper's," said Roger, in a low voice. So, feeling that there might be ears listening in every hedge, the four of them hurried quietly back.

They went to a little shed in Miss Hannah's garden and crowded in there together. "What an evening," said Roger, blowing out a deep breath of relief at being somewhere ordinary and safe. "Those bells ringing out all by themselves like that—and then the woman and the man coming, exactly as if they were the enemies foretold by the bells."

"I wonder if anyone else heard them—the villagers, for instance," said Diana.

"Some of them may have," said Roger. "But the village is a little way away, isn't it—and as the bells are not swung loosely on ropes, but only jammed up there tightly together, they wouldn't sound nearly as loud as they would do if they were pulled and rung properly. They jangled, more than rang."

"They did the best they could," said Diana soberly. "I was awfully scared. I suppose the 'enemy' didn't hear them, because they were coming in the car, and must still have been some way away. I wonder if they would have come into the Hall if they *had* heard them."

"Of course not," said Roger. "Clever bells—to warn us but not them! I say—this is all very *peculiar*, isn't it? What's down that secret passage?"

"You mean *who* is," said Diana. "That man said 'Where is *he*?' not 'Where is *it*?' There's someone down there, doing something."

"I don't know where, then," said Roger. "*We* went right down to the brick wall, and there wasn't anyone. And, as far as I could see, there was absolutely no other passage or cave or anything. Just a tunnel."

There was a silence. Everyone was thinking. "Shall we go down the passage again some time and have another snoop?" asked Roger at last.

"No," said everybody, very firmly. The idea of getting down there again at dead of night, with those bells nearby likely to ring all by themselves at any minute, didn't appeal to anyone.

"I tell you what we *could* do," said Snubby suddenly. "We could try and find out where the *other* end of the secret passage is, and then explore it backwards, so to speak—to the other side of the brick wall."

Everyone thought this was a very bright idea. Roger gave Snubby a little pat on the back. "Now that *is* an idea," he said. "We might find something out then."

"Yes—but wait a minute. We don't know where to look for the other end of the passage," said Diana, after a moment's thought.

"We'll go and ask Grandad again," said Roger, promptly. "Maybe he'll tell us this time."

Diana suddenly yawned, and that set the others off. The church clock struck twelve, very solemnly indeed.

"We ought to go to bed," said Diana. "We'll never wake up in the morning. Where's old Barney going to sleep? He can't go back to Ring O' Bells Hall, that's certain."

"I shouldn't think he wants to, either," said Snubby. "I know I wouldn't."

"Well, I don't," said Barney. "Those bells rather shook me. I just can't understand it. Poor little Miranda is so frightened that she's not moved since I tucked her into my shirt. She must have had a fit when she heard them jangling out!"

" I had a pretty good fit myself," said Snubby. " Well, what about Barney. Couldn't he sleep here for the night? In this shed?"

" Yes—just for to-night," said Roger, considering. " I don't know if Miss Hannah would mind, but as we can't ask her now, we'll just say Barney *can* sleep here. After all, Miranda isn't likely to pop in through her window or anything."

Barney was very tired. He arranged some sacks to lie on, and Diana found an old garden rug to cover him. " We'll go in now," she said. " You'll be all right, Barney, won't you?"

" Fine," said Barney, curling himself up. " You go and get into bed—you'll be getting 'flu again, or something! See you to-morrow."

" Yes—and we'll find the other end of the passage *some-how*," said Snubby. " And down we'll go."

" Though I expect we shall find the roof *has* fallen in, as that woman said," remarked Roger, remembering.

" Anyway, we'll have a shot at finding it and exploring," said Barney sleepily. " Good night, all of you."

Loony gave Barney one last lick on the nose and sniffed at the sleeping Miranda under his shirt. Then he trotted off quietly after the others. What an evening! He would have something to tell Loopy next day, no doubt about that!

CHAPTER TWENTY

GRANDAD'S OLD BOX

NEITHER Miss Pepper nor Miss Hannah had heard the bells ringing the night before. Diana didn't ask them straight out, but the children felt that they *had* to discover if they had been heard.

" I thought I heard bells ringing in the night," Diana said casually at breakfast-time. " Funny! "

" You must have been dreaming," said Miss Pepper. " Mustn't she, Hannah?"

" Yes—she probably heard the church clock striking," said Miss Hannah. " It has a lovely tone. Do you want a fourth sausage, Snubby?"

Snubby did. " My appetite's coming back," he informed Miss Hannah.

"*Coming* back! " she repeated horrified. " You don't mean to say it's even worse than this?"

" He's just greedy—it's nothing to do with appetite," said Diana. Snubby aimed a kick at her under the table, but Diana had already drawn her legs well out of the way, and there was a sudden agonised yelp from poor Loopy. This meant Snubby getting hurriedly down from the table and crawling underneath to comfort him and apologise.

" *You'd* better have the last sausage, Roger, as Snubby has disappeared," said Miss Pepper, whereupon Snubby came back again in a hurry.

" What are your plans to-day?" asked Miss Hannah. " Riding? Walking? Lazing?"

" We thought we'd go and have a talk with Old Grandad again," said Diana. " And then perhaps go for a walk. Do you want any errands done, Miss Hannah?"

511

"No, I don't think so," said Miss Hannah. "You'll do all your usual jobs first, I know—beds and so on."

"Oh, of *course*," said Diana. "And you do know you've only got to ask us to do absolutely anything for you and we'll do it."

"Like a shot," said Snubby, finishing the last sausage. "I do like the way you cook sausages, Miss Hannah—nice and *bursty*."

"What extraordinary things you say, Snubby," said Miss Hannah. "Have you finished? Because if you have you might remove Loony from my feet. He's so heavy."

Loony was removed, and Loopy followed. Diana got up to go and fetch Barney's tray of breakfast things. She had already been out to see him, and had taken him a very fine breakfast. Miranda was sitting licking marmalade off a piece of toast. She offered it to Diana.

"No thanks, darling Miranda," said Diana. "You can have it all. I don't want even one lick. Barney, we'll come out as soon as we can. We've got a few things to do."

"Right," said Barney. "I'm going to mend that bit of fence that's broken. I must do *some*thing in return for my breakfast!"

"Oh— Miss Hannah *will* be pleased," said Diana. That was so like Barney. He always felt he simply must repay any kindness as soon as ever he could.

About eleven o'clock the four children, Loony, Loopy and Miranda were all going up the lane to Hubbard Cottage. They stopped at a little shop to buy a tin of tobacco for the old man they were going to see. The woman knew quite well what he smoked, which was lucky.

They walked up to the front door of the cottage and knocked.

"Come away in!" called Mother Hubbard's voice, and in they went. Mother Hubbard was there, scrubbing her floor. She was pleased to see the children. She got up, wiping her hands, and smiled at them.

" Could we see Old Grandad?" asked Diana politely. "We've brought him a little tin of tobacco."

" Well, if that isn't kind of you! " said the old lady, and she took the tin. " I wish you *could* see him—but he's got one of his poorly turns and he's in bed."

" Oh," said the children, and looked so disappointed that Mother Hubbard felt sorry.

" There's nothing *I* can tell you or do for you instead, is there?" she asked.

" Well," said Diana, and paused. She looked at the others and they nodded. " You see, it's like this—Old Grandad told us about some old books he once had, and we wondered if he still had them and would lend them to us."

" Old books?" said Mother Hubbard, frowning as she tried to remember. " Let me see—those must have been thrown away years since."

" Oh—*what* a pity! " said Diana, disappointed.

" When I came to look after Old Grandad, he had a wonderful lot of rubbish," said Mother Hubbard. " And I had a good turn-out and threw a lot away. But I did put some into an old box of his. You can rummage through that if you like, and see if you can find any old books there. He wouldn't mind! "

" Oh, *could* we! " said Diana delighted. " We'd love to. We're so interested in Ring O' Bells Village, you know."

" Yes—it's a queer old place," said Mother Hubbard. " Do you know what Old Grandad said to me this morning? He said he heard the bells at the old Hall ringing last night. The things he do think! Why those bells haven't rung for years—they've got no ropes to pull them with."

" Didn't you hear the bells too?" asked Roger.

" I sleep sound," said Mother Hubbard. " And if I heard bells ringing at Ring O' Bells Hall, I'd think I was off my head. Will you believe it, when Fanny Tapp came by this morning, and I told her what Old Grandad said, she made out she'd heard them too, and was proper scared in the night. The tales some folks make up!"

The children listened to all this and said nothing. So others had heard the bells too!

"You come along into my washhouse," said Mother Hubbard. "I've got Grandad's box there. And would you like some of my gingers? I made them yesterday."

The "gingers" turned out to be nice, hard, ginger biscuits, almost as good as Naomi Barlow's cinnamon biscuits. The children followed Mother Hubbard into the little washhouse, munching the biscuits.

There were shelves round the washhouse and Mother Hubbard pointed to an old brass-bound box. "That's Grandad's," she said. "Can you lift it down?"

"Yes, thank you," said Barney, and lifted it down. It wasn't very heavy, so there couldn't be much in it.

A loud call came from the little front garden and Mother Hubbard hurried off. "That's the baker," she said. "You undo the box and see what you can find. If there's books there, you can borrow them."

The children opened the box. It had a simple catch to fasten it. They bent over the open box, excited. What would they find?

They found very little. There were a few roughly carved wooden figures, which probably Old Grandad had done himself and was proud of. There was a funny old ship, its sails in rags, its mast broken. There was an old wooden pipe, and what looked like a home-made whistle.

"Not much here," said Roger. "Wait—here's a book!"

He took it out. It was bound in leather that was warped and discoloured with damp. Many of the pages had stuck together. The children pored over it, trying to pull the pages apart.

"Be careful—you'll tear them," said Roger. "Blow! This book is in that difficult old lettering. We can't possibly make out much—and look how messed up the pages are—we can hardly read anything anyhow."

They all pored over the book, trying to make out a word here and there. They couldn't even find out the title. It was in flourishing letters, so decorative that the children couldn't read them.

"No good," said Roger, disappointed. "Still—if Mother Hubbard will let us, we'll borrow it, just in *case* we can make out something. Though how we could ever find out if the secret passage is mentioned here I simply don't know!"

"Found anything interesting?" asked Mother Hubbard, appearing again. "Nothing but rubbish there, I expect. Oh, you've got an old book. Borrow it, if you like."

"Thank you," said Diana. "We'd like to. I hope Old Grandad will be better soon."

"I'll tell him you've been, and give him the tobacco," said Mother Hubbard. "Good-bye—and keep the book as long as you like."

They all went out. Barney took Miranda out from his jacket. He had hidden her there in case Mother Hubbard or Old Grandad didn't like monkeys. She had been as good as gold. The two dogs, each with a bone from the old lady, welcomed the children as if they had been away for a week. Roger laughed and untied them.

"Old Grandad doesn't like dogs," he told them, "so don't bark your heads off like that, or he'll come after you with a stick!"

They went to the village for an ice-cream. Snubby was carrying the book, dipping into it as he went. He suddenly stood still and said "HA!" in a most excited voice.

"What are you ha-ing about?" asked Diana. "Found a recipe for cooking sausages or something?"

"Look at this," said Snubby, and the others crowded round to see. Snubby had got the book open at the very last page. He pointed to the inside of the back cover. "There's a kind of pocket there," he said. "And there's something in it—a map, I should think. Let's sit down somewhere and find out."

They went into a field and sat down. The dogs ran off to the rabbit-holes, delighted. Miranda went with them—not to look for rabbits, but to jeer at the two digging dogs!

Snubby drew out a paper from the old pocket inside the back cover of the book. "It's parchment," he said. "Gosh, I hope it doesn't fall to pieces in my hand!"

"Give it to me," said Diana. "I'm more careful than you are."

With deft, gentle fingers she unfolded the parchment, and spread it on her lap.

It had been folded in four, and the folds were already cracking.

"It's a map!" said Diana, thrilled. "Look—a map of Ring O' Bells Hall! Oh, if only it would show the secret passage!"

They all pored over it in excitement. The map was not so discoloured and faded as the pages of the book, and the children could easily make out the name at the bottom. "Dourley. Ring O' Bells Hall."

"It's genuine!" said Roger. "Now we really *may* find out something!"

Dourley: Ring o' Bells Hall

CHAPTER TWENTY-ONE

A LITTLE HUNTING AROUND

THEY DID FIND out something. They found out quite a lot.
It might be difficult to decipher the old printing on the
pages of the book—but it was much easier to read a plan
or map.

It seemed to be a plan of Ring O' Bells Hall, showing all
the ground floor. The two towers were indicated, one as
a square, one as a circle at each end of the Hall. Bells
were drawn in the square showing that that was the Bell
Tower.

" Where's the little panelled room where the secret pass-age begins?" said Roger.

" Here," said Diana, and pointed to it. " That must be it—it's off the hall, and near the kitchen and it's small."

" Is the secret passage shown?" asked Snubby, screwing his head over the map.

" No," said Diana, in disappointment.

" There's a letter P. in the room," said Roger, pointing. " Why? P for passage, of course. It *is* a P, isn't it?"

They all agreed that it was. But the P only told them what they already knew—that there was a passage leading off the little panelled room!

" Well—it's a thrilling old map, and beautifully drawn —but it doesn't tell us what we want to know," said Roger, in disappointment. " I suppose there isn't anything else in the old pocket inside the back cover, Di?"

Diana looked, inserting her fingers gently. She gave a little exclamation. " Yes—I believe there is! "

Very slowly and carefully she drew out another piece of parchment, much smaller than the other. It was folded in half. With fingers that suddenly shook, she opened it. Everyone bent over it at once.

At first they couldn't make it out. It seemed to be merely the plan of some bit of countryside. Then Snubby's rather dirty finger poked down at the paper.

" P! " he said. " P again. P for passage. Look, it be-gins here, by this house, or whatever it is."

" I should think it's meant to be Ring O' Bells Hall," said Diana. " It's roughly the shape—you know how it sticks out at the back, so to speak. Well, all right—we'll say that P is for Passage—the secret passage. How does that help us?"

" Can't you *see*?" said Snubby impatiently and he jabbed at the map again. " There's a faded red line lead-ing from that P—look, there it goes—right from Ring O'

Bells Hall, over the stream, through the wood—and ends at this other P here! "

" Gosh—you're right, Snubby! " said Roger. " It *is* the *passage*—must be! But it doesn't go over the stream, of course—it goes under—and under the wood—and it seems to end at some little building, if that's what this square indicates."

" What building would that be? " said Diana, thinking. " Could it be—Ring O' Bells Cottage? "

" It could be—and is! " cried Roger. " Of course, of course. Don't you remember what Old Grandad kept saying, when we asked·him where the secret passage went to. ' Ask Mother Barlow, ask Mother Barlow! ' It went to her cottage, of course, that's why we had to ask her—though she's been dead for ages. He'd forgotten that."

" And Naomi Barlow lives there now," said Diana. " I wonder if *she* knows anything about it, But I say— where in the world does the secret passage end in her cottage? Don't you remember the solid stone floor in each of the rooms? There didn't seem anywhere for a passage to open."

" There wasn't," said Snubby. " I'd stake anything that no passage is under the floors of Ring o' Bells Cottage."

" Yet this old map certainly shows the passage ending there," said Roger, puzzled. " Perhaps it ends somewhere nearby—in the wood, under a trapdoor, or something like that."

" Yes—that might be so," said Barney. " Anyway we know the way the passage takes now—it runs from the panelled room we know, avoids the house, goes straight under the garden, runs to this stream, goes under it—must be pretty deep there, I should think, or the water would seep through—then under the wood, and up to the cottage, ending somewhere about there."

" Gosh—it's wonderful! " said Snubby, too thrilled for words. " What do we do next? "

"I'll tell you what we do next," said Diana, a marvellous idea suddenly filling her mind. "We go to Ring O' Bells Cottage, and ask Naomi Barlow if she'd be kind enough to let Barney sleep in her little store-room, with Miranda—because we can't find a place for him in the village!"

"And he can snoop round, and ask her questions and see if he can find the passage!" said Snubby. "What a brainwave!"

"She loved Miranda—she would say yes, I'm sure," said Diana. "Let's go and ask her immediately after lunch."

Feeling very thrilled indeed, they all went home to enjoy a good lunch. Barney had his out in the garden with Miranda, who spent a most enjoyable half-hour peeling the skin off a tomato and eating it.

After lunch they set off for Ring O' Bells Cottage. They were almost there when they saw Naomi Barlow hurrying along, looking like old Red Riding Hood again, because she had on the red cloak! She greeted them kindly.

"I hope you weren't going to see me, children. I am going down to clean out the church, and shan't be back till six."

"We *were* going to see you," said Diana, disappointed. "We were going to tell you that we simply can't find *any*-where in the village for poor Barney and his monkey to sleep in at night—and Miss Hannah won't have him because she's afraid of monkeys. So we wondered, we just wondered if——"

"I'd let him sleep in my little old cottage!" finished Naomi, and she smiled. "Of course he can—he can have the room where *I* used to sleep for years when I was a child. You remember the store-room I showed you? He can sleep there—and I shall have a pet monkey to fuss over again."

"Thank you, Mam, very much indeed," said Barney gratefully.

"You go up to the cottage now, and set the store-room to rights," said Naomi. "Tidy it up, and put down the old mattress you'll see in one corner. That'll save me doing it when I come back tired."

"You *are* kind," said Diana. "We'll love to do that— and is there any job you'd like us to do for *you*—clean the windows, or anything?"

"Oh, no—the only other thing you can do is to help yourselves to my cinnamon biscuits!" said old Naomi with a laugh. "They're in that big tin on the mantelpiece. Now I must hurry. You go along to my cottage—you'll find the door isn't locked."

She hurried off, looking more like an old Red Riding Hood than ever. The children looked at each other in delight. Could anything be better! A bed and shelter for Barney and Miranda in the very place where the other end of the secret passage began!

"We're in luck's way," said Diana, as they turned down the little path to Naomi's cottage.

"Yes—we can have a good look at the floors in each room to make sure there's no passage below," said Roger. "I wish we could do something in return for the old woman's kindness."

"I shall pick some bluebells and put them about the cottage," said Diana, and she went to pick a big bunch. The boys went on with the dogs, Miranda on Snubby's shoulder for a change.

They came to the cottage. The door was not locked, and they opened it and went in. "Let's have a good look round first," said Roger. They were examining the kitchen floor when Diana came in with her bluebells.

"Found anything?" she asked, putting the flowers into a jug, and looking round for some water. She found some n a pail. There were no taps, of course, because Naomi had to draw her water from the well outside.

"Look at this floor," said Roger. He was on his knees, examining it closely. "I could bet anything that these stone flags haven't been disturbed for hundreds of years! You can't shift a single one. They're set so close together too. If there *is* a passage underneath, it can't be got at by us, that's certain."

The floors were the same in every room, solid and firm, though uneven. The stones were hollowed where much treading had been done. "Shows how old they are," said Roger, marvelling.

They went into the store-room and tidied it for Barney. "It smells nice," he said, sniffing at the pickle jars and jam. "I shall like sleeping here. I shall dream of dinner with pickles, and tea with jam!"

They found the old mattress and put it on the floor. There really wasn't much room for anything else then. It was just a cupboard of a room, but Barney was not at all particular.

"Well, that's done," said Diana. "Now what about having a good look round the garden and in the wood nearby, just to see if we *can* find anything else—an old stone trapdoor, or something—hidden under grass, perhaps."

They went out into the sunshine. First they searched the little garden, but there was obviously nothing there. Then they went out of the gate, separated, and examined every inch of the ground all round the garden. But there was nothing to be found there either.

"It's maddening," said Diana. "The entrance *must* be somewhere. Barney, you must get into conversation with Naomi Barlow to-night, and see if *she* knows anything. It's so long since the passage was used, apparently, that people seem to have forgotten all about it. But she may have learnt something from Mother Barlow."

"Right. I'll do my best," said Barney. "Now what about one of those cinnamon biscuits?"

"Oh, yes," said Snubby and lifted down the tin. They each took one and put the tin back, though Loony and Loopy clamoured for one too.

"Certainly not," said Snubby firmly. "You were not included in the invitation to help yourselves to biscuits. Anyway, you've had a wonderful afternoon, scrabbling round the wood."

"Let's go back to tea now," said Diana. "I'm hungry."

So back they went to one of Miss Hannah's good teas. How they hoped that Barney would be able to find out something from old Naomi Barlow!

CHAPTER TWENTY-TWO

BARNEY HAS AN IDEA

THE FOUR MET the next morning in the garden at Miss Hannah's. Snubby had Barney's breakfast-tray all ready, and he carried it out, with Roger and Diana running in front to greet Barney and Miranda.

"Did you find out anything?" asked Diana eagerly. "Did Naomi tell you where the passage began?"

"No, she wouldn't," said Barney. "At first she said she knew nothing about it at all—the passage was known only to a very few at any time, and those were the Dourleys themselves. Then she said it wasn't in existence now as far as she knew."

"Blow!" said Roger. "Not at all helpful. Didn't she *really* know anything?"

"Well, it was queer," said Barney slowly, "when I pressed her a bit about it, because I couldn't help feeling that she knew more than she said, she got all upset, and said something rather peculiar."

"What?" asked everyone at once.

"She said, 'I'd forgotten the drowning for years, and now you've made me think of it. I shall have my nightmares again. I tell you that passage has never been used since the drowning. It's gone, it's gone!'"

The children listened to this in astonished silence. What could it all mean?

"What drowning?" wondered Diana. "And why hasn't the passage been used since the *drowning*? Whatever has it got to do with somebody being drowned? You can't drown in a passage."

"There's just one explanation," said Barney and he

lowered his voice. " It may be wrong, but it's the only one I can think of. Where do you drown? In water. And where is there any water near Naomi's Cottage? Only in the well."

There was a pause. " I still don't see any explanation," said Roger. " What do you mean?"

" I mean this," said Barney, " and it may sound far-fetched, but I think it's worth going into. Suppose that secret passage has its outlet in old Naomi's *well*? And somebody, who was being chased, used that passage and instead of being able to get out of the well, fell down and was drowned? If it had happened when Naomi was very young, and she heard of it, she would never forget it. It would give her nightmares. Maybe even the story of it, if told to her as a child, would be enough to make her dream."

" I think you're right," said Roger. " It all fits together. But good gracious—how could a secret passage open into a well?"

" I don't know," said Barney. " That's for us to find out. If there *is* an opening down that well—and we all know how very deep it is— there must be some way of getting up or down it—some footholds of some kind—iron staples let into the wall, perhaps. We could soon find out."

" This is very, very exciting," said Snubby, rubbing his hands together. " We'll have to be careful not to miss our footing, though—or there'd be a nasty splash! "

" Don't say things like that," said Diana with a shiver.

An impatient voice suddenly called from the house. " Children! Whatever are you doing? Are you *never* coming to breakfast?"

" Good gracious—we forgot all about it," said Roger in surprise. " Fancy *you* forgetting too, Snubby. Unbelievable! "

" We'll be out as soon as we can, Barney," said Diana, and the three of them tore in with the dogs at their heels.

They all had to go riding that morning, because they had arranged it the day before. Barney went too, wearing old jodhpurs belonging to Miss Hannah's nephew, who was now grown up and gone away. He was a perfect horseman, having been trained to the saddle from his babyhood. The children admired him as he rode. Good old Barney, he was a marvel!

As they rode, he told them about his night at Ring O' Bells Cottage. " I slept in that tiny room," he said, " and I dreamt of food all night long, the smells were so delicious. Snubby, you ought to try taking a few pickle jars and spice jars to your bedroom. You'd have wonderful dreams. You'd probably be eating all night long in them."

Everyone laughed. Snubby considered the idea seriously and thought it a very good one. He debated whether to subtract a few bottles and jars from Miss Hannah's larder and give the idea a trial.

Nobody noticed the scenery very much that morning because they were so excited at the idea of examining the well.

They talked and talked about it, and at lunch that day Diana could hardly eat anything, she felt so full of anticipation. However, neither Roger nor Snubby were in the least affected, so the lunch was not wasted.

That afternoon they all went up to Ring O' Bells Cottage with Barney. " Old Naomi is going off to finish cleaning the church," he said. " It would be a good chance for us to have a look at the well."

The cottage was empty when they arrived. Naomi had gone. The children made sure of this and then went straight to the well. They looked down.

It certainly *was* a very deep well. Roger dropped a stone down again and they listened for the splash, which seemed to be a very long time coming.

" There it is," said Barney at last. " Now, let's look for a way down."

The little ferns grew so thickly in the well walls that it was difficult to see even the bricks. Barney felt about, leaning over the well side. Diana held on to him, scared of his falling down.

" I've got something! " said Barney at last. " There's a kind of iron loop here. Wait—I'll pull out these ferns."

He pulled them out and then the others could see what he meant. A loop of iron was fixed to the wall. It seemed very firmly fastened in. Barney gave it a tug.

" Well—if this is a foothold to use when going down, there should be others in a row down the wall. I'm going over to see."

" Oh, Barney—don't," said Diana.

" I'll get a rope from the store-room and tie it round Barney's waist," said Roger, who also didn't like the idea of Barney going down the well. " We'll tie the rope to the well post, and hold on to it ourselves, letting Barney down bit by bit, as he finds something to hold on to."

They got the rope and Barney let them tie him. Secretly he considered this rather silly, for he was a first-rate acrobat and climber—but he could see that Diana was very scared.

He went over the side, treading on the iron loop he had found. He put his foot down cautiously and felt about among the ferns He found another loop!

" Got it! " he called back cheerfully to the others. " This must be the right way down. No wonder nobody knew of it, it's so well-hidden by the ferns."

Ferns did not grow very far down, however. Barney found it easier to feel the iron loops after a time. One or two of them fell away as he trod on them and gave him a little shock. The others heard them splashing into the water, and held very tightly to Barney's rope. Diana's heart beat fast. Oh, dear— this was very dangerous! Surely they ought not to do it? But they must find out, they must!

Barney went down a very long way. "Can you see the water yet?" yelled Roger, his voice sounding most peculiar down the well.

"Yes—just," called back Barney. "I say—I can't feel any more loops for my feet. Blow—don't say the rest of them have rotted and fallen away!"

He felt about again, shivering, for it was icy-cold in the dank, dark well. No—there were no footholds at all below where he was. He called up to Roger.

"Roger! I've not got a torch with me. Tie yours carefully on a bit of string and let it down. I want to see if the entrance to the passage is anywhere here, as there aren't any more footholds."

The torch came down, twisting round and round on its string. It only just reached Barney! He took it and switched it on. Ah—now he could see!

He sent up such a yell that the others nearly let go the rope. Miranda, who hadn't gone down the well with Barney, looked down into the darkness anxiously.

"What is it?" shouted Roger, his voice echoing all the way down.

"There's a hole here, right in the side of the well!" called Barney. "I bet it's the entrance to the secret passage! I say—what a marvellous idea to have a way of escape leading to a well. Nobody would ever dream of that! I'm going in!"

"No, no!" almost shrieked Snubby. "Wait. We want to come too!"

"Not Diana," came back Barney's voice.

"I don't want to come!" cried Diana. "Anyway someone must guide the rope and hold it as you each go down. I'll do that."

Barney stepped into the black hole, flashing his torch. He could see nothing but a tunnel underground. Gosh—this was exciting! They really had found the other end

of the secret passage now. Would it lead back to Ring O'
Bells Hall, as it showed on the map?

Roger came down next, feeling for the loops with his
feet, and holding on to others with his hands. Then
Snubby, who left a frenzied Loony behind. Diana had a
job to stop Loony and Loopy from leaping into the well.

Soon all three boys were standing in the narrow hole. It
was merely a round gap in the brickwork of the well. Did
the water ever reach as high as that? Probably not. The
spring from which the well water came must be very deep
under the earth indeed.

"You can see what old Naomi means by someone
drowning now, can't you?" said Barney. "Probably
someone came hurrying along this tunnel in the dark and
didn't realise he'd come to the end. He must have run
straight out of the hole and dropped down into the well."

"Horrible!" said Roger, shivering with excitement, cold
and horror. "Come on. Let's explore the tunnel. But
hadn't we better keep quiet, in case there's somebody else
about? There may be someone down the tunnel at the
other end!"

"Yes. Keep quiet then," whispered Barney. "Come
along. I'll use my torch, and you can follow."

So down the weird tunnel they went, following each
other in the darkness. What a strange adventure!

CHAPTER TWENTY-THREE

UNDERGROUND

FOR SOME WAY the tunnel ran straight and level. The roof
was low in places and the boys bumped their heads till
they got used to looking out for a sudden dip in the roof.
They trailed on, with only the light of Barney's torch. The
tunnel smelt dank and musty, and Roger hoped the air was
good enough. If it was bad they might faint and fall
down!

" Just as well we left Di behind to raise the alarm if we don't get back," he thought.

The tunnel took a sharp bend, and ran downwards instead of level. The boys went on steadily. They all wished they had warm coats on, for they felt very chilly indeed. Suddenly Barney stopped and pointed with his torch to something.

A tree-root had penetrated through the roof of the tunnel and hung down in front of them! It looked very queer.

" We're under the trees now," said Barney in a whisper.

" We shall soon leave the wood behind and come to the stream. I bet the tunnel takes a big dip under that, to get away from the damp river-bed! "

It did. It suddenly went down very steeply indeed, and became wet and muddy. The roof dripped water. Barney shone his torch on it. " Look," he said. " Someone reinforced the roof just there with great stones. They've made a kind of stone arch. A good thing too, or the roof would have crumbled very quickly."

They went on again, and then came to a full stop. " Blow! " said Barney, shining his torch in front of him. " The roof *has* fallen in here—look! "

So it had. A great mass of rubble lay in front of them, and there was a broken hole in the roof.

" It might not be very serious," said Roger. " Let's just scrabble a bit and see if we can get through."

It was difficult to " scrabble " with only their hands, but they soon found that Roger was right—the fall was only trivial. They could make a way through at one side, by piling the earth and stones in the middle of the fall.

They went on again. Then Barney spoke in a low whisper, almost in Roger's ear. " We must be getting somewhere near Ring O' Bells Hall now—better be very cautious."

The tunnel now began to slant upwards a little, and

curved to the right. Then another roof-fall stopped them. This time it was a bigger one. The three looked at it in silence.

Then, from behind the roof-fall came a noise—a spasmodic noise of quick, regular sounds, painful to hear—the noise that Barney had heard, distorted and muffled by distance and by the fact that it had come up the secret passage to the little panelled room. No wonder Barney hadn't recognised the noise.

It was very simple to recognise now that it was near—just the other side of the roof-fall. It was a man coughing painfully—cough, cough, cough—pause—cough, cough, cough—pause—cough, cough.

Then there was a dreadful groan, and the man on the other side of the roof-fall muttered something in a broken voice.

" He's terribly ill, I should think," whispered Barney. " He ought to have a doctor. What's he doing down here, do you suppose?"

" Kidnapped, probably," said Roger, also in a whisper. " As for a doctor—that's probably who we saw when we hid in the chest the other night—do you remember the man with a small bag? He was probably a doctor called in by the woman."

" But wouldn't a doctor be amazed to be taken to a patient hidden down here?" asked Snubby.

" He's probably a doctor who attends the gang or whatever it is that kidnaps people and hides them here," said Barney.

" Look," said Roger, straightening himself up. He had been bending down, peeping here and there. " Look—there's a little space in this mass of rubble—you can see right through it."

Barney bent down and put his eye to the space. He could make out part of the clothed body of a man, tossing and turning. He could not see his face.

"Shall I speak to him and ask him who he is?" whispered Barney. The others nodded. They felt sure the man was a captive, a prisoner, probably kidnapped and held for some reason or other.

Barney spoke through the hole. "Hallo, there! Who are you?"

The man beyond stopped moving at once. He now appeared to be sitting up.

"Who spoke?" he whispered, in a croaking, frightened voice. "Who is it?"

"Never mind," said Barney. "Tell us who you are. What are you doing here?"

"I've been kidnapped," groaned the man. "I'm a detective, and I've been spying on a gang who are known to be kidnappers. They've got *me* now—and now they want to get out of me all I know—then they'll bump me off. So I'm not telling."

He fell back and began to cough again, a dreadful tearing cough. The boys knew he must be very ill. They didn't doubt his word at all.

"Shall we try and get through to you, sir, and—get you out this way?" asked Barney, realising as he said it that it would be quite impossible to get such an ill man along the tunnel and up the sides of the well.

"No. No, I can't even stand," said the man, beginning to cough again. "Listen—they'll kill me if they think I've been talking to anyone, so be careful. Listen to what I say."

"We're listening," said Barney.

"Three of the gang are coming here to-night to try and get out of me, for the last time, all that I know about them and others," said the man hoarsely. "They'll be here at eleven. Can you hide till they come, and then warn the police? Tell them its Detective-Inspector Rawlings who's sending the message."

"Right—and then if the three are down here in the

secret passage, they'll be nicely rounded up," said Barney, seeing it all. " A very good plan, sir."

" Does the caretaker-woman feed you?" asked Roger, through the hole. " Is she in it too?"

" Everyone's in it! " said the man. " I knew they were using this place for their headquarters, but I'd no idea there was any secret passage here. There's many a poor fellow's been put down here! "

He coughed so badly that he couldn't stop. Barney and Roger and Snubby felt distressed. " If only we could get to him to help him—but this wretched roof-fall is too big to shift without tools," said Barney. He called through the hole in a pause between the coughs.

" We're going now, sir, but we'll do exactly as you say. Good-bye! "

They made their way carefully back, clambering over the side of the other roof-fall when they came to it. They were at last beside the well, and heard Diana calling in a despairing voice.

" Barney! Roger! Snubby! Oh, do come back! Roger, what's happened?"

" Poor old Diana! " said Roger, suddenly realising what a long time they had been, and how scared Diana must be. He yelled up.

" Hallo, Di! We're back all safe and sound, with news for you! "

" Thank goodness! " came Diana's voice, sounding very tearful.

Barney felt for the rope end hanging down the well and tied it round his waist in case he fell. " I'm coming up, Diana! " he called.

He was soon up, going hand over hand up the well wall, climbing like a cat. Miranda leapt chattering on to his shoulder as soon as he appeared, fondling and caressing him lovingly. Loony and Loopy threw themselves on him barking.

534

"I feel like doing that myself, Barney," said Diana, with tears of relief in her eyes. "You *have* been gone a long time."

"We'll get Roger and Snubby up and then tell you our news," said Barney, and he turned to look down the well. Snubby was already coming up. Roger soon followed. All three shivered with the cold, and were glad to feel the hot May sun on their shoulders.

They told the astonished Diana all that had happened. She could hardly believe her ears.

"*Well*! To think that kidnappers use the old Ring O' Bells Hall like that! I suppose that's why that woman put in for the job and got it—it would be easy for any gang to get in and out, and use the secret passage for hiding things and people in, if they had someone actually here all the time, watching over their prisoners, ready to let the gang in and out of the place!" Diana paused for breath.

"Yes—no one would ever guess that an old show-place like that in a country village would be such a cunning headquarters," said Roger. "One of the gang must, of course, have heard about that secret passage and seen its possibilities. And to think that no one could go down there because the woman was always on guard!"

"There's one thing I don't understand," said Barney. "We went down that passage, but we came to a brick wall, bricking it up. There was no one there then, yet I heard that man coughing the night before. Where was he?"

They all thought hard. "All I can say is that some of the bricks in the wall must be easily removable," said Roger, at last. "After all, we didn't examine the wall very closely. It must be possible to take out enough bricks to get through. I'm sure we shall find that's right. It's all very clever and very well planned."

"It's a bad look-out for that detective to-night," said Snubby. "He won't tell what he knows, that's certain—so they'll either bump him off, or leave him there to die.

He's ill enough to pop off at any time, I should think."

"So should I be, down in that cold, dank, damp, chilly place, shut up day and night with no air to breathe," said Barney. He sat on the wall that ran round the old well, and thought for a minute or two.

"I'm seeing a lot of things now," he said. "You know when I got a lift in that van which dropped me at Lillinghame, but which I saw later on, outside Ring O' Bells Hall, late at night? Well, there was something in that van which terrified Miranda when she got into it. All *I* could see was a sort of white thing that seemed to run about on the floor of the van—but it was probably the detective's hand out of its covers! I expect he was lying there under sacks and things, probably doped with something."

"Yes—it looks as if the prisoner was brought here that night," said Snubby. "Poor wretch! What a long time to spend down there."

"We must make our plans now," said Barney. "And —we must make them very, very carefully."

CHAPTER TWENTY-FOUR

THAT NIGHT

THEY DID MAKE their plans carefully. They talked everything over bit by bit, and discussed exactly what would be best to do.

"No good saying a word to Miss Pepper," said Roger. "She would be scared, go to the police, and they'd do exactly what the detective doesn't want—go in immediately to rescue him, and then that woman would warn the gang, they wouldn't come to-night, and not one of them would be captured."

"For that same reason I think it would be best to stick to what the man said, and not warn the police till the gang are actually down the passage," said Barney. "The police might act too soon."

"All the same, I think the poor ill man ought to be taken up immediately," said tender-hearted Diana. "He might die."

"I don't think another few hours would hurt him—and he'd be pretty wild if he thought we'd not done what he told us to," said Roger. "No—I think we must do exactly what he said—wait till the gang is there, and then rush for the police station."

"Where are we going to watch for the gang to come?" asked Snubby. "In Ring O' Bells Hall?"

"Yes," said Barney. "We might be spotted, anywhere outside. You never know. There are plenty of good hiding-places inside. Those chests, for instance."

"I don't like those," said Snubby. "I feel sort of cooped up there."

"Right. We'll find somewhere else then," said Barney.

" But listen—we don't take Loony. If he growls he'll certainly give us away again."

Loony heard his name and ran up at once, wagging his tail violently. Snubby patted the silky black head. " All right," he said reluctantly. " We won't take him. But he'll howl like anything."

" Well, he'll have to," said Barney. " This is too serious a matter to spoil for the sake of taking Loony."

" What about Miranda?" asked Diana. " She gibbered like anything the other night."

" She'll be all right to-night," said Barney. " I'll put her collar on, and a lead, so that she has to stay on my shoulder. I will see she doesn't utter a sound."

" All right. We hide, and we wait, and we watch to make sure the gang are safely down the secret passage," said Roger. " Then we rush and get the police in—is that right? Suppose they don't believe us?"

" They will if we say the detective's name," said Barney. " Detective-Inspector Rawlings- they'll know about him and will have been informed that he has disappeared. Anyway, I'll jolly well *make* them believe us."

" Those bells knew what they were doing all right, when they rang themselves the other night," said Snubby suddenly. " Talk about enemies! I'm not awfully looking forward to waiting in Ring O' Bells Hall to-night, I don't mind telling you I'm scared of those bells."

" Well, don't come then," said Barney. " Stay with Diana. I'm not letting her come."

Diana was relieved. She had thought she really *ought* to come, but she didn't want to in the least. If Barney said she wasn't to, well, that was that. She would stay at home with Loony- and Snubby too, perhaps.

No- Snubby was going, whether he was scared of the bells or not. " You can't keep *me* out of it," he said, putting on a most courageous voice. " I may not want to come very much, but I'm jolly well coming, all the same!"

"Good for you," said Barney. "Where's the police station? We'd better know all these details—the shortest way to get to it from Ring O' Bells Hall, and all that. Pity we can't telephone them—but they'd probably think it was a spoof call. Anyway I don't remember seeing telephone wires anywhere near the Hall."

"What time shall we be there?" said Roger. "The detective said the gang would arrive at eleven. We'd better be there at ten, then, and watch out for them. We shall have plenty of time to arrange our hiding-places."

"Yes—ten o'clock," agreed Barney. "Gosh—this is all frightfully exciting, isn't it? I never thought anything like this would happen when I popped down here to see you for a few days."

"Excitement must be very good for 'flu," said Diana. "I feel perfectly all right now. I bet Snubby still thinks of his poor wobbly legs though!"

"I do not!" said Snubby indignantly. "Except that I keep feeling awful pangs of hunger all day long, I'm just exactly the same as usual."

"I thought you *usually* felt pangs of hunger," began Diana, and then was interrupted by Roger, who had just looked at his watch.

"Wheeee-ew! I say! It's half-past five! Would you believe it? We've missed tea at Miss Hannah's now. It will be all cleared away when we get there. What shall we do?"

"No wonder Snubby began talking about pangs of hunger," said Barney. "I'm feeling some myself."

"Let's go down to that village shop and see if they'll give us something," said Diana. "We could at least get ice-creams. I do hope Miss Hannah won't be too wild with us."

They found the shop open and were able to buy buns, ice-creams, chocolate and orangeade, so they didn't do too badly. The dogs had an ice-cream each too, for being so good and patient all the afternoon. Miranda had half of one, because Barney said they sometimes gave her a tummy-ache and he didn't want her whining that evening!

They went back to Miss Hannah's. Barney went too. He planned to wait in the shed till the time came for him to join the others and go to Ring O' Bells Hall. He would have supper with them first.

"It's such a wonderful evening perhaps we could have a sort of picnic supper out in the garden," suggested Diana. "I believe it's all cold to-night."

It was—so they were allowed to take their plates into the garden and sit on the grass, with Loony and Loopy and Miranda greedily watching every mouthful. Miranda was too clever at snatching, and Barney had to speak to her very severely. She hid her face in his neck and made little mournful noises. Diana wanted to fuss over and pet her, but Barney wouldn't let her.

"No, Diana. She's getting spoilt with all the fuss everyone makes of her. A scolding will do her good. Do you know, at Naomi's last night she actually went to a bottle of cherries, took the lid off—*unscrewed* it, mind you—and began to take out cherries with her paw. And Naomi let her! No wonder she's getting spoilt."

"She's such a darling, though. I do so love her," said Diana. Loony was immediately jealous and came and put his head on her knee, looking up at her mournfully out of melting brown eyes.

"Go on with you!" said Diana, tapping his nose with her spoon. "It's cupboard love! You want a bit of my blancmange."

Loony looked at her, got up and trotted indoors. He came out with Miss Hannah's lovely green bath-towel, treading on it as he ran, and tripping himself up. He put it down at Diana's feet, as if to say, "You're not very kind to me—but look what I do for you!"

"You're very naughty," said Diana. "Now I've got to
540

get up and put it back again. No, Loopy, no—you are *not* to feel you've to play a silly trick too. If you dare to go in and bring out the hall mats I'll SMACK you! "

They almost forgot what was going to happen that evening as they had their picnic supper and played about with the dogs and Miranda.

Miss Hannah and Miss Pepper watched them through the window. They were having their own supper in peace. " How nice to be young and carefree like that! " said Miss Hannah. " No worries, no serious cares—just able to pop into bed and shut their eyes and sleep till morning without a single worrying thought."

She would have been most amazed if she had known the worries and cares the children had that night. They were certainly not going to be able to go to sleep with no worries till the morning. Snubby, in fact, felt that his life was full of fears and worries as the evening drew on!

" Snubby, you're looking tired," said Miss Pepper, seeing a worried frown on his face. " You'd better pop off to bed straight away."

" Right," said Snubby, thinking that he might as well get two hours or so of sleep before he had to face the darkness and silence of Ring O' Bells Hall. He went up in such a docile manner that Miss Pepper was most surprised, and a little alarmed. Surely Snubby was not sickening for something else?

Nobody was late that night. Barney said good night and went out of the gate, presumably to go to Naomi's. He slipped back through the hedge at the bottom of the garden, and made his way to the shed with Miranda. He settled himself quietly on some sacks to await the striking of the church clock. They were all to set off at ten.

Snubby fell asleep, but neither Diana nor Roger did. They both felt extremely wide awake. Diana half wished she was going, then changed her mind as she thought of seeing the " gang," whoever they might be.

" It's almost ten," whispered Roger at last. " I'll wake Snubby. I do hope Loony will be all right without us."

Snubby sprang up. He whispered good-bye to a most surprised Loony, thrust him on to Diana's knee and then while she was making a fuss of him, fled downstairs with the others. They were out in the moonlit garden just as Barney walked out of the shed, and the clock struck ten.

" Good work," said Barney in a low voice. " Got your torches? Come on then. Don't put them on though—we can easily see in the moonlight."

They walked down to Ring O' Bells Hall, and waited while Barney shinned up the ivy and got into the room with the four-poster bed he once slept in. He ran down into the hall and opened the front door to them. They all crept in and shut the door again.

" Let's go into that room over there, and wait," said Barney. " I've just remembered, there's a big cupboard there. We could leave the door of the room open, and watch through the crack for the gang to come in—and then pop into the cupboard till they've gone down the secret passage. Then we'll hare up to the police station."

They went to the room and pushed the door open. Then they got the most terrible shock! There, seated round a candle on a table in the room, were three men and a woman!

The gang must have come early! Run, Barney, run, Roger and Snubby. Run for your very lives!

CHAPTER TWENTY-FIVE

HEADLONG INTO TROUBLE

BARNEY AND ROGER were right in the room before they
realised that there was anyone there. Snubby had suddenly
paused, seeing a light, and had tried to pull back the
others, but they were right in the room by then, and were
seen.

The men leapt to their feet at once, staring in astonishment and anger. Roger was petrified, but Barney saw at a
glance the danger they were in. He turned to run at once.

"Stop!" shouted one of the men. "STOP, I say. Who
are you? COME HERE!"

In real fear the boys fled out of the room. What a blow!
All their wonderful plans were shattered! They would be
lucky if they escaped themselves now.

"Separate- -hide—quickly!" panted Barney. He darted
off towards the kitchen. Snubby fled into a nearby room.
Roger made for the little panelled room where the entrance
of the secret passage was. The chest! He would hide there.

He felt about in the darkness when he got into the room.
Ah—here was the chest! He lifted up the lid and got in.
The lid fell with such a noise that he trembled. Surely the
men would have heard it.

Snubby didn't at first recognise the room he was in—
then as he looked round, panic-stricken, in the moonlight
that flooded through a window, he saw that he was in the
room that contained the secret chamber up the chimney.

He tore to the chimney-place at once, just as he heard
the men outside the room. He pushed himself into the
wide chimney, and felt frantically for the steps at the side.
Thank goodness, it *was* the right chimney! He climbed

up, and squeezed himself into the dirty, musty, secret cavity.

Only just in time! The three men burst into the room, holding brilliant torches that drowned the silver moonlight. "He came in here!" cried one. "I saw him."

"Then he's here still," said another man grimly. "There's only one door—the one he came in by. We'll find him all right!"

Snubby trembled so much that he really wondered if his legs would hold him upright. They didn't! They gave way beneath him and he slid into a sitting position! The men heard the noise he made, sliding down to sit. "Listen —he's quite near!" said one, and opened the door of a cupboard. It was empty, of course.

"*I* thought the noise came from somewhere over here," said another man, walking to the fire-place. He poked his head up the enormous chimney and flashed his torch there. Snubby almost groaned. He expected to feel his foot pulled roughly, and to be hauled out.

But the secret chamber was meant to hide people properly, and it did. Not a sign could be seen of the hidden boy in the light of the torch. Only if the man had known of the chamber could he have seen Snubby, by climbing up one of the steps himself. But he didn't know it.

The woman did—but she had gone after Roger! The men hunted all over the room, opened chests and cupboards, looked behind curtains—and finally gave up the search. "He couldn't have come in here," they said.

"Lizzie!" called one of them. "Where are you? Have you found those kids?"

"I've found one of them!" she called back. "He's in this chest!"

She had heard the banging of the lid and had rushed into the little panelled room. She could see at once that the only hiding-place was in one of the chests. She lifted the lid of the small one. It was empty.

Poor Roger was crouching down in the other, hardly daring to breathe. He heard the lid of his chest lifted, and a torch was flashed in quickly. Then the lid was slammed down immediately—and he heard a key turn in the lock!

Roger clenched his fists. Now he was out of things—locked up well and truly. It was an idiotic thing to do, to let that lid bang down! He could have kicked himself.

The men came into the room and the woman tapped the chest with her torch. " Here's one anyway," she said. " Safe and sound for the moment. What about the other?"

Roger heaved a sigh of relief. So they thought there were only two of them—they couldn't have seen Snubby! Where in the world had he gone? If only he could nip out and go to the police, things would still be all right. But would Snubby be brave enough to do that?

The three men and the woman began a search for Barney. " Who *are* these kids?" demanded one of the men. " And what are they doing here at night?"

" They're probably a couple of young hooligans who got in somehow and thought it would be a lark to steal a few things," said the woman.

" Well—it's just too bad for them, but I'm afraid we shall have to take them off with us to-night and dump them somewhere where they won't be able to split on us for a long, long time," said one of the men grimly.

" We've *got* to find the other fellow," said another man. " Listen—what's that?"

It was Miranda! She was hiding with Barney, not far from the foot of the square tower. He had got behind a great heavy curtain, and was crouching there, his heart beating far too loudly for his liking. Miranda felt that he was scared, and she was scared too.

She didn't like being on a lead when she was frightened. She leapt a little way up the curtain, felt the pull of the lead and fell back again. Barney didn't dare even to whisper to her. She began to gibber a little.

He decided to undo the lead. She might feel happier then. So he slipped the catch and freed her. She was off and away at once. She leapt to the top of a cupboard and ground her teeth in a queer way she had when she was both frightened and angry. This was the noise that the men had suddenly heard.

One man flashed his torch in Miranda's direction, and was amazed to see a little monkey there. " A monkey!" he said. " The owner must be in this room then. Quick, search everywhere! "

Barney felt cornered. Sooner or later they would come to his curtain. He had no illusions about these men. They were tough and cruel. It would go hardly with any of the boys if they were captured.

He decided to worm his way behind the curtain to where the foot of the tower was. If he could sprint up the steps to the platform, he might find a corner to hide in—some niche the men wouldn't see. It was a forlorn hope but the best he could think of.

The men were on the opposite side of the room, examining every cupboard. Miranda chattered at them angrily, keeping well out of their reach.

Barney came to the end of the curtain. He made a dash for the tower. He rushed safely through the open doorway and sprinted up the stone staircase, round and round and round. Miranda heard him and with a bound she was after him, scuttling up on all fours.

Barney groaned when he saw her. No matter where he hid up on that little shadowy platform, Miranda would chatter and give him away!

Then a brilliant thought shot into his head—that little room above the bells! He could get up there, and be perfectly safe. He had only to threaten to push down anyone who came up after him! Nobody could ever get him out of there.

He began to climb up the straight wall of the tower, finding the hand and footholds in the stone quite easily, for he had used them once before. Miranda sat chattering angrily on his shoulder. She couldn't understand any of these peculiar happenings at all.

The men raced up the spiral staircase too, with the woman behind. " You'll get him—there's only a platform at the top—hardly anywhere to hide! " she panted.

But when the first man reached the platform and flashed his torch round, there was no one to see! He shone his torch into one or two shadowy corners—nobody there!

He heard a noise above his head and flashed his torch there in surprise. He was just in time to see Barney's legs disappearing, as the boy clambered through the hole in the roof, from which the bells hung.

" Look there! " he said startled. " The fellow has actually shinned up this steep wall and climbed through the roof. Can he escape from there?"

" No—unless he squeezes out of the window and flings himself to the ground—where he would certainly be killed," said the woman. " We don't need to worry about *him* now! We can shut and lock the big door at the front of the tower, and he'll be as much a prisoner as the other fellow in the chest. Nicely out of our way! "

One man looked doubtfully up at the hole in the ceiling. " There must be footholds up the wall," he said. " I've a good mind to try and shin up myself, and knock the fellow on the head to make sure he doesn't worry us for some time."

Barney heard all this, of course. He kept well away from the hole, in case one of the men had a revolver. He didn't trust these fellows—he had upset their carefully laid plans, and goodness knew what they would do to him if they had the chance.

He called boldly down. " I can hear you—and I tell you

this—if any of you climb up here, I'll knock him down to the stone platform! I've got the advantage of any of you up here!"

There was a silence. " He's right," said one of the men in a low voice. " He could reach out and strike anyone down, once they got up to the top. Well, we'll do as you say, Lizzie—lock the tower door at the foot, and leave him here to stew!"

" Well, that's the two of them then—and the monkey," said another man. " Now let's get about our business. We'd better go down and see our friend. Lizzie says he's pretty bad to-night, so maybe he'll be willing to listen to us."

Barney heard them go down the spiral staircase. He heard the heavy door at the bottom slam, and he heard the grating sound of the big key being turned in the lock. He sat up in the little room above the bells, gritting his teeth together. All their plans were spoilt! They were prisoners instead of setting someone else free!

" Shall we go down or not, Miranda?" he said. " Better go down, perhaps, and see if they *really* have locked the door."

He put his head down to look out of the hole. The bells gleaming in the light of his torch, hung just below him, still and silent. Barney flashed his torch down beside them, trying to see the platform below.

Miranda suddenly gibbered in fright, and clutched at his arm. With all her small monkey strength she tried to pull him back. Barney was surprised. Whatever was the matter?

CHAPTER TWENTY-SIX

THE WARNING OF THE BELLS

" WHY ARE YOU suddenly so frightened, Miranda?" asked Barney in surprise. " I'm not going to fall down."

But still the little monkey gibbered and pulled at him. Barney sat back and looked at her. " Now what's all this about?" he said. " Why be in such a state because I put my torch out of the hole?"

He put his torch out again, and by accident it touched one of the bells, which gave out a very small sound—ding!

Miranda went quite mad. She leapt to the window sill as if she were going to go out. Then she leapt back to Barney, squealing pitifully and pulled at him. What *could* be the matter?

" Are you afraid of the bells, Miranda?" asked Barney at last. " Did they scare you when they rang all by themselves that time? Look—I'll touch them—they won't harm me! "

He stretched out his hand and tapped one of the bells, which said, " DING " a little more loudly. Miranda scampered into a corner, put her arms across her face, and rocked herself to and fro, moaning as if she were human.

Barney was really nonplussed. He had never seen Miranda like this before. He flashed his torch on the scared, miserable little monkey and pondered. Why? Why? Why?

And then he suddenly knew! Of course! Why ever hadn't he thought of it before?

" Miranda, come here," he said softly. " I know why you are so frightened—you're frightened of the bells, aren't you? Miranda—*you* rang them before, didn't you—when we all thought they had rung themselves? You were up here, exploring—you didn't know what the bells were, or what noise they made—and in your usual inquisitive way you leapt on to them—and set them swinging. And they rang! They jingled and jangled and wouldn't stop!" Miranda still went on moaning to herself. Barney was sad for the little monkey. He went on talking in his quiet, soothing voice.

"You leapt from one to the other in panic, didn't you, Miranda—and you made them ring madly and wildly till you were almost frightened out of your skin. Now you can't bear me even to touch them! Poor little monkey. Come here, Miranda."

Miranda came, making funny little noises. She cuddled into Barney's arms, comforted by his soft voice, though she couldn't follow what he said.

"There's nothing to be frightened of, Miranda," said Barney. "They're only bells. Well, well, well—so they didn't ring themselves the other night—*you* rang them, though you didn't guess what a noise they would make."

He sat there with Miranda in his arms, thinking back to the night when the bells had rung and frightened them all so much. Then his thoughts slid back to this unfortunate night. They had had high hopes—and now here they were, captured and locked up! He was pretty certain that Roger, anyhow, was captured, and he couldn't imagine Snubby remaining uncaught for long.

Barney thought of the ill man down at the bottom of the secret passage. He thought of the three men and the woman—the "gang" as the detective had called them. Now they would be able to get out of their unfortunate prisoner all the information they wanted—they would probably leave him there to die—and get away in safety themselves. How long had they been using this place as their headquarters? How many plots had they hatched here, how many people had they imprisoned down in the secret passage beyond the brick wall?

Barney wished he knew what was the best thing to do. How could he warn anyone that something was amiss at Ring O' Bells Hall? Was it possible to squeeze out of the window and climb down the ivy, if it grew strongly there?

Then, as he sat there, just above the bells, an idea came to him. Why didn't he think of it before? It was the only thing to do!

He would ring the bells himself! Not as Miranda had rung them, jingle-jangling them in fright—but ring them fiercely and loudly and urgently without stopping! He would rouse the whole of the village! He would bring the police hurrying to the Hall. He would terrify everyone so much that SOMETHING would have to be done!

Then another thought struck him. The bells would warn the men too. They might come rushing up, and get away, if they had a car. Barney thought hard. They would now be down in the secret passage, far below the foundations of the house—beyond the brick wall, which must have a way through it somehow. They couldn't possibly hear the bells there!

" The bells will warn the whole village—but not the men," Barney decided exultantly. " It's an idea—a wonderful idea. Miranda, darling, I'm going to give you the fright of your life, I'm afraid—but it can't be helped. I'm going to ring the bells! "

Barney lay down flat on the floor of the little tower room. He leaned out of the hole, and stretched his arms down to the short ropes on which the bells were tightly hung. He caught hold of them.

He rang the bells. How he rang them! Surely never, never before had those bells rung so wildly, so madly, so insistently.

" Jingle, jangle-jangle, jing, jing, JING, jangle, JANG,

JANG, jingle, jing, JING, JANG, JING, JANG, JING, JANG. . . ."

The noise up in the little tower was terrific. Miranda gave a loud howl and bounded to the window. She was out of it in a trice. Barney didn't notice. His head was down through the hole, and he was pulling the short ropes for all he was worth, panting hard.

Roger, down in the chest, heard them, and was terrified. The bells! Ringing by themselves again! They must know that enemies were here, right in the very house. He crouched down in the locked chest, trembling, wondering if the men could hear them too.

Snubby heard them, half-standing, half-sitting in the secret cavity of the old fire-place. He was in a most uncomfortable position. When he heard the tremendous loud noise of the bells, breaking the silence so suddenly and urgently, he almost fell out of the secret chamber. He sank down till he was sitting flat again. He shook so much that even his teeth rattled in his head.

"The bells!" he thought to himself. "The bells again! How do they know? How do they guess that enemies are here?"

Neither he nor Roger imagined that it was Barney who was ringing them. They didn't even know that Barney was up in the tower.

Snubby was far too frightened to move out of his hiding-place. For all he knew the men might be waiting somewhere to pounce on him. He was quite, quite determined not to stir from the secret chamber. How well he knew now what fugitives had felt when they crammed themselves into this little secret hidey-hole. Now that he heard the bells ringing, he was all the more certain that nothing, nothing, nothing would make him leave that chimney-place!

The men and the woman down below in the secret passage heard almost nothing of the bells. The place where they were now, beyond the brick wall, was sound-proof to the jangle of the bells so high up in the tower. All they heard was a slightly tinny noise from somewhere which didn't make them suspect any danger at all.

But the sound of the bells went far and wide over the countryside. The jangling leapt out of the old tower and penetrated into cottage windows, and into dog kennels, and into the barns. This was no hurried, flurried spell of ringing such as the bells had given before—it was a summons, a warning, a signal of danger!

Dogs barked. Cows lowed. Cats fled to corners. Men threw the bed-clothes off and leapt out of bed. Women screamed. Miss Hannah and Miss Pepper awoke in a hurry.

Diana comforted the amazed Loony, while Loopy put himself in a cupboard.

Diana was frightened. Those bells again! What was happening down at the Hall? Were the boys all right?

The two policemen at the police station, dozing in their chairs, sprang up, astonished, at the sound of the bells. One reached at once for his helmet.

" Something's up! " he said. " Where's Joe? Tell him to phone through to Lillinghame, just in case we need their help. Something's up! Just listen to those bells! "

Down towards Ring O' Bells Hall went a crowd of scared, wondering villagers. Some of the men had pitch-forks, some had sticks. Why did they bring them? They didn't know! Something was up, at the Hall—and till they knew what it was they were taking no chances.

The police joined them on bicycles. " What's to do?" the villagers shouted to them. " Who's ringing the bells?"

But the police knew no more than anyone else!

They came to the Hall. It was in complete darkness. Not a light was to be seen in any room. But still the bells clashed out urgently.

" Someone must be in the tower, surely! " cried a man.

" The bells ring themselves," said an old man sombrely. " Always did! "

" Here's a car! " cried a woman, shining a torch on to a big car shoved right up against the hedge, not far from Ring O' Bells Hall.

" Ha! " said one of the policemen. " Here—where's Joe! Joe, you take charge of this car. Take out the key, to start with. Now then, where's Bill? Oh, there you are —we're going to get into Ring O' Bells Hall, if we have to break the door down! "

The police hammered at the great front door of the Hall. Barney couldn't hear the noise, up in the tower room, but Roger, hidden in the chest, heard it, and Snubby, trembling violently up the chimney, heard it too. He felt sick. Now what was up?

He heard a stentorian voice outside the front door.

" OPEN IN THE NAME OF THE LAW! "

But the front door, of course, did not open. It trembled under the hammering the policeman was giving it, but it remained firm. The policeman tried again.

" OPEN IN THE NAME OF THE LAW! "

" It's the police," thought Snubby, and was flooded with relief. " The police! They heard the bells and they've come! I'll open the door to them. Oh, WHAT a relief! "

CHAPTER TWENTY-SEVEN

PLENTY OF EXCITEMENT

SNUBBY forgot his fears. He scrambled down from the secret chamber, almost falling headlong into the great fireplace. He rushed across the room, out of the door and into the hall. Very little moonlight entered there, and it looked very dark. But Snubby was feeling extraordinarily brave now.

He ran to the front door, tripping over a mat or two. He turned the great handle and swung the door back.

The police had powerful torches, and they flashed them on to Snubby at once, not quite knowing what to expect. They gaped when they saw a sooty-faced boy of about twelve, grinning joyfully at them!

" Here—what's all this?" said the first policeman. " What are you doing here? And who's ringing those bells?"

" I don't know," said Snubby. " Gosh, I'm glad you came. Those bells are ringing to say that enemies are here. Look out, won't you! "

The villagers began to crowd in too. The policeman swung round. " Where's Joe? Joe, keep these people back. May be danger here for all we know."

The bells went on ringing madly. Barney was doing the thing properly! He had rests every now and again, but he made up his mind to go on ringing them till something happened.

The two policemen went to the foot of the square tower. They meant to find out who was ringing the bells. Snubby followed some way behind. He was quite certain they were ringing themselves, and he didn't particularly want to go near bells that behaved in such a strange manner.

The police unlocked the door at the foot of the tower. They went up the spiral staircase cautiously, torches in hand. They came out on to the platform. Barney saw the light of their torches immediately, and withdrew his hands from the bell-ropes. He looked down warily. Who was this—enemy or friend?

To his great relief, he saw the dark-blue uniform of the police. He almost fell down the hole with joy. The bells gradually stopped jangling, and the first policeman called up in a stern and commanding voice.

" You up there! What do you think you're doing, ringing bells in the dead of night? Who are you?"

" Wait a moment and I'll come down and tell you," called Barney. He slipped through the hole, held the guide-rope, found the first footholds and climbed down the tower wall like a cat. The police watched him in astonishment. He leapt down beside them.

" Another boy! " said the first policeman. " Now you just tell me what all this is about, young fellow! "

" It's serious," said Barney. " Very serious. Did you ever hear of someone called Detective-Inspector Rawlings?"

This unexpected question made both the policemen gape in surprise. " What do you know about *him*?" rapped out the first one.

" I'll tell you," said Barney, and tried to tell his extraordinary story as shortly as possible. It took the policemen some time to grasp what he was trying to tell them.

" Secret passages—Rawlings behind a brick wall down there—ill, perhaps dying—the gang here to-night—who *are* they, anyway? And where are they? Tell us, boy, quick! "

" I'm trying to tell you," said Barney impatiently. " But what you don't realise is that it's all very urgent. The men are down there *now* with Rawlings. You can catch them and rescue him, if you're quick! That's what he planned for you to do, with our help. But things went wrong, so I rang the bells to get somebody here."

At last it dawned on the policemen that things really were urgent. They went down the spiral staircase, almost falling over Snubby, who was half-way up listening to what Barney was saying, with very great interest. So it was old Barney who had done all that bell-ringing! Gosh!

"Hallo, Snubby—where's Roger?" called Barney, catching sight of Snubby.

"No idea," said Snubby.

"Who's Roger? Another of you?" asked the policeman, marvelling at coming across so many boys in the middle of the night.

"He's my cousin," said Snubby. "When we were chased, we all separated and hid. I don't know where Roger hid."

"I'll take you to the entrance of the secret passage," said Barney, and he guided the two policemen to the little panelled room. "The passage begins here," said Barney, "I'll just——"

But he was interrupted by a terrific noise in the chest nearby. Roger had heard Barney's voice and was clamouring to be let out! He knocked with his heels on the floor of the chest, hammered with his fists and yelled at the top of his voice. "Let me out! I'm here. Let me out!"

"Bless us all!" said the policeman, startled. "What's that now? Who's in there? Is this a pantomime, or what?"

"It's Roger," said Barney thankfully, and he unlocked the chest. Roger sprang up like a jack-in-the-box. "What's happened?" he cried. "I heard the bells."

"Tell you later, Roger," said Barney. "Look, did you hear the gang go down into the passage?"

"Yes," said Roger, "the three men and the woman."

"Have they come back yet?"

"No," said Roger. "I thought they might when I heard

557

the bells. But they shut the secret panel, and I reckon the noise of the bells didn't reach them enough to scare them. The tower is a good way away from here. I heard them, of course."

"Where's this secret panel?" said the first policeman. Barney showed him how to slide it back. He was most astonished.

"Such goings on!" he muttered, and was about to stick his head into the hole, when Barney pulled him back.

"Wait- they're coming back. I can hear them. Better be careful, they're tough."

Sure enough, the sound of voices and footsteps could now be heard Silently Barney slid the panel into place again, and they all stood waiting. Could they catch the whole gang- or would the first one give warning so that the others would run back?

A most unfortunate thing happened. The second policeman felt a sneeze coming. It was a large sneeze, he knew that. He groped for his handkerchief, feeling as if he were going to burst- which is practically what he did do, when the sneeze came. It was quite colossal, and almost blew Snubby to one side. He jumped violently.

The first policeman gave an angry mutter, then everything was silent again. There was now no noise from behind the passage The "gang" had evidently heard the explosion and had stopped to consider the matter.

The men apparently eventually decided that the woman had better go and investigate. Soft footsteps came up to the closed secret panel. In a moment or two it slid quietly back a crack, and the woman shone a torch through the crack.

When she saw the silent group in the room she shut the panel with a scream, and called back to the men. "It's the police! They're here!"

She stumbled back in panic. The first policeman slid back the panel with a bang and shouted down the passage.

"You come on here, and give yourselves up. You're cornered. It'll be the worse for you if you don't come now."

A loud and sarcastic laugh came up the passage. "Sez you! Come and get us! Anybody coming down this passage will be neatly picked off!"

That made the policeman hesitate quite a bit. He considered things for a moment and then called down again.

"Bring Detective-Inspector Rawlings up here at once."

"Sez you!" said the mocking voice again. "He'll be a nice little hostage now, won't he? He's ill, you know, and he needs a doctor badly. We'll give you your inspector if you let us go. Otherwise—well I doubt if he'll last till the morning!"

As if to underline what they said, a terrible rasping cough came up the passage way, muffled by distance, but still dreadful to hear.

"He *is* very ill, sir," whispered Barney.

"Well—what are we to do?" said the policeman, exasperated. "No one can go down there without being in grave danger, that's certain. If only we knew of another way to out-flank them."

"I know another way, sir," whispered Barney. "This secret passage runs a long way—up to an old woman's cottage—it comes out half-way down her well."

The policeman began to think he must be dreaming. "Where's Joe?" he said, turning round. "Joe, stay here and see no one escapes this way. You've got your truncheon, haven't you? You know what to do. I'm going with this boy."

Leaving the useful Joe behind, the two policemen followed Barney, Snubby and Roger to the front door, where an excited crowd of people were still waiting.

"You can go home," said the first policeman gruffly. "You'll be told the news to-morrow. Can't tell you anything. Here you, Jim—go and telephone to Lillinghame and tell them we do want them, and the quicker the better."

"We'd better wait till they come, I think, sir," said Barney. "This gang is pretty desperate, according to Detective-Inspector Rawlings. I've got a plan, if you'd like to hear it."

"Come back into the Hall then, and we'll listen," said the policeman. He and his companion, and the three boys went into a nearby room. The policeman sat down and turned to Barney. "Go ahead," he said.

"Well, sir," said Barney. "We know another way into the secret passage, which leads to where the inspector is lying. There are two roof-falls which we shall have to deal with. He is just behind the bigger of the two. Now, what I propose is this——"

He paused, thinking. "Go on, then," said the policeman, and Snubby and Roger bent forward, wondering what plan Barney had thought of.

"These men won't know we're coming from the opposite direction," said Barney. "They won't be expecting that. They'll just be keeping guard on the other end of the passage—so, if we surprise them from the opposite end, we'll capture the lot!"

CHAPTER TWENTY-EIGHT

A VERY NICE EVENING'S WORK!

" PAH! " said the policeman. " They'll hear us coming."

" I'd thought of that," said Barney. " Could you arrange with Joe or somebody to create a disturbance up this end, so that all the gang would think they were going to be rushed, and would have their attention on this secret passage here——"

" And not be watching the other end! " cried Roger. " So that we could break in there and take them from the rear. Good work, Barney! "

" Ah I see," said the policeman. " Yes—quite a good idea. But how shall we make sure that there's a disturbance this end at the same time as we want to break through?"

" Easy," said Barney. " Set a definite time, sir—and we'll count on the disturbance being set in motion here at that time, we'll know the gang will be guarding the secret passage here, and we'll be able to break through behind them nicely! "

" Yes—it sounds all right," said the policeman. " What time shall we say?"

" Let me see—it'll take a little time to get to Ring O' Bells Cottage," said Barney, calculating. " And then down the well, and along the tunnel—remove the roof falls, or it will be difficult for all of us to get through. I should think if you said in two hours' time, sir, that would be about right."

" Good—say three o'clock then," said the policeman, consulting his watch. " All these goings on in the middle of the night! Where's Joe? He'd better be told about this, and told to set his watch by ours."

"I'll tell him," said Roger, and went off to the useful and very solid-looking Joe. He promised to create a terrific diversion at exactly three o'clock.

"Shouting and hammering and such-like?" he said. "Yes, I can do that all right. I'll have one or two of the Lillinghame fellows with me, too, by then."

The Lillinghame men arrived in another two minutes. There were four of them.

"Where's Joe?" said the Ring O' Bells policeman. "I want two of you Lillinghame fellows to stay with him. He'll tell you what's up. And I want you other two to come with me. I'll tell you the tale as we go. We mustn't hang about here any longer."

They set off with the three boys. Barney had suggested taking a couple of spades, and these were borrowed from one of the villagers.

As they were going along the road, a little dark shape dropped down from a tree on to Barney's shoulder. "Miranda," he said thankfully. "So you've come back. I was so worried about you. I knew you were terribly scared."

"Who's Miranda now?" asked the first policeman, feeling that he couldn't cope with much more. He shone his torch on her and gave a jump. "A monkey? What next? Is she coming with us too?"

"She is," said Barney cheerfully. "I'm not losing her again to-night! She nearly went off her head when she heard those bells!"

They walked quietly through the wood to Naomi's cottage. There was no light in her windows. She was in bed and fast asleep.

"To the well, sir," said Barney in a low voice. He lowered himself over the side and went quickly down, holding on to the iron loops that stuck out from the brick-work.

The first policeman stared in horror, flashing his torch down.

"Here—what's all this? Surely we haven't got to go down here? Why, it's a very deep well!"

"It's quite safe," said Roger, and he went down too, followed by Snubby, who was now almost speechless with excitement. What *would* the boys at school say to all this?

The police followed very reluctantly. The two spades were let down on string. At last everyone was safely through the hole in the side of the well, and started on their way through the secret tunnel.

Nobody liked it much, though the three boys didn't find it quite as strange as the policemen because they had been that way before.

The spades came in useful at the first roof fall, which was soon tackled so that everyone could go through easily. As they came near the second one, Barney stood still and warned the policeman behind him.

"We're almost there. What's the time, sir? It's not three o'clock yet, is it?"

"Five minutes more," said the policeman.

"Well, we'd better get as close to the second roof fall as we can—the inspector is lying just behind that—and wait for three o'clock. We may hear something of the commotion above. We may not, of course, but we shall at least hear some exclamation from the men, and possibly hear them leaving the place where the inspector is and going through the brick wall."

"How do they get through that?" inquired the policeman, feeling rather dazed.

"I don't know, sir—I guess they can take out enough loose bricks to get through all right," said Barney. "Now, we'd better move on, sir. It must be almost three."

They moved silently up to the second roof fall. The crack through which Barney had seen the sick man had disappeared. The rubble had shifted a little and covered it.

The dreadful cough came rasping through the roof fall to the ears of the waiting company. "He sounds very ill," whispered the policeman uncomfortably. "Poor chap. We must get him off to hospital at once."

There were muffled voices to be heard behind the roof fall. Then, in the far-off distance, came echoes of some kind of noise. The men on the other side of the roof fall started up at once.

"What's that!" said one of them, in a loud voice. "They're coming! Quick, up the passage! Got your gun, Charlie? We'll soon show them we mean business!"

There was silence after that, except for the distant noises that kept echoing through to the watchers by the roof fall. They came from the valiant Joe and his helpers, no doubt, making their "commotion!"

"Quick, sir—where are the spades? Let's get through now," said Barney urgently. Soon the spades were at work on the rubble, and in no time at all a way was cleared through. Beyond was a small, widened-out chamber in the tunnel, with a rough bed, a bench, candles, and a jug of water. On the couch lay a man, breathing heavily.

"Inspector Rawlings!" said the first policeman. "We're here!"

The ill man turned bloodshot eyes to the company crowding into the little chamber. He smiled feebly. "Good," he said, "good. Get them, Brown. They're tough, so look out. Keep those boys back, though."

He began to cough again. Silently the policemen crossed to the brick wall that enclosed the other side of the little hidden room. There was an opening there big enough for a man to get through.

Barney had a look at it. Yes—it was as he had expected. Certain bricks were loose and could be easily removed. He was about to follow the last policeman with Roger and Snubby when he was pushed back.

"No kids in this," said the policeman's voice, rough but kindly.

"I'm not a kid," said Barney indignantly.

"You're to keep out of this," said the policeman. "You'll only cramp our style. Do as you're told, youngster."

Barney knew when orders had to be obeyed. He sat down beside the man on the couch, who had now closed his eyes and seemed to be in an uneasy sleep. He breathed so loudly and with such difficulty that it was painful to hear him.

"We're out of the most exciting part of all," said Snubby gloomily.

"You wouldn't like it a bit if you were in it," said Roger. "I wonder what's happening. Hark!"

There was suddenly a loud disturbance up the passage, shouting, yelling, and the woman was squealing. It went on for some time, and then a policeman came grinning down to the secret room. He stuck his red face through the hole in the brickwork.

"All finished!" he said. "They were waiting for Joe and the others to attack from above—and we crept up behind and were on them before they could even turn round. They never heard us at all. I'm not surprised, with the din old Joe was making."

"Are they all caught?" asked Barney in delight.

"Yes—and we've got the woman too—Lizzie the Go-Between," said the policeman. "We've been after her for a long time—and here she was at Ring O' Bells under our very noses. Come on up. We're sending a doctor down here now, and the poor old inspector will have to be taken up above and put into hospital. He's in a bad way."

"I'm all right," said a weak voice, and the ill man opened his eyes. "I feel a lot better now I know the gang is arrested. I know a lot about them, and a lot about their friends. I——"

He began to cough. " Now don't you say a word, Inspector," said the policeman kindly. " Doc will soon be here."

He beckoned to the boys, and they climbed through the hole in the brickwork. The policeman then climbed into the little hidden room, to stay with the inspector till help came.

Up the passage went the boys, and behind the secret panelling. A helmeted head was poking inside the open hole in the panelling. " Oh, it's you boys," said the head. " Come on, now."

The boys climbed out. There seemed to be quite a crowd of people in the little panelled room—any amount of policemen, the woman, the three men belonging to the gang, and a man they saw was a doctor. He disappeared into the secret passage at once, carrying a small black bag.

The three men and the woman were handcuffed. They all looked angry and sullen and the woman looked scared. She was astonished when she saw the boys. She recognised them at once.

" You! " she said, hissing at them. " So it was *you*, prying and snooping and——"

" Shut up," said one of the gang sharply. The woman subsided, but she glared all the time at the boys as if she would like to bite them.

" A very nice evening's work," said one of the men from Lillinghame, who seemed to be an inspector, and very much in charge of the proceedings now. " A nice little haul—and a prospect of further hauls, when we get some information from Inspector Rawlings! "

" You go home now, you kids," said the policeman who had directed proceedings in the tunnel. " We'll see you to-morrow. You've done well. Now go home and sleep— if you can! "

CHAPTER TWENTY-NINE

ALL GOOD THINGS END!

IT WAS all very well to say: " Go home and sleep." For one thing there really wasn't very much of the night left, and for another thing, who in the world could go to bed and sleep peacefully after such an adventurous night?

Feeling very much awake and on top of the world the three boys left the Hall and went up the road once more. Miranda was on Barney's shoulder, rather subdued by all the queer happenings of the night.

" She'll never like bells again," said Barney, fondling

her. " Will you, Miranda? She must have made for the window in the tower, and vanished out of it."

" Diana will be wondering what's been happening," said Roger. " I'm surprised she and Miss Pepper and Miss Hannah didn't come down to see what the matter was."

There were lights in the front room, when the boys arrived. Diana was looking out for them anxiously, with a worried and angry Loony by her side. The spaniel hurled himself on Snubby like a cannon-ball as soon as he came into the hall, and Loopy followed suit. For a few minutes nobody could make themselves heard through the excited barking.

" Boys! What *has* been happening? How *could* you go off like that without telling us?" cried Miss Pepper. " Diana told me such a peculiar tale that I could hardly believe it. What *is* all this about secret passages and bells and a sick man and——"

" We can tell you everything now, Miss Pepper," said Roger, grinning. He looked pale and tired but very cheerful. Barney looked the same as usual. Snubby looked incredibly dirty, through having stayed so long in the secret chimney cavity. Miranda was not to be seen. She was curled up inside Barney's shirt, and not even a paw was showing. Miranda was too tired for words!

Bit by bit the strange story came out. Miss Hannah's eyes nearly dropped out of her head. " Such goings on! " she said. " I never heard such things in my life."

Barney explained about the bells, and how he had rung them to awaken the village and perhaps startle the police, and how marvellously his plan had worked.

" The bells woke *us* up," said Miss Pepper. " I was really scared. I couldn't help remembering the old legend. I couldn't imagine there was anyone in the tower at that time of night, ringing the bells—and fancy its being *you*, Barney! "

" Gosh, I did ring them hard," said Barney. " They

absolutely deafened me. I had to ring them by their short little ropes, you see, so I was almost touching them. I'm certain sure it was Miranda who rang them the first time —by accident, I expect. She probably jumped down on to them without knowing they would jangle, then got terrified and did a lot more jumping."

"Poor Miranda," said Snubby, and put his hand inside Barney's shirt to feel the warm little bundle. Miranda didn't stir.

Miss Hannah had got some cake and milk and they all ate as they talked. "Funny how hungry an adventure makes you," said Snubby. "I haven't felt hungry like this for ages."

"Fibber," said Diana. "You're always saying that. Goodness, Snubby, I did have an awful time here all alone, wondering and wondering what was happening to you. I simply couldn't bear it—and Loony was a frightful nuisance. I had to hold his nose into the cushion when he began howling in case Miss Pepper heard him."

"Woof," said Loony mournfully, looking reproachfully at Snubby.

"It's dawn," said Diana, looking out of the window. "The sun will soon be up. I shouldn't think it's worth while going to bed, is it, Miss Pepper?"

"Certainly it is," said Miss Pepper, who was feeling rather dazed with all she had been told. These children! It was really *dangerous* to look after them. You simply never knew what they would do next.

She got up. "Come along," she said. "Get into bed just as you are, dirt and all! Just slip into your pyjamas and crawl in. Sleep till twelve o'clock if you like."

"Good gracious—we'll be awake *long* before then!" said Snubby, and got up, yawning loudly.

They were not awake long before then. They all slept till past eleven o'clock, and they would not have awakened then if Loopy hadn't given such a fusillade of barks that they all sat up with a jump. Snubby rose to the window and looked to see why Loopy was barking so madly.

" It's the police! " he said excitedly. " Three of them— all looking very important. Come on—get dressed and come down."

" You'd better wash your face, Snubby," said Roger. " Hey, Barney, stir yourself a bit more! "

Barney had actually been allowed to sleep on a couch in Roger's room, with Miranda tucked into his arms. Miss Hannah couldn't bear to send him out into the shed, and most heroically said that Miranda could sleep on the couch too.

Soon they were all downstairs, and the police welcomed them with broad smiles.

" What have you come for?" asked Snubby eagerly.

" Oh, just to see if we could persuade you three boys to join the police force," said the inspector smiling. " I feel you'd be a real help."

Snubby really believed this. He gazed exultantly at the inspector. " Gosh—not go back to school, do you mean?"

" Fathead," said Roger, and gave him a poke in the ribs. " Don't you know a joke when you hear one?"

" Oh," said Snubby, and looked so bitterly disappointed that the three policemen guffawed with laughter.

" We came to clear up a few points," said the inspector. " How did you come to guess there was any funny business going on at the Hall?"

Barney told them how a man had given him a lift, dropped him at Lillinghame—and then, to his surprise, he had seen him again at the Hall that night.

" I know it was him—he had the same van, with ' PIG-GOTT, ELECTRICIAN ' on the side," said Barney. The policemen looked at one another and nodded.

" Just what we wanted to know," said the inspector, and wrote it down. " We've had our eye on Piggot for some time. He's always making peculiar little trips to the

Bristol Channel and round about here. Now we know why. When his pals come up to the Channel with one or two men on board who want to get into the country and keep hidden till they've got papers, Piggott is at hand. And when a little kidnapping is done, Piggott is again at hand with his van. It probably has a false bottom. We'll examine it carefully."

"To think that such things go on!" said poor Miss Hannah, who really was upset at all these sudden happenings.

"Another thing we want to clear up," said the inspector, "is about the bells ringing the first time. Who rang them then?"

"Miranda, my monkey, I think," said Barney.

"Were you in the Hall with her?" asked the inspector. "I understand it was at night."

"Yes, sir," said Barney, looking very uncomfortable. "I'd nowhere to sleep, so I shinned up the ivy and slept in a four-poster bed there. I suppose I did wrong, sir."

"You did," said the inspector. "But I understand you're a circus lad, without a home—you sleep anywhere you can."

"That's right, sir," said Barney. "I hope you won't hold it against me, sir. I didn't do any harm."

"It won't even be reported," said the inspector. "You're a good lad and a brave one. Have you anywhere to sleep now?"

"Yes," said Miss Hannah surprisingly. "He's going to stay here with me until the other children leave in about a week's time. I'll look after him."

Barney looked at her in grateful surprise. Diana gave Miss Hannah a sudden hug, and Snubby yelled "Hurrah!" Roger rubbed his hands joyfully. Now they would all be together properly. Good old Miss Hannah!

"Well—if he's under your care, he'll be all right," said the inspector, with a twinkle. "There won't be any more

571

borrowing of four-poster beds—or, er—table-cloths! We noticed how creased and crumpled they were when we found the four-poster bed had been slept in—and that couch downstairs."

"Barney's all right," said Snubby loyally. "You can always trust old Barney, sir."

"I think I agree with you," said the inspector, giving Barney a little nod. He asked a few more questions and then shut his note-book. "That's all," he said. "And I wish you a very happy week—without even the *smell* of an adventure to spoil it!"

"Oh, sir," protested Snubby. "Adventures don't spoil things. I say—could we go to the Hall to-day, and get down that secret passage again—we didn't really examine the hole in the brick wall properly, or the secret room beyond. Did you see that little cupboard, sir, with the candles and things?"

"Oh, yes," said the inspector. "We probably saw as much as you did, though not quite so soon. Those candles were kept there, I imagine, to light the secret room when it was occupied. You can certainly go down to the Hall if you wish, and explore anything you like—on one condition."

"What's that?" asked Roger.

"That you will at once ring the bells if you find any prisoner, crook or suspicious person hiding in any secret cavity, chamber, passage or room," said the inspector solemnly.

"Good gracious," said Miss Hannah, half-alarmed. The children laughed.

"We promise!" they said, and took the three policemen to the front gate. The children watched them go ponderously down the road, while they stood there talking. Loony and Loopy got tired of it and ran off.

Presently Miss Hannah called to them. "Are you coming in to brunch?" The children turned in surprise.

" Brunch?" said Diana doubtfully. " What's that?"

" Just a mixture of breakfast and lunch," called back Miss Hannah cheerfully. " It's nearly twelve o'clock, you know—too late for breakfast, too early for lunch—so you'll have to make do with brunch."

Brunch proved to be a really wonderful meal, beginning with bacon and eggs, going on to tongue and salad and finishing up with tinned pineapple and cream. Snubby approved highly.

" Why don't we always have brunch?" he said. " I say, Barney—Miranda's helped herself to a handful of pineapple chunks. Greedy thing—I was going to have a second helping! "

Miranda sat nibbling her juicy pineapple chunks, her bright monkey eyes keeping watch on Snubby, as if she were afraid he might snatch them from her. Loony put his head on Snubby's knee. Loopy immediately put his head on Snubby's other knee.

Snubby sighed happily. " Gosh—another whole week of brunches and rides and games with Loony and Loopy and Miranda, and Barney living with us here—it's too good to be true."

" Woof," agreed Loony, licking Snubby's bare knee. Loopy at once licked the other one.

" Well," said Barney, reaching for his glass of lemonade, " good luck, everyone—and here's to our Next Adventure! "

THE ENID BLYTON TRUST
FOR CHILDREN

We hope you have enjoyed the adventures of the children in this book. Please think for a moment about those children who are too ill to do the exciting things you and your friends do.

Help them by sending a donation, large or small to the ENID BLYTON TRUST FOR CHILDREN. The Trust will use all your gifts to help children who are sick or handicapped and need to be made happy and comfortable.

Please send your postal orders or cheques to:

> The Enid Blyton Trust for Children,
> 3rd Floor
> New South Wales House
> 15 Adam Street
> London WC2N 6AA

Thank you very much for your help.

Have you read all the adventures in the "Mystery" series by Enid Blyton?

The Rockingdown Mystery

Roger, Diana, Snubby and Barney hear strange noises in the cellar while staying at Rockingdown Hall. Barney goes to investigate and makes a startling discovery . . .

The Rilloby Fair Mystery

Valuable papers have disappeared – the Green Hands Gang has struck again! Which of Barney's workmates at the circus is responsible? The four friends turn detectives – and have to tackle a dangerous criminal.

The Ring O'Bells Mystery

Eerie things happen at deserted Ring O'Bells Hall – bells start to ring, strange noises are heard in a secret passage, and there are some very unfriendly strangers about. Something very mysterious is going on and the friends mean to find out what . . .

The Rubadub Mystery

Who is the enemy agent at the top-secret submarine harbour? Roger, Diana, Snubby and Barney are determined to find out – and find themselves involved in a most exciting mystery.

The Rat-A-Tat Mystery

When the big knocker on the ancient door of Rat-A-Tat House bangs by itself in the middle of the night, it heralds a series of very peculiar happenings – and provides another action-packed adventure for Roger, Diana, Snubby and Barney.

The Ragamuffin Mystery

"This is going to be the most exciting holiday we've ever had," said Roger – and little does he know how true his words will prove when he and his three friends go to Merlin's Cove and discover the hideout of a gang of thieves.

Armada

Have you read all the "Secrets" stories by Enid Blyton?

THE SECRET ISLAND

Peggy, Mike and Nora are having a miserable time with unkind Aunt Harriet and Uncle Henry – until they make friends with wild Jack and discover the secret island.

THE SECRET OF SPIGGY HOLES

On a holiday by the sea, Mike, Jack, Peggy and Nora discover a secret passage – and a royal prisoner in a sinister cliff-top house. The children plan to free the young prince – and take him to the secret island.

THE SECRET MOUNTAIN

Jack, Peggy, Nora and Mike team up with Prince Paul of Baronia to search for their parents, who have been kidnapped and taken to the secret mountain. Their daring rescue mission seems doomed to failure – especially when the children are captured and one of them is to be sacrificed to the sun-god.

THE SECRET OF KILLIMOOIN

When Prince Paul invited Nora, Mike, Peggy and Jack to spend the summer holidays with him in Baronia, they were thrilled. By amazing luck, they find the hidden entrance to the Secret Forest – but can they find their way out?

THE SECRET OF MOON CASTLE

Moon Castle is said to have had a violent, mysterious past so Jack, Peggy, Mike and Nora are wildly excited when Prince Paul's family rent it for the holidays. When weird things begin to happen, the children are determined to know the strange secrets the castle hides . . .

Armada